To... Enjoy

VACANT EYES

*Blessings,
Chux!*

VACANT EYES

CHRISTINE MAGER WEVIK

Vacant Eyes

ISBN-10: 1-9761-6710-8

ISBN-13: 978-1-9761-6710-2

Copyright © 2017 by Christine Mager Wevik. All rights reserved.

Second Print Edition: March 2018

Editor: Sharon Olbertson and Kathryne Squilla

Cover and Formatting: *Blue Valley Author Services*

This is a work of fiction. Names, characters, places, and incidents either are the product of the author's imagination or are used fictitiously, and any resemblance to locales, events, business establishments, or actual persons—living or dead—is entirely coincidental.

DEDICATION

To Mom and Dad Wevik –

~ Thank you for your generosity, love, and guidance—and warm custard in times of need.

~ Thank you for your humor, grace, faith, and class—and your gentle way of telling me "Frick and Frack" sounded like swear words. (They're still not. I googled it. They're Swiss ice skaters.)

~ Thank you for being our go-to people—and never failing to inquire about the rains. Farmers forever.

~ Thank you for raising an extraordinary son who loves me anyway, just as you do—even when I do swear (really loud) right in your ear on the phone. By accident, I might add.

God kissed the earth when you were born. I thank Him for you, my parents in every way.

I love you.

Chris

ACKNOWLEDGMENTS

Several people are responsible for the ultimate publication of this book.

First of all, me. I did most of it. It was hard, fun, painful, exhilarating, butt-numbing, and empowering. Writing is a solitary, disengaging vocation, and we, as writers, need to be our own best cheerleaders. Good job, Chris. Well done. Moving on.

To my editors: Sharon Olbertson, the English teacher (although not mine) who always said, "Never say in an article, 'A good time was had by all.' You don't know that! Did you ask everyone?" All who know her said she'd be the perfect (tough, sharp, maybe a *little* scary) editor. She was. And she became a dear friend and advocate in the process. Also Kathryne Squilla, of LWS Literary Services, who was necessarily tough but fair. And I still like her. Both of these fine ladies made this a much stronger book, and gave me permission to be me. (Actually, they forced me to be me. "It's called 'voice,' Chris." Plus, no one else wanted the job.) Thank you.

To my beta readers, of which there are many, thank you and I forgive you:

Bonnie Cook, Terri Frank, Mindy Houser, Shelley Jensen, Marilyn Kratz, Susan Miskimins, Julie Morren, Donna Neuman, Doreen Ronning, Teresa Schlup, Loretta Sorensen, Doug Wevik (husband and most honest and loving critic), and Rose Ross Zediker. I'm sure I forgot someone. You're in the next book, top of the list. Not even alphabetically.

To my cover designer, Victorine Lieske, of Victorine Originals, who skillfully extracted my vision from my head, much as my protagonist did with her house's memories. It's a gift. And not unlike my MC, her patience was not only a virtue—it's probably what saved her. Thank you, Victorine.

To my technical advisor, Sheriff Dan Limoges and the Union County Sheriff's office. Thank you. I wish we all knew each other better. (P.S., If you saw my research browser history, I'm pretty sure we would.)

To Dean Koontz, the author who hooked me with *Strangers* and has since kept me happily dangling from his perpetual string of beautiful words. Thank you for coming down from the mountain to greet little me. Not all great authors can fish from a mountain, but you can and do. Often, I've heard.

Finally, thank you to my husband, Doug, and my children, Valerie, Ashley, Kara, and Daniel: You save me daily. I love you.

CHAPTER ONE

"**K** IDS," CONRAD GRUMBLED AND SHOOK his head at the litter in the ditch on the narrow dirt road. Different route, same garbage. He'd seen all kinds on his daily drive to get a look-see at crops. Mostly beer cans, fast food packages, water bottles. Water bottles. Bottled water that people bought in stores. Water they could get for free at home. Stupid. Next they'll be spending good money on bottled air.

But this was a different kind of trash.

He slowed his pickup to get a better look at the unusually large bundle at the side of the road ahead. Sleeping bag? He'd seen recliners, usually at the end of the college school year. Even saw a hide-a-bed once. Ugly, though, as most were. Plaid. He left it for the county workers.

This was no chair or sofa bed. Odd to find something this big discarded here on this low-maintenance, back road. With ruts axle-deep, farmers hardly used the road, much less city folk.

Stopping short of the lumpy mass, he parked and got out, engine running. He hiked his sagging jeans up over his narrow hips as far as his bulging gut would allow. The door squealed as he pushed it shut.

"Dud, stay," he mumbled to the Blue Heeler mix pacing in the back of the truck. The grizzled dog stretched his head over the edge of the bed, itching to jump out and explore.

Conrad's squinted gray eyes swept the countryside. Uneasiness crept over him at the sense of isolation on this unfamiliar road. Except for an overturned grain cart blocking his usual route, he wouldn't be here. Could be a trap … people these days …

He yanked his grungy cap down to his brow to block fall's morning sun, and walked around the front of his truck.

Conrad stopped at the corner of the pickup and steadied himself, his arthritic hand on the warm hood. He struggled to make sense of the sight.

"What in the … " His hand flew to his mouth. The crumpled body of a young woman lay at his feet.

Dark hair matted with blood, mud, and leaves, her head was tucked in toward her small, curled up frame. An oily, burgundy clot of blood puddled under her battered face and upper body. What clothes she wore were ripped and stained with blood and dirt.

Conrad bent over her. Outright horror and disbelief mingled with shameful, morbid fascination. A dead body! He couldn't help but stare.

"Sweet Jesus," he muttered. Now what? Call someone! He patted his pockets for that phone Maggie made him carry. He found it in his shirt pocket, flipped it open, and after two tries, his thick and trembling fingers dialed 911.

"Yes, I need to report a body! Conrad. Conrad Dahlum. On the dirt road – that low maintenance road west of Archer Road and 312th ... I don't know! I just know it's a body! A girl. Yes, looks dead. No, I didn't touch it, are you crazy? What? Oh, for the love a'.. yes, I'll hold." Good night!

Conrad squatted close to the corpse. *What in the world happened? How could anyone ...*

A raspy, gurgling moan emanated from the girl's swollen and crusted mouth. Dudley bayed in response.

"Holy Hell!" Conrad scrambled backward from the girl, landing hard on the dirt and dropping his phone. He picked it up and puffed into the receiver, waiting for the dispatcher. Come on, come on— "Hello? Hello? Yes! It's alive! I mean, she's alive! Get someone here quick!"

18 MONTHS LATER

"I'M NOT DYING. I'M NOT dying," she told herself as she ran. The affirmation was part of her litany when she wanted to stop jogging and walk. She mentally went through the checklist that was her coach:

Do your legs hurt?

No ...

Does your side hurt?

No ...

Can you breathe?

Yes ...

Then keep running!

She hated her coach.

Brynn ignored protocol when it came to running. She didn't care about technique, what part of her foot she landed on, or what the experts on the internet said. She ran the way her body told her to, the way that felt natural and comfortable, the way cavemen ran long before Nike invented sports. *And if I look like a caveman when I run, oh well.*

Running wasn't even the goal; she simply lacked the patience for walking. Besides, it was more of an escape from the smothering. Blessed time alone. Freedom.

Brynn stole a quick look over her shoulder, hearing the rumble of a vehicle over her playlist tune.

An unfamiliar pickup swerved around her. Out of state license. The second that day.

It's nothing. I'm fine. They want me to be afraid. A victim. It's over. Like it never happened.

She glanced over her shoulder again, shook the tension from her arms, and pressed on in determined stride. Dialogue from her last counseling session with Dr. Stokes echoed in her mind, interrupting the flow of lyrics streaming from her headphones. "So do you feel that your husband and your mother are unreasonable in their concern for you?" he had asked.

"No, but it's been a year and a half. I'm fine. And the guy who ... He's probably long gone."

"Have you considered that he might not be? That it might even be someone you know? Try to understand their perspective, Brynn. They're scared. You almost died."

She had felt him staring at her as she picked at a loose thread on the chair. "I just want life to be like it was before. Like it never ... " She shook her head. No one understood and never would.

"I'm afraid that's impossible. You're in denial."

5

Brynn cranked up the volume, picked up the pace, and left his words behind.

So they won. For now. She stayed on the relatively busy paved road in front of their farmhouse—to appease *them*—and usually only went a mile or so in either direction. And as usual, where her mid-run pep talks started to fail, her playlist took over, giving her the energy to reach her driveway with some semblance of dignity and enthusiasm. She was always a better runner when someone was watching. And, like today, it seemed someone was always watching.

She slowed her steps and walked up her driveway as she cooled down, reaching the porch where her big brother, Wes, stood, leaning against a post. "How was your getaway?" He grinned.

Brynn smiled, panting slightly. She put one foot on the step and stretched. "Perfect. I lived."

"Great. Can I go home now? I have a pasture to fertilize."

"Sure. Thanks for watching the kids for me. I hadn't been out for a few days. I was getting—"

"Flabby?" he cut in.

"No, I was going to say—"

"Ugly?"

"No, I—"

"Gassy?"

"No! Stop!" She smiled. "I was going to say that I was getting anxious for some time alone! You make me want to leave again. Where are the kids?" she asked, stretching her other leg slowly.

"Inside, eating pudding. So is Mom watching the kids when you go to your counseling next week? If not, I could probably—"

"I'm not going. I'm cutting back." Brynn stretched, avoiding his gaze.

"'Cutting back'? Yeah, those dang bad habits ... smoking, Facebook, counseling ... "

Brynn stopped and glared at him. He pressed his lips together in a forced smile. "You maybe want to talk to Jackson about that, though, huh?"

"Wes."

He held up his hands in defense. "Just sayin' ... " He sauntered toward his pickup. "See you tomorrow, Binny."

"Yup," she said as she moved toward the door to check on her two children. She stopped abruptly and yelled, "Wessy!" back at his retreating pickup. He honked his horn and drove out.

She smiled to herself as she went inside. "Turd," she said under her breath.

The moment Brynn entered the kitchen she was indeed tempted to leave again. Buddy, five, had just peeled the skin from the top of his pudding and flung it in the direction of his seven-year-old sister, Ellie. "Dog poop!"

"No!" She reached out to stop him just as it landed in Ellie's red, ringleted hair.

Brynn stuck her fisted hands on her hips. He stood facing her, doe eyes staring up at her, his softly curled, fluffy brown hair framing his cherub face. Dang that sweet face. The child, however, tested her daily. How her children could be so different in every possible way was as baffling to her as math and black holes.

"Jack Jr! You do not throw pudding! Why would you do that?" Brynn shook her head, exasperated.

"Because I don't like that part," he said simply. "It's gross."

"Time out, Buddy. To the chair. Right now."

"But, Mom! It's gis-DUSTING!"

"That's 'disgusting', and still naughty. Go." She pointed toward the break she already needed.

Buddy trudged to his well-used time out seat as Brynn pulled the clump of pudding skin out of Ellie's hair.

"Mom! Get it out, get it out, get it out! It's dog poop!"

"Oh, for heaven's sake. We'll wash it out. It's just pudding." Brynn led Ellie to the bathroom.

As Brynn washed Ellie's hair over the edge of the tub, she heard the back door open and shut. Any moment, she would hear her husband's boots thumping to the floor as he removed them. She waited a few seconds after the second thump and shouted out from the bathroom, "He's in time out, Jackson!"

"What's the latest offense?" Jackson said from the bathroom door.

"Throwing dog poop," Brynn said soberly. Ellie gasped and whipped her head around to look at her mother with a shocked and sickened expression on her freckled face.

"What?!"

"Just kidding. It's the skin from the top of his chocolate pudding." Brynn stifled a laugh.

"Oh. Well, can't say as I blame him. That's gross."

Brynn rolled her eyes at her husband of 10 years. He was too soft with the kids, but she loved him for it, despite its effect on her disciplinary strategies.

Jackson took note of Brynn's attire. "How was the run? Did Wes watch the kids for you?"

"Good, and yes," she answered both queries and added, "I figured I'd take advantage of the opportunity since he came by after fixing fence and offered. He'll be back tomorrow. He had to fertilize the pasture.

"So are you ready for duty? I'll start supper when I'm back from hog chores. I thought we'd grill out tonight. Steak, asparagus ... .." Brynn patted her daughter's wet mass of curls with a towel.

"You had me at steak," Jackson said. "Why ruin a perfectly good meal with vegetables?"

"Yeah, Mom, we can just have meat and bread. And ice cream," Ellie grinned conspiratorially at her father.

"Yes. Strawberry ice cream rib eye sandwiches, no yucky vegetables." He winked at Ellie.

"Stop encouraging her, J," Brynn said to Jackson and left the bathroom.

Ellie squealed as Jackson threw her over his shoulder and followed Brynn to the kitchen where Buddy was serving out his sentence.

"Buddy, do you know why you were put in time out?" Brynn asked, squatting down to face her son.

"Yes, Mommy." Buddy searched the ceiling for the right answer. "Throwing gis-dusting pudding?"

"Yes. Are you going to do that again?" and realizing her mistake as Buddy opened his mouth, quickly added,

"No, you will not. Now go apologize to your sister and give her a hug."

Brynn hid her grin behind her hand as she watched Buddy. With his best goin'-to-the-gallows footsteps, arms hanging motionless, he reached his sister, now standing near her father. Looking at the wall behind his sister, Buddy said, "Sor-ry, El-lie." Insincerity at its finest. He turned to his mother and tipped his head. A pained expression of distaste and embarrassment came across his face.

Brynn crossed her arms. "Yes, you have to hug her."

Brynn got home from chores, dropped her smelly clothes in the washing machine, grabbed a robe from the mudroom closet, and went to shower. She boosted the volume on the iPod dock in the bathroom. With two, and sometimes more, showers a day, she had learned to make them fast but efficient and enjoyable. Although pork production wasn't a passion like her artwork, it was interesting and profitable, as well as a perfect means to her goal of raising her own children and working from home. It was also extremely dirty and stinky work. Brynn sang along as the tunes bounced off the shower walls. She knew that she was probably behind the door when God was handing out singing voices. Singing and math: she couldn't be good at *everything*.

As the warm water from the shower's enormous rain head sluiced over her, Brynn distractedly traced the lines of the angry, purple scars in her skin. Her doctors, particularly the plastic surgeons, were wizards with their stitches and surgical glue and matching up of jagged edges, but they were not miracle workers. The marks from numerous lashes, cuts, scrapes, burns, and surgeries were a part of her now. Despite her bitter salve of anger, annoyance, and grief, nothing other than time would lessen their visibility or existence, so she endeavored to embrace them. She named them, claimed them as her own, and chose to see a certain anomalous beauty in them. Although she didn't choose the scars, the macabre map of lines left in her skin by a vicious pseudo-cartographer a year and a half before were all hers and no one else's. Everything she had been through made them symbols of survival. The fact that she didn't remember one moment of the pinning of those gruesome badges of honor was of no consequence to her now. She had to decide that she was beautiful—maps, badges, and all.

CHAPTER TWO

"**P**OOR BABY." BRYNN LOOPED THE rope's slipknot around the dead pig's back foot. She'd always felt the need to offer some kind of tender, if cursory, condolence to a dead pig, especially if it was from the sick pen, one that she was trying to nurse back to health. Selfish sendoff, really. It only made her feel better, but did nothing for the pig at that point.

It was hard to not get attached. Having always been an animal lover, it wasn't a stretch to imagine herself as a caretaker of *some* kind of creature, but she never imagined being a pork producer, manager of their 2400-head hog facility. She had envisioned something completely different for her life, her vocation. John Lennon's words, "Life is what happens while you're busy making other plans" resonated with her. He seemed to have written it with her in mind. Raising pigs was a great way to make a living while she was busy making plans to be an artist, or more specifically, a *money-making* artist. In the meantime, pig chores called while Jackson ate breakfast with the kids.

She dragged the pig to the compost pile where it would eventually become fertilizer for the crops and went back into the massive building. Brynn and Jackson put up the 50-by-400-foot building a few years earlier and she loved its modern conveniences. She smiled as she thought of her father-in-law who liked to razz her about how "rough" she had it. "Ya know, years back when we had pigs, we had an open-front shed that we had to scoop snow out of and change bedding every single day. We had to thaw out frozen waterers, add new straw, and shovel manure by hand out of the pens every single day." He probably also had to walk to school through waist-high snow "every single day"—uphill both ways, to boot.

She had it made. The building was state-of-the-art, with temperatures monitored and controlled by a computer that called her if it fluctuated outside of a healthy range, if the electricity went out, or if the water pressure had dropped. The computer also turned on the circulating fans and opened curtains when the building was too warm, and in the summer, even turned on misters to cool the pigs— almost as if it knew instinctively that pigs can't sweat. The feed refilled automatically as the pigs needed it. The manure went into a pit—away from the pigs—to be pumped out and used for fertilizer on the fields.

Most importantly and her main concern, the pigs were happy and comfortable in this precisely managed environment. They might be livestock, raised to feed the masses, but in the meantime, they were hers. More like pets than produce.

She enjoyed swine immensely, marveling at the innate behavior of pigs, barking like dogs to alert the herd when they sensed or heard something strange to them. Even in confinement they attained and displayed their inherent traits, and even more so when someone strange was in the building. She announced herself every day upon entering the building with "Piggies!" They barked, the sound spreading down the room, until all the pigs froze in place, the room a spiky sea of rigid, upright pinkish-white ears. She strolled resolutely and pompously down the service alley like a powerful commander, all attention on her as she inspected her troops, arms crossed, at her leisure. Of course, once they knew it was Brynn, they went back to whatever they were doing: eating, sleeping, or fiddling with something—anything—that moved. Because pigs were curious, playful, and easily bored, Brynn hung chains in the room and occasionally threw in a small tire or wooden post as toys.

Brynn went back to the sick pens to check on the pigs that had been sorted out of the herd. "Babies!" she cooed. They began their side of the dialogue with grunts of contentment and excitement.

Her patients waited for her attention and affections. She scratched behind their ears and rubbed their tummies as they rolled over like needy puppies. They ran to greet her, if at all possible, eager for the pampering. She hand fed and watered only the pigs that were too weak or sick to be mobile—usually new to the pen—the others, however, she forced to get up and get their own.

"Okay, Chubby, you're getting up today!" She played the tough guy, wedging her rubber work boot under the hind end of one of her more stubborn pigs as he sat upright. Slowly pushing his shoulders forward, she helped him to his feet as he squealed in protest. He trembled and danced, but put his head in the wet-dry feeder and ate greedily. She scratched his back as he stood and ate. "Good boy! Look at you!" Little victories were her bonuses.

One by one, each with assigned names that matched their personalities, she tended to all in the pen. Mama, whose hoof had been caught in the slats in the floor, was first. With no open wound Brynn merely made sure the pig got up on a regular basis to keep her from getting lazy and stiff. Stubs, a pig with a chewed tail, would soon be back in general population. His tail was better and he was growing obnoxious. She gave shots for lameness or infection where needed, giving treats of ginger snaps and soggy apples where wanted, and making sure the rest were comfortable until she could come back later in the day. She finished with Lucky, a pig that would soon need a different name. She'd continued to lose weight despite Brynn's best efforts, and unfortunately, it seemed the only shot that could help would come from Jackson's 22.

Tenderness to creatures in need was second nature to Brynn, but she had to work at maintaining a practical perspective in pork production, especially in the case of the inevitable euthanizing of suffering animals. That she left to her husband.

Brynn checked the rest of the herd, then went to the building's office and did her daily record keeping, charting water use, high and low temps, treatments, and mortality count. After she checked the feed level in the bulk bins outside, she changed out of her coveralls, rinsed her boots, and cleaned the office floor. Just because the office was *in* a pig sty didn't mean it had to *be* one—and it wasn't. The hog facility's office was cleaner than any she'd seen in any other confinement unit. It was painted a soft shade of lavender, had an easy-to-clean vinyl floor, and was equipped with a coffee maker, a refrigerator stocked with sodas and water, and a bathroom. The office, the building, the pigs—they were hers and she felt an enormous sense of accomplishment and pride in her work and the healthy, happy pigs she raised. She made the rules and everyone who entered the building, including the men who worked on equipment and those who helped load the fattened hogs onto trucks, knew that she was in charge. She felt a twinge of errant pride and satisfaction that many other pork producers envied everything she'd done in her operation— everything except, perhaps, the lavender paint color.

Brynn finished in the confinement unit, locked the door, and walked the quarter mile driveway back to their house. The day was young and promised to be exceptionally warm and sunny for the end of March. The pigs were doing well, the kids were restless and ready to be outside, and Jackson would be at Wes and Deidra's all day, working on equipment. With the sunshine warming her and seeping into her mood, Brynn decided that after she showered, she would take the kids to her mother's, grab her camera, their American Bulldog, Bingo, and scout for a house that needed to be immortalized in a painting.

Brynn's mother, Adelle, poured another cup of coffee for Brynn in a poorly disguised attempt to stall her long enough to talk her out of going. "Are you sure you're ready? I'm happy to watch them, you know that, but maybe you should wait until Jackson gets home and have him go with you." This would be Brynn's first official photography outing since her abduction.

"Mom, I won't go far, promise. I have my cell phone, the car, and the dog with me." She looked at the dog, smiled, and shrugged. "At least she looks badass. I told Jackson I would call him when I found a house. I'll be fine." She planted kisses on her mother's and children's cheeks, pausing to wag a finger in Buddy's face in a silent pledge of some serious mom-business if he didn't behave. The kids raced off to see what needed breaking, and Brynn trotted to her car, excited at the surge of creativity bubbling up within her once again. As she drove out, Brynn purposely avoided looking at her mother who she knew would be standing on the steps, holding her coffee, her tongue, and her breath.

So far, it had been a productive day. Her first subject had been a massive refurbished barn, retrofitted with tall, arched church windows. She'd remembered that the loft was now a basketball court and the lower floor was a vintage furniture and junk shop. It was like a playhouse for adults. She'd wanted to shoot it ever since discovering it months ago on a shopping excursion with Jackson. She could envision a unique, humorous—if not altogether irreverent—painting; one with farm animals streaming from the door after a long-winded sermon by the proverbial pastoral bull. Maybe title it "The Holy Cow Congregation" or "The Gathering of the Flock" or something.

Brynn then went to a house she'd passed on the way to the church-barn. She parked on the side of the gravel road, let the dog out of the car, and grabbed her equipment. In her excitement, she fought the urge to run toward the ditch that separated her from the vacant house. Bingo bounded through the brown grass, chuffing and sniffing, thrilled to be away from the farm and in an absolute high from the car ride—her favorite. *That's exactly how I feel, Bingo!* Brynn grinned. She fished her phone from the pocket of her blue jean jacket and called Jackson.

"Hey, J. I just left The Church Barn. I found a new house. It's that old place just south of Steever's? Yeah, I'll just be here a few minutes. Not much I can do from the road … No, I won't go in … .probably. No, honey. Okay … Okay! Don't worry. I'll call you when I leave here, all right? Yeah, bye."

"Honestly, Bingo, all this fuss. You'd think I almost died or something," Brynn smiled, but it immediately faded in light of her poor taste in jokes. She *had* almost died eighteen months ago, abducted, beaten within an angel hair's breadth of her life, and found on the side of the road two days later. She had also been sexually assaulted and brutally tortured. The ordeal had left her in a coma for over two weeks.

Though Brynn remembered nothing of the abduction or the attack, she recalled the look in Jackson's eyes when she finally awoke. That look caused her more pain than any she could recall ever feeling throughout the weeks and months to follow. It was a look that still brought her to tears when she thought of it: Jackson's eyes, red, watery, sunken deep into their sockets. This big, strong man of hers—6'3", 190 pounds, capable, resourceful, intelligent beyond his years, ruggedly handsome, hard and tough but soft where it counted—looked like a prisoner of war. Beaten, hollowed out, pallid, emptied of every joy God had graced him with, and desperate. She wanted never to see that look again. Ever.

The weeks after she awoke were a fog: surgeries, therapy, and rehab, combined with visitors, cards, flowers, and phone calls too numerous to count, remember, or want. She also endured endless, exhausting, and agonizing—as well as pointless—interviews with local and state police detectives, FBI officials, and the media. She was home by Christmas. The phone was taken off the hook, the mail was screened, the bad guy was never caught, Bob's your uncle, and that was that. She didn't dwell on it and everyone else did. Maybe she didn't *because* everyone else did.

Maybe, Brynn thought—not for the first time—*there's something wrong with me! It happened to me, yet I'm the only one not freaked out by it. I'm the only one not looking over my shoulder, not jumping at every little noise or worried about every weird thing that happens. There* might *be something wrong with me.*

She was just scaring herself; it wasn't really the truth. Probably.

Although, now, with her first time out taking pictures, she started to feel a little tingle of trepidation creeping up from her gut. She thought about the strict precautions she was constantly instructed to take. A very real possibility existed, that whoever did this was still out there, still watching. Perhaps always watching. It felt good to feel something that was a normal response to such a traumatic event, and yet, it was not a welcome feeling. She was in uncharted waters. Was it better to be blissfully ignorant, or wise and afraid?

Nothing bad would happen to her this minute, probably not this hour, almost certainly not this day, if ever again. For the time being, she was going to focus her camera and try to do the same for herself.

She jumped across the standing water in the ditch, her tall leather boots sliding a little on the slope. It would be so much easier to go up the driveway to the house, but the trees obstructed the view, and this was the only way to shoot the house with a clear view. Besides that, she had hoped to keep her promise of not going into or up to the house. And she really hoped not to be shot for trespassing.

The perfect house stood before her. And this was the perfect time of year to shoot houses for painting. It was like the picture wanted to paint itself. Earth sought to trust the warmth with a slight five o'clock shadow of green that lightly touched the ground; the sky was the palest of blue, and everything in between, a delightful monotone. Painting watercolor images over black and white photos of landscapes and old buildings was not only her hobby. It was a way for her to give the world what it was promised when she was born—a little sliver of something good that might make a difference. What began as a tight, hard bud of a notion had blossomed into an art—a love and passion for breathing life into things that looked dead.

Brynn's old Nikon whirred and clicked. She'd missed that sound. The zoom lens compensated for the stupid promise she had made to her husband. Brynn inched along a sagging barbed-wire fence, using the viewfinder as her guide, listening to the chatter of her camera, and hoping she didn't step into a badger hole or a deep puddle.

She paused to absorb the moment in a memory her camera could never catch or convey. A few small, dirt-encrusted snowdrifts still hid in the shadows near brush and buildings, but most of the land was clear of snow and dark with moisture. The birds fluttered from tree to tree, finding no foliage in which to hide. Bingo had her nose stuck down a hole of some sort nearby, her body still and rigid, but her tail wagging with anticipation that she would be blessed with a good chase. A soft breeze stirred the sunshine with the air, a faint loamy scent wafted up from the ground, and ahead of her, the beguiling old house waited patiently for her consideration.

The house was weathered gray, white in its past life, with several dormers. A story and a half. The porch, missing a post, slumped in slightly on itself like a kinked umbrella.

Some of the fretwork on the porch and peaks was broken or missing. Even with missing shingles, the roof looked in surprisingly good shape.

The house held few redeeming qualities, as with any long-abandoned home, but its saving grace was the windows. They were like eyes, sad and empty, longing for just a glint of light or life. Every house she'd ever photographed and later painted in faint, soft shades of watercolor came back to life on her easel. The houses spoke to her with their eyes. They beckoned her to visit, to share, to come and sit a spell and listen to their stories. They were so like the rheumy, desolate eyes of the residents at the nursing home, those residents desperate to matter to someone, to have someone hear what they lived and know who they once were.

When she found a house to paint, she was giving it a second chance, if not a second chance at a life within its own walls, at least a second chance at life on someone else's wall. She wanted to grasp it, paint some life and breath back into it, save it, and watch it thrive.

These houses, this work, her art—they were like a lit match to a sparkler. She could feel the sizzle of glowing possibilities. She would be their breath. She would be the life they craved, the story they wanted to tell, the listening ear, the color that was drained from them by age and years of neglect. She would be the light that was lacking in their vacant eyes.

Brynn was jolted from her reverie by skidding tires on gravel, a dog's panicked bark, and a horn blaring. No doubt her dog was responsible for all three. Brynn's heart raced, but probably not as much as Bingo's, who stood quivering in the grass near the road where a dark blue Ford pickup idled, angled oddly on the road.

The window rolled down and the driver, grinning, leaned out the window to talk. She recognized him right away. "Brynn, your dog wants in my front seat. The hard way!" he laughed heartily. Arlo Emmick farmed nearby and attended the same church as Brynn and Jackson. He was one of many who helped Jackson with harvest the fall Brynn was in the hospital recovering from her attack.

This farming community was like a family, and she was grateful to belong. Farming is one of the most dangerous occupations. Fatal and crippling farm accidents were not uncommon, and the agricultural community was also not immune to its share of urban-variety violence. Aside from her own harrowing ordeal, Brynn had experienced rural tragedies firsthand when her best friend, Lanea, disappeared 16 years earlier. Break-ins, vandalism, attacks like Brynn's, suspected abductions or runaways, and even murders, though rare, were sad reminders that no one is safe from the iniquities of humanity. If anything, they acted as bonding agents in rural areas, cementing families together in a protective huddle against outside evils.

"Hi, Arlo. Sorry about that! She must have found a rabbit to chase." Brynn patted her thigh to summon the dog. Bingo hurried to Brynn's side, leaning her boxy head against Brynn. She rubbed the dog's ears in forgiveness. *I'm no better than Jackson—soft, through and through.*

"Out taking pictures again, I see." Arlo nodded toward the dilapidated house.

"Yeah, such a nice day and all ... "

"Why don't you go on in, get a little closer? Uncle Cole would love to see his old place painted in a portrait by you. I haven't been up there for a while, but I could go with you, if you want," he offered. Apparently, paranoia was rampant in these parts, and Arlo was a member of her posse of protectors. She appreciated the offer nonetheless. Snooping was her favorite hobby.

"Are you sure? If you're busy ... " She really hoped he wasn't. And she didn't actually recall *specifically* saying the word "promise" to her husband.

"Me? Busy? Ground's too wet and cold to plant, and you know me—I'd rather hang around with a pretty girl than work on my tractor," He grinned, his big teeth flashing through his bearded face. Arlo was like a big brother— "big" being the operative word. Just a couple years older, he towered over Jackson by 6 inches and outweighed him by at least 100 pounds. He reminded her of a chubby cousin to Chewbacca from the Star Wars movies, although she would never tell him that. He was brawny, barrel chested, and scary looking, but he was as warm and gentle as he was large, almost part of their family. He was the protective type, and she had always felt safe around him, especially since his wife, Eva, was one of her best friends.

"I didn't know this place was in your family," Brynn said as they walked up the driveway. Bingo had plundered ahead, nose to the ground, hot on the scent of an animal that was undoubtedly smarter and faster than she.

"Yeah, Uncle Cole still owns all this land, and we rent from him. He's in the home now, but sharp as a tack, that guy."

"I'll be sure to take him a copy of my picture when I get it done. "

"He'd like that a lot. Plus he doesn't get too many visitors. Sally died years ago, and they never had kids, so ... " Arlo pushed his hands deep into his pants pockets and glanced around at the property as though he were seeing it for the last time.

"That's too bad. Yes, I'll take him a picture," she said quietly as she stared at the house. She imagined an old man smiling at the memories he shared in his old home. "I don't believe I know him. He wouldn't mind a visit from a total stranger?"

"Are you kidding? That's like asking Dingo Bingo if she would mind catching a rabbit." They chuckled and climbed the porch steps.

Arlo pushed open the heavy wooden door, and they entered the living room. The room was small and dusty, and the corners were draped with billowy cobwebs.

Arlo, Brynn, and Bingo checked out the surroundings, with Arlo narrating as they toured the main floor. "Our boys come over here now and then. They like to think of it as their hideout, but we always know where to find them. No one seems to bother the place. Then again, there's nothing here for anyone to steal. No nice woodwork, antique light fixtures, nothing like that."

He was right. This house had nothing to offer in the way of character. The wood trim was handmade with pine 1 x 3's tacked around the doors and windows. Basic brass ceiling-mount light fixtures had long lost their glass shades. There was no open staircase that she could see from which to pilfer old, unique balusters. The structure was beyond repair. Chunks of plaster had fallen from the ceiling, exposing the rotted skeleton of lath underneath.

No plaster littered the floor, though. Somehow, this house had escaped the vandalism and disrespect that plagued most abandoned properties. It likely helped that the house was in close proximity to the Steever's home.

Now in the dining room, Brynn could easily imagine the mid-century furniture filling the rooms. In the living room she imagined a square-armed couch and matching chairs with doilies on the backs, an oversized television console stood in the corner, and she could envision in the kitchen, a chrome and yellow laminate dining set.

Her imagination had always been what her mother called "rich," but it provided her with a very colorful picture of how homes of that era must have looked. Details and images seemingly right out of a magazine filled her head.

"Brynn?" Arlo snapped her back to the present, and announced he was going upstairs to look around. "Want to come along?"

"Uh, no. Go on ahead. I'm going to take some pictures down here, if that's all right," she lied. She enjoyed the ride her imagination was taking her on far too much to abandon it.

Arlo and Bingo plodded noisily up the stairs as Brynn continued to soak up the atmosphere of the home, envisioning with exquisite detail the décor, even the typical clutter a home acquires. She imagined a man, tall and thin, with long sideburns, and a woman, petite and attractive, her dark blonde hair done up in a French roll on the back of her head. She pictured the man sitting down at the table, removing his hat, and the wife promptly picking it up and tossing it to the floor. They share a smile as if in a private joke. Brynn smiled at the imagined scene. She must have seen it somewhere.

A crash of shattering glass broke the spell, and Brynn twirled to face the door to the upstairs. Bingo hurled clumsily down the stairs, sliding the last few steps on her fat rear, and darted out the front door. Arlo trudged down afterward, shaking his head.

"Bingo," was his only explanation as he jerked his thumb over his shoulder.

"I'm sorry. I'll pay you for that," Brynn offered. Arlo just shook his head and laughed.

"Big chicken. It was only a broken window leaning against a wall. Some watchdog you got there ... " he teased.

Brynn jumped at her ringing cell phone.

"Hello? Hi, honey. I'm fine. Just looking through the house. I mean ... ." Brynn felt her face flush, remembering her promise, or *implication of a promise*, as she chose to think of it.

"I'm with Arlo," she interrupted. That shut him up.

CHAPTER THREE

J ACKSON PUT HIS CELL PHONE back in his pocket and
went back to work on the planter.

"So how's Brynn doing?" Wes asked. His forced
casual tone and intense focus on his work wasn't lost on
Jackson. Wes was as concerned for Brynn's safety as he was,
especially now that she was out and about.

Jackson was just getting used to the idea of Brynn being
well enough to function normally at home, say nothing of
venturing out. He wasn't sure he was ready for her to be
that well.

"Seems to be doing okay. She's out taking some photos
today. For the first time."

"And? You're not okay with that?"

"Yeah. Yeah, I am … "

"But?"

"Exactly. We still don't know who took her, although we have a pretty good idea of what happened ... " he trailed off, the image of a battered Brynn flashing in his mind. "Who knows? The guy could still be out there looking for her. And she's out taking pictures, for God's sake." Jackson pulled on the wrench, tightening the nut as if to fuse it to the washer.

"You gotta let her, Jack. I know my sister. You go along to get along. She's tough, but more than anything, she's stubborn. She's got to be able to do what makes her happy. You know what they say: if Mama ain't happy, ain't ... "

"Shut up, Wes."

Jackson could almost hear Wes grinning on the other side of the planter.

Wes was right. Jackson just couldn't forget the phone call telling him that she'd been found. And he couldn't get that image of his fragile wife on the gurney as they wheeled her into surgery. He'd had a hard time believing it was her, his Brynny—bruised, broken, almost unrecognizable.

It was a miracle she'd survived. She might be strong, but she was petite—5'1", 105 pounds fully dressed, soaking wet. There was no way to know everything that had been inflicted upon his wife; the doctors' reports detailed enough of it to make him wish he didn't know. With obvious signs of a brutal rape, ligature marks, burns, cuts, broken bones, bruises and contusions, he couldn't bear to even imagine what she'd been through. Jackson clearly remembered feeling like he needed to find whoever had done it and break the law in so many ways it became shards as fine as dust. That feeling was easy to remember because it was never far below his conscious thought.

Why couldn't she just be happy at home? Why couldn't she just stick to the two-mile stretch in front of their house? Why couldn't she just take pictures of their own house?

"So where is Brynn shooting at today?"

"Arlo's uncle's place. Just south of Steever's."

"Oh. That's good."

They both knew what he meant by that. Neither of them wanted her to go anywhere near where she had been found. Seeing the house where she was held might bring back unwanted memories for her. Although they clung to the hope of finding her attacker, they preferred to have it come about through DNA searches in criminal databases, eyewitnesses, and forensic evidence of some other sort.

Brynn was tough. There was no doubt about that. Jackson was continually mesmerized by her courage, her stalwart desire to squeeze passion and joy out of every minute of every day. He'd admired it from the day he met her years ago. He'd seen her, even as a teenager, as a strong, spirited creature—a small but willful filly. She bounced and trotted everywhere behind him and Wes in her ratty jeans, high-top tennies and her dark, shiny hair pulled up into a perpetually messy ponytail. But eventually, long after high school, he found that she'd grown (although not much) into a graceful, young woman, and realized he couldn't stop looking at her.

He was still enthralled with her, sometimes maddeningly so. Those gold-speckled green eyes. She knew how to use them, how to work him. She deserved to live her life. She was right. *Everyone* was right, damn it. But he didn't have to like it. It was her stubborn, independent ways that had helped her survive. They were also part of the reason she'd been taken. Jogging when the "wind went down and it was finally cool." Jogging when everything to the west was a black silhouette, and everything to the east had been gobbled up by the night. Jogging when, apparently, all the riff-raff came out to play with the moon.

She had no healthy fear of anything except for math and ticks. It was her fearlessness that scared him the most.

Deidre came into the shed with brownies and coffee, and forced the men to take a break.

"How's Brynn? I hear it's her first day out. Maybe I should ask, 'How are *you?*'" she asked Jackson as she poured the steaming brew.

Jackson shot a glance at Wes. *Blabbermouth.*

"She's great. That's what she keeps telling me, anyway."

"Don't worry. I'm sure she'll be careful, Jackson," she said, though her tone lacked conviction halfway through her sentence.

"Right. Like she was … ." He shook his head. "You're right."

Anxious to get back to work, the men finished their snack and handed Deidre their cups.

Wes cleared his throat. "Not sure I should say anything, but … Brynn said she's cutting back on counseling sessions. Said she's not going next week. Did she mention this to you, Jack?"

"Wes, that's none of your business," Deidre said.

Wes glanced at her, then Jackson. "Thought he should know."

Jackson picked up his tools. "I'll talk to her." He didn't hold out hope that it would do any good.

CHAPTER FOUR

BRYNN AND JACKSON SAT ON the porch drinking colas. "Honey, I appreciate that you were worried, but I was never in any danger."

"You don't know that!" Jackson shook his head in exasperation.

"Please don't make me mistrust our friends. I swear— it's like everyone is trying to make me paranoid!"

"Yes! That's exactly it! Finally you get it! You're in denial, Brynn." There it was again. "You're lucky it was Arlo who stopped, but it could have been anyone. I don't know who attacked you. Hell, even *you* don't know who attacked you, and yet you walk around the countryside ... " The pitch in Jackson's voice rose.

"It was my first day out! It's been a year and a half. When are you going to let me grow up?" Brynn turned away from him. Her eyes stung with tears of frustration. She blinked them back and turned to face her husband.

"I refuse to be a victim, Jackson. I won't do it! The police, the media—the whole world knows—that I don't remember anything about the attack. I am not going to live in fear that some wacko is coming back. There's no reason for him to come back. He was probably some freak that hopped off the interstate. Anyway, I would have called you if it had been anyone besides Arlo, okay?"

"What if you don't get the chance to call? I just want you to be careful." He paused. "And what's this I hear about you not going back to counseling?"

Brynn stared at him.

"I didn't say I was not going back. I said I'm cutting back. I think I can make some of my own decisions. I'll talk to Dr. Stokes. We'll work something out. Can we stop fighting? Please?" Brynn stopped, finding it hard to speak around the massive lump in her throat.

"I'm sorry to keep harping on you about this," Jackson said as he went to her and wrapped her tiny body in his big arms, "I just want you to realize that it's possible that it could have been someone we know, much as I hate that thought."

She didn't believe he was sorry. She was sure this would not be the end of this issue—it would always be this way when she was out on her own. Brynn wanted to wriggle free from his embrace and set him straight, but she chose— once again—to sacrifice satisfaction for peace.

Ellie and Buddy burst onto the scene, chasing Bingo, who had one of Ellie's dolls dangling from her mouth.

Brynn stepped away from Jackson and clapped her hands. "Bingo! Drop it!" The drool-soaked doll plopped to the porch floor. Ellie and Buddy stopped in their tracks, looked at the doll with disgust, and it was clear that they didn't want it back all that badly. They went back to chasing the dog, apparently with no particular goal in mind.

Brynn gathered up the slobbery doll and soda cans. "Do you know Cole Emmick? Arlo's uncle? He's the one who owns that old house. I'm going to take him a copy of the picture when I get it done." The nonchalance was probably obvious, but she was relieved to be momentarily free from his suffocating concern, and discussing anything on a lighter note.

Jackson stared at a spot on the porch floor. "No. I kind of forgot about that place. I'm never in that area," he said, his voice mechanical.

"I'm going to work on my painting for a while before chores. Any requests for supper?" Brynn stood with her hands full, waiting for a response. "J?"

Jackson returned from his daydream. "Hm? Oh, meat and potatoes. Or am I being too specific?" he said, smiling weakly.

The supper menu was not what Jackson was brooding about, but that's exactly where she was leaving the conversation.

Brynn looked over her photos later, chose a few of her favorites, and printed them on watercolor paper. She decided to paint more than one this time, particularly since she was giving one away, and she didn't have any other photos to paint, besides the church-barn. That was a much bigger project. She needed to use as much of her recent resources as she could. Who knew when she would be allowed out of the house again?

The visions of life in this house floated through Brynn's mind like ghosts. Her painted images upon the watercolor paper would need to be just as delicate and otherworldly. Ideas, impressions, and fantasies flowed smoothly from the brush onto the paper.

She absorbed herself in her watercolors most of the afternoon. After chores, she made a supper of cheeseburgers and sweet potato fries. Brynn smiled as she did the dishes, feeling pleased with the day, the progress on her artwork, and the fact that no one seemed to notice they'd actually eaten vegetables.

Jackson offered to bathe the kids and get them ready for bed, and Brynn quickly took him up on his offer. The familiar yearning for her art was returning for the first time since her abduction. She felt drawn to the painting, to the house and its sad, beckoning eyes and the stories it wanted to tell her. She was getting excited to meet Arlo's uncle, Cole, and see the look on his face when she showed him the life that she'd rendered to his dying homestead.

Later that week, Brynn had a finished product that she could present to Arlo's uncle. After breakfast, she went to her mother's with the framed and matted eleven by fourteen painting in the front seat of her car, out of reach of her son in the back seat.

"Thanks, Mom, for watching Buddy today. Do you need anything from town?" Brynn hoped she didn't need to rush back home right away.

"No, Hun. Thank you, though. Do you need me to pick up Ellie when she gets home from school?" Adelle scooped Buddy up in her arms. Brynn watched her mother with admiration. She was a devoted mother, a patient and loving grandmother, and above all, a good friend. Not unlike Brynn in stature, she was about 5'3", thin, with dark hair and eyes, and gifted with endless energy and enthusiasm. She was so like Brynn's maternal grandmother, who lived to be 97, and said her secret to longevity was to put her two feet on the floor every morning and get going. So far, Adelle seemed to be adhering to the same secret recipe for long life. It seemed so unfair that her mother would likely live the better part of her life without a companion since Brynn's father, Ted, died in a car accident when Brynn and her brother were still in high school.

"I'll be home before the bus gets there with Ellie. Mom, do you know Cole Emmick? Arlo's uncle? I did a painting of his house, and I'm taking a copy to him. Come see it! It's in the car!" Brynn was as giddy as a calf on new pasture, literally springing from the ground in excitement.

Setting Buddy down, Adelle followed Brynn to her car. Brynn took the painting from the car and handed it to her mother. Adelle studied the picture, looking closely at the delicate, translucent strokes of color added to the black and white photo. "Brynn, this is stunning! I'm sure Mr. Emmick will love it." She handed the painting back to Brynn. "No, I don't know him personally, but I've heard the name. He's in the home, right?"

"Yes. I'm going there now. I think I'm going to start selling my paintings again, Mom. I had so much fun with this!" Brynn beamed.

"Good for you, Brynn! You know I'll help in any way I can," Adelle hugged her daughter tightly and then sent her on her way.

As Brynn drove the eight miles to Perris, their hometown in southern South Dakota, she tried to imagine what Cole Emmick would be like, and hoped he wasn't a crotchety old grouch, like her own aged uncle had been. "Sharp as a tack" could have more than one meaning.

Three miles from town, she passed the Think sign marking the spot where her father had died and blew a ritual kiss. The diamond shaped Think signs were part of a SD DOT "Drive Safely" program started in the 70s. The markers were grim but meaningful monuments to lives lost on SD roadways. Although not her father's home or his grave, the spot was sacred to her, the spot he took his last breath on earth.

She arrived at Perris Manor, and entered the facility with the painting in her arms and butterflies in the pit of her stomach. She found an aide who directed her to Cole Emmick's room, discovered it near the end of the wing, and knocked lightly as she peeked in the half-open door.

"Mr. Emmick? Hello?" Brynn stepped slowly into the room. Two elderly gentlemen sitting in the double occupancy room stared at her expectantly. Their room was like a small apartment: each side of the room equipped with everything they needed in life, or everything they were forced to choose when their lives were reduced to a 10 by 12 foot space. Both beds were made with the sheets tightly tucked, and cozy, knitted blankets folded at the feet. Family pictures in various sizes and from different eras adorned the walls and dressers, but none looked immediately familiar to Brynn. Coffee mugs sat on a card table near a backgammon board along with a chicken feeder-type candy dispenser filled with pastel M&M's.

Each in their own half of the room, the men were seated in wheelchairs. Apparently they were not bound to them, Brynn assumed, seeing two walkers standing nearby.

The man nearest the door spoke first.

"Well, hello! Come in, come in!" It was obvious that he didn't get many visitors, but at least he didn't appear to be a crotchety old grouch. "How are you? Have a seat!"

Brynn was relieved that he seemed to expect her. "Mr. Emmick?" she said as he prattled on and motioned to the various places she could sit. "Did Arlo tell you I was coming? I'm Brynn Young. I'm a friend of Arlo and Eva's. I brought you something." She found herself prattling too.

"My, how you look like my own granddaughter! Such a pretty little thing, like you ... " He grinned and rambled on. He looked small in the wheelchair. There wasn't a trace of Arlo in him. With his thick jowls, sagging nose, bushy eyebrows, and only a narrow band of thin, white hair that wrapped around the back of his head, he looked like one of the Muppets. He sported a sweatshirt and sweat pants, though she doubted he would be doing any strenuous workouts any time soon. It would not be difficult to like him, Brynn thought, but she hoped she could get in a word before suppertime. She waited, her mouth slightly open, ready for the opportunity to speak.

Brynn fidgeted, standing in the middle of the room as he continued to talk. The other man just sat quietly in his chair, observing, with mild amusement on his face, as if he knew something she didn't.

Her new friend couldn't contain his excitement. "Would you like to sit? There's a folding chair in my closet, Honey. Or sit on my bed. Please, sit, sit! It's so good of you to come. Would you like some candy? Peanuts! Here! Have some peanuts!" He held out the dish, putting his slippered feet on the floor and scooting closer to her with his wheelchair. Overwhelmed with the sudden and intense attention, Brynn felt like a new kindergarten teacher with infatuated students. She smiled awkwardly, uncertain, and glanced at the peanuts and then at the other old man, who looked her straight in the eye, wrinkled his nose a little, and gave a quick and subtle shake of his head.

"Uh, no ... No thank you, Mr. Emmick. I'm just here to give you something ... " Brynn tried to break into the man's endless dialogue, grateful for the hint from the quiet one.

The other man finally broke his silence, and smiling at Brynn, said calmly, "Spencer, she's not here for you. Why don't you go see Hazel? I saw her pass by our door just now. I think she's looking for you."

Spencer turned his head toward the door. "Hazel? Are you sure?" He turned back to Brynn and Cole. "Yes. Yes!

I think I'll go find her. Nice meeting you, Miss. You be sure to come back. You're such a pretty thing, just like my granddaughter. You must meet my friend, Hazel. Hazel would just adore you ... "

"You'll miss her," the real Mr. Emmick said.

"Oh, yes. Of course." Spencer said, and raised his eyebrows as if suddenly remembering something he had forgotten to do. He left the room, using his feet to move his chair. He looked both ways in the hall, as if waiting for a break in heavy traffic.

"Mr. Emmick?" Brynn faced the old man, holding out her hand for him to shake, which he promptly accepted. His hands were soft, but the handshake was firm and confident. She was impressed with his elegant appearance; white cotton dress shirt buttoned up to his chin, a half-buttoned pale yellow sweater, gray dress slacks, and shiny black dress shoes. He was thin, long-legged, with neatly cut silver hair and an overall refined look about him.

"Yes. Nice to meet you, Miss Young. Arlo told me you were coming. Sorry about all that ... " he chuckled, "There isn't much entertainment here, I'm afraid." His voice was deep and smooth.

"Well, it's not like either of us could have stopped that train wreck, right?" she played along, already liking him immensely.

"Spencer is a good man." Cole Emmick shook his head slowly, then added, "But just a tip: don't eat the peanuts." He looked at her, grinning faintly, as if he expected her to know why. "Never heard the joke?"

"I don't believe I'm familiar with it." Brynn sat down on Spencer's bed. "But I love a good joke ... or even a bad one."

"You don't spend much time here, do you?" he asked, but continued, "It's just a very old joke about a pastor who visits a resident, but the resident is sleeping. So while he's waiting for the old man to wake up, he sees some peanuts in a dish nearby and helps himself. When the old man wakes up, the pastor confesses that he has eaten all the old man's peanuts. The old man says, 'Oh, that's all right. I was done with them.' 'Done with them?' the pastor asks. And the old man says, 'Yeah, I already sucked all the chocolate off of them.'"

Brynn choked on a laugh, grateful she hadn't eaten the peanuts. Cole laughed as well, apparently pleased that he could still tell a joke, albeit a bad one.

When their laughter subsided, Brynn got around to the reason for her visit.

"Mr. Emmick,"

"Please, call me Cole."

"Cole," she smiled, "Arlo was kind enough to show me your old house—I hope you don't mind. I painted a picture of it, and wanted to bring you a copy," Brynn picked up the picture and held it out to him.

"You painted it? Are you an artist?" He reached for the picture, his eyes sparkling. She could feel his eagerness to see his home again.

"Of sorts ... " Brynn demurred, and noticed the man's hands trembling as he held the picture, studying it closely. He took in the colors she'd added to his former home:

the faint green water color over the naked trees, the subtle white shades of the siding on the house, the slightest hint of smoke coming from the chimney, and an almost imperceptible, ethereal image of a person standing in the window. His chin puckered slightly and his gray eyes glistened with tears. She didn't know what to say, hoping she hadn't hurt or insulted him.

"Oh. My word. This is … " He cleared his throat and continued, his hoarse voice an octave lower, "Beautiful. Just beautiful."

He started to hand the picture back to her.

"Oh, no, Cole. That's yours … if you want it … ." Brynn reminded him.

"Well, you don't say! I'd be honored. Thank you! Thank you so much." He paused to look longingly at his home once more. "Sally and I lived there for many, many years. We built that house, you know. It was nothing fancy, mind you, but it was ours. Sally died a few years back. She would have loved this."

Brynn wasn't sure where to go from here, but she didn't feel at all inclined to leave. "So how long were you married?" she asked, partly out of curiosity, partly out of awkwardness, anxious to lighten the mood with small talk.

"Fifty-five years," he said, solemnly, "She was a few years younger than I. I should have gone before her." It was clear that he felt the same sense of unfairness that Brynn felt for her mother.

Cole turned his chair and wheeled himself over to his bedside table, picked up a framed photo, and held it out to

Brynn. She rose to receive it and lingered on his side of the room while he spoke.

"That was taken on our 50th anniversary, back in 1985."

"She was a lovely woman."

"Are you in a hurry? I must be keeping you ... ."

"No, not at all!" Brynn took a seat in a chair on his side of the room, suggesting that she had all the time in the world, and compared to him, she did.

Cole opened the drawer on his nightstand and retrieved a photo album from it. "Would you like to see some photographs? I may even have one or two of the house." The brown leather binder was crackled with age and worn at the corners. The care with which he handled it was a touching testament to his cherished memories. He moved his chair close to Brynn's and handed her the album. The thick book was heavy and tattered.

"I would love to." Brynn opened the book carefully. Most of the photographs were held in place with corner tabs, but some were merely stuck in the book like an amendment to his life story.

"We never had children." Cole broached the subject that Brynn was too polite to address. He was quiet a moment as Brynn looked at the old photos.

"Here's a picture of the house in, oh, I'd say, 1942 or 1943, just a few years after we'd built it. See that pretty fretwork? My wife chose to have the fretwork outside on the porch rather than the fancy things indoors. Not much money in those days for extravagance, after the Depression and so forth, but it was my wedding present to her."

"It's lovely. She must have been so proud." As Brynn looked at Cole's face, she saw a change in his expression. He was somewhere in his past, reliving a happier time.

She turned back to the book, lifted the next page, and suddenly felt her hands begin to shake, her face grow hot, and her heart begin to thump wildly. She stood abruptly, knocking the book from her lap, sending photos fluttering and sliding across the floor.

"My goodness! Oh, Mr. Emmick ... Cole ... I'm so sorry! I ... I don't know what's wrong with me ... ." Brynn got down on her hands and knees to gather the items.

"No harm done, dear. None whatsoever." Cole took the book that Brynn recovered from the floor and set it on his nightstand. Brynn could see the bewilderment on his face.

Brynn scrambled to pick up the photos, but she could hardly find the coordination to pick them up, much less arrange them neatly. She put the messy stack of photos on his bed and rose to her feet.

"I just remembered ... I need to ... I'm sorry. Can I come back sometime?" Brynn struggled to appear calm, but she could tell that Cole was not blind to her distress.

She offered her hand in parting, but instead of shaking it, he gently kissed it, held it for a moment with both hands, and said, "Ms. Young, nothing would make me happier. Thank you so much for your gift." He had to have felt her trembling.

In an attempt to appear blithe, Brynn pointed at him in a mock lecture and said, "No peanuts!"

Cole winked and smiled. She appreciated his graciousness, but she knew her false bravado was not lost on him. Brynn quickly turned and left the room, fighting the urge to run to the parking lot.

Once in her car, Brynn put both hands on the steering wheel, closed her eyes, and pushed her head into the back of her seat. She forced herself to slow her breathing, inhaling through her nose, exhaling through her mouth.

She opened her eyes and put her still-shaking hands on her lap. She couldn't believe it. She couldn't believe that the people she thought she had *imagined* in Emmick's home looked *exactly* like the Emmicks in the photo album.

CHAPTER FIVE

HOW CAN THAT BE?!
How can that be?!
As Brynn drove home, only those four words streamed through her brain, like a news crawler on the bottom of a television screen.

How is it possible, she thought, finally able to interrupt the ticker, *that I saw two people in that house who actually existed, or at least imagined them so clearly, exactly as they had looked in real life?*

It's not possible. It was a fluke. Lots of men had sideburns in those days, and women wore their hair in French rolls, and lots of men set their hats on kitchen tables—tables that were chrome and yellow laminate. Lots of people looked like that in those days ... .*but they didn't look exactly like the Emmicks.*

"Maybe I saw a ghost. That's it. I saw ghosts. No, wait. Cole is still alive. Not ghosts. What *was* that?" Brynn talked aloud to herself, and she wasn't ashamed of it this time. It helped her to think clearly, and now was a really good time to do just that.

Brynn picked up Buddy from her mother's and went home, made a cup of coffee, and sat at the kitchen table. Several thoughts raced through her mind. The one at the forefront was to go back to that house—alone.

And then what? What if I see them again? Scream and run? Talk to them? Ask them "How's it going?"

"What the *hell* ... " Brynn spoke out loud and Buddy answered.

"Uh-oh, Mommy."

"Oh, I'm sorry, Baby. Mommy's sorry. I wasn't talking to you."

"Is there someone else here?" He looked around.

"No, Hun, I was talking to myself. I'm sorry I cursed."

"That's okay. I won't tell Daddy," he whispered and ran away, as if he were going off to hide her secret in a special place to be used against her at a later date.

Okay, Brynn. Get a grip. You need to think this through. What if you go back there again, and you see them again. What are you going to do? What if you don't *see them again?* That thought scared her almost as much as the prospect that she would see them again ... maybe more.

If I don't see them again, how do I know I saw them to begin with? Maybe I imagined the whole thing? Maybe I'm losing my mind. Maybe today was all just a big dream. Or the last three days was just a dream. Not likely, dang it.

Compelled to look at the pictures she had taken of the Emmick's home, Brynn fetched them from her cabinet in the family room and spread them out on the table, hoping she could glean some clues from them. Maybe refresh something in her mind that would give her an answer she could live with until she knew more.

She was still poring over the photos when Ellie arrived home from school, and still when Jackson arrived home from Wes'. Supper was not made, chores were not done, but more concerning to Brynn was the fact that she still had no idea how to explain what she saw.

Jackson joined her at the table and looked at the photos. He studied them with her, as if he knew what they were looking for.

"How did Mr. Emmick like his picture?"

"He liked it a lot. He's a very nice man ... " Brynn looked at Jackson and tried to imagine herself telling him what happened.

"Well, when I was in the house, you know, after I told you I wouldn't go in, but we won't talk about that right now, I imagined I saw some people who looked a lot like how the Emmicks looked back in the 50s, except they weren't real, they were like ghosts, but they can't be ghosts, because one of them is still alive, and technically, one of them could be a ghost, since one of them is dead, but that wouldn't explain why I saw both of them, and we don't really believe in ghosts do we, since we're Christian and all, or do we?" Yeah, that ought to go well. Brynn just stared at her husband blankly. She took a deep breath.

"Brynn?"

"He's a very nice man. I better get supper started and go do chores, huh?" Brynn avoided the subject altogether and decided she needed more information before she could confide in anyone about this strange occurrence.

While Brynn did chores, she went through all the possible explanations. It could have been ghosts, or one ghost projecting images of things that happened. Maybe it was just her imagination, or perhaps, she, at one time, saw a photo of Cole and Sally at Arlo and Eva's, and that would explain how she knew what they looked like. And the furniture. And Cole putting his hat on the table, and Sally removing it. C*rap. I have to go back.*

During their simple supper of vegetable beef soup and crackers that night, Brynn was quiet, contemplating how and when she was going to go back to the Emmick's house, and more importantly, how she would react to whatever happened then. Brynn saw Jackson watching her, obviously noticing the usual table chatter and chaos was at a minimum tonight. *One more thing for him to obsess over.*

"Ellie, how was school today?" Jackson asked.

"It was okay. We learned about fires, and Jessica and I got pushed off the swings," she said as she lined up her saltines in a neat row.

Brynn watched Buddy as he ate. He took a sip of milk after every bite of soup.

"And Mrs. Carmichael made *those boys* apologize to us … " Ellie continued.

Buddy was oblivious to his mother's watchful eye and Ellie's banter as he ate and drank.

"So what did you learn about fires?" Jackson asked his daughter.

"Well, there was a fireman there and he showed us his cute outfit ... " Ellie buttered two crackers and laid them down, then crumbled two more into her soup.

"You mean his uniform? His fire hat and gear?" Jackson smiled, amused by Ellie's girlish vernacular, but refrained from laughing.

"Yeah, that stuff ... "

"Buddy," Brynn said quietly, looking her son in the eye.

"Hm?" he answered, his mouth full of soup.

Brynn raised her eyebrows and tipped her head in the direction of his glass of milk.

Buddy raised his eyebrows in reply, lowering his chin, as if to imply they had a deal and he was still good with it. He tried to wink, which looked more like he was being poked by a needle, smiled at his mother, and brought his glass to his lips. With an if-you-can-swear-I-can-spit-my-vegetables-into-my-milk look, he emptied his mouth.

"And Jessica said her butt *still* hurt ... "

"Jack Jr."

"Mommy swore!" Buddy shouted.

The chaos at the supper table calmed Brynn. It made everything that happened at the Emmick's house now seem overblown. She appreciated the distraction. She was reading far too much into whatever it was she thought she saw, and until she had an opportunity to go back to the house, she wasn't going to stew about it anymore. It was a strange coincidence, but nothing more.

51

The following day, Brynn did her chores early, and went for a run while Jackson was there with the children. She decided she would paint another picture of Emmick's home place after getting Ellie off to school. It was another beautiful spring day, cool but sunny, and Brynn felt refreshed and as ready as a robin.

As she gently colored her black and white, she reasoned that she was overreacting, that she basically imagined everything, including the man and woman in the kitchen and their resemblance to Cole and Sally in the photo. She chided herself for thinking it was so real. She would simply go back sometime and prove that it was all just silly.

If it's all so silly, why do I keep trying so hard to discount it?

Eventually, concentration proved as elusive as answers. Brynn put her half-finished painting away and called her mother.

"Mom," Brynn released her rambunctious son from the car, noting how he was like a bull bursting from the chute at a rodeo. "I'm just going to spend a couple hours taking pictures. I'll call you, okay? Often." Brynn watched her son scramble up the steps to her mother's house, grateful for the reprieve, but also grateful for a mother who wanted to be useful. "Wear him out and there's a bonus in it for you."

"Where will you be? In case someone asks ... " Adelle was only doing her duty as a concerned mother, *and* as a spy to a certain paranoid husband, Brynn thought. She was hoping to avoid that type of question.

"Oh, all over, really. I'll call you." Brynn hopped in her car and sped out the driveway, narrowly escaping a fib.

Brynn pulled up the driveway to the old Emmick house and parked her car out of sight from anyone who may pass on the road. She picked her way through the tall grass, glancing back at the road several times, feeling like a common criminal. She was more than a little nervous, but tried to appear casual as she walked up the front steps to the house, as if someone was watching, which she hoped with all her being was not the case.

"Hello!" she called as she entered, and immediately felt foolish, but at the same time, was greatly relieved when no one answered. *Who would answer, Brynn? A ghost? A murderer? Really.* Brynn again felt foolish, but smiled at her own embarrassment, and enjoyed her moment of folly. It calmed her nerves.

The house looked exactly as it had a few days ago, but it seemed emptier somehow. It was as empty as any house that had nothing in it could be, but the emptiness was something she felt, not something she saw or didn't see. It felt that way because of what she knew about its owner and what his life had become. As hollow and forsaken as a tomb, the house echoed with her footsteps. Dust floated in the cold sunshine that streamed through the dirty windowpanes.

She walked cautiously into the living room, just as she did the other day. And just as she did the other day, she imagined furniture, décor, a mid-century setting. She walked into the kitchen and waited to see if she was crazy.

She saw the man enter the kitchen, the woman pour his coffee and set muffins on the table, saw the man sit down, set his hat on the table, saw the woman toss the hat to the floor, saw them share a smile. *Reruns. Again.*

Brynn wondered if she was merely remembering what she saw the other day, but then something different happened: the woman slowly sat down at the table and set her delicate hand on his. They paused for a moment, the woman's smile becoming strained as her eyes filled with tears. She said something to the man that Brynn didn't—or couldn't—hear. The man, whom Brynn knew now to be Cole, stood, went to his wife's—Sally's—chair and pulled her up into his arms. They wept silently, as Brynn searched the room for a distraction. She noticed a small, cardboard box on the table with layette pieces draped over the side. Brynn felt like a voyeur watching this very private exchange, and briefly considered finding a way to slip out of the room unnoticed. As soon as the illogical idea came to her, the vision went away.

She stood motionless in the kitchen. Brynn wasn't sure what she saw, what it meant, how she saw it, if she saw it, if anyone else could see it, what caused it, or what to do about it. Coming back to the house didn't answer her questions. It created more. She was also surprised that she wasn't more alarmed or scared or worried about her sanity. The whole thing *seemed* as natural as a memory.

As promised, Brynn left the kitchen, went outside, and dialed her mother, a call that was essentially as evasive and non-committal as any parolee's. What Adelle didn't know wouldn't hurt her. Regardless, Brynn snapped a few shots of the house to assuage her own guilt about misleading her mother.

Brynn reentered the house, and although she wanted to know more about the story in the kitchen, she also wanted to see if any other visions would come to her in other rooms.

She went to the steps that led upstairs from the kitchen. She stopped and listened, then began ascending slowly. She was nervous once more. In the movies, this was the part where something jumped out at her or a door slammed shut, except here, there was no loud music to warn her. She hated being manipulated by sad or suspenseful music. She always muted those parts of a movie—a habit Jackson detested. Consequently, he preferred to go to the theater rather than watch movies at home: she couldn't control the volume—just as she couldn't control what would happen here. At least loud music would be a sign to run.

Brynn reached the top of the steps without incident. Nothing jumped out at her, no doors slammed, no goth ghouls crawled down from the ceiling. She stood in the upstairs hall. Doors to three small bedrooms and a small bathroom stood open. Nothing happened. She wasn't sure what to expect or what to do, if anything, and she stood for several minutes.

Eventually, Brynn could picture a few framed portraits on the walls, and a small table in the hall, holding a clunky, black telephone. *This is how it started,* Brynn recognized, *things appeared to me as if I imagined them, or like I remembered them, even though I've never been here.*

Brynn waited while the scene unfolded before her. Sally appeared near a doorway, came to the phone, picked it up and answered it. Brynn heard nothing. Sally smiled, her chest heaved with emotion, and her eyes filled with tears. She spoke, set the receiver back in its cradle, and turned to Cole, who had entered the hall. They embraced, and once again, Brynn felt out of place and intrusive. Cole gently placed his hand on Sally's abdomen. It was Brynn's turn to smile.

The vision disappeared just as the vision in the kitchen had. Leaving, Brynn was eager to see what more she could witness in these chilly, dark, and dusty rooms.

She went to the room from which it seemed Cole had emerged, and walked to the center, waiting, while she processed what she had seen in the hall.

The room began to take shape around her, and Brynn saw atop a braided rug, a double bed with a spoon-carved headboard, fitted with floral sheets, and a thin, hand-tied quilt. On the wall opposite from her sat a dresser with attached mirror, the surface draped with a lace scarf and adorned with family photos. Fresh-cut, pink peonies were placed in a mason jar on the nightstands along with matching hobnail lamps.

A younger Cole than she had seen in the kitchen sat in his pajamas on the edge of the bed. Brynn instantly questioned her decision to come into such a private place, but then she noticed that Cole looked uncomfortable. He sat stick straight, his hands on his knees, his head down. A younger Sally materialized in the doorway, her pale pink nightgown stained red below her waist. Cole rose from the bed, facing his wife, and she slowly shook her head in answer to his unspoken question. She backed up to the wall for support and slowly slid to the floor, her face contorting in grief as she wept. Cole went to her, smoothed her hair from her wet face, kissed her tenderly, and picked her up and carried her to their bed.

Brynn couldn't bear to see more. She left the room and hurried down the stairs in tears.

"What was that?!" she shouted as she reached the kitchen. She was no longer embarrassed by her own voice in the empty dwelling. "And why am I seeing it?" There was no answer from the dust, the gloom, or the cold, desolate house. She felt like she was being taunted. She was angry and confused, but, oddly, unafraid. Were the events in the bedroom before or after the phone call in the hall? Was any of this related to the events in the kitchen? Brynn didn't recall whether the Cole and Sally in the hall were the older or younger version. She was becoming more confused.

Brynn paced through the house, hesitant to stay in one room or in one place for more than a few seconds. She should be calling home soon, but she knew better than to try to talk on the phone right now. Unable to calm herself with her pacing, she stepped outside into the warmth of the sunshine, feeling as though she'd been away from earth for a week. She wiped her face and defiantly stuck her hands on her hips as she glared at the house, daring it to answer her.

When no response came, even though none was expected, Brynn pulled her phone from her jacket pocket and called her mother. She kept her eye on the house, as if it might pull up its tethers and bolt.

"Hi, Mom. Just checking in ... Yeah, things are fine. I'll be home within the hour probably." She didn't know if she would be able to figure anything out in that allotted time, but that's all the time she was going to devote to a house that manipulated her feelings and did its own muting. She was beginning to understand how her husband felt when she muted the volume on the television.

Brynn was determined to use the next hour productively. She went back into the house and stood in the living room, willing it to give her something. Hopefully something boring. She didn't have to wait long. She noticed the room had evolved into something a little newer in décor, although not much better, perhaps late 1960's to early 1970's design. Within seconds, she saw Cole and Sally enter the room, turn on their color television, and sit down on the sofa. A western show, "Bonanza", played silently on the television.

Brynn waited for something more to take place, but was only rewarded with the two grasping each other's hands. *Well, you asked for boring,* she thought.

As she stood in the living room, more images came to her. She saw the couple lugging heavy suitcases into the room and preparing for a trip. It was apparent that they had traveled.

Brynn went back into the kitchen, and along with a replay of the previous vision, similar pieces of the couple's history came to Brynn, not as though it happened around her, but in her mind, and of this room. Visions, memories that were clearly not her own, appeared to Brynn: Sally running rinsed clothes through a wringer of an old washing machine and dropping them into a basket, Sally canning vegetables and cooking meals, with Cole coming and going, sometimes helping. They were all moments that one would think of if they were to reminisce about their lives. *Whose memories were they?*

It was plain to Brynn now that these were memories— seemingly, memories borrowed from the couple or the house. *But how? It's absurd! A house can't have memories!* She couldn't comprehend how she saw them, or why. What determined the order in which she saw them? Did it work like her own memory seemed to work, her mind bringing the most powerful, compelling, and moving moments of her life to the front of the memory bank?

Brynn tried to understand what she'd witnessed in the house. She could assume that Cole and Sally had lost at least one child to miscarriage, and that they traveled, but beyond that, she knew little else. She wanted to know more. Most importantly, she wanted to know how much of what she saw was real.

Or is it all in my head?

CHAPTER SIX

T HE NEXT COUPLE OF DAYS were blessedly uneventful for Brynn, with the exception of pig chores. The change in weather had triggered a few minor health issues in the barn and Brynn needed to spend more time tending to the herd. Her pigs had runny noses, mild coughs, and were listless, much like her own children when they got colds. As with the colds in her children, it was viral and there was little to do for her pigs except treat them with aspirin to alleviate their symptoms.

Brynn enjoyed learning about pigs and their idiosyncrasies. The psychology of the swine family fascinated her. While some people—especially people who were never around hogs—assumed that pigs could be vicious and untrustworthy, Brynn knew them to be intelligent and affectionate. They made excellent pets. They were a social, playful animal, but even in confinement, as in the wild, they resorted to the survival-of-the-fittest behavior, weeding out the sick or maimed, picking on it until it ultimately died of a heart attack from the stress.

Pigs were also very territorial. Before Brynn had the sorting system, which allowed all of her pigs to be in one group, there was a pecking order that they all adhered to in their former pens of approximately 30 pigs. One could put different pigs in a new pen and they would establish their own rank, but to put a pig into an established pen was basically sentencing the new pig to a cruel, horrible death. Pigs were very adept at picking out a stranger, using their keen olfactory skills to sniff out the new pig to the group, and would once again, bite and chase the new pig until they killed it.

Brynn knew some tricks to outsmart the pigs and their bullying tactics. She collected old perfumes, dumped them into separate spray bottles, and when the pigs started to single out a new pig, she sprayed the pigs with different scents, particularly their ears. It didn't hurt them in any way; it only confused their senses and made it impossible for them to detect any scent that wasn't familiar. It was *all* unfamiliar. It was really quite funny, thinking of her pigs smelling like little old ladies at a church luncheon. Eventually, they would give up trying and take a nap, and by the end of the day, they all smelled the same—like manure.

Odors ... scents ... aromas. Brut cologne reminds me of Dad. Certain odors could elicit a long-buried memory, like the smell of wet ashes after her uncle's house fire or her father's favorite cologne. Her mind flashed back to her visions at Emmick's home.

Did she smell something that made her see those visions?

And why couldn't she hear what was happening seemingly in front of her? From her own memories that she could recall the sound of a scream, the inflection in someone's voice, a distinct sound linked to a powerful recollection, or the unique melody of a specific tune. She mused over this as she finished chores, showered, and went to her mother's to pick up the kids.

Perhaps I can't hear them because they aren't my memories. No, that can't be it—if that was the case, I shouldn't be able to see them either.

Why am I even wondering why I can't hear them when I should be wondering why I am even able to see them! It must have something to do with the house. Or my connection with the Emmicks. The whole thing is so bizarre!

Brynn's brain ached from thinking about it. It was far easier to just accept it and not dwell on the complexities. That didn't stop her from wanting to learn whatever she could about the house, however. Eva, Arlo's wife and her friend, might know more about Cole and Sally and the house, but Brynn was unsure about how to broach the subject without divulging what she'd seen. She didn't need one more person worried about her safety or sanity. It would be easier to deal directly with Cole, especially since he was not one of the people who could "mother" her. She was merely biding her time until she could manage another visit to Perris Manor.

That opportunity presented itself that day, when Brynn found that she needed to run to town for a few groceries. She grabbed her list, loaded the kids in the car, and drove to the nursing home.

Brynn parked her car and unbuckled her children from their car seats as she tried to think of a way that she could ease into a conversation with Cole about what she witnessed in his house. She wasn't having any luck.

"Now, kids," Brynn wondered why her lectures always started with the word "now." As she turned the children to face her, she took turns looking them each in the eye as she spoke. "When we get to Mr. Emmick's room, you mind your manners, play quietly, and if you can behave, I'll have fruit snacks for you, all right?" She also wondered why her lectures always ended with "all right" or "okay" when it was basically an order. "And don't eat the peanuts," she added quietly, unsure if she should be serious about that last directive. She was nervous, second-guessing her every word and action.

When she reached Cole and Spencer's room, she knocked and was greeted warmly by both men. She found them in the midst of a card game, and wished that she had phoned ahead.

"Sorry to interrupt your card game. Should I come back another time?"

"No!" they practically yelled, pushing the cards to the side and waving the three into their makeshift bachelor pad. Brynn smiled and guided her children into the room, feeling like she had just come home for Christmas.

"Cole, Spencer, these are my children, Ellie and Buddy."

"I'm Buddy!" Buddy announced, apparently worried that he might be mistaken for his sister, and the three adults chuckled. Spencer held out his hand for Buddy to shake, and Buddy gladly accepted. The children took the opportunity to show Spencer the "cooler" way to shake—the fist bump.

Brynn noticed that Spencer was once again—perhaps always—dressed in comfortable sweats, and Cole looked as though he were ready for church in his gray trousers, dress shoes, buttoned-up light blue shirt and argyle sweater vest.

Cole was the first to speak this time. "So what brings you by?"

"Oh, we were just in town getting some groceries and I thought I'd bring the kids over to meet you."

"I'm so glad to see you again. When you left last time, I was worried I had said something ... ."

"Oh! Psh! No!" Brynn had spent so much time worrying about how to begin *this* conversation with Cole, she had completely forgotten about how she was going to explain the last one. "I'm so sorry about that! I had just forgotten something and needed to run ... ." She fumbled through her explanation just as she fumbled through her oversized leather purse, hoping both would be an adequate distraction.

Brynn pulled a couple packages of dinosaur shaped fruit snacks from her bag and handed them to her children, completely forgetting that they had yet to prove themselves deserving. Buddy and Ellie opened them and dumped the contents onto the card table and began to trade flavors as Spencer gathered the cards together. "You kids like Slap Jack?" Both declared themselves masters of the game. He shuffled and dealt the deck three ways, slowly enough to give the children time to eat their fruit snacks, but Ellie and Buddy stuffed their mouths full in order to get right to the game.

Brynn took a seat in the chair on Cole's side of the room.

"So how are you doing, Cole?" Brynn was anxious to steer the subject of conversation away from their last encounter.

"Quite well. Say! That painting of yours has gotten lots of attention here. I've had several compliments on it, you know. Where did you learn to do that?"

"Well, I've always loved photography, but I wanted to make it more … interesting. I learned a little bit about it in college." They turned their attention to the painting.

"It's similar to the hand-coloring done in the late 1800's, like on daguerreotypes, or more like Wallace Nutting's work, but you've gone even further with it … ." Cole gazed at his print as a surprised Brynn turned to him.

"You're familiar with Wallace Nutting's work?" A faint grin touched her face, astonished that he knew of the artist's work, but she didn't want to insult him by appearing as such.

"Oh, yes. He was very popular in our day," he said, as though today wasn't still his day, "He hand-colored black and white photos to make them look like color photos— you have put in life and color and light where there is none. You have a talent, young lady."

With a new appreciation for her own work, Brynn brightened and turned to study her painting, and decided to use the subject as a natural segue into her questions about the house.

"Cole, I hope you don't mind, but I went back to your house. I took a few more photos, looked around a bit..." She was still unsure how to tell him about her surreal experiences in his home. She looked at her children. One thing she was sure of now, however, was that it would be difficult, if not altogether unwise, to discuss those experiences with her children present. Brynn was annoyed with herself for being so impulsive and impatient. She glanced at her children and Spencer playing the card game, wishing she had thought ahead to this moment. She could have predicted this dilemma.

"Kids, no hovering. Ellie, Buddy, move your hands. How's anyone supposed to slap the jack if you're practically laying on it?" The children moved back a fraction of an inch.

"Did you get anything different this time?" Cole looked at her intently.

Brynn gaped at Cole. Her mouth hung open a bit, and she shut it quickly, realizing she probably looked like her brain cells had just stopped functioning.

"No, not really … ." she lied, staring back at her brood.

"You have beautiful children." Cole said. "Your son looks a lot like you."

Brynn smiled. That was code for " … your daughter doesn't." They heard it often. Ellie looked nothing like her brother.

"Thank you. He does. We tease Ellie about being adopted." Brynn remarked, a little louder than necessary.

Ellie looked up briefly from her hovering hand and smiled at her mother.

"She's not, of course," Brynn laughed a little, "That's what we tell everyone, and she's gotten used to the joke.

There's red hair in both my family and Jackson's, but she certainly looks a lot different from Jack Jr., doesn't she?" They were quiet for a while, watching the game since there was no other activity to occupy their attention.

"I regret not having children, especially now," Cole said.

C'mon, Brynn. Spit it out. "Okay. I lied." She couldn't look at him.

"What?"

She felt him staring at her.

"I did get something different ... saw something ... I can't explain." She turned to face him. "I know about the miscarriage."

Cole's expression was one of puzzlement and pain.

"I'm sorry," was all she could muster. For what, she wasn't sure.

A loud slap interrupted the quiet.

"Winner!" Ellie pointed to the sky and did a little victory dance.

Spencer gathered the cards and set them aside. "Perhaps the children would like to go to the lunch room just down the hall and have a cookie with me?" Spencer looked as hopeful and excited as her children, but Brynn saw understanding as well. She suspected he wasn't as addled as he let on.

"Of course. Kids, behave. Got it?" Brynn was relieved that she and Cole would have a moment alone to talk, and nervous for the same reason. The kids each grasped a handle on Spencer's chair, and he guided them out into the hall as other residents passed by on their way for the afternoon coffee time.

Cole wasted no time. "How do you know about that?" Cole's voice was almost a whisper, as if a conspiracy theory were about to be revealed. "We told no one."

Brynn had no defense. She knew things she had no right to know or reason for knowing them. She felt bad for Cole as well, sensing that he felt his vow of secrecy with his wife was violated without his consent or knowledge. Her eyes glimmered with hot tears of humiliation as she searched for words to explain. She knew she had to tell him what happened at his house, and do it fast. Cookies don't last long.

Brynn took a deep breath and exhaled slowly, steeling herself for whatever might come. Anger, distrust, being thrown out on her ear.

"Cole, I have to tell you something. I don't know how to explain it, really, but something weird happened when I was in your house. At first I thought I was imagining things, imagining what your house looked like back in the 50s. And then I saw a man and a woman in the kitchen, like I remembered it or something, but I still thought I was imagining it. Until I came to see you last time with the painting. When I was looking through your photo album, I saw that picture of you and your wife and I realized that the people I imagined—saw—in your kitchen were you and your wife. It scared me, and I ran ... " Confessing was like sliding down an icy hill; at the utterance of the first word, there was no stopping or turning back, and it was a hard, fast, and scary ride all the way to the bottom.

The old man nodded slightly as if to encourage her to go on.

"So I realized that I had to go back to your house. I went back a couple days ago. The same thing happened. Except this time, I saw more. I saw your wife in her pink nightgown ... the night she lost the baby ... I saw you and Sally in the hall when you got a phone call—I guess the call telling you she was pregnant, maybe? I'm not sure. I can't hear what's happening, I can only see it. I saw lots of things, but I haven't told anyone. I promise. I'm so sorry." And no soft landing.

Cole was no longer looking at Brynn, but at the print of his house. He looked melancholy, but not angry. He rubbed his chin, then propped his chin on the hand. Brynn waited. Finally, Cole dropped his hand and spoke quietly. "My wife didn't want to see the pity in people's eyes when we told them about the babies, so we eventually told everyone that we weren't having children, not that we couldn't or had lost them. When we lost the first one, early on, we decided that we wouldn't say anything about any future pregnancies until we were sure ... .."

Brynn felt a bit better, but that did nothing to stop the tears.

"We lost three ... .that we know of ... ." He paused, lost in thought for a moment.

Finally, Cole faced Brynn and patted her arm. "You've nothing to be sorry for. Now—about what you saw ... ."

"I didn't see anything, well, you know ... personal ... " Brynn tried to smile, but her quivering lips and her tears belied her attempt.

"Oh, heavens. I am an old man, completely beyond embarrassment," he chuckled briefly, and waved his hand in dismissal. "What do you think caused it?"

Brynn pulled a tissue from a nearby container and gathered herself. "I don't know. I only know that it didn't feel like I was seeing things, because it was in my head, not in the room. It's like I said: it felt really natural, like it was my own memory. But I've never been in that house, and I've never met you or your wife. All I can figure is that I was able to see ... memories that aren't mine."

Brynn knew how ridiculous it all sounded, and she was a little embarrassed to even tell anyone about it, but it felt good to be able to share the bizarre story. She waited for his laughter.

Cole gave her no reaction that indicated he didn't believe her. Brynn felt herself relaxing slightly.

"It is odd ... " he finally said. "I've never heard of anything like this."

"I know. Me neither."

Cole raised his eyebrows. "I'm not sure I believe in this sort of thing, but do you think you're psychic?" He looked excited at the prospect.

"I guess I never really believed in that stuff, either," she said. *But it sounds more appealing than the other options ... like brain damage, hallucinations ...*

"Couldn't hurt to look into it. It's never happened to you before?"

"No. But I'm not opposed to seeing if I could do it again ... " Brynn smiled for real this time.

Conversation paused as they thought.

"What does your husband think?" Cole asked.

"I haven't told him. He'd worry about me, and I don't think I can stand any more of that." She shook her head.

It's ironic, she thought dolefully, how her family had become like Ellie and Buddy's hands in their card game over her. They hovered over her, ready to strike at the sight of any "Jack" in her life: ten minutes without visual or verbal contact with her, strangers in the area, a random hang-up on the phone, a car driving by their house too slowly … . Everything made them worry, even the slightest intimation that perhaps she's remembering something about her abduction, which she never had and probably never would, according to her doctors. She'd silenced her phone, but that too, was becoming a nuisance.

"I remember hearing about your ordeal," Cole stated, a look of concern on his face.

"I'm fine." She fiddled with the tissue in her hand.

Brynn was relieved when Cole went back to the subject of her misplaced memories.

"Well, I would suggest going into other houses and seeing if you can recreate this … occurrence. That's the only way to find out—and please don't take offense—*if* this is real, what is causing it, why you see it, and so on."

She appreciated his honesty, but most of all, his friendship and trust. "None taken. That's not a tough assignment. I suppose I just need to be able to find out if what I see actually happened, and … " she thought a minute, " … I suppose I'll have to do it in a home that I don't have any memories in?"

"Not necessarily. You should be able to judge whether you were there or not, right?" Cole was leaning forward in his chair, obviously excited with their plan.

"True. I can go anywhere, actually. I could even go back to your house, but that wouldn't help much. I'll try to think of a new place." Brynn smiled, finally at ease.

"I really wish you would tell your husband about this," he pleaded.

"I will. In time." Brynn looked at the time and stood up. "I better find my children and let you get your coffee and cookies."

"I'll join you. Let me get my walker and take a stroll with you, if you're not in too much of a hurry."

"I would love that."

Standing, he looked like a different man. He was taller than she had guessed—about six foot three. He seemed more distinguished, stately. Age and time had not found his posture. His steps were purposeful and steady, and his expression was one of confidence. She knew that this relationship had turned an important corner and that he would become an integral part of her life. Walking side by side, they made their way slowly down the corridor to the dining hall where she found her children entertaining the residents. She was glad she had come.

CHAPTER SEVEN

U PLIFTED BY HER VISIT WITH Cole, Brynn arrived home, unloaded her car of kids and groceries, filled her cupboards, and got out her painting supplies. It would help her think while she figured out what to do next.

Whose home would she go to? Her mother's? Did she really want to know things about her mother, her parents, that she was never meant to see? And if she did go to someone's home, and then see, or rather, remember something, how would she verify that it happened without revealing her ability? More puzzling still to Brynn was the fact that she didn't recall seeing any "memories" when she'd last been in her mother's home, or her brother's home … .or any other homes, come to think of it. She didn't force these visions. They came to her as easily as a dream in sleep, as unconsciously as a thought, as involuntary as a blink. She didn't control them; she simply waited for them to occur. It didn't seem as though she could will them to come to her, and conversely, she couldn't keep them from happening, except to leave the room or not give them time to form in her mind. So the vision, the memory, apparently belonged to the room where she was at the time. Had something happened to cause this ability since she was last in someone else's home? Why did it not happen here, at home? Unless it was because the house's memories melded with her own and she simply failed to distinguish between the two.

First things first. Brynn needed to see *if* she could do it again, and worry about the rest later. For the next few hours however, she intended to work on her painting before making supper and checking on her ailing pigs.

Painting and pondering turned an easy, graceful dance, and a rapt Brynn absorbed the mood they created. Panic and self-doubt were gone. The only thing hovering over her at this moment was hopefulness. Tomorrow she would make a plan to visit someone's home.

It was not the thunder that awoke her very early the next morning, but the large, quivering canine on her chest. She struggled to squeeze out from underneath Bingo, and the petrified animal moved with her, stuck like an industrial magnet to steel. She stood and Bingo reluctantly lumbered to the floor. She rubbed the dog's velvety ears, and bent down and kissed her massive head. "Bingo, a turtle would make a better watch dog. It's only thunder, you big baby." Bingo rolled over onto her back, inviting Brynn to prove her love for her. Brynn rubbed the smooth tummy, and the moment she stopped, Bingo leapt into bed next to a still snoring Jackson.

Brynn covered her cotton shorts and tank top with a soft, oversized terry robe and pulled on a pair of fuzzy stockings that slouched thick and warm around her ankles. She loved mornings like this—slow, relaxed, and hushed— even amidst the booming thunder and hissing rain.

Lightning streaked and sizzled across the sky, and thunder rumbled through their hundred-year-old house, rattling the windows.

Coffee had no competition when it came to priorities on any given morning for Brynn. She padded past the sleeping monsters, down the stairs to the kitchen, and started her coffee. She sat at the kitchen table, watching the light show and savoring the aroma of the fresh brew that dripped ever so slowly into the pot. Coffee in hand at last, she went to the porch and sat down in the antique wicker chair. Although it was now only early April, it was surprisingly warm outside. Tornado weather, she thought, a little excitement pulsing with every flash of lightening.

Common sense eluded her when bad weather came around, with Brynn typically clinging to the windows like a child on Christmas Eve, waiting for something exciting to happen. Blizzards, thunder, lightning, downpours, tornados—they were all equal forms of entertainment. Her children were direct products of their genetics and environment, loving the storms, sleeping better when it was windy, noisy, raining; snuggling down further into their cocoon, safe and warm against the elements. The dog, though, was not related to her by blood so she at least had an excuse. Bingo was a rescue pet from the local animal shelter, the unfortunate name predestined by the old song, as their past two dogs were, and as would all future dogs, no doubt. Too many times singing "B-I-N-G-O ... " had decided that. Although Bingo's looks were imposing, she was as cuddly, lovable, and harmless as a fat baby.

The warmth and comfort of quiet ritual coaxed a relaxed Brynn into contemplation of what would be her next course of action. She would go to her mother's house for a visit today, and hope that she wouldn't learn anything that she wasn't supposed to know. She hated knowing what she was getting for Christmas—how would she deal with knowing some secret like an affair; or *worse*, what kind of sex life her parents shared? Perhaps she would visit her brother's if that didn't provide satisfactory results. If all else failed, she could go to Arlo and Eva's, and at the first hint of anything that even suggested *their* sex life, she would be fighting to escape before any ghastly images could be burned into her brain for eternity.

A roguish wind reached in to tease her hair as she sat watching little rivers of rainwater forming in her gravel driveway and on the sidewalk. Like a fussy child, the wind instantly changed its mood, yanking on her hair, and grabbing the rain and throwing it at her in angry gusts. Brynn walked around the corner of her wraparound porch and looked to the west from where the storm was coming. The black western sky was full of menacing clouds, approaching fast. She was transfixed by the roiling storm clouds, but decided it would probably be best to watch the tumult from inside. As she reached the door, she considered the fact that her family was likely still asleep; the house was hers to wander, to research, to utilize. She opened the door slowly, deliberately, and stepped inside. She would try to see her home as though through a stranger's eyes.

The décor was largely European in design, a soothing blend of muted tones, and the furnishings, a charming, romantic marriage of elegant and rustic, with a dash of whimsy. Brynn was madly in love with her home. It was hard for Brynn to appreciate this home as though through another person's eyes—the lovingly-collected pieces in these rooms told a story, held special meaning.

Matching furniture was a fundamental sin to her, with the exception of the side chairs in her dining room set, which were white-washed wood. The head chairs were upholstered linen arm chairs with button tucks, and all of them cozied up to a weathered farmhouse table with a distressed plank top. To Brynn, the whole concept of distressed furniture was form and function at its best. The idea of each scratch and nick and dent creating more character in a piece was design brilliance. Her family provided those elements of character for free.

Her living room was a graceful mix of antique, new, and thrift store and travel finds. The sofa was a neutral beige camelback with down-stuffed cushions and nail head trim, the chairs were Louis XV style that Brynn had reupholstered herself in a playful leopard print fabric, and the room was grounded with a worn tapestry wool rug that she found at an estate sale in the south, covering the ebony hand-scraped hardwood floors. Brynn was drawn to anything patinaed that proudly showed its age and flaunted its imperfections, like mirrors with etched silvering, metal with rust, wood with dings, and paint that was chipped. She briefly wondered if her affinity for old things was really an unconscious hope that someday, she could demonstrate such grace when she herself was ancient and obsolete.

She didn't take herself or her home too seriously. She also wasn't a fan of ruffles, or fussy opulence and grandeur that some Country French design exhibited. She was proud of her home, and the two rooms she now surveyed were indicative of her style throughout the whole house—comfortable, warm, and elegantly casual. A subtle smile curved her lips as she closed her eyes. To Brynn, home was like cocoa with a plump dollop of whipped cream, and right now, she was taking a long, delicious sip.

Knowing that, as memories go, one could retrieve them at any time, with or without seeing, she walked into the room, eyes closed, and waited to see what memories would come to her. She could recall practically any memory she chose to, with the exception of a few weeks surrounding her abduction, but hoped to see what the house would share with her nonetheless. She waited.

Nothing. Nothing that she herself didn't conjure up in her mind: birthday parties, family get-togethers, and the typical daily riot she called life. Feeling somewhat distracted by the storm outside, Brynn found it hard to concentrate on the task at hand, but nothing came to her that wasn't her own.

Perhaps this phenomenon was unique to Cole and Sally's home, Brynn thought, feeling somewhat sheepish in the realization that she hadn't thought of this before.

Regardless, she would do her research and hopefully come up with some kind of reasonable explanation that she could give to Cole, her only confidant in this mystery. She decided that she would not go back to Cole's house until she had exhausted all other options.

Assignment number one: Mom's house. Guilt singed Brynn's conscience for using her mother's home for her bizarre experiment, but as she turned her son loose from the car, she determined that it was just another visit—with a little paranormal activity thrown in, if she were lucky.

"Hi, Meema!" Buddy shouted as he kicked off his shoes and ran past his grandmother, Adelle, on his way to the snack cupboard, as usual.

"Hold on, Buster. First, kisses. Then, wash your hands. Third, where are your pleases and thank yous?" Adelle reminded him. Buddy ran back to Adelle, hugged her fiercely, and gave her a wet kiss on her cheek. "*Please* can I have a treat?"

"After you wash, you *may* have a treat." She hugged him, tousled his soft, curly hair, and let him escape. Adelle was born a grandmother. Brynn watched her mother with admiration. Adelle had always attested that Wes and Brynn were both very much like Ted, with Brynn being graced with more than her allocated share of stubbornness. But Brynn preferred to attribute her strengths to her mother, including the gift of tenacity, which she preferred to call it.

Months ago, Adelle had stated that it was Ted's stalwart drive in Brynn that saved her life throughout her ordeal; that a small part of her believed he was watching out for his baby girl as well. Adelle fancied that Ted was there with his only daughter, along with the angels and God Himself, giving her mettle and might, upholding her, just as he secretly held the bicycle seat when Brynn was learning to ride, letting her think it was an accomplishment that she alone could claim. Brynn knew Adelle was comforted by the notion that Ted's death could enable him to help his child in a way that he could not in life. Who was Brynn to argue?

Adelle also became a stiff advocate for Jackson, saying he was right to be concerned for Brynn, knowing how her fearlessness bordered on recklessness. In response, Brynn pretended not to know what they were talking about.

Adelle poured coffee for the two of them as Buddy raided the snack cupboard. "So what brings you by today? Are the men getting itchy to get in the field and driving you crazy?"

"Yes. Buddy is old enough to drive the Case, isn't he?" They chuckled at the idea of Buddy driving a tractor, but both of the women knew how fast children grew up on a farm and how they wanted at an early age to be included in the excitement of planting and harvesting. Buddy was already the official seat warmer in the farm equipment, and he rarely let Jackson out of the house without a promise to let him ride along in the tractor or the combine.

Strategic planning was not one of Brynn's strengths. She stood with her coffee, feeling restless and anxious to get on with her experiment.

"Mom, how long have you lived here?"

"Well, let me see. Your father and I married in 1971, and we moved here shortly after that. We bought this house from Bietler's. Remember them?"

"Yes. They scared me. They always wanted to keep me whenever we'd go visiting. I thought you'd leave me there." Brynn casually inspected various objects set about, hoping her mother would leave the room for a few minutes so she could have some time to absorb or see or whatever it was that was going to happen. She briefly considered trying to "wander" into another room alone, but her mother would follow her to every room except, of course, the bathroom. Experiment or no experiment, Brynn was fairly certain she didn't want to see what that room had to share.

"They were sweet. They just never had any girls and you were their favorite. So anyway, 40 years I've lived in this house. Why do you ask?"

"Just curious." She wandered around the kitchen, continuing to aimlessly examine things she couldn't care less about. "How old do you think this house is?" Brynn didn't know how long she could keep up this nonsense.

"It has to be over a hundred years old."

"Hm." She turned to look at her mother who was smiling faintly. Adelle was suspicious. Brynn fully expected the need to scramble for a reasonable explanation for the odd conversation, but Buddy came to the rescue by creating a diversion: sticky fingers on Adelle's arm.

"Okay, mister, let's go wash up, shall we?" Adelle led the sticky boy to the bathroom. Brynn set her cup on the table and waited for something to happen. She closed her eyes, held her breath, opened her eyes, breathed deeply, held perfectly still, and stepped into the middle of the dining room. She tried everything she could think of short of chanting, liturgical dance, and incense to prompt the visions or memories. She didn't see anything that she hadn't witnessed firsthand, and was hard pressed not to prompt her own memories out of frustration and lack of results with her experiment. It seemed to be so easy in Cole's house. They just came to her then—unsolicited, organic, and effortless—regardless of other people, distractions, want.

"So what's all this curiosity about the house?" Brynn startled when Adelle entered the room with Buddy again, picking up where the conversation left off. *Dang it!*

"Oh, nothing much. Your house is about as old as ours. Did you have any issues when you remodeled your bathroom? Jackson and I are thinking about re-doing our main floor bath." As far as explanations go, it was weak at best, but seemed to work ... so far. And it was the truth, for whatever that was worth.

Disappointment set the tone for the remainder of Brynn's visit with her mother. Buddy had a full tummy, however, so the afternoon wasn't a total wash, and Brynn was at least grateful that she had no irreparable damage done to her brain by uninvited carnal images.

"I'm stopping at Wes', Mom. Do you need me to take anything over there?"

"Thank you, Honey. Yes, take the paper. Wes hasn't read it yet."

One more chance to try this thing out. Whatever it was.

"Hello!" she called into the kitchen from the door. Deidre was still at work and Wes was probably helping Jackson. Handy. She stepped inside the doorway, stood still, and waited.

Breathe.

Buddy called from the car.

Concentrate. Memories ... memories ...

The horn blared.

Oh, Good Lord.

Again.

How did he get out of his car seat?

Exasperated, Brynn went back to her car and drove to Arlo and Eva's for one last try.

She rang the bell, clutching Buddy's hand as they stood on the step.

Arlo answered the door. "Hello, Brynn, Buddy! C'mon in! Eva's at work and I was just leavin' for parts, but ... "

Brynn stepped inside before he could rescind.

"I can't stay. I'm just wondering if ... uh ... if you and Eva have any ... um ... new kittens you're hoping to find homes for?"

"Kitties!" Buddy shouted.

"Uh, no, not that I know of," Arlo answered.

"Oh, that's too bad. Can we use your restroom? Buddy here ... " Brynn stammered.

"Sure. Down the hall on your right."

"But I don't have to—" Buddy protested.

"Yes, you do," she said to Buddy.

"Thank you, Arlo." Brynn hurried down the hall with Buddy. She sent him into the bathroom and waited outside the door. This wasn't the ideal scientific experiment she hoped for, but it would have to do.

Nothing came to her.

"Mom, I can't go." Buddy whined from behind the closed door.

Brynn opened the door a crack and whispered, "Just try, Buddy. Hurry."

She looked at the floor, concentrating. Nothing.

A couple minutes passed, and she heard the toilet flush, then the faucet running. The door opened and Buddy exited.

Buddy grabbed his mother's hands with his wet hands, jumping up and down, "Are we getting a kitty?" Brynn pretended not to hear.

"Thank you, Arlo. We'd better let you go get your parts. Tell Eva hi!" She rushed out the door before Arlo could ask any questions and she ended up with a cat she didn't want.

With chores and supper still undone, it was too late in the day to go anywhere else, so out of desperation and resignation, Brynn decided that she would go back to Cole's house early the next morning after chores. Buddy could go with his father in the tractor. Like ants from the earth, April drew busy farmers out into the field with the applications of fertilizer, and cultivating to turn the soil, warming the earth to ready it for seed. The Jacks could bond over their usual meaningful discussions about front-wheel assist tractors, what GPS was, where worms come from, what's for lunch, what's for snack, why God made dirt, and a barrage of other questions, for which five-year-olds are famed.

The prospect of going to Cole's old farm was not as exciting as the previous visits, expecting that she'd see the same things, or worse, nothing at all, both of which would offer no new explanations to the strange events. Brynn decided to take an alternate route. The extra time and fresh scenery of going the long way around might also refresh Brynn's enthusiasm about going back to Cole's farmstead.

The long way around proved to be the best way, as Brynn discovered another abandoned property to photograph and possibly inspect. She was glad she'd brought her camera.

Parking part way up the driveway to the house, Brynn got out of her car and slung her bag over her shoulder. She recognized the house. It had belonged to the family of Bradley Voog, a boy she had gone to school with, but it had been vacated when the family lost their farm operation during the farm crisis of the 80s. Having never been bought by another family or corporation, the building site, like many small family operations in the 80s, became obsolete and worthless to other farmers and banks as well. Multi-generational family homes were like the farmers of that era—cast off like a mink coat in the desert, considered more of a burden than a treasure. Many farmers, after losing more than any human should have to—homes, belongings, their source of income—and watching them be auctioned off along with their dignity to the highest bidder, gave up the only collateral they had left: their life.

Over a million American farmers went bankrupt in the 80s, and during that time, domestic abuse, assault, suicide, and murder in rural communities increased dramatically. Even though Brynn was just a child, she remembered the hushed conversations of the adults about the turmoil in her community.

She knew well the history of the agricultural depression from school, the news, and her father. Farming was profitable in the 70s, when technological advances in agricultural equipment encouraged farmers to invest in newer machinery. Unfortunately, the market bottomed out with soaring interest rates, a 25% or more drop in farmland values, and a surplus of grain due to an embargo to Russia, which caused grain and cattle prices to fall. Unable to make a profit, farmers defaulted on loans, forcing creditors to foreclose.

Tragic examples of the farm crisis were evident in not only the national news stories, but in the very county where Brynn and Jackson lived. The abandoned farm to the north of them once belonged to the Kludts, who had lost their farm to creditors. George Kludt, distraught and over $450,000 in debt, loaded his shotgun, drove to town and shot his banker. He then came home, shot his wife and two young children, and finally shot himself. The crumbling farm still stood on the other side of the section from Jackson and Brynn. After foreclosure, no one cared or dared to live there. That was one farmstead that Brynn hoped never to visit for any reason.

Brynn valued the mystery that ignorance bought. She was unaware of the strife that brought Bradley Voog's family to ruin, and preferred to keep it that way, but hers was a mission that trumped prudence. She would likely learn no more than the average coffee group of men and women alike had, that met at 10 and 3 every day at Collette's Corner Café. They gathered to discuss critical socioeconomic issues, such as why Marcene Biggle sat in a different pew last Sunday, or whose car was parked in Dan Forney's driveway all night long only one week after his divorce became final, and what in the world Clarence Kessler was thinking, buying a new combine when everyone knew he couldn't afford it. Whatever, if anything, she discovered here, it would remain private, unlike the information passed around and reshaped by every single person seated at Collette's Circle of Knowledge.

Dodging puddles, Brynn hurried up the driveway toward the house. She hoped that she could glean only enough information to prove or disprove her theories and get out before she either learned more than she cared to, or was caught trespassing.

Unable to get through the front door with the collapsed ceiling acting as a barricade, she went to the back door and entered just off of the kitchen. The house was cold, even though the day was warming with the bright sunshine and tepid breezes. Her footsteps echoed and the floors creaked. She could smell the musty basement from here.

Shattered glass, broken furniture, and animal droppings were everywhere. Refuse either discarded by vandals and partygoers or abandoned by the previous tenants littered the entire house. The walls were a tapestry of graffiti, old wallpaper, water stains, and dirt.

As Brynn carefully navigated through the war zone of time, neglect, and sabotage that was once a kitchen, memories of events she'd never witnessed flashed before her. Bradley's family members drifted in and out of focus, the clips jumbled and vague. Brynn considered the possibility that her hurried attitude might be affecting how years of memories came to her. She slowed her breathing, relaxed her mind, and tried to forget that her car was not far from the road, and quite visible.

She recognized Bradley's father, pacing across the cleaner kitchen of the past, his wife standing off in a corner, watching and weeping. His lips moved, though no sound was heard. The tension in the room was palpable, even with the passage of more than twenty years. He stopped pacing and stood motionless for a moment. Grasping the back of a kitchen chair as if to steady himself, Bradley's father shook with what appeared to be anger, frustration, sadness, or a mixture of all of these. He put his head down as if in prayer, then abruptly heaved back, the chair in his hands, and slammed it across the table, then the floor, slamming, slamming, until all he was holding was a broken stick. His wife, dodging flying pieces of shattered chair, ran from the room as Bradley's father stood sobbing, clutching the stick to his chest as though it was the only thing he had left in the world.

Brynn's eyes flooded with tears for them and for the shame she felt at using this family's personal and private drama as a way to learn more about her new ability.

She backed out of the room, as if to discreetly and politely leave and save them embarrassment. A silly thought, but it felt right.

Scrooged. As she walked back to her car, Brynn suddenly had a recollection of a scene in one of her favorite movies, as Frank—Bill Murray—was taken back to his childhood home by the Ghost of Christmas Past. In one scene that Brynn recalled, Frank was concerned that they would be heard and seen by those in the room, his younger self included—when the ghost reminded him that they weren't really there—that it was more like a rerun. The scene was one of Frank as a four-year-old boy. It was Christmas Eve, and Frank's father came home and gave him veal as a Christmas gift. This moment, as silly and brief as it was, was obviously pivotal in the shaping of Frank's future. Why the ghost chose this moment over others was inconsequential, being merely one moment in a series of integral moments that created the story of Frank's life.

There was so much to understand and ponder. What determined the order of the memories that appeared to her?

Brynn deduced that the memories she saw weren't necessarily in any particular order of importance or chronology, but perhaps more in order of how strong they were, how powerfully charged they seemed to be. Her abilities seemed limited to homes no longer occupied. She'd learned more than she needed and deserved to know here, and chose to leave the rest of the memories inside the walls of this home, untouched and sequestered.

Back in her car, Brynn paused, feeling almost sorry for the house as she stared at it. It seemed to stare back, sad and lonely, as though it was a living, feeling being. *This is ridiculous. It's a house, not a person. If I'm going to witness these memories, then I have to suck it up and not get so wrapped up in what's happening. It's the past. It's not happening now. It's a rerun.*

Brynn had a thought. She started the car, backed onto the gravel road, and abruptly left the building site. She drove the short distance to the site of her next experiment, and parked in the driveway approaching another abandoned building: an old, one-room school house. No paint remained on the structure, the windows were missing entirely, sunlight streamed in through the ravaged roof, the door lay on the ground next to the cracked walkway. The only identifiable feature on it was the bell tower, the bell long since gone. She grinned, pleased with herself for thinking of this, and got out of her car. She grabbed her camera, and began taking pictures as she approached the building. She imagined the painting of this archaic school that she could pull from the watercolor paper. She mounted the crumbling concrete steps leading up to the front door of the schoolhouse.

What was once a place of learning and youthful energy was now a haven for rodents and pigeons. The interior was filthy with scraps of nests, bird and animal droppings, and the usual party garbage, but it would do. She was surprised that the floor was still intact, having been exposed to the harshest elements that South Dakota's seasons could throw at it. The hardwood floor was warped and buckled in places, and sagged like a trampoline mat. She decided it was best not to assume that it was strong.

Her experiment proved successful: she envisioned students and teachers in period clothing of various decades, desks, writing on the chalkboard, books, lunch boxes, coats, smiles, and frowns. She even saw a dunce hat, setting atop some poor fellow who more than likely neglected to mind his manners. *Times have changed indeed.*

She stuck close to the walls as she inched her way a little further into the room, hoping that the floor wouldn't collapse. She didn't need to be anywhere in particular, she now understood, to see what the room wanted to share with her. No earth-shattering, heart-wrenching, or downright private memories came unbidden, thankfully. The most traumatic events she saw was a yardstick being used for spanking, a Christmas program sidelined by a goat that didn't want to be a lamb in the manger scene, and someone's awkward first kiss in the coat room.

She took mental note of dates on the calendar in various scenes, names and dates written on the chalkboard, the styles of clothing, brief glimpses of teachers and students. It was a flurry of activity on a timeline of which only this one-room schoolhouse kept track. She was just the television displaying a broadcast over which she had no control. If she chose to stay, she reasoned that she could probably sort out certain times and events, but there was no need. She understood all she needed to know about what her ability encompassed, although there were still many questions she had about *why* she was capable of seeing these memories.

What would make a house or building release its memories to someone, especially her, and especially now? Was it something within her that caused the house to allow her access to its secrets, or was it something within the houses? If indeed it was in the house and not simply her oddly-acquired ability, why did no one else seem to see them, like Arlo, when they toured Cole's home? From that perspective, she reasoned that it was her own ability that allowed her to see the home's memories. The mystery now was what caused her to acquire this bizarre ability. She'd been in empty or abandoned houses before and never experienced this phenomenon—until recently.

She felt the hair on her arms stand up, and an icy tingle down her right leg. It occurred to her, at that moment, that the only thing that had changed for her recently was her abduction and near-death.

CHAPTER EIGHT

ON BRYNN'S HARRIED DRIVE HOME, theories swirled in her head. Could head trauma cause such a thing to manifest in a person? Lacking an *insane*, trustworthy confidant, Brynn would have to trust Google to help her investigate—because what *sane* person would even *attempt* to help her answer these questions? Why or *how* she obtained this bizarre talent was her most pressing question. Following that, the implications of this ... *thing* ... were abundant, if not altogether alarming. *If* Brynn were able to enter any abandoned property and see its memories, what possibilities (and ramifications!) could this entail? *Could* it be a gift, or would she be forever haunted by visions that were not hers every time she entered an empty building? As with any unnatural—or rather, *supernatural*—gift that one doesn't understand or necessarily need, would it become a curse? She'd seen television shows about psychic mediums. She would be a pariah. *Calm down, Brynn. Get home, get Google, maybe get a beer ...*

Brynn's hands were shaking, and when she got out of her car at home, she found her knees were rivaling her hands. She strode directly to the kitchen. Despite the fact that it was only a little after eleven a.m., she had not yet eaten, and she was not much of a drinker, she opened a beer and drank directly from the can—olives and frosty mug be damned. Google could wait.

Thankful not to have her children to contend with, she grabbed her laptop and settled into the window seat in the bedroom. Brynn googled "special abilities head trauma."

Google must have been expecting her: it had several suggestions before she even finished typing. The very first post was about a savant talent acquired after a severe brain injury, and on the second page was a link to an article written about six different people who gained amazing skills after traumatic brain injuries. Listed in the latter article were people who, after suffering head trauma and recovering, demonstrated various skills that they did not previously have. One could recall details from his childhood in remarkable detail, being able to draw or paint exactly how a building or scene looked when he was four years old. Another was able to play the piano exquisitely, having had no previous experience. Yet another could draw fractals and suddenly knew complex math equations. The fifth person listed became a painter/poet/sculptor, and the sixth became a digital artist.

Why couldn't I get the gift of sculpting? I've always wanted to sculpt! And I suck *at math! Why not that? No, I suck at it because I hate it. Why this, though? Why not something else?* Anything *else!*

None of the articles mentioned a person being able to see memories that didn't belong to them.

Brynn searched the first four or five "nexts" and couldn't find anything related to her specific malady. She was completely unnerved by the sites that mentioned epilepsy or vampires. Any sites that suggested the occult or anything that was not God-given, Brynn rejected, refusing to believe that God would allow her to survive such a horrific ordeal only to be given a tool that Satan had forged. She was briefly fortified by a site that seemed to have certain information slightly relevant to her search, only to have it lead her to a page that said "Click Here for Enlightenment". *Enlightenment. It's probably a porn site. Pass.*

Brynn's fingers typed against her will. And better judgment. *"Freak: curiosity, rarity, oddity, mutant, aberration, anomaly ... "* Although disheartened and a little worried at her last impulsive entry, she continued reading: *"one-off, enthusiast, fanatic, fiend, nut, lover, buff ... "* The latter terms, oddly enough, made her feel somewhat better (except for "one-off," which was the most offensive and unsettling, even though she'd never heard the term).

Brynn had two more options to research. She chose the least painful first: psychic. Wikipedia started out their definition with "a person who claims to have an ability to perceive information hidden from the normal senses ... "

"Claims?" What do they mean by that? She scrolled down through a myriad of ads for psychics to find the Merriam-Webster definition. "Relating to the psyche, lying outside the sphere of physical science or knowledge; immaterial, moral, or spiritual in origin or force. Relating to, affecting, or influenced by the human mind." *I'll say ... So I must be making it up?*

Neither definition answered her question. She didn't know much about psychic phenomenon, but from what she'd seen on television shows and in movies, it was more like a feeling, an interpretation of something someone saw or felt. Brynn simply felt like it was a memory. Like she had been there. But she knew she hadn't.

Brynn took a deep breath, and the last entry jumped from her jittery fingertips onto the screen: insanity. *Wow.* *"mental disorder ... delusions ... crazy ... "* Brynn's hands were shaking again. Her face grew hot. She swallowed, fighting panic as she scanned the page of information. "... *hallucinations ... psychosis ... madness ... "* She stared at the words. Finally, she looked up.

Wait a minute. I'm only crazy if those things I'd seen never happened. I know what I saw at Cole's house, and it wasn't imagined. As long as I can prove that I'm seeing events that actually happened, I needn't be concerned.

She logged off, took the computer back to her desk, and plopped down in her office chair in a pout. She felt like Jack Jr. in a time out. Questions and doubts plagued her, and Brynn did not want to explain the occurrences away any more. She wanted to believe that what was happening was real, not imagined; that what she saw was fact, not fiction; and that she was normal, healthy, and sane, not … the alternative. It was disturbing enough to realize that she had the weird ability, but for some reason, it bothered her more to know that it might have been caused by the head trauma.

The thought that her injury brought about her ability was an epiphany for Brynn, her first real admission of the reality of her ordeal. She began to wonder how it would affect the way she viewed her abduction from now on. What other repercussions or side effects could she expect? Maybe she *would* eventually have seizures, like the doctors predicted. Maybe this "gift" was only one of many complications she might develop over time. What else? Hallucinations? Paranoia? Schizophrenia? *Math??*

Brynn allowed herself only a couple more minutes of self-pity, fear, and indecision. She finally forced herself from her chair, stomped into the kitchen, and made herself a turkey bagel sandwich with fresh asparagus spears and a touch of honey mustard. Milk was the chaser this time.

Brynn cleaned up her dishes and wiped the granite counter. The wiping and polishing of the surface was soothing. *Whatever happens, at least I have Cole to confide in.*

She stopped suddenly and looked at her watch. Brynn grabbed her purse and phone, checked her clothes and boots, and left for town to visit Cole.

The aroma of the Perris Manor's dinner—something that smelled like chicken soup—still hung in the air as Brynn entered the building. Some of the residents were eating yet as she passed the dining hall. Other residents were lingering in the hall and in the lounge near the nurse's station as she made her way to Cole's room—all good signs that he might still be awake. She supposed she could have called ahead, rather than rudely presuming that the residents didn't have plans, and that an impromptu visit to a nursing home was socially acceptable behavior. It had become a habit borne of the time when her grandmother was in the home. She gladly welcomed visits any time they were nearby, and insisted on being woken up or interrupted. She had always said that no nap or card game was worth missing the one thing they all bragged about and lived for.

Brynn peeked into Cole's room before knocking and found him reading in a recliner next to the window. He noticed Brynn before she could announce herself and waved her in. Spencer was resting in his bed, so she tiptoed to Cole's side of the room and sat down near his chair.

Cole looked happy to see her. "How have you been?"

"Great! The pigs, the kids, the farm, they keep me hopping ... " she whispered. "How are you? Have you had many visitors?"

"No, not much of that. I see Arlo, Eva, and the boys about every week. My brother now and then. Visitors are a pretty hot commodity in here, you know." He smiled, but she saw a sadness in the way his mouth curved. She instantly felt guilty for having personal reasons for visiting.

She didn't know what to say that wouldn't sound contrived. She smiled and nodded.

"It's good to see you again so soon. So what brings you by?" He lowered his voice. "Anything new in the 'visions' area?"

"Yes!" She clapped her hand over her mouth briefly, then continued in an urgent whisper, excited to finally be able to talk about it. "Sorry. Yes, I saw more of those … visions … memories. I wanted to talk to you about them."

Cole held up his hand as if to silence her, and said quietly, "Should we go to the chapel? No one will be in there this afternoon. We'll be able to talk there." He slowly pulled himself from the deep chair, got into his wheel chair and they rolled out the door quietly, leaving Spencer still asleep in his bed.

The chapel was designed in nursing home fashion; rows of individual, movable chairs made it easy to replace them with wheel chairs. It was a solemn, peaceful place with stained glass windows, flickering electric candles, soft lighting, silk flower arrangements, and an old upright piano in the corner. The sanctuary walls, covered in dark, wood paneling, held several neutral serene prints of the "misty gardens, clasped hands, and floral arrangement" category, hung about the room. To appear as non-denominational as possible, a simple cross was mounted on the wall at the head of the room with a pulpit nearby. Brynn mused that it smelled like every other church: a mingling of stale books and old cologne.

The chapel's seating arrangement was versatile enough for tables in case a rousing game of dominoes threatened to break out since it also served the home well as a secondary gathering place. The community room was always a constant construction zone of jigsaw puzzles and family gatherings, if things hadn't changed from the days when her grandmother had been here.

Cole rolled halfway into the room and turned his chair to face the doors. Brynn pulled up a folding chair near his and sat down facing him.

Cole seemed as excited to hear the new developments as she was to report them. He leaned forward in his chair. "Now. Tell me everything. Did you go back to my place? Did you go somewhere else? What happened?" A child-like look of expectation came over his face.

Brynn smiled at his enthusiasm. She hoped, though, that he might have answers as well as questions.

"Okay ... " She began, as she recounted everywhere she had been, everything she had seen, including all that she had sensed, worried about, wondered, researched, found, and feared.

Cole listened, only nodding occasionally as Brynn relayed her fantastic story. It sounded crazy. Even to her. When she finished, it was as if a boulder had been lifted from her.

She waited for Cole's calm, worldly, rational words to bolster her wilting confidence. Silence reigned—for an uncomfortable amount of time, in Brynn's opinion. She turned her head slightly to the side and waited for a sound. Any sound. She felt like a safe cracker, listening for the faintest clicking noises of tumblers ready to surrender their sentinel.

Cole's face was drawn into folds of deliberation.

"Hm," was all she got.

Brynn nodded slowly.

"Okay. I know what you're thinking. You're probably right. I'm ... I'm ... " She tapped her temple with her finger. "Wacka-doodle-do."

Brynn laughed, which sounded more like a hiccup, and got up from her chair. "You know what? Never mind what I said. This is just silly." She began to pace. "It's okay. You can say it. 'Maybe she's not dealing with a full deck.' 'Maybe she's a couple bricks shy of a full load.' I know what people say. It's kind of funny, actually. 'The lights are on, but no one's home.' 'She's got a screw loose.' 'One taco short of a combo.' 'Her elevator is stuck between floors'. ... ... let me see ... 'She's a few peas short of a casserole.' ... .um ... 'The wheel is turning, but the hamster's dead.' Oh, here's a good one: 'Half a bubble off plumb.'"

Brynn stopped her pacing, hands on her hips, and stared at the ugly, industrial-brown sanctuary carpet. The silence was deafening.

Brynn put her hands over her face, embarrassed and disgusted with herself. This was completely out of character for her, even if she did have a good excuse. She turned to face Cole, hoping he wasn't shocked or angry. He must be so ashamed of her.

Cole sat slightly slumped in his chair, his left thumb on his left cheek, and his fingers curled over his mouth, his eyes watery and slightly squinted, and his shoulders shaking. Brynn rushed to him and knelt down near his chair. "Cole, I'm so sorry! That was just cruel and insensitive. I don't know what got into me."

He shook his head, and moved his hand and she could see that he was laughing. He opened his mouth to speak, but the giggles overcame him again, and soon Brynn was giggling in spite of herself. Their laughter escalated and echoed in the solemn space, adding to the absurdity of the moment. Tears spilled down their flushed faces as random words escaped between their hoots and snorts. "Taco combo? Where did you ... oh, my goodness!" Cole cried.

Finally, they sighed in exhaustion.

Their apologies met and crashed in the air between them.

"I'm sorry. I didn't know what else to say. I wasn't implying anything." Cole worked on his part of the defense. "I was stunned, is all."

"No apology necessary. My hypochondria is showing." Brynn paused. "So what do you think?" She hoped he would have more than one word this time.

Cole pondered a moment. "'The most beautiful thing we can experience is the mysterious. It is the source of all true art and science.' Albert Einstein. Have you ever read anything about him or by him? He was brilliant, but more than that, he was benevolent. We don't have to figure out why or how you got this ability. See? You know what you saw, and I know you are being truthful with me. You have proved it to me in the things you've told me about my wife and me in our home. Now we just need to acknowledge it, and decide what to do with it."

There was no ambiguity in Cole's demeanor, and that was all Brynn needed.

"So now what?" She finally asked the question that she'd come to ask.

"Well," Cole grasped the question that had dangled annoyingly in their faces for the past half hour, "that depends. What do you want to do with it? If you simply want to use it to gain information about a home's history, then just gather bits and pieces when you go into the empty houses. Don't stay too long. But if you want to do something more with it, like, say, investigative work, then you will have to stay longer, and find a way to go back into a house several times, either with permission or—not that I'm advocating this—without. It's just a matter of what you are willing to disclose about your purpose in going in, if anyone asks. In other words, if you want to pursue this ability of yours, and you don't want to expose your secret talent, you will likely have to lie, trespass, or both." He had a wry grin on his face, and it was refreshing to Brynn to see this wily side of such a reserved man.

He thought for a moment, and then added, "Why do you suppose that certain memories come to you first? I mean, what determines the order in which they are revealed to you? And why you? And why only empty houses?"

"I wondered the same thing. I imagine that it was, in fact, the head trauma that gave me this … .thing … and I haven't been in any deserted buildings since before my … before I got hurt. And I suspect that the order in which they are revealed have to do with how emotionally charged the moments were, not by importance or chronological order. Like any memory of mine, the bigger the moment, the easier it is to recall. I have no idea why it only works in abandoned homes. Maybe there's too much energy in an inhabited home for me to see them. I don't know. This is all so bizarre."

"So you must be psychic," he said soberly.

"Maybe it's not me. Maybe it's the house. You know, like the memories belong to them and somehow, they can give them to me? Maybe the old, abandoned houses are like old people sharing their memories—telling their story before they die.

"Sorry," she winced.

"Makes as much sense as someone who can see someone else's memories by stepping into an empty room." Cole said, graciously accepting the explanation.

"Or I'm psychic," Brynn murmured. The possibility seemed more frightening than a house that could remember, but being here with Cole calmed her. Like her father calmed her.

Brynn felt herself relaxing as they talked a few minutes more about the endless possibilities, like how useful it could be in solving mysteries, settling disputes, and clearing up misunderstandings. They wondered aloud about opportunities to use it, such as going into the room where Lee Harvey Oswald supposedly stood, or entering the last known whereabouts of Jimmy Hoffa. Even the rusty, ruined, submerged rooms of the Titanic, not that she'd ever go to the bottom of the ocean—even for that. Knowing that Brynn had only a few more minutes before she had to leave to be home before Ellie got off the bus, they wrapped up their conversation with more practical matters.

Cole encouraged Brynn to tell her husband about her abilities when she felt the time was right, but urged her to make it soon.

"So, have you contacted your doctor about this?" he asked.

"No, and I don't plan to. If I told my doctor about this, even if I could prove it, it would complicate things. I think something like this goes beyond doctor-patient confidentiality. It would be all over the place. And it still wouldn't change the situation. It wouldn't help. I mean, who knows? Maybe it won't last. Maybe it will go away as mysteriously as it came. Which wouldn't be all bad ... " Brynn shrugged.

Cole grinned. "I suppose another bump on the head is out of the question?"

They chuckled, but they both knew that she was— they were—on the precipice of a dark, yawning chasm of unknowns. And the bottom and the other side were nowhere in sight.

CHAPTER NINE

SOMETHING HAD CHANGED. HE DIDN'T know what, but something had changed in Brynn. He knew nothing of what to look for in the way of serious side effects of her attack. Maybe her behavior was nothing more than preoccupation. He hoped, anyway.

In any case, he found Brynn's neurologist's number in his list of contacts and called the office, leaving a message for the doctor to call him back on his cell phone.

Brynn was on the road to recovery. That was a good thing. Wasn't it? She was taking up her artwork again and she was getting out and visiting neighbors and friends, and even making new friends. However, she was gone more from home, forgetting things, becoming more distant and distracted, and taking more chances. What if she had a seizure? What if she developed personality traits that were dangerous to herself or others?

What if she remembered what had happened to her? He couldn't protect her from herself. There were things that she would eventually have to deal with, and there was no way to be there when it came time to do that. He had work to do. Fieldwork this time of the year was unavoidable. Spraying, fertilizing, planting—it was all done far from the security of their farm yard. What if she needed him?

Jackson drove the tractor into a field that was more than four miles away from their home. He had filled the seed boxes at home, saving an extra trip to the field with a pickup loaded with bags of seeds. He lowered the planter into the warm, moist soil. Those seeds would grow a major part of their income for the coming year. In with a "please" and out with a "thank you." It was a silent prayer upon the lips of every farmer who was at the mercy of too many variables to even make this occupation prudent; farmers who did it anyway for the sheer love of it. Some would say it was the definition of insanity. Farmers would say it was heaven.

Jackson was one of those farmers. He felt his pulse trill every time he dropped the planter. He hoped his children would grow to love agriculture, and Buddy was already showing signs of this sweet insanity. Even Ellie, who was as prissy as they came, loved the country and the animals and the outdoors, much like her mother.

Jackson knew he'd hit pay dirt when Brynn agreed to marry him. His family loved her, well, most of them; his sister didn't, but that was her problem. Brynn became his priority and that was understood and, for the most part, respected.

Now with the abduction and attack, it became more imperative to put her first. She wasn't out of danger by any means. Just because she couldn't remember what had happened, or who had abducted her, it didn't make her less of a target. The fact that she'd survived made her even *more* of a target.

Jackson was nearly done with the field by the time Brynn's neurologist called him back. Jackson stopped planting to talk.

"Dr. Metheney … yes. I … yes, very well … m-hm … " The good doctor loved his small talk. "Yes, she's doing well … that's why I called. I was wondering … yes, getting out and about … " The doctor chattered on. Jackson looked outside to see if it was fall yet. "Right. Say, Doctor, I have a couple questions. Is there anything I should … " *Oh, good Lord.* "What symptoms should I be looking for, again, in after-effects of head trauma?" There. He said it, even with the doctor talking right along with him. "M-hm. Yes, seems to be … I'm wonderi … No, none of that … All right. Great. Thank you. Right. M-hm … .right … . Well, I really have to run … Thank you, tha … " Jackson hung up. Such go the great conversations with the busy doctors. At least he knew that there were no significantly worrisome symptoms that he was witnessing. No seizures, no irritability, depression, anxiety, nausea, headaches, dizziness—at least none that he knew of.

Jackson started planting again. He should have felt relief at what he'd learned. He felt ashamed. He was hoping for some reason to keep her at home, where she was safe. Worry was the only thing growing for Jackson now, and his usual feelings of excitement were buried along with the seed.

CHAPTER TEN

"**T**HESE TRACKS ARE FRESH," SHE said, stooping to get a closer look at the marks in the damp trail. She touched the faint impression in the soil, examining it carefully.

Buddy looked at Brynn, his eyes wide with wonder. "What kind of animal made them, Mama?"

"Oh, the worst. I'd say a six or seven year old, uh…" Brynn smelled her fingertips, touched them lightly to her tongue. "Yup. Homosapien. We'd better keep moving. I hope we're down wind of them. Usually harmless, but when they're cornered, they can be trouble." Her mouth twitched in an effort to hide her smile. She put on her best adventurer face—serious, confident, and fearless—and briefly scanned the woods. Ellie and Buddy looked around uneasily, but the excitement was visible on their faces. "Should we try to get to the top of this ridge before we make camp and eat some grub?" Brynn asked, standing and slinging her backpack over her shoulder.

"That's a great idea, Mama," said Buddy, but then whispered to his sister with a concerned look, "Did you bring grub? I only have peanut butter and jelly samwiches."

Ellie smiled at her mother as she informed Buddy that grub was just another word for food. It was clear she thoroughly relished being the older, *smarter* sister.

They continued for a short while on the path near the river and then took the trail at the fork that led to a clearing at the top of the hill. There was no risk of encountering any wildlife—dangerous or otherwise—with Brynn's two children chattering incessantly as they hiked in the state park near their home. "Do you think there are bears in here?" Ellie asked. "I wanna see a moose!" said Buddy breathlessly, putting his toy binoculars up to his eyes. Ellie wore blue jeans, a t-shirt, boots, and a cap, just like her mother, but had on her Dora the Explorer backpack. Buddy had his Sponge Bob backpack strapped to his back, and wore his camouflage shorts and t-shirt with his favorite light-up shoes, in case they got lost and needed to light their way. They trudged up the hill on the narrow path, talking about what a great adventure it was, and how long and hard the hike had been, although they'd only been in the park a total of forty minutes, at the most.

"No, I don't think there are bears or moose in these parts," said Brynn, enjoying her role as expert and guide a bit too much. As she navigated over boulders and large tree roots, and tramped around on slippery, damp trails, she marveled at how the hike made her feel strong and invincible in a way that vacuuming, bathing kids, and tending pigs didn't.

Their adventure stalled on the hilltop, where they spread out a soft blanket under a massive cottonwood tree and unpacked their lunches of peanut butter and jelly, juice boxes, and homemade strawberry cupcakes with strawberry cream cheese frosting. They rested for a few minutes after eating and read *Where the Wild Things Are* before packing up their gear.

"Take only pictures ... " Brynn prompted.

" ... and leave only footprints, we know ... " the children finished the quote as they gathered up all of their belongings and trash.

Their adventure was precisely what Brynn needed. She breathed deeply the musky, sweet scent of the woodlands, and drank in the soft breezes that refreshed her like a long drink of cool water. The copses smelled of decayed, moss-covered wood, wet leaves, and new cedar growth that reminded her faintly of red licorice. They climbed trees, studied previously-undiscovered life forms under their Dora magnifying glass, hunted for T-Rex bones, took photographs of each other and nature, and finally made their way home to nap on the porch hammock. It was the perfect Saturday. May would be over soon and school would be out. Summer would be consumed with activities and events, without anyone having any knowledge of making any such plans.

In the meantime, spring was frenetic, with energy and life bursting from the earth. With calving, planting, hog chores, and school events, there was little time for Brynn to do much more than think about her ability to see memories in old homes. With so many factors to consider, she was beset with doubts about it—not whether she had it, but her justifications for using it. Discovering details that were entrusted to the past and the lives that lived it was a moral issue Brynn struggled with. When she did find a worthy reason to use her talent, revealing her ability and to whom would be a dilemma. It would be nearly impossible to use the information she gained without divulging how she learned it. Case in point: her own abduction and attack. Especially since everyone knew she had no memories of her own to rely on.

Jackson was another concern—her biggest by far. If and when she shared her attributes with him, what would his reaction be? Brynn could just about guess. He would probably make her stop. He'd most likely make her go to the doctor, because he would think she was either ill or nuts or both. He would almost certainly obsess about her, worry about her, hover over her—even more than he did now—and the wounds of her abduction would be scrubbed raw again for him.

She would keep this to herself until it became necessary to share it. Her ability was her boon as well as her bane, but for now, at least, it was hers alone.

"Please stand as you are able ... " During church the following day, the pastor prepared the congregation for her sermon with a prayer. Brynn stood with Jackson and the congregation.

"Heavenly Father ... "

Why am I here? I could have stayed home and brooded with a lot less hassle.

Brynn went through the motions of standing and sitting and bowing her head for prayer. She wasn't hearing or feeling what she needed. Church wasn't always a balm for the aching soul or a recharging of the spirit. Sometimes, like today, it was an exercise in frustration and discipline for parents of young children. The kids were restless and crabby, likely the result of too much fresh air and not enough sleep. Keeping them quiet and somewhat still in the pew was foremost in Brynn's plan, but taking something home besides a case of the grouches was always the goal. Today, she just didn't care. She was grumpy, too.

" ... be with us today ... " the pastor continued.

Brynn felt the crushing weight of the responsibility of her ability. Standing in the midst of her church family, she felt more alone than ever.

Is this a curse or a blessing? I know what I should do with it, but do I want to? I don't want it. I don't want to know what happened. Not to me, not to anyone, not if it means doing it alone. Some mysteries would have to go unsolved. Mysteries.

Lanea's face flashed in her mind. The familiar tilt of her head, the wispy hairs in her face. The memory of Jackson's face replaced the vision. The worried, sad face she'd seen hovering over her bed in the hospital.

Brynn pointed at Ellie, instructing her to stand, and pulled Buddy to his feet. She folded her hands and pinched her eyes shut.

It's not a curse. If I use it ... Help me.

" ... Oh, Holy Spirit, breath of God, breathe on us now, and move within us while we pray ... "

With that, Brynn felt a cool, gentle breeze touch her face, move her hair. She gasped softly and looked up. Had anyone else felt that? She looked at Jackson. His head was bowed. She looked around. No one appeared to have felt a thing. Is it possible? Had she just experienced a miracle?

"You may be seated," the pastor said after finishing the prayer.

Brynn sat down slowly. She couldn't believe it! It was a sign. What did it mean? She should tell someone, but who would believe her? She felt ... honored! Blessed!

Jackson turned to her. "Air just came on. Feels good," he whispered.

Brynn gaped at him. Her mouth fell open.

"What?" he asked.

She stared at the back of the pew ahead. "Nothing."

"What?"

"I just thought ... " She felt silly for even wondering. But in the excitement and hopefulness of the moment, she considered telling him everything. No, not here, not now. "Never mind."

His lips formed a "wha..", but the word never met the air. He shook his head in bewilderment and turned back to the pastor.

Brynn crossed her arms and slumped back in the pew. How could she expect a miracle? Answered prayers, maybe. Miracles? Doubt it. She'd have to make her own. Never pray for strength: you'll get trials.

" ... a mystery is something you stand in awe of; it's not always a puzzle to be solved ... " The line from the sermon drifted into Brynn's distracted thoughts. It eerily echoed Cole's Einstein quote. She smiled and jotted it down in her bible margin. Perhaps it wasn't exactly word for word, and perhaps it wasn't meant to apply to Brynn's gift, but she nevertheless took it—and the coincidence—to heart. She reflected on the previous day and all of the wonders she and her children witnessed. She didn't need a miracle. She thought of her life and how undeniably and immeasurably blessed she was, and she thanked the Lord for all of her treasures—her new ability included. It was then that she decided that this was a gift, a precious and useful tool, and she knew that she could use it to draw the truth from walls that could tell no lie.

It was a mystery, no doubt. And by days end, there would be no doubt as to how and where Brynn intended to use it.

CHAPTER ELEVEN

N O CHILD LOVED ASPARAGUS MORE than Buddy. He loved to eat it, but more than that, he loved to hunt for it. It was a springtime ritual that Brynn and her children relished—like hunting Easter eggs, but without the bright, pretty colors to tip them off. This was a more challenging sport, definitely worthy of higher merit than that of some silly Easter tradition, so bragging rights went to the one with the most poundage, and that was usually Buddy.

With Ellie in school, Brynn and Buddy put on their hunting clothes—long pants, boots, and long-sleeve shirts to guard against ticks—and hit the ditches in search of wild asparagus unwittingly planted in the fence lines by birds. Especially adept at hunting this type of prize, Buddy was all too willing to get on his hands and knees to crawl into the last year's dried tangle of asparagus growth to reach the new, crisp shoots. He had been well trained in the fine art of snapping off the spears near the ground, and instructed to not eat it until they had at least washed it. The latter law wasn't always adhered to, but Brynn couldn't fault him for that minor infraction. She too loved the raw, tender spears. They often came home with scarcely enough for supper.

If asparagus had been the ultimate goal this day, they would have been much wealthier for it, but the quest was just a ruse. Brynn was in pursuit of details, and she wasn't going to find them in ditches. As a matter of fact, the ditch in front of the old Covey home had no asparagus at all, not that it deterred Brynn from her objective. Their hunt landed them here after only a half hour of scavenging.

Brynn studied the modest story-and-a-half Covey house and farmstead. No one had lived there for several years and it was in dire condition, which was no surprise, considering the dreadful state it was in when it *was* occupied. Brynn had never been in the house, had never even been invited, which seemed odd to her even as a child. But she knew where it was and remembered what it looked like from the road, and it looked as though nothing had changed with the exception of an increase of grass and weeds. Well, and junk. If anything, the grass and weeds were an improvement, helping to camouflage the hoards.

Lanea Covey, a childhood friend of Brynn's, was 16 when she disappeared from this home, and never seen again. No trace of her was ever found, the case still considered open and unsolved, although open didn't necessarily mean active. This mystery was Brynn's objective.

There were many variables at play here, Brynn mused, conscious of the fact that she was never very good at math. She realized that first of all, the house had to be abandoned, and in this case, she was fortunate to have that in her favor. Secondly, and probably most importantly, there had to be clues within those walls of the house Lanea went missing *from* for Brynn's gift to be useful in solving this puzzle. The house Lanea went *to* would be preferable, but lacking that, Brynn would have to use the only link she had. Moreover, Brynn was unable to hear the memories that the walls projected, so deciphering those clues and clips would be time-consuming and speculative work. This would be a long shot. Since there was no proof either way that she was abducted or simply a runaway, Brynn hoped that she could learn something concrete about at least one of those theories.

Brynn casually kicked the dried grass as she eyed the derelict farm. Buddy stared at her, baffled. "Mama, there's no 'sparagus here." He squinted up at her, now suspicious of her motives.

"You are *right*, little man! Just seeing if you were paying attention," she said, "You scout around a little bit more over by those trees there, and if we don't find any, we will move on, okay?"

Brynn dawdled near the fence at the edge of the property as she watched to see how much traffic was nearby. She decided, after Buddy reported for a second time that there was no asparagus to be found, that she would finish their hunt quickly at their favorite spot, and then take him to her mother's so she could come back alone.

With Buddy secured at her mother's, and Brynn's alibis in order, she was ready. Nervous and scared, but ready.

Four miles was a long way to walk if you wanted to get there fast, but not far to drive. Driving, however, meant a vehicle that could be spotted by passersby if she parked onsite. A bike seemed to be the best option for Brynn—easily stashed in the trees, grass, or a building to hide her presence at the farm.

After an early and quick dinner, Brynn prepared for her covert assignment. She loaded her backpack with her camera, phone, a notebook and pen, and a bottle of water. As a last thought, she threw in some fruit snacks. Her heart raced, thinking about the detective shows and movies she had watched, remembering favorites like *Get Smart*, *Mission Impossible*, *CSI*. "Cool your jets, girl … " Brynn whispered to herself. This was not a television show; it was her life. She put the embarrassment aside, determined to view this as a community service … a civic duty … maybe even a Christian mission, and left home on her bike.

Gravel and skinny-tired 10-speed bicycles didn't play well, but they needed only to get along for the last two of the four miles. Brynn reached the edge of the property without encountering any other vehicles on the gravel road that passed the Covey house.

Her heart beat a little faster, not so much out of effort as fear, as she pushed her bicycle past the post holding the No Trespassing sign, and lifted her 10-speed over the stretched barbed-wire gate across the driveway that held the *other* No Trespassing sign. Pretending not to see them, or downright ignoring them, didn't make it right. But it was a justification that she was aware she would have to make at some point. She would make it later. Right now she had to get out of sight.

The tall, tangled grass pulled on her legs and bike pedals as she hurried to reach cover. The aged, half-dead windbreak and the rusted cars and machinery stashed within obstructed the view from the adjoining fields. She leaned her bike against the house's back entryway, confident it would not be seen. And except for the fact that her bike was not rusty, it could be mistaken as one in the graveyard of dead equipment in the yard. She took a breath, wondering if she had breathed even once since getting off her bike at the road. The scariest part was over. She hoped. Getting caught in the house might be rather scary, but there was little reason for anyone to come looking for her.

Like any good detective, Brynn got out her notebook and pen and jotted down everything—the date and time, observations about the house, and a rough layout of the farm—as she walked toward the back door of the house. The farm looked like a scrap metal yard. Scattered amongst the many obsolete, worthless buildings were corroded skeletons of machines and cars, big and small parts for things that were also worthless, and many objects that could only be classified as junk. Save for the root cellar mound near the back of the house, the small building site was relatively flat, loosely hemmed in by the dying, scanty windbreak, which clutched its rotten treasures like withered, skeletal fingers.

As she pushed the half-opened door and stepped into the back entryway, her first observation of the inside of the house was one of disgust. From what she could see, the interior of the house was also filled with junk. Though the door and most of the windows of the entryway were intact, they were almost impassable with all of the refuse left behind. The back entryway was clearly an addition to the house—a common practice with the smaller, eventually-obsolete farm houses of the past. The dead giveaway was the double-hung window between the addition and the kitchen. The addition included a meager bathroom, fitted with a toilet tucked into one side of the tiny washroom, an undersized, wall-mounted porcelain sink in the middle, and a cheap plastic shower stall on the other side. A cracked and yellowed accordion-style vinyl door hung limp from the doorway. The whole bathroom was hardly bigger than a closet, probably essential at one time, now dilapidated and repulsive. Adjacent to the bathroom sat an ancient, rusted washing machine and dryer under a mountain of debris and dirty clothing.

Had Brynn a fear of mice or rats, their abundant droppings would have been ample excuse to turn around and leave. But other than the vile evidence left behind, they were nowhere to be seen. But not absent. The thought filled her with disgust.

The building still held the winter cold in all the rubbish. The chill did nothing to hide the odors, however. Damp from the open door and a few broken windows, the house exuded a moldy stench that mingled with the distinct mousy smell.

Ruffled peach (orange?) curtains still hung on the windows, frayed with age and abuse from the sun and exposure to wind and rain. A tarnished brass light fixture, sans light bulb and globe, barely clung to the wall next to the doorway into the kitchen. The state of the room—the house—sapped Brynn's mood at the evidence of the dismal life Lanea, the only child of the Coveys, must have endured. She shook her head, as if to force the smothering gloom from her mind, and concentrated on her objective: to see what visions she might be able to gather from the home about her friend's disappearance. *Focus, Brynn!*

There seemed to be no profoundly memorable moments in the entryway besides the typical comings and goings of various people: mostly Lanea's father, Bertis; her mother, Genevieve; Lanea; and the part-time hired hand, a man Brynn vaguely recognized, but whose name she'd forgotten. With the few experiences she'd had in the abandoned homes, she had gathered that the strongest memories seemed to come to her first, and when nothing truly memorable happened, she saw everyday movements and happenings, such as in this case.

Before entering the kitchen, Brynn made notes of her thoughts and visions in the entryway, and prepared herself for the stories the kitchen might tell. If this house was like any other, the kitchen was the soul of the home. Knowing this family's history, it would be tender, and heavy with emotion.

She made her way to the kitchen door and peered in, hesitant to enter. Brynn sighed with relief. It wasn't as packed with trash as the addition, although still littered with junk. At least the grimy, hideously outdated linoleum floor was visible. Most of it. Well, some of it.

Stepping into the room was like stepping into a whirlwind of images: visions of Bertis, alone, weeping at the table, Genevieve clutching her daughter then fainting to the floor, and Lanea crying as she cooked meals. She also saw brief visions of a younger Bertis with his siblings and his parents, who apparently built and owned the home before Bertis inherited it. With so many emotions in so little time, Brynn reeled with sensations as she sorted through the images of past events. She calmed herself and focused on the events surrounding Bertis, his wife, and his daughter. As she stood there, the room seemed to lose some of its urgency, almost as if, instead of trying to seduce her with fancy trailers, it trusted Brynn to stay long enough to see the whole show.

Brynn peeked out the kitchen window to the road and nearby field. No one came in any direction, as far as she could tell from where she stood. She had never been much of a rebel. Granted, trespassing on abandoned property wasn't exactly homicide, but she didn't want a record. Or a reputation. She just wanted to get done and get out. This was going to take some time. Sorting out these visions was going to be like putting loose, jumbled pages of someone's autobiography in order and trying to figure out, in the end, which pages were missing.

Brynn picked up a rickety chair from the floor, wiped the grime from the seat with her sleeve, and sat down tentatively. Ignoring the visions momentarily, she removed her phone from her backpack and quickly called her mother to report in. Then she set up her temporary station in the kitchen, notebook and pen on her lap and water nearby. She was too repulsed to even consider the fruit snacks.

As the memories came to her, Brynn jotted brief descriptions. She hoped to remember them well enough to investigate without returning too often. Time would be her best ally in this assignment. She just needed to be patient and allow the visions to come to her, and try not to be distracted by the thoughts of being discovered here.

Brynn found that even though she was in real time, the memories she saw were in fast forward, happening like a lightning-fast flash in her mind. What would seem like hours of replay were, in actuality, minutes of present time.

Visions came to her as she made notes, including one of Bertis sitting at the kitchen table, weeping, with the police across from him making notes as well. The room, although neater than in present day, was in its pre-hoard stages. Tidy—no doubt attributed to the ladies of the household—stacks of magazines, boxes, and clothes filled the corners of the room.

Brynn's eyes filled with tears, watching Bertis cry. It was particularly difficult in this case, knowing Bertis' story. His loss seemed insurmountable. Brynn couldn't imagine losing a child and a spouse in such a short time, Genevieve to cancer, and Lanea to God-knows-where. Bertis, for a big man, looked bent and frail. He sat at the cluttered table, answering questions from the police as he stared at an invisible spot amongst the junk in front of him, tears welling up in his eyes. She wished she could hear what they were saying. The silence of the visions was frustrating.

She could only imagine that he was relaying information about Lanea.

Brynn stared into the room, her mind replaying events that it had never witnessed firsthand. As quickly as the memory came, it faded and a new one came into focus: Genevieve folding laundry at the kitchen table and Lanea cooking at the stove, a slight smile curving her lips as she stirred something in a kettle. Brynn had a fleeting moment of awe. Lanea stood directly in front of her in the memory, seemingly almost within arm's reach. She wished she could pause the spectral moment and affect it in some way. She wanted to grab hold of Lanea and protect her from whatever fate had planned for her, or whisper in her ear that danger was stirring as surely as she was. If this had been one of Brynn's own memories, it would have been easier for her to accept—and harder to recall—since it had dulled with time, as did the ache for answers. These memories were as fresh and new as two minutes ago to Brynn, and it revived her pain. However saddened by the vision of the friend, it was good to see Lanea again, looking just as she did when they were in high school together. She'd forgotten how lovely Lanea was. This dispassionate room had remembered her more clearly than Brynn's own thinking, sensing, comprehending, and intricate mind.

At 16, Brynn looked to be 12, but Lanea at 16 was the absolute opposite: she was a woman. Long, wavy, blonde hair, ice blue eyes, and fine features overlaid with flawless, silky skin—she was exquisite. Tall and slender, Lanea was, in every sense, more mature than other girls her age. She carried responsibility like a torch—never concerned with duty, workload, or commitment. Ostensibly, she welcomed them as challenges to be trounced, or items to be gladly checked and scratched from a list. Brynn was in constant amazement at Lanea's tenacity and brilliance. She was at the top of her class in school, strong, unpretentious, courageous, and accomplished in everything she attempted. Yet she was unassuming, soft-spoken, and often dismissed as reticent. Education was important to Lanea; school was not. Her dreams were what some would call ordinary to downright insipid, but to Lanea, they were sublime: she wanted to marry the beautiful boy down the road and raise a family.

As captivated by the memory as Brynn was, she was also immediately puzzled. The memory impressed upon her when she entered was Lanea crying, but she looked happy here. Then, as suddenly as the thought occurred to her, the memory changed. Lanea turned toward her mother as Genevieve began to fall. Lanea lunged to grab her.

"Mom!"

Brynn jumped and screamed as the sound of Lanea's voice traveled inexplicably through the years and from the walls. She quickly searched the room to see if by some weird chance her kids had followed her here, giving her a slightly less preposterous explanation for the sound. Brynn scrambled to her feet, desperate to find logic and composure in the silent, filthy room, but found neither.

She took a few deep breaths as the memories continued to play soundlessly in her mind. She talked out loud to herself, feeling foolish but better at the same time, "Sound is good. Sound is normal. I'm not crazy ... ", though not completely convinced of all of it.

Shaking but determined, she sat again in the chair and watched the memory replay for her, this time without hearing Lanea's voice. Until now, she had supposed that she would never hear sound while witnessing a house's memory. Then again, she would have never thought it possible to *see* a memory, much less the *hearing* of a memory that she absorbed from a house.

It was clear, now, that the memory of Lanea smiling was merely a part of a much bigger remembrance that the house retained within its depths. Perhaps the picture of Lanea crying as she cooked was the remembrance of the many times she stood crying at the stove. Brynn saw the latter memory played over and over, but with no climactic beginning or end, and apparently from different times, possibly after Genevieve's diagnosis. Brynn's theory—that the emotionally charged moments were the first to be conveyed—seemed to be accurate.

In the hopes that she would see more memories that the kitchen had to impart, Brynn waited. She saw the familiar, though sedate, moments the family shared throughout the years. Mealtimes, chores, holidays, seasons, family discussions and daily devotions, the kitchen saw it all and recorded it perfectly, unaffected by emotion, unchanged by opinion, suggestion, or influence, unembellished by ego. Provided Brynn could retain her ability, the memories within the walls would retain the truth, and that was something upon which she could depend to help her solve the disappearance of her friend.

She noted times that Lanea and her father were here alone, likely the two months' time between Genevieve's death and Lanea's disappearance. After Genevieve died, and especially after Lanea was gone from the picture, the kitchen was no longer a place of warmth and comfort. Rather, it was a utilitarian necessity for Bertis to cook his paltry meals and eat them alone, or to prepare his meals to take to the field, which he often did, according to the sad accounts the room kept.

With such a short amount of time between Burtis' two losses, the lack of significant memories of Lanea with Bertis in the kitchen wasn't surprising. Neither was it surprising that when they were together, the warmth and joy was gone from the room, and apparently from their lives as well. Genevieve's death had permeated the house, taking not only Genevieve, but all the delight and contentment of everyday living for the family. Of the few memories with only Bertis and his daughter, Brynn saw them quietly eating together, having devotions, and doing daily chores, but all were absent of any happiness or verve.

Sensing that the room had shared its most important memories, Brynn sought out the next room for her assignment, the living room. The house was not big, thankfully. She was becoming increasingly nervous about being here, although she'd only been in the house for little more than a half hour. There was no dining room, with the fairly large kitchen leading directly into the living room, and from there, to an enclosed stairway to the upstairs.

The living room was as cluttered and disgusting as the kitchen and entryway, but even more so with the couch.

All kinds of disgusting creatures loved couches, and any one of them could be living inside it. Mice, rats, opossum, raccoons, cockroaches, spiders—the couch made for a soft, insulated, stinky, fluffy, warm nest for them to live in year round, like a lovely vermin campground. One couldn't live on a farm and not know of the revolting nature of the entire rodent species. The very thought of it was nauseating to Brynn, but she was resolute in her mission. She avoided the critter-infested cushions and found a bucket to overturn and use as a seat as the memories found her.

For a living room, it didn't know much living. Memories indicated that there had never been a television in the room. There seemed to be no radio, no musical instruments, no game playing, no storytelling, no puppet shows or plays, and no big, loud family get-togethers like Brynn had for holidays. The gatherings, quiet and solemn, were only limited to Bertis, Genevieve, and Lanea. Did they have no other family? No other friends? It seemed as sad an existence as Bertis' after his family was gone. The memories within the room were subdued, like those of the kitchen.

How boring can they be? Brynn was dismayed at the absence of spirit and *fun* in this family's life. She now had another reason to feel bad for Lanea. She knew nothing of her friend's melancholic family life. Not only because Lanea was quite private, but also because Brynn had never been here to experience the girl's family dynamics. Lanea had been to Brynn's house several times, and was polite, helpful, and cheerful. The story that Brynn was uncovering stung her with guilt for not knowing her friend's plight.

Guilt or no, Brynn felt she had a job to do, and she could redeem herself in some small way if she could discover what happened to Lanea. She hoped to at least find a fluttering thread that would unravel the tangled knots of this mystery.

Utterly bored by and frustrated with the lack of details contained in the room after just a few minutes, Brynn chose to venture upstairs, her final frontier, except for the basement, if there was one and if it was accessible. An hour had passed since arriving at the house, and Brynn had earlier promised to be home within two hours. She felt confident she could keep that promise, with only the upstairs and possibly a basement remaining. She could always come back if necessary. *With a Hazmat suit, dual-cartridge respirator, and triple dose of antibiotics*, she thought.

Brynn hovered on the steps, hesitant to ascend. They were littered with animal droppings, and Brynn thought the only thing more that the animals could have done to declare this their domain is to hang a no vacancy sign. She didn't care to be sprayed by a surprised skunk or chased by an aggressive woodchuck. She crept up the stairs, prepared to run at the slightest noise or skittering of fur in her peripheral vision. *And maybe bring a stick next time. A stick would be lovely.*

She reached the top without incident, and slowly surveyed the small upper floor. The stairway ran parallel to the hall, which led to two small bedrooms and a closet. The upstairs replicated the lower floor, in an L shape, each bedroom under a gable. The vertical walls reached only to about three feet. The larger of the two bedrooms was near the head of the stairs, and the smaller was located at the other end of the hall, which was still only about ten feet from the larger room. Between the two rooms was a small bathroom, and a large closet—or small room—under the eaves, which Brynn assumed was storage, since there was an excess of junk spilling from it.

Supposing the larger room to be the parents', Brynn wavered about entering it. Recognizing the importance of getting all of the facts, and that the most important of those were probably in Lanea's room at the end of the hall, which Brynn wanted to end with, she decided to disobey her instinct to delay it. If what she saw downstairs was any indication of what stimulating proclivities may lay beyond the bedroom door, she wholly believed she would be completely safe from any gross images scarring her mind. Brynn reckoned that a good detective would put aside his or her own squeamish tendencies in the line of duty, so she lowered her chin, and charged through the doorway.

Just as she suspected, and for which she thanked sweet Jesus, there were no surprises in the master bedroom. Lanea's parents seemed to spend little time in the bedroom besides sleeping, reading—mostly the Bible—and praying. Brynn witnessed a couple of lively, although silent, discussions which were as close to arguments as Brynn had seen in this house, though not quite reaching the point of anger, with this head of the house asserting his place and this wife knowing hers. As with Brynn's parents, Lanea's parents' disagreements had taken place in the privacy of the bedroom.

Growing up, Brynn knew Lanea well, but little of her parents. Bertis was a tall, just-short-of-handsome, barrel-chested man: quiet, and reserved, but friendly, just the same. Genevieve was petite, gentle, soft-spoken, and pleasant in appearance and demeanor. Brynn remembered hearing that Bertis was a long-time bachelor and considerably older than Genevieve when they met at a local diner where Genevieve waitressed. They courted for a short time, married, and he was in his fifties by the time Lanea was born. Lanea and her parents were once members of their Lutheran church, but left when their ultra-conservative needs and ideals were not being met, and joined a more fundamentalist sect in another county. When they left Brynn's church, Lanea and she were fairly good friends. Although distance wasn't an issue in their friendship, common interests and opportunities were. Lanea went to the same school, and there the friendship had endured, but after school, Lanea had chores and was rarely seen outside of her farm.

And then there was Marshall. Marshall was the beautiful boy down the road that Lanea had met at the age of 14, and who she had planned to marry. How they managed to have a meaningful relationship for two years with Lanea's strict restraints was a mystery for another day. Brynn was confounded by that, but glad that Lanea at least had that relationship to sustain her and maybe provide some insight into what normal was. And that if Brynn had to be replaced, it was with someone who would save Lanea from a dismal life of boredom.

That was all moot now. Beautiful Boy Marshall eventually married another. Lanea would never know the full, happy life she could have shared with him. She would never know, with him, the bliss and madness of marriage, the sheer serenity and insanity of parenthood, the hopefulness of the future, or the lush rewards of the playfulness and divine work that grew and defined a family. Maybe she never knew it with anyone. After 16 years, the fragile, enchanting hope that she was alive, but either held or hiding, had wilted like a morning glory's ephemeral bloom.

Brynn shut the door in the face of those wretched reminders and stepped through the doorway to Lanea's room.

With all the refuse in the room, Brynn chose not to sit as the memories came to her. Among them came the poignant moments showing Genevieve on her deathbed, and the tender care given to her by Bertis and Lanea. It was obvious that Genevieve had been moved to this room during her infirmity, which, as Brynn recalled, was only a couple of months. The bed had been moved near the window for her, and the room was bright and cheerful, being south facing, and most importantly, it was nearest the bathroom. Genevieve had been stricken with a virulent form of leukemia. The prognosis wasn't good even with treatment, nor did it include any therapy that would lengthen her life or make it more comfortable. They chose to forego the expensive drugs and endless, painful procedures. Even as private and disconnected as the Coveys were, Brynn remembered that the community had gathered around them, providing meals, farm help, and support as Genevieve and her family struggled with the disease. Unfortunately, the support ended at the front door of the Covey home. No visions of outside help were ever seen inside the house.

Brynn fought to contain her emotions as she watched Lanea with her dying mother. The young woman washed her mother's hair and gently brushed it, bathed her and helped her dress. She fed her, held her hand, sang soft, silent hymns to her, prayed with her and for her, read to her, and watched her sleep. On better days, Lanea and her mother laughed and crocheted together, or Lanea told stories. Her mother watched Lanea intently, asking questions and making comments that Brynn couldn't hear. It was a paradoxical twist, Brynn reflected, that Genevieve's illness brought more spirit and ardor and cheer to this room than the whole house had probably seen in its entire existence. The bond that it bolstered between mother and daughter was even more of a precious gift, valuable beyond measure.

In one deeply affecting moment, Brynn watched as Lanea bent over her mother's fragile body and whispered in her ear. She slowly drew back as her mother's eyes opened wide, and they both began to weep. Genevieve placed her bony hands on Lanea's damp cheeks, wiped away the tears with her thumbs, and gently held her only daughter's face as she searched it for a long while as if to commit it to memory for all eternity, a weak, sorrowful smile touching her lips. She pulled Lanea to her, wrapped her thin arms around her, and Lanea nestled close to her mother's tiny, ravaged body on the bed. Genevieve kissed her daughter's forehead, and they lay in peaceful silence until they drifted off to sleep. Only God and the grave were privy to those words, but Brynn imagined that both God and the grave were privy to countless sad goodbyes.

Within moments, Brynn witnessed Genevieve's death, and it was apparent, by Genevieve's feeble state, that it was soon after the day that Lanea had spoken the hushed words in her mother's ear. Bertis and Lanea were sitting at Genevieve's side. Bertis was praying as he held Genevieve's hand, and Lanea was crying and stroking her mother's soft hair as she watched her mother slip into another world far, far away from her. Brynn watched the light flicker and fade out of Genevieve's eyes, and out of Bertis' and Lanea's lives. Brynn understood much more clearly the visions of Lanea crying at the stove; that she was either preparing food for a mother that she would soon lose, or later, preparing food for only herself and Bertis who were later lost themselves.

Amidst the powerful memories contained within the room, Brynn saw Lanea as a small girl, playing with dolls, reading books, coloring, and otherwise entertaining herself. As a young girl and into her adolescence, Lanea spent endless hours alone, reading, doing homework, and writing in her journal. Brynn couldn't decide whether that was a good thing or a bad thing.

Emotionally exhausted, Brynn desperately needed a short break before finishing up. She took a step to leave and was struck by an image that she had not previously seen. Lanea was sitting on her bed, which was near the window where Genevieve had occupied it, so Brynn took this to mean that it was after Genevieve had died and after Lanea had moved back into her room. Lanea, her face flushed and wet, was writing a note. She stood, placed the note on the nightstand, stuffed some clothing, personal items, and her Bible in her backpack, and tiptoed to the door.

Despite her trespassing, gray-area alibis, and other sundry sins of the day, God still favored Brynn. He answered her morning prayer with the gift of a clue: Lanea had run away.

CHAPTER TWELVE

BRYNN PEDALED VIGOROUSLY, THE EXCITEMENT spurring her to go faster. But the further she pedaled from the Covey home, the less sure she was of her theory, and the more her excitement and energy waned. *Wait ... she was never listed in news reports as a runaway ... Didn't the police get the note? ... Why wouldn't Bertis show them the note? ... Had Bertis not truly believed that she had run away ... Unless ... maybe* Bertis *never got the note ... Did Lanea change her mind? ... Why wouldn't I see that? ...*

Brynn fetched Buddy from her mother's, dodging the tiny detail that she hadn't taken even one snapshot of any house. She went home with more questions than her venture had answered. She would have to return to the house eventually. Perhaps there were no more clues within the house, and maybe whatever happened to Lanea had happened outside those walls and those memories were not captured but had dissipated like a flimsy dust devil into the vast openness of the universe just as the girl seemingly had. However, Brynn was not allowing her determination and her momentum to be derailed by maybes.

"Do any of you remember Lanea Covey?" Brynn's casual mention of the subject during a lull in the usual dinner noise had a less than casual reaction, freezing everyone at the dining table in mid-motion like a game of Simon Says. Except for the stony silence and Brynn's mortifying feeling that she had just flunked Nonchalance 101 right in front of Jackson's family, it would have been comical. Someone gulped. *You're out!* came to mind, but she said nothing as she poked at her salad, her eyebrows raised in forced, subtle curiosity. She smiled, trying to temper the graceless moment, but their response to her innocuous question began to feel wrong, as did her innocuous question.

Brynn's father-in-law, Ever, said gruffly around the salad in his mouth, "Of course. It wasn't *that* long ago." Sixteen years wasn't that long ago to an old guy like Everett—or Ever, as everyone knew him—but it was half of Brynn's life ago. Ever was in his upper seventies, retired, and now living in Perris with his wife. He was never done with farming, although the farm was pretty well done with him. The back and shoulders of his small frame were bent, and his gray hair was thin. The lines in his weathered face had been deeply chiseled by the many hours of work and worry, and he'd had more parts replaced than a vintage car. He would die a happy man, probably in Jackson's tractor. He occasionally operated it when he got an itch to play in the dirt on his old farm, now Jackson's and Brynn's home place. Brynn hoped that wouldn't be for a long, long time.

"It *was* sixteen years ago, Everett," said Cleo. Jackson's mother never used his nickname. She had always asserted that it was disrespectful and silly. Ever was the nickname given to him by none other than his parents. Ever. Young. It was just too clever. So they named him Everett and dubbed him with distinctiveness. Witless. Cruel. That's what Cleo thought of virtually all "clever" names. "Cleo" was short for nothing, but that didn't stop the childhood taunts, she'd recounted, calling her "Cleopatra" or "Cleo the Cow." She grew up strong and practical and productive, forthright and feisty—all valuable attributes for a good farm wife for which she prided herself. She was tall—taller than Ever by almost four inches, and sturdy, a bit old-fashioned with her orthopedic shoes and her homemade paisley aprons and matching pot holders. But she was keen to current happenings and trends. She even learned to text and use Facebook—much to the surprise of her children and grandchildren—but avoided the silly abbreviations. She refused to even consider Twitter on the basis that the very name of it sounded nonsensical.

Cleo turned to Brynn. "Why do you ask, Honey?" Although the tone had lightened slightly at the Young dinner table where the family was gathered with Jackson's sister's family to celebrate Ever's 79th birthday, it was still fraught. Furtive glances flew around the table like a bowl of creamed onions. Brynn pretended not to notice.

"I was out earlier today to take pictures and went by her house and got to thinking about her and wondered if anyone has heard anything lately about her disappearance. That's all."

Oh, my God, Brynn, eat something!

Brynn bit off a large chunk of bread, hoping to fill the space from where the endless, inane words seemed to spill uncontrollably. Amidst the embarrassment that her topic of conversation was completely arbitrary was the unsettling suspicion that it was inappropriate for reasons beyond her grasp.

"No ... no, I don't believe so," said Cleo. *I knew I could count on her,* Brynn thought. "Last we ever heard was right after she went missing, maybe a few months later, and the article just said that the authorities couldn't say for sure if she was a runaway or was abducted. There was no proof either way. Shoot—she could have fallen in a well, for all we know. I do remember, though, that there were a couple boys that they suspected may have had something to do with it." A fork clattered off a plate and Ever cleared his throat a little more loudly than necessary.

"Well, it's true," Cleo continued, defending her last statement. "Marshall was her boyfriend, you remember, don't you, Jackson? And that other boy, what was his name ... Ryker. That's it. He was a neighbor boy who had a little thing for her. He was kind of odd, I recall. Remember,

Jackson?" Jackson nodded discreetly in agreement, his mouth conveniently full.

Brynn answered, "I remember them, Cleo," when it became obvious that everyone else was suddenly riveted by the food on their plates. "I remember the investigation focused on them. I knew them, but didn't hang out with them. They were older than me. More Jackson's and Wes' age." When no one spoke right away, Brynn continued, determined not to let the topic drop, "I looked up some old articles I had after I'd been by the house. They didn't say much about her running away. Didn't they find a note or anything? I wonder if they searched her room ... ." Afraid she was already saying too much, she reassured herself that they had no idea what she had seen in the Covey home.

"So, Dad, are you planning a trip to the cities to see a Twins game this summer?" asked Rhonda, Jackson's sister. Ever started to speak, but as Cleo continued, he reconsidered, probably knowing that he was no match for his wife in the grueling sport of gossip. He sipped his coffee instead.

"Poor Bertis," Cleo clucked her tongue and shook her head slowly, ignoring Rhonda's detour, "He lost Genevieve and then just a month or so later, little Lanea ... "

"Little? I thought she was a teenag ... " Ted, Rhonda's husband, seemed to suffer a sudden attack by some unseen force under the table. Probably the pointy end of his wife's shoe.

"You know what I mean," Cleo replied. "She was such a young girl, only 16, wasn't she, Brynn? Weren't you friends? Just loses her mother, then falls into a well or whatnot.

It's just so sad. Bertis was just beside himself." Brynn was grateful for whatever got Cleo going, although she wasn't learning anything she didn't already know. "No, Brynn, they never found a note from what I recall. And they searched the house completely, and never found anything missing that one might take if they ran away. Besides, Bertis and Genevieve were such good parents. Why would she run away from home?"

Excruciating boredom? Brynn thought dryly. "I know Marshall. He's a nice guy. I can't imagine him hurting anyone, especially her. They were great together. I guess I don't know Ryker real well, but I know him. He's shy and a little slow, but that's a bit of a leap from introvert to abductor."

"A lot of people wondered about those two boys after she went missing. There was never any proof they had anything to do with it, but that doesn't mean anything either way. Fact is," Cleo was pointing with her loaded fork, " ... they quit talking to police after a while. Wouldn't cooperate. Lawyered up." *Oh, good night, another Law & Order junkie.* Brynn suppressed a smile and raised her chin in polite acknowledgement. "Even today, they keep to themselves, won't talk about it. I imagine they just got tired of people suspecting them of things, whispering around them, talking about them, you know." Cleo finally took a bite of her dinner, but added, "And they won't talk to each other, either. Some bad blood, there." Practical as she was, Cleo still loved her drama.

"Surely they questioned everyone in the area. Weren't there any other suspects?" Brynn wondered aloud.

"Really? Do we need to have this discussion today? Here? Right now?" said Rhonda from across the table. She stood, dropped her napkin on the table, and left the room, leaving her husband and teenage son at the table with their mouths agape, looking like they had just been dropped in the middle of a vast desert and told to find their way home.

"Excuse me," said Cleo and went to the kitchen.

Muffled conversation drifted into the dining room. Dishes clattered in the sink.

"I'm done with all this! Either change the subject or tell her. Or I will," echoed Rhonda's voice from the kitchen.

Jackson hollered toward the kitchen doorway. "That's enough, Rhonda!" Ellie and Buddy sat back in their seats, wide-eyed and startled, and Jackson reached over and squeezed Brynn's hand and whispered, "We'll talk later."

Cleo came back to the table and sat. No one moved. Suffocating silence filled the room.

"What did I ... ? I don't understand. I'm sorry," Brynn stammered, bewildered by everyone's behavior, as she quietly set her fork down and folded her hands in her lap, her appetite gone. She searched Jackson's face for a clue as to what had just happened as her eyes filled with tears. Jackson simply shook his head at her and smiled reassuringly at Brynn and the children.

Ever called to Rhonda, "Bring the catsup back with you, will you Ronnie?" taking charge of the situation in tacit fashion and not allowing Rhonda's outburst to add any more drama to the already tense atmosphere. Rhonda returned with the catsup, slammed it on the table, plopped back down in her chair and crossed her arms. She crossed her legs as if to emphasize her stance and the end of the subject. Her eyes traveled the room, defiantly avoiding contact with any other's. Jackson shot her a hot look that went virtually unnoticed.

"Pass the roast. Please." Ever smiled, graced Brynn with a sympathetic wink, took the platter from his wife and carved himself a hearty portion of beef rib roast, his favorite meal.

"I'm so sorry, J. Why didn't you tell me?" Brynn said quietly as she fingered the hairs on Jackson's chest. After their sweet, peaceful lovemaking, they lay in their room, emboldened by the darkness and comforted by the closeness of their somnolent bodies. Jackson's arms were wrapped around his wife protectively as he stroked her cool, silky hair, her head resting on his shoulder.

After they had arrived home and gotten the children to bed, Jackson had told Brynn that he was a suspect in her disappearance, as well as the disappearance of Lanea Covey. Brynn's disappearance was the springboard to the renewed interest in Lanea's case, since the cases were, as authorities put it, "eerily similar"—if only in the respect that they were within four miles of each other and they were both female—and he was a common factor in both.

"You didn't need to know. It wasn't your fault, and there was no point in adding to your burden." Jackson's voice was distant, soft.

"But you never told me you were a person of interest in Lanea's disappearance."

"It was before we started dating. I was questioned only because I'd asked her out a couple times, and she had always refused. She was interested only in Marshall. Marshall, Wes … and Bertis, too, probably … they all knew I liked her, so it wasn't hard for the police to discover that, but that's as far as it went." Jackson paused, but after a moment of silence, continued. "Then when you disappeared, they thought it was all too convenient. The only thing that kept them from arresting me was proof. And our kids. They were my alibi, since I was watching them when you went running that night. By the time the investigation got rolling, you were found. It settled down after that, but it wasn't over, of course, since they never found who'd … taken you. I even had trouble getting them to let me see you in the hospital." Jackson's voice caught in his throat. Brynn kissed his chest.

The silence that lingered between them was as soothing as their gentle caresses. Brynn's and Jackson's relationship had transcended the self-consciousness usually felt in the absence of dialogue. The hushed moments gave them a mutual feeling of intimacy, tenderness, and serenity that no words ever could. Brynn's heart ached for her husband, and she knew his was hurting for her.

"I'm so sorry, Baby—"

"Shhh … " Jackson interrupted her apology.

She could never apologize enough. She could say it every hour of every day for the rest of their lives and it would forever be abysmally inadequate. She'd still feel responsible for everything he—they all—had been through. A small part of her wished she could remember the attack, or at least her attackers, so that she could share in the burden of that dark time in their lives. She began to wonder if her blissful denial was a selfish indulgence. At what price, though, would that memory come? Maybe Rhonda had a point.

It's early for fireflies ... thought Brynn lazily as their breathing slowed simultaneously. The firefly wandering aimlessly on their bedroom window looked like the stars were realigning themselves. She wished they would. It might change everything, including the past.

Rhonda had every right to feel the way she did. She was the older sister, the firstborn, and she relished her starring role as protector of her brother and her parents. Rhonda was the only child for many years before Jackson came along, and when Jackson, the long-awaited son, was born, though she resented it, she had no choice: she could be a part of his life or not. Being the bossy, independent child that she was, she declared Jackson her onus, almost as if the decision to have Jackson join the family was hers and hers alone.

A teller at the Perris Community Bank, Rhonda was a stickler for detail, which made her vocation a perfect fit. Ted, her husband of 21 years, was a CPA in Perris as well. They had only one child, probably to vicariously fulfill Rhonda's desire to perfect the only-child intellectual. Their son, Zane, rejected that dream wholeheartedly, preferring to live at his friends' homes as much as legally possible, and holing up in his locked bedroom the rest of the time, playing video and computer games and listening to angry music. When he was around his parents, his main form of communication was shrugging and rolling his eyes.

Rhonda couldn't be more different from Brynn: she was tall with hair that was horse-coarse, kinky and fiery red, and the freckled, anemic skin that usually came with it. She inherited her mother's build, but with less padding, giving her a pinched, severe appearance. She reminded Brynn of that sour schoolteacher on Little House on the Prairie, a suitable tip-off to her personality.

Brynn could not account for the blatant resentment and hostility that Rhonda exhibited toward her. It didn't begin with her abduction, which she would be able to understand from the viewpoint of blame. Jackson once told Brynn that it was because he no longer followed the "Gospel of Rhonda." Brynn smiled at the recollection, remembering Rhonda's tirade about their choices in wedding music, bridesmaid dresses, flowers, honeymoon plans. Jackson, instantly recognizing the essence of Rhonda's rant, remarked that maybe they should just forget the wedding, not get married. Rhonda shut up faster than a clam in fresh water. Jackson laughed loud and hard, having outed her, and then quietly and firmly told her that Brynn made him happy and that Rhonda could either be a part of their lives or not. There was no in-between. Rhonda lived as close to that line of in-between as she could, seeming to test Jackson's loyalties to one side or the other, but his allegiance always and only landed squarely on Brynn's side.

Jackson was the lambswool between the two points of friction. Brynn's and Rhonda's mutual love for him would be enough to sustain a polite respect for each other, the fiasco at the dinner table notwithstanding. Friendship, however, wasn't necessary to survival. There would be no sharing of the fermented batter of Friendship Bread between the two. If Jackson was aware of the festering animosity Rhonda still held for Brynn, he was unconcerned. Brynn knew that his love for her was as clear and infinite as the universe outside the window, and as simple and innocent as the lightning bug pretending to be a star.

"I love you, J," Brynn said tenderly, imagining the vow seeping directly into his softly thumping heart right below her lips. She liked to fantasize that those would be the last words she would ever hear him say and the last words he would ever hear from her. However, knowing how spitefully serendipitous and cruel death tended to be, it would most likely be "holy crap," "oh, we're out of dog food," "move over," or some other stupid phrase that he or she would carry into the next world to be posted for all perpetuity on the "Pathetic Last Lines" board. Regardless, or rather because of that fact, she quietly said it again for added measure.

"I love you." She smiled as her eyes closed, the warm heaviness of sleep settling over her like the wonderful heft of her Grandma's four flannel quilts on a frigid, winter night.

A soft snore was his response, but she could live with that.

CHAPTER THIRTEEN

THERE WAS NO WAY TO hurry through chores. They took as long as they took whether she was anxious to get on with her investigation or not. Brynn walked the pens, gave a good scratch to her favorites, and did her record keeping as usual. She enjoyed her job, but sometimes had to be reminded by her pigs. She was thorough, finishing before 7:00 a.m., in plenty of time before Ellie left for the bus.

"Mama, stop." Ellie held up her hand authoritatively like a stern crossing guard as Brynn poked her head into the kitchen from the mudroom. Ellie was ready to leave, her backpack bulging with likely more amassed show-and-tell than actual schoolwork. She wore a light blue shirt and matching floral ruffled skirt—that, no doubt, had a pair of shorts underneath in case cartwheels became too much of a temptation—and pink cowboy boots. "Don't come any closer. You're stinky. And I'm wearing perfume." She looked and acted far too grown up for Brynn's taste. Brynn grinned, stepping into the doorway and opening her arms in a playful plea for some morning love. Hugs were not allowed in Brynn's crusty, pre-shower state. They threw air hugs and blew kisses as Ellie walked out the front door on Brynn's customary "Have an awesome day!" send-off. By Ellie's senior year, that line would be either as annoying or unnoticed as a squeaky floorboard, but cherished traditions always started out that way.

Jackson finished his coffee, standing as he gulped the last in his cup, and grazed Brynn's cheek with a perfunctory kiss. Planting season was a time of quick exchanges and distant affections. Daily plans, intimate discussions, and minor disagreements were often condensed and conducted with one hand on the doorknob, as Jackson's was now.

"Where are you planting today? Should I bring dinner out to you when Buddy gets up?" Brynn was making plans in her head as well as out loud.

"We'll be at the south eighty. Yeah, you can bring something out." He was already opening the door. "Are you bringing Buddy out, too? He wanted to ride with me today."

"I was hoping you'd ask. I have some errands to run in town." She tried not to sound too glad.

"What do you have to do in town?"

I was afraid of this. I shouldn't have said anything about going to town. Now I wonder if I should tell him about my plans to try to find out what happened to Lanea, and my plan to visit the sheriff's office to see what he can tell me. But that would lead to a discussion about my weird ability. He deserves to know. Now would be the perfect time. If he wasn't in a hurry. If the door wasn't open. If I thought it wouldn't land me in a doctor's office somewhere. I can't. Not yet.

"Oh, stop at the library, get some groceries ... " She realized too late that the "oh" probably made her story less believable, but he didn't seem to notice.

" all right, then. See you in a little bit," Jackson said as she moved in and grabbed his shirt to collect a real kiss.

"Don't come any closer. You're stinky and I'm wearing perfume," Jackson leaned back, repeating his daughter's orders. They laughed as Brynn wrestled a proper kiss from her husband, and Jackson trotted off to his pickup. "No egg salad!" he yelled over his shoulder.

"Buddy likes egg salad, I thought," she called, stepping out onto the back stoop.

"He does. He doesn't like *me* to eat it ... " Jackson was already pulling away from the house.

"Ah, yes ... " Brynn waved him off, understanding his meaning, having witnessed firsthand the grievous after-effects of that particular meal. "And he said *I* was stinky ... " she muttered to Bingo, who had followed her outside. Brynn felt a tickle of apprehension in her stomach. It was probably because of the half-truth she'd given Jackson. She shook it off and went back into the house to shower.

Bingo hovered around Brynn's feet as she prepared Jackson's lunch, staring intently at the floor, as if believing that the beautiful gifts from the meat gods above sprang miraculously from the hardwoods below her nose. Brynn made a ham sandwich for Jackson and a peanut butter sandwich for Buddy, along with bags of pretzel chips, halved grapes, and a fun-size candy bar for each of her men, adding two bottles of juice, and a jug of water to share. Knowing that—at least for Buddy—food was the most important part of the day, she included a couple containers with banana bread and chocolate cake for their mid-morning and mid-afternoon snacks. The cooler bag bulged satisfyingly like Ellie's backpack when Brynn was finished, lending her the heartwarming feeling that a hefty dinner pail was tantamount to a full tummy and, therefore, love in its purest form.

She dropped a piece of ham on the floor. The dog snatched it up as fast as a frog eating a fly. The morsel disappeared with no chewing, savoring, or appreciating involved, her focus in life, always, not on the current treat, but the next. Her eyes were now glued to the floor in anticipation of the next. The only evidence of the offering was a wet spot on the floor and a pithy thank-you-wag of her tail. "You're welcome, you ungrateful beast," Brynn quipped.

Buddy shuffled into the kitchen shortly before eight o'clock, his curly shocks flattened on one side of his head and his eyes still puffy, as Brynn finished cleaning up.

"Morning, Sunshine!" Brynn wiped her hands on a towel and picked up her son for a cuddle.

"Where's Daddy? I'm going with him today. We're planting and stuff," Buddy announced. Brynn smiled, noticing that although Buddy was still rubbing the sleep from his eyes, he was set to go with his boots pulled on over his camo-print footie pajamas and his blue jean jacket crookedly buttoned up to his chin. Brynn suspected he had put his boots on before bed the night before. She wondered how many a dark, quiet, spring night had claimed a little boy and replaced him with a little farmer.

"Yup, I'm taking you out as soon as you've eaten breakfast."

"But I'm not hungry!" he whined in his raspy morning voice.

"Daddy ate breakfast … " Brynn said, setting a bowl of cereal on the table. Buddy sat, committing only one cheek to the chair, and gobbled his food, milk dripping from his chin.

Brynn gathered his clothes for the day, put the lunch supplies in the car, and made a list of things to do and get in town. Again, her stomach fluttered. She made sure to list the stops to the library and grocery store.

Within minutes, Buddy finished his second bowl of cereal. She changed his clothes, washed his face, and combed his hair, which he promptly messed up. "Mama. Farmers don't comb their hair," he admonished. Brynn raised her eyebrows in doubt, but refrained from saying anything that might sully his idea of his future occupation.

She couldn't resist a tease. "What if you meet a pretty girl?"

"In the tractor? No way. 'Sides, girls are gross. Daddy doesn't like girls," Buddy grabbed his mother's hand on the way to the car.

"Your daddy likes *me*."

"You're not a girl. You're my mom. He has'ta. Daddy likes cows and stuff." Buddy was so confident in this assertion that Brynn knew she wouldn't win. She conceded, acknowledging that she stood somewhere between mom and cow in the order of her husband's affections. At least in the little farmer's eyes, which was high praise.

With Buddy and the food delivered to the tractor, Brynn went back to the house and gathered the necessary items for the day: notebook, purse, phone, and list. She briefly thought of all the chores around the house she could be tackling, but put them out of her mind. She wanted to learn what had happened to Lanea.

As she drove to town, she tried not to think of the prospect of walking into the courthouse in Perris. Although she'd been there numerous times and knew almost everyone on a first name basis, it was the first time visiting there since her abduction.

As she neared town, she realized that maybe her nerves were strung a little tighter with the idea that they would treat her differently, as was fairly common these days. She couldn't blame them. She had achieved almost a celebrity-status in town. In a town of a little more than three thousand people, it was understandable. Big-city crimes rarely occurred, and most people in a town that size either died or didn't—not much of that in-between-or-almost excitement. Didn't take much to fuel the fire of gossip, the nefarious eternal flame of every small town. She knew well the heat of that flame. Grocery shopping or dining in town shortly after her recovery made her feel as if she had forgotten to dress.

Brynn pulled up to the curb in front of the courthouse and stared at the building. She shook her head, berating herself for the melodrama, and got out of her car.

Walking up to the courthouse doors, wearing her faded jeans, a jean shirt, and flip-flops, Brynn slowed her pace, then stopped in her tracks. She wondered if she was underdressed, even though she wasn't there in any legal capacity. It was also about coffee time—the sheriff could be gone on break. She hadn't thought of that.

She began to feel as though this trip to the courthouse was just a silly waste of time. *Who am I to waltz in here all business-like, wanting to know details about an old case that's basically none of my business? I'm not an investigator. I'm just a nosey housewife with too much time on her hands.*

She turned and went back to her car. She started the engine, but couldn't seem to do more than sit unmoving in the driver's seat, staring at her clenched hands in her lap. She felt a foreboding that she couldn't name, a panic that she didn't understand, and a sense of dread that made her want to avoid the building as fervently as a funeral.

What are you so afraid of? She didn't know. She knew only that she didn't feel ready to go in.

A rap on the car window startled her from her thoughts.

"Brynn?" Bonita, a clerk at the courthouse and long-time friend of Brynn's, had a look of motherly concern on her face.

Brynn lowered the window.

"Hi, Bonita. What are you up to?" She couldn't imagine a feebler, more pathetic greeting, but there it was.

"I just took some things to the post office. It's so good to see you!" Bonita paused, perhaps hoping for input from Brynn and getting none, she added, "Are you coming in? I saw you going in, then you turned around ... "

"Yes. Yes, I was. I'm just ... making some notes. Before." Brynn smiled, a nervous twitch in her upper lip belying her casual demeanor. There was no pen and paper in her hand. Bonita didn't seem to notice.

"Well, the coffee's on, Hun. It would be great to catch up with you, if you have time. What brings you here? Anything I can help with?" Bonita's cheerfulness put Brynn at ease, as always. She was slightly older than Brynn, but their friendship was so comfortable that no amount of time between meetings seemed to affect its fit, and they slipped easily into it again.

Bonita Laverdure and Brynn had become friends when they worked at the local diner together. Brynn was in high school, and Bonita was putting herself through college. Bonita had trained Brynn in the finer points of waitressing—like how to get more than a dime tip from the two-and-a-half-hour coffee drinkers, and that happy cooks make happy customers. Had Brynn believed in reincarnation, she was certain that Bonita would have been a ballerina in her former life. She was refined and lissome, as gentle and graceful as silk ribbon. Brynn had never heard an angry or disparaging word cross Bonita's lips; she could make an order for creamed chipped beef over toast sound like a love sonnet. All of that made it doubly hard for Brynn to hate Bonita for the amazing tips she could rake in.

"I'm here to talk to the Sheriff. Is he in today?" He probably wasn't. She had plenty to do at home anyway. She needed to get tomatoes planted, and the winter grime on the windows made a sunny day look foggy. A quick run would be wonderful.

"He is. Should I let him know you're here?" Bonita half-turned, waiting.

"Oh, well. That's ... He is?" Brynn was surprised by the news. Then disappointed. She briefly wished she had left when she had the chance. She thanked Bonita and urged her to go ahead. She took her time gathering her things and making her way into the building.

The courthouse was spotlessly clean, sparsely but tastefully decorated with local artisans' work. It smelled like the waiting room of a doctor's office. She couldn't think of better incentive to make people want to avoid going to court.

She waved at acquaintances who worked in the one large room with the three utterly-unnecessarily-separate windows of the auditor's, treasurer's, and register of deed's offices. They couldn't see her apprehension as she calmly strolled to the end of the corridor where Sheriff Raske's office was located.

If he was surprised to see her, it didn't show. Sheriff Arthur Raske looked eager and delighted, but not surprised. Brynn reasoned that he had been given a heads-up by Bonita.

"Brynn! What a wonderful surprise!" Raske shouted. "Come in. Have a seat!" He held a chair for her.

"Sheriff. Thank you." Maybe he'd ask what kind of pie she wanted with her coffee.

As if reading her mind, he said, "Coffee? Bonita told me you were coming in, so I checked the pot. It's early enough in the day. I won't have to use a spatula to serve it." He grinned at his own joke. "She said you wanted to speak with me?" He grabbed the carafe from the coffeemaker on top of a file cabinet near his desk and poured coffee into a disposable cup.

Brynn smiled, feeling considerably more relaxed than she was a few moments ago. Brynn and Jackson both knew the sheriff, a soft-spoken, lanky man in his forties. She doubted he could elicit fear in a shy child if he tried. He had been born with a defect, if one could call it that, bequeathing him with a faint perpetual smile on one half of his smooth, boyish face. To call him handsome would be an exaggeration, but his full lips, wide blue eyes, dimples, and slight overbite made him attractive in the same way that made nerdy virgins attractive to sexy flirts.

"Well, yes. I had some questions I wanted to ask you." Brynn dug her notebook from her bag as the sheriff set the unrequested cup of steaming coffee on the desk, and took a seat across from her.

"If a person had questions about a case—" She paused, unsure how to proceed in a situation where she obviously had no experience or business. "How much would she be able to find out from your office?"

"Depends on the case, depends on what you want to know. Open cases have certain restrictions, of course, since it's considered an ongoing investigation," he answered, his hand on a thick file that he glanced at more than once during his explanation.

"I believe it's an open case," she began, testing the waters.

"I take it you remembered something about your case, your abduction?" he plied. He worked at being cool, professional, but she could read his hopeful countenance.

"No," she stated, emotionless. They were both perplexed, momentarily dazed into confused silence.

She spoke first.

"I'm sorry. I'm here about a sixteen-year-old case. Lanea Covey's case."

"No, I'm sorry. I shouldn't have assumed you were here about your case. But, since you asked, I'm afraid I can't help you much with Miss Covey's case unless you are immediate family. Her case is still open. *Your* case, however, would be a different matter." He placed his hands on the file in front of him.

"No, I'm not family. Just a friend who wants to know what happened to her." Brynn paused, eyeing the file. "Why would my case be a different matter?"

"Well, basically, because it's yours and you lived it. Not much we could share that you wouldn't already know, if you … could remember." He cleared his throat. "Naturally, we wouldn't disclose details, evidence that only the perpetrator would have knowledge of, those that we wouldn't want to become public." Raske leaned over the brown folder and fiddled with a pen as he stared intently at Brynn.

Brynn picked up her Styrofoam coffee cup and took a sip, grasping it with both hands when she noticed a tremor in her grip. The coffee was an industrial version compared to her own anemic brew, likely the standard recipe for law enforcement offices world-wide, where circumstances called for something to chew on while mulling over difficult cases.

The seconds felt like a twelve-hour standoff, like she was being dared to prove her bravery, her will, her wit. She knew what he was doing. And she wasn't going to be baited or sidetracked.

"So where can I find information about Lanea Covey's case?" Brynn finally asked.

"Well, I imagine the best place to get information would be the newspaper. Search their archives for stories about her from that time period, ask around to her friends and family, things of that nature." His eyebrows furrowed. "Can I ask why you're looking into this? Now, I mean? Did something happen that we should know about?"

"No, nothing happened. I paint houses, you know, artistic images. I was out last week photographing houses and went by Lanea's place and it got me thinking about her, and what happened to her. No. Nothing happened." She tried to ignore the file that taunted her as mercilessly as did the sheriff's expectant expression.

"As long as you're here, I was hoping to talk to you about your case. Have you noticed anything suspicious, or remembered anything that might help our case? Your case?" he elucidated.

"Suspicious?" The question startled Brynn.

"Unfamiliar vehicles or people in your area, suspicious behavior in anyone you have come in contact with, things like that."

"No, not that I recall ... " The mention of behavior triggered in Brynn the memory of the unpleasant incident at her in-laws a couple of days previous. "But now that you mention it, I do recall a discovery that I wanted to ask you about."

Brynn took a breath. "Sheriff, you've known my family and Jackson's family most of your life. I can't believe you would think that my husband had anything to do with my disappearance, my attack."

He seemed unfazed by her complaint. "I understand your feelings, and I would rather not have to look at spouses as suspects in cases like yours, but sadly, more times than not, it is someone the victim knows that ends up being the culprit. It's my job, it's nothing personal."

"Nothing personal." Brynn nodded, as if she agreed but didn't believe it. "So can I assume that he is no longer a suspect?"

"I didn't say that," Raske countered. "Everyone's a suspect until someone's convicted. And we will explore all possibilities until your case is solved. I'm sorry." Brynn sensed his apology wasn't as sincere as it sounded.

"Then can you tell me who *isn't* a suspect?" To speak of the file was like speaking of ghosts in a dark cemetery. She sipped her coffee, feigning poise and a vague disinterest. "What's all in that file?"

Raske overlooked her first question. "Facts about your abduction, your injuries, notes about the people who were questioned in connection to the case, pictures. There are a few sensitive things that I can't disclose with you, as I said, things that only the perpetrator would know. Those things, we wouldn't want accidentally leaked. But other than that, you are free to see or know what's in here."

Raske pulled a smaller file and a few sheets of paper from Brynn's case file and placed them in a drawer.

He moved the file to the middle of the desk.

Raske's hand rested on the thick sheaf as he chose his words.

"I don't have to tell you that the things in this file are pretty shocking, even for us. You are welcome to look through here, or you can ask me any questions you may have if you'd rather not. But I'll be honest. I'm hoping it will help you remember something that might help us get a break here." He looked her in the eye, warning her of the gravity of the situation.

"I understand. I'm a big girl. Even if I don't remember, I'm quite aware of everything that happened to me." She pulled the file to her, and catching the corner of the folder under her finger, felt a tingle go down her leg. Her pulse quickened. She looked at the sheriff and time seemed to stop. The air, the light, the day, all manner of life and her surroundings solidified as if atoms had ceased bombardment. The nanosecond between now and never was frozen in a moment that seemed to last forever. Like that flash of The Detonation, that ephemeral twinkling between life and death, that fickle trice between "I" and "do." That moment was a thick layer of paper separating her from "no going back."

She opened the file.

Documents that were hard copies of a computer file, copies of emails and correspondence, and copies of medical records filled the folder. X-rays with unmistakable images of broken bones—a skull fracture, ribs, a wrist, and two fingers. Words, like flashes of hot light, scored her mind. *"Head trauma ... Internal injuries ... Rape ... Torture ... Burns ... . Abrasions ... Contusions ... Lacerations ... Fractures."*

Although at first dizzying, they gradually melted together into slurry. She slowly scanned the documents, trying to digest the specifics of her experience. Facts, clues, suppositions, leads, and notes by investigators were interesting, even fascinating, but in relation to her, fundamentally unimportant. Just words. This was history, a telling of heinous events that she lived, but it may have well been someone else. However colorful the story, it didn't change the fact that there was no end to it. It didn't change the fact that there would be no recovery of the deleted files in her mind. She had been told that by her doctors. The gratifying conclusion to this mystery might never be written, at least not by her.

She glanced at the sheriff, whose mannerisms revealed his aim. He was assessing the effect of the file on her. More for the reprieve than the sustenance, Brynn finished off the last sip of her coffee.

"Can I get you more coffee? I'll get you another cup." The sheriff jumped up and left.

Although she didn't need another cup, he at least wasn't hovering for a moment as she continued to leaf through the papers.

She lifted a sheet of paper that revealed a stack of photos beneath. The first was a photograph of a grassy ditch with a patch of flattened grass near the edge of a gravel road. Brynn looked closer. The spot was tinged with red. The next was a photo of a house—a large, dilapidated Foursquare. It looked familiar, but as Foursquare designs go, she reasoned, if you've seen one, you've seen them all.

The sheriff returned with the coffee.

"What's this picture of, besides a house, I mean." Brynn showed him the photo.

"We found evidence in that house," he answered succinctly. "Does it look familiar?"

Brynn shrugged. "Not particularly." She wasn't going to fill him with false hope. She did wonder, briefly, about asking where it was. She waited for that moment to pass.

She lifted the photographs and looked carefully at each—photographs of a room much like the rooms Brynn had seen recently in empty houses—rooms filled with trash and destroyed by vandals, animals, and the elements. She studied photos of items like clothing, a mattress, an excised chunk of hardwood flooring with a red boot print next to a ruler. It reminded her of painted handprints from Ellie's kindergarten class. She realized that this was not paint, but it was hard to reconcile herself the fact that this was her blood.

Her hand stopped on the next photograph. It was a close-up of a ghastly wound, a deep jagged gash in a part of the anatomy that she did not recognize. Moving on, she noted that there were several photos of wounds, wounds which were cleaned, but not yet stitched or treated. Some wounds depicted were almost perfect circles—like chicken pox scabs—but she knew they were not. Some were angry slashes and scrapes. These photos were oddly, morbidly compelling. She was at the same time curious and disgusted.

The photo that came next stunned Brynn into paralysis. A face, battered into swollen lumps of raw meat, came into view—split and bloated lips that looked like shiny, engorged water balloons; eyes that were nothing more than slits in puffy, purple tissue; rasped cheeks that looked to be stuffed with cotton in a ridiculous parody of a fat man. Brynn stared for a long while at the face, but then relaxed with relief. She had been in a coma for two weeks following the attack, but she doubted she'd ever looked like that. It wasn't her. Somehow, the file had been mixed with someone else's, someone who had suffered brutality and evil beyond anything she could imagine. She felt sorry for the girl.

Brynn's eyes flooded with tears. Sheriff Raske touched her arm.

"Brynn? Are you all right?"

Her voice was thick. "Yes, I'm fine. It's just ... " she wanted to use the word "sad," maybe the word "appalling," or even the word "frightening," but out of respect for the girl, she left her statement unfinished. She swallowed hard, consuming her emotion, then sat up straight. She blinked back the tears.

"I'm sorry. I wish I could help, but I can't." Brynn closed the file and slowly pushed it back toward the sheriff. "So you think the newspaper is my best bet for information on Lanea's disappearance?"

Raske nodded. Brynn stood and thanked him as he stood and wished her luck. Brynn knew that his best shot had just fallen short of the target. It wasn't even in the same forest. She refused to feel bad about his failure. It was nothing personal.

Brynn left the courthouse and walked down the block to the newspaper office. Her legs felt heavy and the sunshine didn't seem as warm or bright as when she'd gone into the courthouse. She felt deflated, depressed. Brynn pulled out her list and forced herself to move on with her mission.

After reaching the newspaper office, she searched the archives for articles relating to Lanea's disappearance, finding little more than what she had discovered at the catastrophic birthday party. Her motivation squelched by her meager results and by the cloud that seemed to follow her from the courthouse, she stuffed her notes into her bag. She then finished her errands with a trip to the grocery store, buying only the basics. The thought of a short visit to Cole crossed her mind, but she was exhausted and it was early afternoon, soon time for Ellie to arrive home from school. Brynn drove home, her mind numb from fatigue. Unmoved by the radio's ploys to cheer her with happy tunes and annoyed by its manipulation, Brynn punched the on/off button. She might have time for a nap; or perhaps a cup of tea and a good book would serve her just as well.

The shower after chores that evening helped her spirits as much as the run had earlier. She had opted for a punishing run to a few choleric choices in music. Her skin tingled deliciously with the hot water as she soaped and smoothed the lather over the faint lines and marks on her body. She traced the paths of unknown weapons and deeds, stopping at one on her hip. She stared at it. The hip. That was the unrecognizable part of anatomy she couldn't make out in the photo. She examined the scars on her legs, then her stomach, her breasts, her arms. These wounds were the ones she saw in the photos. These scars, the hieroglyphs, the sacred carvings that she had tried to revere as symbols of her courage and determination, were now repulsive. She knew them; she knew their history and their intent. She hated them. She wanted them gone. The hot water of the shower now mingled with her burning tears of shame and revulsion as she scrubbed at the mutilations, furiously pawed and scratched and rubbed at them. They were marks that she did not choose—they were evidence of an evil that dirtied her soul and marred her temple. They were someone else's symbols of power, some mad man's mark of terror and control. These engravings were his dedications to himself. As good as branded by the monster's searing, red iron, he would forever be able to claim them, and her, as his own.

Brynn collapsed on the shower floor, hidden in the steam, silenced by the water, and drenched in self-loathing and grief. When she at last was purged of all the hatred and sadness that would go down the drain, Brynn emerged from the shower, wiped the haze from the mirror, and quietly searched the reflection for any trace of the girl.

Brynn had never noticed how loud the ticking clocks were before that night. Even when the children were tiny babies needing nighttime feedings, she was unaware of the audible reminders of the measured passage of her life. That night, however, the clocks ticked, the dog snored, the wind sighed at the windows, and the old house creaked. Brynn wandered, unable to sleep. The darkness and solitude soothed her aches. Brynn wrapped herself in her robe and a quilt and went out into the cool, breezy night and sat on the porch swing, waiting for sleepiness to arrive as if by midnight delivery. Unbidden thoughts and images tumbled over and over in her head like balls in a bingo cage. The incubus of her own making was more horrifying than any she could have read in her file, the possibilities—nay, probabilities—of what had been done to her far exceeding the facts anyone, besides her assailant, knew. Who was he? Did she know him? Was her family justified in their fear for her? How long would this go on?

The blackness outside the sanctuary of her home's walls suddenly seemed different than that of inside—darker, more withholding, and much less benign than just moments before. Clouds shrouded the scanty moonlight, and the wind carried a mist. Something was coming—rain, for sure, maybe something more.

She went into the house and locked the door. Did she even have a key? Settling into the rocking chair near the fireplace, she clicked the remote and turned on the gas flames. She lay open the damp quilt, stretching her cold feet toward the fire. The warmth massaged her and the flames mesmerized her, fixing her gaze and her mind on the tranquil flickering, flickering. He was not here. She was safe. It was over. Over.

The house creaked again.

CHAPTER FOURTEEN

T HE CHILL WAS HARD TO shake off. Brynn trotted home from the hog house, hoping the brief quarter-mile jog would warm her and rev up her spirits, but the lingering morning showers dogged her. Gloom shadowed her like an irritating neighbor kid who asked too many dumb questions—persistent and inescapable.

Brynn paused before turning the knob on the mudroom door. There was no rush, since Jackson was with the kids while she did her chores, unable to go to the field because of rain, but she knew well the madness of mornings. She prepared herself for the chaos that always waited on the other side, and however annoying the cold drizzle was, it didn't whine, ring, spill, demand attention, or need its nose wiped. She turned the knob, and as expected, chaos welcomed her in.

Ellie couldn't find her reading book and Bingo had slathered her new pink and orange rain coat in slobber, Buddy refused to put his underwear on and was riding bareback on the dog, and Jackson was late for an unexpected appointment.

"The bus will be here any minute, Ellie! Just take off your raincoat, put on your wind breaker, and you can take the book tomorrow. Buddy, get off the dog!" Jackson boomed, and then said to Brynn, "I have to go. Right now." He shot Brynn a look that talked: *"You're a mother! Fix this!"*

"But my jacket doesn't match my rain boots!" Ellie wailed, leaving the drooled-on raincoat firmly in place.

"Where are you going?" Brynn pulled off a few sheets of paper towel and wiped dog slime from Ellie's coat as she addressed Jackson.

"A meeting. Do you hear the bus honking?"

"Where?"

"Ellie, the bus is here. Buddy!"

"I have this, Jackson. Go."

"Do you need anything in town? No, never mind. You were in town yesterday. I take it you got everything you needed at the courthouse?" Chaos whirled around them as they stood motionless in its fury, staring at each other.

"Were you ... how did ... " she stammered.

The bus honked again.

"Raske called me this morning. Wants to talk. I'll be home ... later, I guess. Ellie, I'll give you a ride to the bus."

Jackson took Ellie's hand. He kissed Brynn's cheek with a curt "love you," and went out the front door, waving at the bus. His pronouncement of love sounded as passionate as a courtroom swearing-in.

In the pickup on the way to town, Jackson fumed about the past two days: First Brynn's inquiries at his parent's home that led to an outburst by his snarky sister, and then Brynn's surreptitious trip to the sheriff's office.

What the hell was going on?

He didn't understand Brynn's sudden interest in Lanea's disappearance. What had made her so curious about this case, and now, of all times? Had someone said something to her? And what had she talked to the sheriff about?

It was bound to come up. He had no one to blame but himself. He should have been honest with her about it long ago. Timing, reasons, relation—it was all just semantics. There was no logical reason why he hadn't told her that he was a suspect in Lanea's disappearance. It was long before he and Brynn had started dating, and she was just a kid then. *Just a kid. She was the same age as Lanea. And for some reason, I thought of Lanea as worthy, and not Brynn. She was my best friend's little sister, and yes, I thought of her as a kid. I am a jerk.*

He eased his foot off the gas and took a deep breath, trying to slow his pulse and his pickup. He knew his anger was more toward himself than Brynn or Rhonda.

Both of them, though, had opportunities to stop or avoid the conflict: Brynn with the questions, and his sister with her malicious dramatics.

And yesterday, before he left for the field, there was plenty of opportunity for Brynn to tell him of her plans to talk to the sheriff. Not only had she talked to Raske about her case, but she could have remembered what happened without Jackson being there to ... whatever. Maybe there was nothing that he could have done. When—*if*—she remembers, he might not be there. Then what?

Arriving at the sheriff's office, Jackson leaned his head back and rubbed his neck before getting out of his vehicle. It was too wet to plant, but there had to be something better to do than sit in the sheriff's office, answering questions.

"Jackson. Have a seat." Raske sat behind his desk and leaned back in his office chair. Jackson sat in the chair opposite the sheriff's desk and leaned back as well, mimicking Raske's confidence.

"Coffee?" the sheriff asked.

"No, thanks. Can we just ... " Jackson crossed his arms.

"Right. Thought you should know that Brynn was in here, asking about Lanea Covey's disappearance." Raske made it clear he was waiting for a reaction from Jackson, and Jackson wasn't in a giving mood.

Jackson looked blankly at Raske. He shrugged. "Is that a problem?"

"No, not really. Aren't you at all curious as to why she would be inquiring about a missing girl just months after being abducted and attacked herself?"

"What are you getting at?"

"Just got me thinking that maybe she's wondering if the cases are related, that's all."

Jackson could feel his teeth clenching. Arthur Raske knew that he'd never be able to see a reaction over the phone and that's why he called him here. Jackson took another deep breath for the sheriff's benefit and said, "Maybe she does. Is that all you wanted?" He stood up.

"Well, no. I also thought you should know that she ... saw her file. You know, pictures, reports and such."

"She *saw* them, or you showed them to her? That was no accident, I'm sure."

"I told her that they were hers, and she made that decision on her own. Has she said anything about her case? Has she remembered anything?"

"No. But it's so good to know that someone's looking out for her, Sheriff." Jackson turned and left.

The trip to town was not going to be wasted on a nosy sheriff. Jackson got into his pickup and drove to the Perris State Bank. He went inside and went directly to the window with the cheap brass placard marked "Rhonda Fossey" and stood waiting for her to look up and notice someone at her station.

"Oh, I'm sorry sir," she said, looking up and smiling, obviously expecting a customer, then dropping the saccharine smile when she saw it was Jackson. "Jackson. What are you—"

"What the hell was that about the other night?" he whispered, although the other tellers' glances told him he wasn't quite as discreet as he thought. Then again, he had no intention of sparing her any indignity. He held more concern, at the moment, for the other customers than for her.

"Jackson, she is just ... " she stammered.

"Just what? Just not dead? Not stupid? What? What's she supposed to do to please you?"

"I just ... " she looked around, " ... don't understand why everyone indulges her. She doesn't need to know anything about Lanea. What does that have to do with her? She's going to open up a whole can of worms if she goes digging around in that." Rhonda tried smiling through her embarrassment.

"It doesn't matter. When are you going to get that through your head? She knows, okay? She knows about Lanea, and she knows that I was a suspect in both cases. It doesn't matter. Now this is where it stops. Drop the hostility. I mean it."

"It's all her fault, you know! Her stupid jogging, getting taken, now poking around ... " Her eyes filled with tears. "She's going to put you right back in their spotlight, Jackson," she hissed. "They'll ruin us."

He pointed at her. "I mean it." He turned and walked out.

Brynn felt like she'd swallowed a fist-sized rock. The heaviness of conflict weighed upon her. It was a familiar sensation, more familiar when it was dense with guilt.

Brynn pulled Buddy from Bingo's back, marched him to his room and handed him some underwear, instructing him in no uncertain terms that he *would get dressed*. Buddy dressed while she showered.

Dishes clattered as she loaded the dishwasher haphazardly, splashing leftover milk and soggy cereal onto the floor, which the dog happily lapped up. *It would have been so easy to drop that little detail about going to the sheriff's office when I was telling him my plans for the day. Why didn't I tell him?*

Brynn looked out the window for the third time, wondering how long the meeting could possibly last. *"I didn't tell you I was going to the sheriff's office because you were in a hurry ... "* A fresh pot of coffee was done brewing. Brynn poured a cup and added creamer, stirring slowly, lost in thought. *"I didn't tell you because you would want to know why I'm so curious about Lanea's disappearance ... " " ... because then maybe I'd have to tell you about my visions ... "*

Going to the kids' bedrooms, Brynn yanked the bedcovers up over the pillows without the usual fuss. *Why did Raske want me to see my file? Well, obviously, he wanted me to remember something ... What is he going to talk to Jackson about? I hope I didn't get him in trouble ... I hope Jackson doesn't think I was there about him ... .*

After putting a mindless, animated movie in the DVD player for Buddy, Brynn went back to the kitchen to wait. She sipped her coffee as she watched the rain trickle down the windows. *... because you'd worry about me ... I didn't tell you because maybe you would think I was crazy ... I didn't tell you because ...*

Brynn's eyes filled with tears. She felt ashamed and saddened at the realization that in some small way, she didn't trust Jackson enough to tell him the truth about her visions. Not yet. Not until she knew more, not until she knew if it would help find her friend, not until she knew for sure … that she wasn't crazy. Or at least that he wouldn't think she was.

Jackson arrived home an hour after he'd left. Brynn braced herself for the discussion that was sure to follow, an apology on her lips as he walked in the door.

He hung his wet coat, walked into the kitchen, and sat down at the table.

"Coffee?" Brynn asked cheerfully, scrubbing the finish off of the inside of the kitchen sink. Her apology was stuck to her lips like dried mustard. "How about a cookie?"

"Sure," he said quietly.

"Um, I don't have any cookies. How about some nuts or crackers and cheese?" Brynn dug through the cupboards as if looking for that apology.

"I don't care. Brynn—"

Here it comes.

"I don't have any nuts or cheese and crackers either. I'm sorry." Brynn wasn't sure if the apology was in response to not having anything to eat or for her offense, but it seemed to fit so perfectly in that little space between the food and the fear. It gave her the necessary courage to turn to Jackson and finally ask the obvious: "What did Arthur want?"

"He wanted to know if you remembered anything about your abduction and attack, and why you are so focused on Lanea all of a sudden." Jackson stared at Brynn expectantly.

Brynn pretended that it wasn't a query.

"Brynn?"

"No, I haven't. And I told him I hadn't remembered anything. And I told you about why I was thinking about Lanea." She went back to scrubbing the spotless sink, forgetting about the coffee and snack.

The silence that followed was not the usual comfortable silence. It felt like the Grand Canyon between them.

Jackson rose and stood next to her at the counter. She added more powdered cleanser to the basin.

"He said you saw your file. That had to be—" His tone was softer.

"I'm fine." They were both entitled to their curt answers. "What would you like for dinner today?" She turned to him and forced a thin smile.

"Okay. You don't want to talk about it."

"Why do you say that? I can talk about it."

"Really? You always ask me about what I want to eat when you're avoiding something." Jackson smiled, diffusing the tension. "I'm not five. I'm not that easily distracted."

She said nothing.

Jackson grabbed a cup and poured his own coffee. "Well, it was a waste of good gas, that's for sure. He didn't imply anything about my involvement, but I did get the feeling he was probing." Buddy ran into the kitchen and Jackson's attention was momentarily diverted as he picked his son up and threw him into the air.

"Chili okay?" Brynn rinsed the sink and started preparations for dinner, which was still three hours away.

"Chili!" Buddy shouted.

The light rain had dwindled away by the time dinner was finished, but the gray hung in the air, muting everything in the mid-May landscape. It did little for her mood, but made for perfect photographs. With Jackson working on some odd jobs in the machine shed and watching Buddy, Brynn packed her photography equipment and changed into some work clothes and boots. She stopped into the shed before leaving and gave the boys a goodbye.

"Be careful, Hun," Jackson said as he hugged her. "You taking the mutt?"

"No, she's a freak. She'll show up in every picture and muddy up the car. No." Brynn also suspected there might be an unscheduled stop at Lanea's house, and possibly a meeting with Lanea's former boyfriend as well. The dog would just complicate things.

Brynn pulled her car into Lanea's driveway, nosing up to the barbed-wire barricade that scolded her, "No Trespassing." With her car in plain view (and having already broken that command), she was satisfied with photographing the house from the road. She struggled to ignore her dour disposition that was compounded by the weather, determined by her curiosity and sense of duty. She got out of her car and took a deep breath of the damp air. The weather was a good thing. Fog and gloom would supply that melancholy tone so crucial to her photographs and artwork.

She trod the length of fence in front of the building site, her rubber boots squeaking on the wet grass as she allowed her shutter to whir and click as if it were the one in control. She backed away and allowed the weathered fence posts and rusted wire to frame her subject like homely bridesmaids in a photo of an aged and ugly bride.

The small area of unobstructed view of the building site permitted only a limited number of unique shots of the house, but Brynn stayed for a long while, taking up nearly an entire memory card with virtually identical images of the property. She would probably delete half of them. It wasn't more photos of the house that she wanted anyway. When the dampness had permeated her jeans and her jacket, she was forced to admit that her stalling was a way to avoid visiting Lanea's old boyfriend. Time was running out. She would have to return home soon. She put her camera in her shoulder bag and trudged back to her car.

The hiss of tires on wet gravel startled her as she was opening the door to get into her car. She turned and saw an old silver pickup pulling up behind her car. Bertis Covey got out of his vehicle and tiredly lifted his arm in a friendly wave.

"Hello, Mr. Covey! How are you?" Brynn shouted, trying to compensate for his age and the lack of cheer in the atmosphere. She felt a measure of relief.

"Brynn, isn't it?" he asked as he rounded the front of his pickup and ambled his way toward her. Bertis wore bib coveralls, a flannel shirt, boots, and a jacket and matching Kruger cap that likely came from a seed company as a gift. Although in his mid-80's, he was still large and robust, though his shoulders drooped and his back curved forward. Brynn knew the creed and breed of farmers—it was work that kept them alive, and she knew that work was one thing he still enjoyed. His face bore the scars of loss and anguish; the years of solitude pulled on his features like heated wax.

"I hope you don't mind, I was taking some pictures of your home place. I don't know if you remember—I'm an artist? I take photos and paint over them?"

"Oh, yes." He walked to the fence and placed a beefy hand on the wire between the barbs, staring at the house. "I remember." Brynn imagined he was remembering far more than her artistry. She joined him at the fence, holding it as well as if in solidarity against the pain it encompassed.

His watery gaze, his defeated posture, the grim weather, the dismal building site, his words—they balled together to form a lump the size of an egg in her throat.

"Glad to see you doing better." He looked at Brynn directly. His weary gray eyes matched the sky—clouded and lackluster. "What brings you out here?"

Brynn cleared her throat. "Just taking photos, trying to get back into my artwork," she said, leaving out the "like I said ... " preamble.

Bertis was quiet. He turned back to the house as if it called his name, which Brynn didn't doubt for a moment. She didn't doubt that it whispered to him in his sleep, that it cried to him when he passed by, that it echoed when he thought of it. The fence trembled slightly.

"Sixteen years, you know. My girls are gone sixteen years now. I'll see them again. God's promise." He nodded gently, the mist in the air gathering in his eyes. "This place is all I have of them. I should tear it down. It's not safe in there. Nothing of value, just memories ... "

Brynn wondered if the fence was electric, the irony of his statement tingling through her. She stared quietly at the house in respect for his solemnness.

"Just taking pictures then?" He wiggled the fence as if testing it.

"Yes, sir. If that's all right." It seemed absurd of her to ask permission to take pictures from the road, but given that she had already breached an unspoken promise, it was a small token of penance she was willing to pay.

"Can't hurt nothin', I don't suppose." He smiled slightly as he moved to return to his pickup. "You take care now." Bertis climbed into his pickup and waved goodbye, watching her as he drove away.

His message was as clear as the "No Trespassing" sign touching her front bumper. She looked back at the house. She thought she could hear it calling to her as well. She would do what she had to do. He would thank her in the end, if she were successful.

Brynn called Jackson to check in, and informed him that she would be a little while yet. She hoped to get some shots of another empty house, and then visit Marshall's house, which was only four or five miles away. She did not inform him of the latter.

Brynn made it to Marshall Nord's house half an hour later, pulling up the long driveway to a home at which she would likely not be welcome. Although they knew each other, Marshall being Wes and Jackson's age and their former friend, she knew that he was tired of the public scrutiny related to Lanea's disappearance. He had quit cooperating with authorities when it had become clear that he was a suspect, although there was no proof linking him with his former girlfriend's case. Over the years, articles in area papers detailed his frustration with finger-pointers and backbiters, which made him retreat from the community and do his business in faraway towns where he was an unknown. When he was forced to deal with locals, he said very little, paid in cash, and left no waves in his wake—that he knew of. Brynn held no illusions that this would go as she hoped.

I'll just let him know that I only want to find out what happened to Lanea, that I don't think he had anything to do with it—just a friend looking for a friend. The butterflies in her stomach felt more like angry, wildcats fighting it out in a burlap bag. It didn't help that her reasoning didn't even sound convincing to herself.

As she pulled into the farmyard, she noticed a tractor near the machine shop, with a man underneath. She pulled her car up to the shed and got out.

Marshall pulled himself out from under the tractor and stood, wiping his hands on a grease rag and throwing it on the ground near the oil pan under the tractor.

"Hi, Marshall."

"Brynn. What can I do for you?" Marshall's mien was businesslike, but not unfriendly. Marshall looked to have stopped growing at 16. He was, at most, 5'8 and 170 pounds. His face was striking, his build solid but well-chiseled. He would be handsome well into his 90's. It was easy to understand Lanea's attraction to him, even 16 years later. He had thick, wavy, black hair that curled over his collar and his forehead; his blue eyes were startlingly bright, and every feature in his face was perfectly sculpted.

"How have you been?" Brynn couldn't hide the quiver in her voice. She was ashamed to realize that his transcendent good looks only added to her anxiety.

"Good. What's up?" He eyed her cautiously. *Just spit it out, Brynn. He knows something's up.*

"Well, I was in the area, taking photos of farm buildings for my artwork, and stopped at Lanea's old place, and it … I was wondering if you would be willing to talk to me about Lanea."

Marshall walked over to Brynn's car and opened the driver's door.

"Go home, Brynn."

"Marshall, I'm so sorry. I just want to know what happened to her."

Marshall held her door, waiting for her to get in.

Brynn walked to her car, hoping the closeness would soften his resolve.

He stepped back from the car door and crossed his arms.

"She was my friend," Brynn said.

His jaw muscles twitched. He shook his head slowly.

His eyes darkened when he finally spoke. "She was my girlfriend. I loved … " He paused, shaking his head again. "Please go."

He went back to his tractor to work, making it clear that he was done talking. Brynn got into her car and began to pull away from the building. Noticing that Marshall's wife had come outside onto the front step of their house, Brynn waved politely to her and continued out the driveway.

She wasn't surprised at the outcome, and although she couldn't have expected any better, it was still disappointing. She had one more stop, however. She wasn't giving up.

After checking the time, Brynn drove to Ryker Otten's home. Brynn knew of the Ottens, and knew that Ryker still lived on his parents' farm, in a separate house once built for his grandmother. She saw the small house about 30 yards from the main house. Both houses were well-kept and freshly painted in a crisp farm-white and the lawns, green and neatly clipped. Red, yellow, pink, and purple tulips bobbed merrily, like little birthday balloons, in the beds under the windows of both homes. The vibrant, happy scene seemed immune to whatever gloom that hovered.

Brynn went directly to Ryker's house and knocked. The spotless age-waved glass rattled in its frame on the door. She peered through the door's window and between the lace curtains—the kitchen was sparsely furnished, but tidy and homey. The lights were not on.

"Can I help you?" a woman's voice called from the front of the main house. A woman, most likely Ryker's mother, stood on the porch, waving.

Brynn walked from Ryker's porch to his mother's. "Hello. Mrs. Otten?"

"Yes. Fern." she answered, wiping her hands on a towel and hanging it over her shoulder.

"Hi, I'm Brynn Young. I live a few miles north of here," she started, unsure how to proceed.

"Oh! I remember. How are you? So glad to see you're doing so well!" Fern opened the door. "Come in! Come in!"

Brynn hesitated to divulge the nature of her visit. And even though the reputation that preceded her was becoming tiresome, it might come in handy.

Brynn stepped inside the door. It was apparent that the happiness that frolicked outside was born in this room. The walls of this kitchen were a soft banana yellow with red accents of a cherries theme dotting the pristine surfaces. The look was vintage, but Brynn suspected that its design was unintended, that the furniture was held over from past eras. Brynn smelled coffee and cinnamon. The mood the homey room created was heavenly.

"Have a seat!"

"Oh, I can't," Brynn glanced at her grubby boots, which seemed incredibly out of place in this Heaven.

"Sure, you can. Floors were meant to be washed." Fern pulled out a chair and Brynn gingerly stepped out of her boots, refusing to muddy the floors. She sat on the edge of a chrome and vinyl kitchen chair, feeling like she was interviewing for a job. Fern sat at the same corner of the table, facing Brynn.

"You're looking for Ryker? Are you looking to hire him? He's such a busy boy. 'Boy.' He's 30," she laughed softly. Fern was small and delicate-looking. Her ash-blonde hair was cut in a pageboy, parted on the side; her modest clothes hung on her small frame, and her face—smooth and youthful—was pleasantly ordinary, punctuated with charming dimples. She was what some would call cute, but being middle aged, it was probably a term she disdained. It seemed impossible for a person with such cheerful surroundings to disdain anything or even form a frown. Her contentedness with life was unmistakable.

"How's your mother?" Fern asked politely. "Coffee?"

"No, thank you. Mom's well. You know each other?" Brynn's knee was bouncing.

"Yes! Our husbands … I'm sorry, your late father … and Hirum went to school together. And your mother was so helpful to us when we adopted Ryker." She sat back in her chair and folded her hands comfortably in her lap like it was going to be a long, glorious, afternoon visit.

"I see. So Ryker's adopted? I guess I didn't know that." Brynn's patience for small talk was waning. In any other circumstances, it would be wonderful to sit in this sunny kitchen and shoot the breeze and lollygag the day away, but she was finding it hard to stay focused on the conversation, distracted by her unasked and unanswered questions that interrupted her train of thought like pop-ups on a computer screen.

"Oh, yes. We tried for years. It was tough. I won't deny that. My friend, Ardis, and I would get together and console each other. We had the same, well … female issues … and it helped to talk with someone who understood. You know?"

"I'm sure." Brynn chewed the inside of her lip.

"We were, *are*, so blessed. Our son loves the farm, he's such a big help. He does work for area farmers on occasion. He even has a girlfriend now! Lovely girl." Fern beamed. Life was good.

Perhaps time didn't exist in Heaven, but back on earth, Ellie would be getting off the bus in 40 minutes and supper was still a necessity. Brynn took a deep breath, and against common sense and lifelong advice, dove head first into unknown waters.

"I was wondering if Ryker was around. I wanted to talk to him about a friend of mine." Brynn readied herself for an interrogation, her circumventing tactics and excuses all warmed up.

"He's out back in the milking parlor, helping Hi." Fern blinked, smiling, waiting. "Round back," she said, pointing sheepishly, as if Brynn didn't understand her prepositions.

"Oh. Of course. I'll just go out there and talk to him." Brynn rose and went to her boots near the door. She was confused by Fern's lack of curiosity, but grateful for it, nonetheless.

Slipping her boots on and opening the door, Brynn muttered her appreciation to Fern and turned to leave, her face slamming into a hard wall of denim.

Ryker stood over her, his face showing none of the blissful countenance his mother displayed. He was as burly as a buffalo. Disturbing images of a woman giving birth to him came to mind, and Brynn wondered if the poor woman had lived through it. Fern most certainly would not have.

Ryker stood 6'4 or 5, easily 270 pounds, and not altogether unattractive, though, Brynn thought, a smile—any expression at all—would help immensely. His dark hair was an unflattering but efficient buzz cut, his eyes were deep-set under heavy brows, and his lips were full and pressed firmly together.

Flustered, and feeling very puny and vulnerable standing toe to toe with the bull, Brynn suddenly forgot everything she wanted to ask.

"Ryker, Brynn, here wanted to talk to you about a friend of hers." She turned to Brynn and asked, "Who's your friend, Hun?" as if Brynn needed an interpreter.

"Lanea Covey." She had nothing more. But that was enough.

Ryker's face finally had an expression, and it was not heartwarming. His brows, already Neanderthal-heavy, drew down on his face, which was turning a dark shade of red and scrunching in anger.

"You knew her, Ryker. You worked there now and then," Fern explained to Ryker, as though he were four years old. It was obvious by his stance and the look on his face that he remembered. "Unfortunate situation. Ryker was questioned, but he didn't have anything to do with it, of course," she continued, still smiling. *Is the woman high?* Brynn was almost more rattled by Fern's apparent nirvana than Ryker's temper.

Ryker moved out of the doorway, motioning for Brynn to step outside. She guessed he preferred to discuss it privately. Just as well.

"Thanks, Ryker. This is nothing … official … I just want to find her. She was my friend," Brynn stated lightly as she stepped out onto the porch. She turned around to face Ryker when she hit another wall. He had shut the door in her face.

The conflicting worlds she'd just experienced made Brynn feel like she'd been thrown from the hearth of a warm, cozy fireplace into a frigid mountain lake.

Stunned, Brynn stood motionless on the porch for a moment, wondering if it was a mistake, the door shutting like that. When it didn't open, she took the hint, plodded back to her car and drove home.

During chores that night, Brynn replayed the day's events in her mind. The hog house was the perfect place to think. Except for the contented grunts and occasional shrieks of bickering pigs, it was quiet. Strolling down the alley and checking pigs and feeders was undemanding and cathartic work. Brynn climbed into the sick pen, cosseting and cooing to her eager patients.

As Brynn finished hand-feeding the last sick pig, she heard the abrupt bark of alarmed pigs spreading through the building. She looked toward the door to see a solid mass of Ryker standing in the alley. He filled the passageway with his mammoth body. His mood was visible from several feet away.

Brynn wondered how he knew she was there, whether Jackson had *told* him to come out there, why he was there, what he wanted. Most importantly, she wondered what she could possibly say that wouldn't make him mad. Correction: madder.

Brynn's mouth opened, but nothing came out. She closed her mouth (flies!) and swallowed, nervously brushing the feed from her pants. She placed her hands defiantly on her hips, which she knew probably looked pretty ridiculous—she, with her 105 pounds of bravado next to his ... *immensity*—but it made her feel better.

Ryker came to the edge of the pen where she was frozen in place. The only thing that stood between Brynn and the very large man was a couple of scrawny pigs.

"My mom ... I apologize for being rude. I don't know nothin' about Lanea bein' gone, and don't come 'round my house no more." He turned to leave.

Brynn's knees were shaking, but opportunity was about to walk out the door. "Ryker?"

He stopped, but didn't turn around.

"I'm not looking to get anyone into trouble. I miss her. I just want to know what happened to her ... " Her voice caught. She was surprised by her emotion, assigning it to the anxiety of the moment, but she realized she really did miss Lanea after all this time. Seeing her in the house's memories had refreshed that sense of loss.

Ryker put his head down as if he were thinking it over, but then started walking away.

"Please," Brynn called to him, "I promise I won't tell anyone anything." He gave no indication he heard any of her pleas as he walked out the door. Brynn swiped angrily at the flies that swarmed around her face. She sniffed, wiped her nose on her sleeve, and kicked the steel gating.

Brynn's quaking legs could hold her no longer. She slumped to the floor of the pen and leaned against the gating. He—or anyone that had a notion to find her here—could have been responsible for abducting her. He could have finished her off here in this building and she'd have been pig food. Only her bones would have remained. Her ordeal, even unremembered, was coming back to haunt her.

CHAPTER FIFTEEN

THE FOLLOWING MORNING, BRYNN AWOKE to see the sun shining and the wind stirring the branches, a perfect recipe for fieldwork and freedom. With only a few days of school remaining in the school year, and therefore only a few more days of investigation unfettered by children, Brynn was anxious to get back to her clandestine research. She refused to be daunted by roadblocks whose names were Marshall and Ryker.

After morning chores were done and the boys had gone to the field, she decided that a vigorous run would be great exercise for her brain. She donned her running shoes, yanking on the laces as if they were the reins to the demons she was determined to control. Lanea's case, her own case, and all the questions and feelings surrounding them seemed to be like little gremlins that hid themselves inside her every thought, pushing out everything mundane and setting fire under the things she tried to tuck away. A little discipline was in order. Brynn set her phone's mp3 player to her favorite playlist, went outside and stretched, and after warming up, fell into step with a tune by Pink, warming up with a stiff walk.

The air was freshly washed, the mild breeze and warm sun refreshing her senses as well as her spirits. Earthworm trails formed abstract artwork in the gravel of her driveway. She would have to remember to photograph those when she had time. She broke into a jog as she came out of her driveway onto the paved road, feeling more energy than she had expected.

In an unplanned assertion of independence, Brynn rounded the corner at which she usually turned around. She ran north on the intersecting paved road, and when she reached the next corner, she turned again, deciding to go around the section, a total of four miles and a route she rarely took—a route she had not taken since before her abduction. It was exhilarating not only to have run this far, but also to have reclaimed some of her autonomy in the process. Now on gravel, Brynn slowed a bit to accommodate the looser footing.

Half a mile down the gravel road, the windbreak from the Kludt farm site stood near the road on her right, century-old trees surrounded by a tangle of volunteer saplings, dead brush, and weeds. It was a small forest, a black veil of vegetation so thick that it seemed even sunlight considered it too much work to breach. The house was tucked into the overgrown grove, not easily visible from the road. A lonely barn stood out away from the windbreak, seemingly outcast and adrift in a sea of last year's corn stubble. The roof sagged like that of a sad, old, swaybacked horse, and much of the siding either lost in the wind, or relegated to quaint birdhouses and rustic furniture custom-built by thieves. The only buildings remaining were that of a chicken coop, a granary, and a small shed, which were equally dilapidated and forlorn, leaning and pitching like drunkards after an all-nighter. Although the only life they likely contained was that of squatters of the vermin variety, the buildings all held a certain eerie quality to them, as though they watched her pass by. Unnerved by its dark history, Brynn picked up her pace and focused on the road in front of her feet.

Four miles was maybe a bit ambitious, Brynn thought, aware, though, that it was possible that the route more than the distance had her feeling a little uneasy. Even before her abduction, Brynn normally kept to the paved roads, and though this was just a mile north of her home as the crow flies, the countryside felt foreign.

In an instinctual habit of glancing over her shoulder as she ran, Brynn noticed a car coming up from behind. She inched closer to the ditch as the vehicle passed her. The license plates indicated it was from out of state. She'd seen a few more vehicles from out of the area lately, and it was a reminder that both of the cases on her mind could very well involve someone they *don't* know, someone— maybe even the same person—from outside their area. She realized that it was her first instinct to suspect a neighbor or someone close to the case, but she needed to broaden her focus. It was a defense tactic, but it would be so much easier if the person involved with her case or Lanea's case was someone she didn't know. Or care about.

Rounding the last corner onto the last stretch of road to her house, Brynn felt her shoulders loosen and her stride become longer and more relaxed. She could see her home. She cranked up the volume on her mp3 player and poured all of her energy into the remaining half-mile, reaching home with a renewed sense of resolve—and legs that felt like overcooked noodles.

Brynn saw the light flashing on her answering machine when she came in. She turned on the machine and it played while she took off her shoes.

There was a noticeable pause before the unfamiliar voice spoke.

"Brynn, this is Marshall. Uh ... my wife and I talked. Before I change my mind ... if you can be here before dinner, we can talk. Can't guarantee anything, though." It was quiet a moment longer before he hung up.

So far, it seemed the women were on Brynn's side. Brynn erased the message and ran to the shower.

The mere act of showing up would make her appear anxious, so Brynn decided not to bother with formalities and impressions. She was on their front steps 20 minutes later.

She rang the bell, waiting and looking at the newly planted window boxes and planters around the front of the house, the little bedding plants barely peeking over the rims. Ranch style, the house was a taupe color with grayish-green shutters and trim. It was a nice house—not fancy, but pleasant. She couldn't help but wonder what the place would have looked like if Lanea had lived there with Marshall.

Marshall's wife answered the door. Brynn pushed aside her mild resentment for the woman's intrusion into Lanea's dream life and stuck out her hand. "Hi, I'm Brynn Young."

"Hi, Brynn. I'm Dena. Come in." The woman, who was tall and slender, not unlike Lanea, shook her hand, opened the door wider and moved aside. She was dressed in a simple, white cotton blouse and blue jeans, her light brown hair clipped loosely to the back of her head in a claw-type clip. She wore little makeup, yet she was beautiful in her simplicity.

Brynn entered the home and slipped off her shoes. They walked from the foyer into the beige-carpeted living room, which was similar to the outside of the home: pleasant, but not extravagant. Overstuffed furniture and golden oak side tables lined the edge of the uncluttered room, and Christian-themed prints adorned the walls, candle sconces and crosses placed as accents around them. Over the sofa was a collage of framed family photos of Marshall, Dena, and their two children, a boy and a girl who looked to be slightly older than Brynn's.

"You have a lovely home." Brynn didn't know what to do with her hands. She clasped them together in front of her body.

"Thank you. It's not fancy."

Brynn felt slightly embarrassed, as if Dena had read her mind or gotten some vibe from her body language. Noticing Brynn looking at the photos, Dena pointed.

"That's our son, Brayden, and our daughter, Ella. He's nine, she's seven."

"They're beautiful children. Are you in our school system? I don't recall our daughter mentioning her. She's seven as well."

"No, we're in the Edman school district. The kids go to school there, and I work in the hospital in Edman. I'm a nurse." Dena crossed her arms. Brynn wondered if it was a defensive posture or if she was feeling uncomfortable, but her look didn't appear to be hostile. So far.

The lull in conversation lent a palpable awkwardness to the moment, and Dena finally said, "I'll call Marshall in. He's in the shed getting ready to go plant. Should we go into the kitchen?" She led the way to the kitchen, motioned for Brynn to sit, and went out the back door. Brynn went to the antique pedestal table and lowered herself into a press back chair. She faintly heard Dena call to her husband.

Brynn's stomach did flip-flops and her knee took on the habitual twitch that Jackson so detested. Brynn took in her surroundings, trying to distract herself like she did when she was waiting in her scratchy, paper gown for the doctor to come into the exam room for her yearly checkup.

The kitchen was warm and ... pleasant as well. Simplicity was definitely the prevailing theme. Subdued but tasteful, it was decorated in browns and beiges, the cabinets oak with a beige countertop. Surfaces were clutter-free and spotless. The place was downright boring. Although feeling only slightly guilty for passing judgment, Brynn was sure that Lanea would have added some life to this home. Even roosters or butterflies would be an improvement.

More and more, she felt as if she were at the doctor's office. She wished she had a magazine to flip through.

Brynn heard a door open and some muffled discussion. Soon, they entered the kitchen, Marshall in his dusty jeans and navy button-up shirt. He pulled out a chair for Dena and they both sat.

"Okay. What do you want to know? And why?" Marshall asked abruptly, skipping over the small talk as he leaned back in his chair.

"Well, I know what the newspaper articles said, but I wanted to ask you what you think happened to Lanea. If you think she was abducted or if she ran away."

"I don't know. I went back and forth at that time and never came up with any idea either way."

"Nothing? Not even a feeling?"

"Look. The police, the newspapers, they all thought and said and did what they wanted and never cared about what I thought, what I felt. I would never hurt Lanea." Marshall's face reddened, and Dena gently laid her hand on his arm. Calmer, Marshall said, "I was the only one they really looked at. They never seriously considered Ryker, in my opinion. He's no angel. Have you talked to him? He had a crush on Lanea and she knew it. She was just too nice to tell him to take a hike."

"I talked to him. He had nothing to say to me."

"What's this all about? Why the sudden interest? Let it go." Marshall blinked slowly, tiredly shaking his head.

"Well," Brynn began, an impromptu explanation as good as the truth forming on her lips, "I recently started up with my artwork again, and I had been around the country side looking at old houses to photograph. When I came up on Lanea's house, it made me start thinking about my own case, and I wondered if they were connected." Saying it out loud made the connection feel much more plausible. "Finding out what happened to Lanea might help me find my ... it might help me in my case."

"Sixteen years later?" Marshall asked incredulously. "You really think they're connected?"

"Why not? Jackson was questioned in both." Brynn immediately felt like she had just turned a chicken loose in the house. There would be no catching it now. But she saw a look pass between Marshall and Dena, and noticed a shift in their mood as well as their positions in the chairs.

"So was Marshall," said Dena, tentatively.

"Is that why you're here? Hoping to shift the focus off Jackson?" Marshall stared calmly at Brynn, his voice flat and his eyes lacking trust.

"No! No. I never thought you ... or Jackson ... had anything to do with it. Either of you. I just wanted to try to get a sense of what you thought happened. You never heard anything about a note she may have left? Do you think she ran away?" The thin line she walked was starting to disappear.

"From what I hear, nothing was missing. All of her belongings, clothes, money, ID, those things were all accounted for. Why don't you ask her father? Or Ryker? I couldn't have been the last one to talk to her."

"She never said anything to *you* about running away then?" asked Brynn.

"No, but like I said … " Marshall slapped his thighs lightly, his elbows bent as he leaned forward, ready to push up from his chair. The conversation was about over. "What makes you think you can get any further in this than the sheriff?" he asked.

Brynn felt as transparent and weak as her flimsy line of questions. "I don't. Just thought it was worth a try."

"Hey. She made her choice. If she ran away, I wasn't part of that decision. If she didn't, then I wasn't part of that either." Marshall's words were clipped, his simmering anger an arrow aimed at an unknown target. Even as taut as the bow was, Brynn braved one more question as Marshall stood up.

"Do you think Bertis would be open to talking about it?"

"Not with me, he wouldn't. He never liked me. Not religious enough, even for him. He was a bit of a zealot. Strict, tight-lipped … . But have a go … and good luck with that."

Marshall turned and started walking away. "That's all I know," he said sideways as he went out the kitchen door.

Brynn blinked, dumbfounded. She rubbed her forehead in exasperation. "I'm sorry if I upset him," Brynn said to Dena.

"It's not you. It's just so hard for him, how it all ended, that's all." Dena stared at the door as if her heart were stuck in it.

"Thank you for your time."

"Of course. Good luck." The more sincere blessing was a small consolation for the lack of any new information.

Brynn got into her car and checked her wristwatch. It was late morning, much too early to hang it up for the day.

She took a notepad from her bag under the seat, and scribbled some notes, but it was hard to put any order to it.

What now?

Cole sat up straight and smiled when she came in the room.

"Well, look who's here!"

Spencer spun his chair around to face the door. "Brynn! Where're those kids?" He glanced around Brynn.

"Hi, Cole, Spencer. Sorry, I didn't bring them with me today," She went to Cole and shook his hand.

"So good to see you!" Cole's eyes were brilliant with delight.

"I'm sorry I haven't been around for the last couple weeks. I have no defense."

Cole, reluctant to let go of Brynn's hand, turned his head toward Spencer. "Spence, would you mind giving us a minute? I'll be down for dinner in a bit."

Spencer waved his hand, "Oh, sure, sure," and wheeled himself out of the room. "Come see us again, Brynn."

Brynn bid him farewell and turned back to Cole, excited to tell him all of her news.

"So what's happening with you lately, my dear?" Cole asked.

"There's so much. I don't know where to start. How are *you?* I shouldn't be keeping you from your dinner."

"Don't you worry about me. A day without tuna casserole is one more day added to my life. Besides, I have a stash in my bottom drawer," he chuckled. "Cashews, black licorice, and Cheetos." Brynn cringed.

Cole pointed at the chair and she sat.

"So tell me what you know. Have you found out any more about your uh … condition? Have you told Jackson about it yet?" Cole propped his elbows on the armrests and clasped his hands together in anticipation of something, *anything*, more stimulating than dominoes and cafeteria food.

"No, I haven't told him about it."

Cole's eyebrows lifted in surprise. "Why not?"

"I'm not ready. I don't want him treating me like I'm crazy. I'd have to prove it to him, and how would I do that? He'd have me checked into the hospital before you could say 'Boo'. He for sure wouldn't let me out of the house. He's just now getting used to me going out on my own without having to call him every 20 minutes to check in."

"Trust him, Brynn. At some point, you will need to. If he's all you say he is, he'll believe you."

Brynn stared at her hands, her insight from the previous day echoing in his words. She remembered her fear and guilt for not telling him, and she remembered his kindness and concern for her at finding out she had seen her own case file. She looked up, swiped at her eyes, shook her hair out of her face, and changed the subject.

"I've decided to use this ability to find out what happened to my friend, Lanea. Do you remember Lanea Covey?"

"Yes, the girl who disappeared several years ago?"

"That's her. She was a friend of mine, and I want to see if I can find out what happened to her." Brynn lowered her voice. "I've been to her house."

"Did you see anything?" By the eagerness on his face, this morsel of gossip would satisfy Cole's appetite much more than would any dining hall fare.

"Oh, yes. I saw lots of praying, Bible reading, work, and total boring-ness going on, but something *much* more important. Get this ... I saw Lanea leave a note on her nightstand after packing a bag. It seemed pretty obvious to me that she ran away." Brynn's chatter got faster as she progressed, the excitement of her journey starting to catch up to her.

"So now what?" Cole asked.

"I don't know. I'm not sure what to think of it. I went to the Sheriff's office to ask about her case, but since I'm not immediate family, I wasn't allowed to see her file. I did go to the newspaper office, though, and look at the stories they had about the case. None of them mention any note. She left it on her nightstand. I don't know how they couldn't have seen it." Brynn scratched her head and ran her fingers through her slippery hair.

"Do you think it's a detail that the police just aren't sharing? Or do you think she changed her mind and threw the note away? But if she didn't run away, where did she go?" Cole asked. They were both thinking out loud now.

"They never classified it as a runaway. They wouldn't have involved federal authorities if they believed that. They didn't exclude that possibility, but if they'd found the note, they wouldn't have invested so much time and manpower into it. Right? Besides—Marshall said none of her things were missing."

"Marshall? Who's he?"

"Oh, sorry, that's Lanea's former boyfriend. I talked to him today. Talked to Bertis, too. Not about Lanea's disappearance, though. He didn't seem too eager to have me anywhere near the house. I guess I can understand that. Do you know Bertis? He's probably about your age." She couldn't stop her rambling; it felt good to confide in someone.

"I know him." Cole rubbed his face as if wiping cobwebs away.

Brynn shook her head to prompt an explanation.

Cole shrugged. "He's a bit of a religious nut, but other than that, a nice enough fellow. What makes you think he doesn't want you near the house?"

"Oh, just a feeling. I might try to talk to him. Do you know where he lives? The house is full of … crap … but it's obvious no one has lived there for quite a while."

"He lives in the Perris Manor apartments, attached to the home, here. Not sure if you'll find him there, though. I understand he is usually out in the country, working, if that's what you want to call it. I imagine he's just puttering around at Hagebak's, his old hired hand's place. Spends a lot of time there, from the sound of it."

"How do you know so much about him?"

"Residents at the Perris Manor apartments are invited to eat here if they like. Kind of an assisted living thing. He comes around here from time to time, sits with the men who *don't* sit near the women. He's funny that way. Got to know him a little. You know. Talk."

"Cole, I appreciate your time, but I really should let you get to your dinner before a nurse or aide comes in here and bawls you out." Brynn smiled, looking around to see if she were endangering his life.

"Wait! You haven't told me all that Marshall had to say. You don't expect me to try to eat that dry stuff without some juicy hearsay to wash it down, do you?" Cole pleaded, his face painted in keenness.

"Sorry, not much juice here. Marshall wasn't exactly thrilled to be talking to me. His wife and he talked, and he agreed to see me, but not much to learn there. He just told me that none of Lanea's things were missing, and that I should talk to Bertis or Ryker, the kid who had a crush on her. He said he couldn't have been the last one to talk to her. I don't know. He seemed kind of mad. Not really at me, directly. I got the feeling that he was mad about something else. Probably the investigation?"

"Is he still a suspect? I assume the case is still open?"

"Yes, it is. As a matter of fact, he was questioned in *my* case. There seems to be some consensus that the two cases might be related. Jackson was questioned, too ... " Brynn's words trailed off, as if she were in thought.

"Brynn?" Cole brought her back.

"I was just thinking. Marshall didn't seem mad about that, either. I can't figure it out. When I apologized to Dena, Marshall's wife, she said something kind of odd, now that I think of it ... " Brynn's eyes flitted around the room, searching her memory for more details.

Cole opened his mouth to revive her again as Brynn remembered.

"She said that he was upset with how it all ended."

"That's how she put it?"

"Yeah. How *what* ended? It's not like Lanea was found, dead or otherwise. Nothing ended. The case is still open." Brynn puzzled.

"Could she have meant something else? Maybe that's not how she meant to say it ... " Cole offered.

"She looked like she was heartbroken for him. Like she meant to say it in just that way." Brynn searched Cole's face now, as if for some help with a puzzle to which she alone held the pieces.

"Something ended that we don't know about. Could you go back and talk to her or Marshall again?" Cole was now looking for clues.

"It would make sense, if something—like their relationship—had ended, especially with him saying he couldn't have been the last one to talk to her. The only reason someone would put it like that is if they knew for certain that someone else *had* to have talked to her after he did." Brynn and Cole stared at each other, their minds seemingly in sync with each other's.

A nurse in cupcake-print scrubs entered the room, startling them both. "Cole, are you coming to dinner? We were wondering where you were!" Fluffy and squat, her build was analogous to her attire. The similarities didn't end there, with her cheer and smile as synthetic as the frosting on her cupcakes, but there were no handcuffs or Tasers dangling from her back belt. The situation was not as dire as they feared. Cole rolled his eyes with a fine-honed skill rivaling that of any teenager as the nurse unlocked the brakes on his chair.

"Please don't tell me all of the tuna hot dish is gone..." Cole chided the nurse as she began to turn his chair.

"Would your friend like to join us?" Nurse Cupcake asked. He was going; there is no "if" in dinner.

"Friend? Would you like to join us?" Cole asked facetiously.

"No, thank you," Brynn smirked. "I have an appointment." She winked at Cole.

Driving into Marshall and Dena's driveway, Brynn realized that Marshall would likely be out planting, and if Dena wasn't home, she would have to wait to ask one of them what was meant by the statement. Moreover, if she couldn't find out anything from them, she would be forced to talk to either Bertis or Ryker, neither of whom she was anxious to speak to again so soon.

No tractor sat in the yard. Brynn had no inkling which fields might belong to Nord's. She stopped at the house, went to the front door and knocked, saying a small prayer that someone was home and that she wouldn't have another door shut in her face. Dena came to the door, opened it, but didn't invite her in. Better than nothing.

"Did you forget something?" Dena asked, a slight look of annoyance on her face.

"Hi, again. Sorry to disturb you ... again ... but I wanted to ask you something that has been bothering me since I left."

Dena was wordless, but raised her eyebrows as if to say "Speak." Brynn didn't understand the change in her mood, but didn't care.

"After Marshall left, you said something ... curious. You said that he was upset with how it all ended. What did you mean by that?" Brynn looked her in the eye, unfazed by Dena's apparent irritation. Brynn struggled to keep her excited breathing under control.

"Did I say that?"

"Yes. You did." Brynn waited.

Dena looked down at her feet, still for a moment. She stepped outside, tucked a loose strand of hair behind her ears, and crossed her arms.

She looked at Brynn. "Lanea broke up with Marshall two weeks before she went missing. She called him up, crying, said she didn't want to see him again, and told him not to try to contact her or come by. Look, it's no secret. The police know that she broke up with him. But it's not something that reporters know. They'd have a field day with that. We've endured enough. Please."

"How did you manage to keep that detail away from the press?" Brynn said softly, hoping to spare Dena from any more agitation.

"It wasn't our decision. Marshall was cooperating with the authorities, told them everything. They were *nice* enough to not leak it to the press. They verified the phone call with phone records. Marshall and Lanea didn't have any issues to speak of, so he was surprised ... and hurt ... that she broke up with him. Marshall is pretty sure her father was behind that. He didn't approve. He was pretty strict to begin with, but almost obsessive after Genevieve died."

Brynn shoved her hands deep into her jean pockets and stared out onto the freshly tilled fields that held so much promise, wondering where the promise was for her friend. She wasn't sure what her next move should be, but it seemed almost impossible to make any move to leave the step.

"Marshall is a decent man," Dena said, "I really don't want to open up this ... mess ... for him again. I hope you're not intending to try to solve this on your own, Brynn, and I *sure* hope you're not intending to take any of this to the papers."

"I'm not looking to get Marshall into any trouble ... I just want to find my friend. I promise." Brynn knew that a promise like that didn't necessarily exclude the former statement, but it was the best offer she could give.

CHAPTER SIXTEEN

T HE NEXT DAY, ELLIE CAME down from her room and put her hand on her stomach. Before the words, "I don't feel good," could finish coming from her mouth, vomit had raced out ahead of them, spoiling the surprise, along with everything in Ellie's line of fire. The stomach flu made its rounds, and everyone but the dog had their turn to purge themselves over the next few days. The down time, however, had given her time to think of a reasonable way to approach Bertis.

May 15th was upon them. With one week of school left, Brynn felt more pressure to pursue whatever leads she could without having to make up excuses and justify being gone so often.

Year-end events such as the spring concert, track and field day, and field trips filled up all the empty spaces on the calendar. Brynn was grateful for a day of no commitments and, especially, no puke.

With the children gone and daily chores out of the way, Brynn called Bertis' apartment and was surprised when he answered. He reluctantly agreed when Brynn asked to meet him at his apartment to talk. She left before she could chicken out or he could call back to cancel.

Brynn found his apartment easily enough with his directions. Before knocking at his door she wiped her hands on her jeans, feeling the clamminess of nerves collecting on her skin. With Bertis' meaning about going onto his property quite unmistakable, Brynn tried to assure herself that his disposition about discussing Lanea's disappearance might be a little softer. She knocked a little louder than she had intended. After a considerable amount of time, he answered. Brynn jumped, surprised by his abruptness as he yanked the door open, as if in the midst of a squabble that her knock had interrupted.

"You didn't waste no time. Come on in." He apparently wasn't known for being a smooth talker. He rubbed his stubbly head and stepped aside.

"Thank you for agreeing to see me, Mr. Covey. I won't take much of your time." Brynn stepped inside and waited as he closed the door behind her.

"Not sure how you think I can help." He shuffled into the tiny, cluttered kitchen near the door. Brynn followed, with no invitation or indication that she was welcome. Without his cap and coat, he looked less imposing, almost vulnerable. His hair was clipped short, military-flat on the top, and his pale, freckled scalp showed through. He wore the familiar bib overalls and flannel shirt, although the shirt was a different color than last time they spoke. The bulkiness of a once-young man's torso had settled upon the old man's waist. He was in his work boots. No doubt, he was the type of farmer who had work in his blood and the boots helped keep it there. Like Brynn's grandfather, their bare feet likely never touched the floor; the boots went on upon rising, and they came off when bedtime came around again.

He motioned to one of two chairs near a small table off of the kitchen. "Why don't you have a seat." It sounded more like an order, but she thanked him and sat. Brynn noticed his hoarding habit had spread like mange on a mongrel to his current home.

Bertis sat opposite her and leaned forward, hands on the table, folded together as if in solemn contemplation, and stared at Brynn expectantly.

Brynn took the hint. "Well, I've been thinking about my case." She paused, hoping to convince him that it was her sole objective. "Apparently, the authorities think there may be a connection to Lanea's disappearance." She had decided earlier that this is all she would say to begin with, and allow him to say whatever came to mind. She hadn't considered the likelihood that he might not want to say anything.

"I suppose that's possible," Bertis said, "but I don't think I know nothin' that could help ya'." So far, so good, but she could feel her knee begging to be bobbed.

"I'm just curious, I guess, to find out if there was anything strange going on before she disappeared. Any strange phone calls, any people or vehicles you didn't recognize going by, anything like that?" Brynn was reluctant to mention anything that alluded to Lanea running away, knowing it would probably strike a defensive chord in him.

"No, not that I recall." His expressionless gaze told her that he had nothing to add.

Good grief. Brushing a cat's teeth might be easier.

"Did you have any suspicions about anyone ... in the area?" Brynn asked, averting his gaze momentarily and playing with the rings on her finger. She looked back at him, loath to appear as timid as she felt.

"Why do you ask that?" Bertis' brows furrowed, and he eyed her guardedly.

"I talked to Marshall a few days ago ... " she said, and with that, Brynn lost the battle with her knee.

Bertis squeezed his hands together slightly. He seemed to study a pile of clutter nearby, apparently choosing his words.

He looked up, his gray eyes locking with Brynn's. "I told the police all I know about him and that other boy, the Otten kid."

"Uh ... right. But I can't see that file. Is there anything you can tell me?"

"Like what? I can't prove nothin'. Marshall and Ryker, they was the only ones I ever thought mighta' had somethin' to do with it. I seen that Otten kid come around a couple days before she went missin'. And Nord, he was nothin' but trouble. Both of 'em were. Heathens." Bertis' face was flushing. Then he looked almost hopeful. "You thinkin' one of them could'a been your attacker?"

Brynn ignored the question. She crossed her disobedient legs and plunged ahead.

"You must have known that she was seeing Marshall. Did you know that she broke up with him two weeks before she disappeared?"

"I heard that, yeah. Probably for the best." He paused. Bertis' chin crumpled as he fought to keep his composure. He shook his head. "She was a good girl. A good, Christian girl. Don't make no sense to me, why anyone would want to hurt her or take her."

His lower lip quivered. He rubbed his mouth as if to wipe away his sorrow, and straightened in his chair. "And the police tried sayin' that she mighta' ran away, but she wouldn't. Couldn'a. All her things was there. Her clothes, her bags, her personal things, her Bible ... She never went anywhere without her Bible. Still have it here."

Unconcerned with whether Brynn cared to see it or not, Bertis got up from the table and left the room. He came back moments later with a white Bible and handed it to Brynn. She opened the front cover, carefully turning the first few pages. She reached the page on which Lanea's name was hand written. The penmanship, smooth and elegant, looked familiar, and Brynn felt a stab of loss. She couldn't imagine how uncomfortable Bertis' well-worn boots must have been these last sixteen years.

"Mr. Covey, I want to find who abducted me, but hopefully, it will help me find out what happened to Lanea." She quickly closed the Bible and laid it on the table to distract him from the tremor in her voice.

"Well," Bertis nearly shouted, seemingly embarrassed by his show of emotion, "you wanna know what happened, I suggest you look at them boys. Both of them was after her, and far as I'm concerned, one of them has to know what happened to her." He paused. "But as for the two cases having anything to do with each other, I don't know nothin' about that." He got up from the table.

"I appreciate you talking with me, Mr. Covey." Brynn said to his back as he led the way to the door.

"So did you get some good pictures the other day? What'ja say you were doin' with those now?"

"I take photos, then print them out onto watercolor paper and paint over them. Artwork." She hoped her irritation wasn't evident in her words, having told him for the third time, and then wondered if he had the beginnings of Alzheimer's.

"Huh," he said as he opened the door. "Sounds a little … highfalutin." He stepped back with the door, holding it for Brynn, as much as telling her it was time to go. "There's a lot of stuff there on my property. Wouldn't want someone stealin', gettin' hurt, or falling in a hole or somethin'. So I got Wade checkin' the place from time to time … "

She understood. Brynn said goodbye and left for home. After a quick bite and change of her clothes, she pulled her hair into a ponytail, hopped on her bicycle, and headed for Bertis' old farm site. It was the implied directive—and compliance—she was having trouble with.

The warm morning had changed to a windy and cloudy afternoon. Off into the west, a wall of rain hung from the heavens like a sheet of indigo silk. Brynn watched the portentous skies as she pedaled south toward Lanea's, hoping the rain would hold off until she was home again. Fat raindrops pelted her as she neared the abandoned farm.

She reached the back door as the skies opened up. Brynn pushed her way into the half-opened door, stumbling over refuse and falling onto the litter-padded floor of the laundry room-porch. The stench of mildewed clothing and animal waste filled her nostrils. She'd forgotten the hazmat suit and mask she'd promised herself.

Brynn stepped over mounds of debris, slowly working her way into the kitchen. She used the house's memories to see all that had happened throughout the years, paying particular attention to the events surrounding the time that Lanea was present. Again, she saw Genevieve collapse, Lanea scream, the mourning that both Bertis and Lanea endured after Genevieve had passed. She saw Bertis at the cluttered table, talking to police. Brynn studied the room, the people, the items within the room, everything she could stuff into her brain for future reference. In her haste, she had forgotten her notebook and pen as well.

No new memories immediately came to her, and knowing that she would see more events if she lingered, she remained for a while. She watched, with sad longing for her friend, as Lanea went about her daily chores and rituals in this room, her lithe form as real as a reflection in a time-dusted mirror. She eventually witnessed what she assumed to be Lanea's phone conversation with Marshall. Lanea was crying and talking, clutching the handset of the phone with both hands as if it were Marshall himself. After a brief conversation, she hung up, and turned to face her father, who was seated nearby, watching her. They glared at each other, the sizzling current of anger between them not weakened by time. Lanea stormed from the kitchen, and Bertis immediately removed the phone from the wall, wrapped the long, coiled cord around it, tucked it under his arm, and left the house. Brynn tried to memorize the time on the clock, the clothing they wore, the items in the room so that upon referring to this memory, she could hope to form a timeline of events. With all the junk in the room, in the house, there was little hope of finding a working pen and somewhat clean sheet of paper. What Dena had said, about Bertis being behind the breakup, appeared to be true.

She moved on to the living room, seeing the same things as before: a whole bunch of nothing. She waited to see if there was anything she had previously missed. She suspected that no amount of time in this room would produce memories of any value to her investigation.

Outside, the rain had gotten heavy. The thought of riding her bicycle home in the rain was only half of the problem she now faced. The other half was trying to explain to her husband where she had been and why she was riding her bicycle in a thunderstorm. She decided to call Jackson with the one thing she had remembered: her phone.

"Hey, Honey ... Oh, I'm at an abandoned farm, snooping ... No! No, you don't need to come get me. It'll stop soon. I'll just look around to see if there's anything I want to get pictures of later. I'm fine. Don't worry ... Yes, I will. Gotta go, my battery's about to die." She hung up before he insisted on coming to get her.

She crept up the filthy stairs, hugging the wall in case there happened to be one of the culprits inhabiting the upper floor—a creature that might want to hastily exit the building by way of the same staircase. She encountered no other creatures on the second floor, but the odds of not coming face to face with a wild animal in this house eventually were going to diminish if she kept this up.

There were some chances Brynn was willing to take in this venture, and some that she was not. Going back into Bertis' and Genevieve's room was one risk she was not willing to take. Something much more frightening and traumatic than a rabid animal was undeniable if she chose to let the room put any images in her head. Brynn sidled past that door with no regrets about that decision.

Other than the bathroom—a last resort—the only room remaining was Lanea's ... and the closet under the eaves. Standing in the hallway, remembering her last visit and recalling the events she had witnessed, Brynn realized that it was entirely possible that the closet or small room was Lanea's room while her mother was infirmed in her room. Near her mother, private, near the bathroom, it seemed logical.

Little light from nearby rooms was shared with the hall and even less with the cave-like room. Peering in and using her phone as a flashlight, Brynn saw enough of it to know that there was room for a single bed or cot, though little else. It was difficult to imagine anything fitting in the room, with all of the debris spilling from it. It was heaped at least three-quarters of the way to the ceiling with clothing, boxes, and rubbish.

The room was at most five feet deep by eight feet wide, with a short wall adjacent to the door, which, at about three feet up, slanted up as a ceiling, running the eight feet length, judging by where the wall ended at the doorway to the next room. If it had been a bedroom, the bed would have had to have been tucked under the slanted ceiling on the three-foot-tall wall opposite the door, an awkward arrangement at best, but completely plausible. This *could* have been Lanea's room for a while.

The notion of climbing that pile of undoubtedly-mouse-infested garbage to get a glimpse of the happenings in that room was almost as repulsive as the idea of going back into Bertis' bedroom.

Hoping to sidestep the unpleasant task of climbing the mountain of junk, Brynn leaned over the spillage outside the door and stuck her arm into the room on the remote chance that she could grasp the memories in that way. It didn't work.

Balancing on her right leg, gripping the door frame with one hand, and stretching her left leg inside the door, Brynn attempted the laughable and almost-contortionist method of absorbing whatever memories she could. With the landslide extending past the door, this allowed only about four toes inside the room. Four toes were apparently not enough to absorb even a fleeting glimpse into the past. Brynn stepped delicately onto the avalanche outside the doorway just enough to get her head inside the room and found even that wasn't working.

Brynn hit the wall in frustration. Obviously, her whole body needed to be inside the room in order for her memory machine to work, and the only way her whole body was going to fit was sitting in a hunched over position or lying down in the room, which meant on top of the pile. Brynn felt a gag tugging at the back of her throat. Eating lutefisk and enrolling in an advanced calculus class would rate better on her list of unpleasant tasks.

The zap of a close strike of lightening and clap of thunder startled Brynn from her near-nausea. The reminder that she was stuck here waiting out the storm only intensified her desire to leave. The chore facing her was enough to make Brynn consider the risk of getting hit and fried alive by lightning on her bike ride home in order to avoid it.

Brynn tried to make herself light as she stepped carefully onto the extruded trash. Once inside the doorway, she crawled the remainder of the way into the dark room. It was possible, even likely, that there were mice beneath her. Brynn cringed at the thought of families of mice being squished below her hands and knees, but she took twisted comfort in the thought that *at least they were being squished.*

Perched in the center of the room, she tucked her head down and sat in a squat, reluctant to lie down. Mouse droppings stuck to her hands and she brushed them off. The thought of never eating with her fingers again crossed her mind.

Almost immediately, the past began to swirl around her. The flurry of memories was like brittle leaves caught in a fall wind, bumping and lifting again, and Brynn's mind grasped what it could. Brynn saw Lanea sitting on a cot, the head of the bed against the innermost wall. She was writing in a flowered journal, her knees pulled up in a makeshift desk. It was an innocent memory upon first glance, but then Brynn saw the glimmer of grief on Lanea's cheeks. However brief Lanea's stay was in this room, it was anything but uneventful as Brynn witnessed Bertis entering the small room, wrenching the journal from Lanea's clutch, and shoving a black book into her hands in its place. Lanea sat up straight, clearly appalled at her father's forcefulness and nerve, but also clearly bewildered by it at the same time.

The black book was a Bible. Brynn had seen it before—in Lanea's bedroom when Genevieve was dying, and also when Lanea was packing to leave. And somewhere else. *Where? Bertis' apartment?*

A sudden quivering on Brynn's leg caused her to leap in alarm, her head thudding against the ceiling, as she pawed and swiped at the unseen critter. Brynn's heart raced wildly by the time she realized it was the rhythmic buzzing and trembling cell phone in her pocket, set to vibrate.

"Hello?" The word seemed overly loud in the claustrophobic room. It was Jackson. "Yeah, still waiting out the storm ... oh, just down the road ... some old house ... I'll be home as soon as it lets up ... "

And then she screamed.

Her own scream, reverberating against the walls that were mere inches from her ears, seemed to scare her as much as had the shadow that scurried across the mountain on which Brynn crouched. "Spider," she explained, forcing calmness, "I'll be home soon."

Brynn stuck the phone into her back pocket, taking deep breaths then wishing she hadn't.

Where was I?

"Lanea, Lanea ... " she said softly out loud while her mind thrummed *hot shower ... hot shower ... .*

The interruption forced a refresh of the memories. Brynn grabbed at the whirling past with her mind as if to collect the memories like elusive dollars in a carnival money booth. An image of Bertis in Lanea's small room alone caught Brynn's attention. He was sitting on the edge of the cot reading Lanea's journal. There was no way to judge when this had occurred, but it was important to the story of the room.

As he read, Bertis' expression morphed over the seconds from puzzlement to fear then rage. His eyes bulged in apparent disbelief; his face was that of a strangling man, purpled and struggling for breath. Trembling, he carefully replaced the book in its original spot and lowered his head into his hands, rubbing first his face, then his entire head in obvious desperation and frustration. He lifted his head, shaking it slowly as his lips moved in soundless lament too seething to be prayer, too anguished to be curse. Whatever he had read in those pages crushed his heart then set it afire. Even without knowing the content of that sacred text, Brynn knew this was what precipitated the confiscation of the journal and its replacement with the Bible.

Again she saw the exchange of books, Bertis turning and leaving the room and Lanea following shortly thereafter. Brynn ignored the impulse to follow them, knowing that the sequence of events was only in her mind, that they could be followed at any time, providing she kept track of what they were wearing and the approximate timing of each of their actions. Why hadn't she remembered seeing anything in the hall like she had in Cole's house, besides the blur of everyone's comings and goings? Perhaps the hallway walls saw the same thing over and over, and blended it all together. The hall's recollection of the family's movements was like the hazy line of headlights in a time-lapse photo of traffic on a roadway. Brynn found the intricacies of her ability hard to understand. It was as convoluted, confusing, and mind-numbing as trying to figure out the complexities of time travel, the endlessness of the universe, or perhaps, the arcane religion of football.

Brynn lingered in the room, gathering whatever memories it cared to share with her. She saw Lanea suffer more distress and sadness in this tiny room than anyone could possibly deserve in their lifetime. This hole was a dungeon and the torture was isolation. Lanea's only warmth came from a handmade quilt, her only light came from a bare bulb in a porcelain socket, and her only friends were an empty, eager page and a pen full of surging emotions waiting to be freed. Lanea's dungeon wasn't limited to these dismal walls, and as full as it seemed with remnants of the past—the memories *and* the junk—this was the emptiest room of all. Nothing was left in this cell that anyone, least of all Lanea, would care to cherish.

After Bertis had taken the journal, the black Bible had become Lanea's friend. Reading, studying, and margin notes had replaced her journaling time, and it was clear that Lanea's mood had changed with the surrogate. Her countenance was grim, her face drawn and devoid of any happiness, often tear-streaked. Brynn bristled at the notion that this Bible—any Bible—could be ostensibly used as a weapon or punishment. The memory of Bertis' exchange of books played over and over like a wordless political or pulpit sound bite, as if to emphasize the moment. But the fact was that this room had seen very little life beside that memory, and the life it did know was bleak and unsympathetic.

Brynn was starting to dislike Bertis and his authoritarian and fanatical methods of parenting, but it didn't explain what had happened to Lanea. Judgment of Bertis would have to be reserved for now.

Thunder growled like a hungry gut, and Brynn felt as though she'd been swallowed whole by a garbage truck and slowly digested with a lifetime of stinking trash. Her back and legs were aching, burning. She had seen enough. Lanea couldn't possibly have done more than write in a room that required bending over and walking sideways just to enter and exit. The Bible and the journal, although opposites in function with one telling and the other listening, were the only constants in Lanea's life. Brynn was grateful that Lanea had them to comfort her, however cold solace they were.

Brynn crab-walked legs first toward the door, finishing her exit with an ungraceful slide to the floor of the hall. She got up and stretched, slapping the dust and dung from her clothes. She felt like she'd been trapped inside that tiny room for hours, but checking her phone, Brynn found it had only been about fifteen minutes. She paused in the hallway, hoping to relive the moment of Bertis and Lanea exiting the closet/dungeon. The time-lapse blur was all she could make out.

Brynn stepped into Lanea's bedroom. Sifting through the visions of the misery of Genevieve's death and Lanea's equally miserable childhood, she paused on Lanea packing to leave. Back pack, clothing, money, and not the white Bible that Bertis mentioned Lanea was never without, but the black one. It was the same Bible that Lanea had read aloud to her dying mother. It was Genevieve's. Although Brynn saw no reason for the seizure of the journal, the Bible did not seem now to be as much Bertis' weapon or a punishment as a visceral reaction, a link to her mother, a celestial lifeline to a flailing child by a scared and lonely father who knew only stern and unwavering faith as the answer to everything.

Brynn waited out the recollections. The order and timing didn't always make sense, but some moments, such as the vision of the police searching the room and her belongings, were easy to interpret. Eventually, Brynn got a glimpse at more commonplace events, like one of Lanea pacing and glancing out the window. The vision was emotion-filled, and it was the oddness of the nervous, repetitive motions that caught her attention, as if Lanea was watching for someone, or waiting for something to happen outside. The room appeared to be set in the same arrangement as when Genevieve was dying, obviously after her death, but maybe before Lanea had moved back into it. The chronology of events was becoming jumbled and confusing. Lanea paced from the door to the window several times, looking in the same direction each time. Brynn stepped to the window and looked in the same direction. The barn.

The prospect of gathering evidence from a barn was questionable, but promising. The rain continued, guaranteeing that Brynn would be a muddy mess by the time she got home. But it was also serving a useful dual purpose: it was unlikely that the hired hand, Wade, would expect anyone to be prowling the farm site in the rain. It gave her opportunity that a clear day might not, and the ongoing rain also gave her time to investigate without Jackson expecting her any time soon.

The barn would be next on her list, right after the basement. The fun was never-ending.

Brynn checked the time on her phone, noting that it was less than an hour ago that she had phoned Jackson and maybe half an hour since he had called her. It was not unreasonable, given that it was still raining that she was not home, but time was running out. If it stopped raining altogether, he would expect her home within minutes and she needed to be ready to leave as soon as possible.

She trotted down the steps and went to the open door below them that led to the basement. There was not a space within the old house that the hoarding disease hadn't infected, and in this case, the basement was near death. The cluttered steps prohibited easy passage, but in the spirit of not-wanting-to-come-back, Brynn traversed the littered slope to at least have a look at the basement.

A few steps into the descent, Brynn decided that she had gone far enough to see the basement. She crouched on the steps, peering below the basement ceiling to scan the room. Most of the basement was visible from this position, although the space was dimly lit by a few small, dirty windows. The aroma was that of rot with the familiar stench of dead mouse overriding the fusty, stagnant dampness.

The basement was filled with buckets, cans, lumber, broken furniture, cardboard boxes, appliances, anything and everything that one could discard. It was as if the house had been set upon a gigantic dumpster, and she was the reluctant diver in search of fetid buried treasures. What little wall was visible was painted the sickly color of hospital green—a shade somewhere between mint and puke.

Brynn wasn't sure if her entire body was far enough below the basement ceiling in order to allow the visions to come to her. Without descending any further, she struggled to hunker below grade while on the steps and get a peek at the past. Finally, she saw brief moments of Bertis hauling his loot to the basement, snippets of him working, fixing things, and repairing foundation and painting the nauseating infirmary color on the blighted basement walls. Not surprisingly, there were no visions of either woman in the space in the few moments Brynn had given it, and they weren't going to get much of a chance to surface. She was repulsed and couldn't imagine anything of value happening here. Brynn moved to stand up and heard a noise.

She froze, crouched on the steps. The floor above her creaked under the weight of heavy footsteps.

How would she explain herself? She'd just been at Bertis' and heard his dimly-veiled warning. And ignored it.

She felt her face grow hot and her heart flipping in her chest. More footsteps. Was it more than one person? They seemed to come from different areas of the room above. Bertis and Wade. Had to be.

She was trapped. She couldn't call Jackson. They'd hear her. There was no way to navigate over the heaps of junk in the basement and hide without making noise. She felt her pounding heart and ragged breathing would betray her long before she had a chance to hide.

Only one way out of this. Own it. She was out riding bike and it started to pour. She came in to get out of the storm. Easy. Now to convince *them*. Brynn stood slowly as she called out, "Hello?"

As abruptly as the footfalls began, they stopped.

They heard. They were waiting. A terrifying thought occurred to Brynn: What if it *wasn't* Wade and Bertis?

Brynn ascended the steps. "Bertis?"

She reached the top of the steps and peeked into the living room. No one. *How could that be?*

With all the junk in the room, in the house, they couldn't have exited so quietly. Or they were still there. *But where?*

Brynn felt a tickle up her spine and the hairs on her arms stood on end. She hadn't imagined it. There would be no point in not confronting her if it were Bertis or Wade. Why would they hide? And if it were anyone else, they couldn't have gone upstairs without making a sound. No one was here.

Chills overcame her and she knew opportunity when she saw it.

She had to keep moving.

In the kitchen, Brynn saw that the rain had almost stopped. Jackson would be expecting her soon and it would take at least fifteen minutes to get home. She took a last look around the room, observing fundamental happenings once again as she passed through the room: the phone call, Bertis and the police, and Lanea's movements, committing it to memory.

She left the house and headed toward the barn, taking her bicycle with her, the wet tangle of grass holding her back as if in warning. She glanced nervously behind her. After the ghostly incident in the house, she couldn't shake the feeling she was being watched.

She needed only a few more minutes and she would be safely away from the property, away from all the discarded debris and past affairs and actions and drama. And spooks. She was looking forward to resolving this mystery, but with what she had learned inside the house, she was no closer to resolution than she was before this visit. She depended on the barn for one last chance at a clue, badly needing the building to hold more than junk, pigeons, and dried manure.

Inside the doorway of the barn, Brynn leaned her bike against the wall and walked casually toward the center. A main alley ran the length of the building, with stalls to the right and an enclosed tack room to the left. At the back of the barn was a stairway to the hayloft. The outbuilding was refreshingly empty. There were a few cast-off items, but with the building missing some of its siding, the only logical reason for its lack of junk was probably due to its lack of weatherproofing.

Before Brynn had a chance to step into the stalls, she saw the first of her visions. Major events like Bertis and his hired hand filling the hayloft and doing chores were the first to appear, but within moments, Brynn saw more significant clips of the past. She saw a younger Ryker standing rigid and surreptitious, peering through chinks in the wall planks into the tack room. Why a flash of this event was important to the structure was puzzling, but as Brynn questioned that, another flash occurred of Bertis standing outside the door of the tack room with a pitchfork in his hand. The look of agony and horror contorting his face, and his ears the same bright red she had seen earlier in the day revealed that what he was hearing or seeing had pierced him as deeply as would the implement he clutched so desperately. Without the image of what he had witnessed, Brynn could only assume that the cause of his distress occurred in another room, likely the tack room, into which Ryker was peering, possibly moments before.

Immediately, the vision of Lanea running into the barn came into view. She was visibly upset and anxious. Clutching at something hidden inside her sweater, she was clearly worried about being seen as she quickly ducked into the tack room.

Brynn's heart slammed against her ribs. As excited as she was to see what tale the tack room had to tell, she was equally as apprehensive. The mystery of Lanea's disappearance could possibly end there. The tack room's battered wooden door was closed for the most part, but hanging half-off its rusted hinges.

Brynn paced the alley, looking toward the tack room and then again outside to the road. Her clothes were damp and smelled of mouse, her hair was plastered to her head, her feet were wet and cold, and she had to pee.

The rain had stopped and Jackson would be expecting her any minute. Wade could drive in. Questions, motives, goals, answers, feelings of dread and exhilaration—they settled upon her like a sixteen-year-layer of dust, and she couldn't breathe. She didn't know what to do. Brynn held no illusions that the minute or two she had left would allow enough time to properly sweep away all doubt about what may have happened in that room.

Brynn yanked the phone from her back pocket and called Jackson.

"On my way, Honey ... yeah, I'll see you in 15 or 20 minutes ... K, bye."

The tack room door squealed as Brynn opened it.

CHAPTER SEVENTEEN

T HE THUNDERSTORM GAVE JACKSON MORE than the usual reason to be concerned. He had no idea where Brynn was, but *she* knew where she was and wasn't telling him. Somewhere, Brynn was in an abandoned house waiting out the storm. It would have been easy for her to ask him to come and get her. It would have been easier for him to insist.

He wasn't the type to tell her what to do or assume that she needed him. *And why not?*

Jackson rummaged through the cupboards looking for something to give the kids for an after school snack. Fudgestripe cookies. Juice boxes. *That'll do.* He threw them on the counter. Brynn would have preferred fruit or even pudding or ice cream, but she wasn't there.

The secrecy and reserve was wearing as thin as April ice. Other than the recent flu that they all had recently encountered, he couldn't remember the last time Brynn had stayed at home and been completely engaged in family.

Anger, worry, and confusion ate at him. Her artwork seemed more and more to be an excuse and not an actual hobby or side job. Was she having an affair? *Oh, man, Jackson. You're stretching, there. She wouldn't. We're happy! ... Aren't we?*

He couldn't bear to think of that scenario. But the other possibilities didn't offer any comfort either.

Think, Jackson, think! What has she been doing lately ... what's on her mind?

Jackson ran a hand through his hair, pausing at the back of his neck and rubbing. What was with all the questions about Lanea? What about the file she'd seen on her own case?

Was she investigating her own abduction and attack? What could she possibly learn?

Jackson paced the kitchen as he and Buddy waited for Ellie to arrive home from school. Thunder boomed like he wished he could. The lightning sizzled and flashed and Buddy clung to the window like a tree frog.

"Buddy, get away from the windows."

"But Mama lets us ... "

"Your mom's not here!" The force with which he said it and the feelings behind that force frightened Jackson more than it had Buddy. He picked up his son and carried him to the living room. "Just sit here on the couch and look at this book," he said softly, handing him Dr. Seuss from the end table. He ruffled Buddy's hair and attempted a smile.

Jackson shuffled through the mail, flipped through the newspaper, and turned the television on and off three times before he'd finally decided to call Brynn back and check on her.

Her voice had echoed on the other end and although she had startled and screamed at an apparent spider, nothing seemed overly wrong with the situation. The only wrongness was in his not knowing where she was and what she was doing, besides waiting out the storm.

Give her time. Give her time.

He wasn't sure how much more time he had. If she was looking into the cases and trying to find connections, she might find them before the authorities did and there would be no way to help her then. What if someone out there, somewhere, knew of her efforts? To what lengths would they go? No doubt as far—further—than they had before.

The waning rumble of thunder drew Bingo out from under the dining room table and onto Buddy's lap, and Buddy used the opportunity to teach the dog how to read.

Jackson knew that the dying storm would bring Brynn home soon.

This had to end. He was going to give her time, but it would not be much longer. It was the last week of school, and before the weekend was over, this was going to end.

The phone rang again half an hour later and Brynn announced that she would be home within a few minutes. There was something odd in her voice. A certainty. There was an inflection of assurance or maybe even a bit of nervous determination that he hadn't heard before. Had she found something?

Where was she?

CHAPTER EIGHTEEN

PREPARING HERSELF FOR GRISLY VISIONS of a possible murder, Brynn pulled slowly on the dangling door. The large, rusty hinge complained but relented. She waited outside the door for a moment, scanning the walls and contents. Unlike the rest of the barn, this room had interior wall boards and a wooden floor. Nails acting as hooks were haphazardly hammered into the upper wall, but only a few were being used for their intended function. A dirt-encrusted, brittle leather bridle, bull nose rings, and corroded tools now served only as support for the cobwebs that decorated the building in macabre lace. A window with dirt-grayed panes permitted enough light for Brynn to see that there were no woodchucks, raccoons, or skunks lying in wait. She eased into the room, swiping at webs that clung to her damp face and netted her matted hair.

Eyes open or closed, it made no difference: Memories fluttered through her mind. Surprised but relieved, Brynn saw no attacks or blood or violence. She then realized, with a trace of shame, that she was disappointed—not that there were no visions of violence, but markedly no visions that answered the mystery of Lanea's disappearance.

As with her other visions, they seemed to appear in order of importance. The scene of the authorities searching the property was there along with the decades of goings-on by Bertis and his family and hired hands. But the vision of Lanea entering the room—as Brynn had seen her moments before—became the most prominent. She was wearing the same clothing as when Bertis had taken her journal. It was the same day.

Lanea had gone immediately to the window and peered out, then pulled something from her sweater. It was her journal, covered in a gray-black dust that looked like soot. She brushed it off hastily, and wrapped it in a hank of burlap that was draped over a nail. Frantically, she rummaged through tools, finally pulling a rasp from a wooden peach crate that hung on the wall as a shelf. She pried loose a wall board near the floor in the corner of the room. She stuffed her bundle into the crevice and replaced the plank, kicking it into place and setting an oily cardboard box in front of the loosened panel.

Brynn knew she would have to pedal fast and hard most of the four-mile ride home to keep her projected arrival time. She didn't care. Her excitement at knowing there might be a journal hidden within these walls would be sufficient fuel to pedal fast enough to win the Tour de

France right now. Late, fried by lightning, wet, cold, feeling as if she was covered like a salted nut roll in mouse turds— none of that mattered. A journal would be a Godsend.

Uninvited memories continued to play while Brynn searched for her own tools to pull the plank loose. There were no rasps or even peach crate shelves, only a bladeless hacksaw and a rusted spring-steel curry comb. Brynn snatched the hacksaw, went to the spot where Lanea had stashed her journal, and found the board, which was merely wedged into place. No nails secured it, but it was stuck, fixed in place by sixteen years of moisture and dirt.

She couldn't concentrate. The visions came at her like startled bats, swooping and dodging, as she tried to pry the board loose with the end of the hacksaw. Brynn saw Lanea stand and brush off her clothing, nervously glancing in all directions out the window, as if waiting for the right moment to leave. Brynn plucked and picked at the edge of the board as she saw Lanea, paused at the window in the sunlight of a brighter day, though not a brighter time. Lanea's face bore the burden of her secrets. Her skin was ashen, deep rings settled under her eyes, and her cheeks were hollowed. Her graceful, chaste beauty was lost somewhere inside her worry.

The board popped loose, and Brynn almost shouted for joy.

Just as her fingers plunged into the void to search for the book, Brynn saw Lanea turn around to leave the room and found Ryker standing in the room near the door. Brynn stopped.

Ryker stood motionless as Lanea spoke to him. The urgency in her actions was unmistakable. She was reasoning with him, perhaps trying to get out of the room without impediment? Lanea's face was wet with tears as she spoke. Her words to Ryker were silent, but the meaning was deafeningly clear: she was pleading. He nodded almost imperceptibly after a few moments, stepping aside and allowing her to pass. She peeked out the door, and ran out of the room into the past. Brynn suspected she would see the exit as well, if she chose to wait for it outside the door, however, that seemed to be the least important part of this puzzle.

Brynn felt inside the wall for the burlap bundle, but found only spider webs and dead bugs. And mouse poop. *Of course there would be mouse poop.* No journal. The one piece of Lanea that could speak for her was gone.

"Damn it!" Brynn shouted.

Brynn rose, wiping her nose on her sleeve and her hands on her filthy jeans as defeat overcame her and her eyes filled with tears.

Even through the tears cresting in her eyes and the deep shadows of a past nighttime, Brynn saw Ryker once more.

He had come into the tack room in the middle of the night and taken the journal from its hiding place.

The bike ride churned up the murky uncertainties of Lanea's past, and Brynn mulled over the questions that bubbled to the surface.

There's no way to know when he had come. Lanea would have known it was he who had taken it, since Ryker was the only one around when she hid it—as far as she knew—so why would he risk it? Then again, why would she hide her journal in the first place? Had she detailed her plans to run away and didn't want her father to learn of them? Of course, Lanea had to assume that her father may have already read it, but in the event that he hadn't, she probably wanted to assure that he wouldn't.

How did she get it back? It looked sooty. Perhaps he'd thrown it in the burning barrel and she'd retrieved it. That makes sense. Why not just burn it then? Burn the only one that listened without judgment, opinion, or advice. Burn the only one that kept vigil with her during her dark times and rejoiced with her when she danced. Burn the only confidant that she could trust with absolute certainty to keep her secrets. Yeah. That would be like setting a match to the woodpile underneath a best friend. Never mind.

Thankful for the quiet time on the ride home, even with the burn of exertion in her thighs, she raced to make up the minutes she'd spent in the tack room.

By now, Jackson and Buddy would be home and Ellie would be arriving any minute. Coherent thought would be a casualty of that chaotic war. After hours of being immersed in another time and place, Brynn felt as though she'd been gone for days. She missed her kids, she missed her husband, and most of all, she missed feeling clean, but she had to try to sort out some of the clues she'd been given in the house and the barn.

Why would Ryker take the journal and when had he taken it? It had to have been after Lanea was reported missing. Perhaps she had written something in it that had implicated him, and if that was the case, he had probably destroyed it. She remembered Bertis saying that Ryker had been to the house a couple days before Lanea went missing. Was this the day Bertis was referring to? He had been outside the door, she recalled, and overheard something. Was Lanea in fear for her life? Had Bertis overheard Ryker threaten her or make inappropriate comments?

There was no way Bertis would have any more to share with her. Whatever suspicions he had of Marshall and Ryker, he was going to hang onto those as vehemently as he did his caches, his memories, and his grief. His caches *embodied* his memories and his grief. She'd have to learn what she could from Ryker. The phone call to Marshall, the seizing of the journal, and the incident in the barn were likely all the same day, since Lanea was wearing the same clothes: black leggings and baggy white blouse and black sweater. Marshall hadn't heard from Lanea after she broke up with him, and she went missing about two weeks after that. So if she broke up with Marshall the same day that the journal was confiscated, but didn't disappear for two weeks after that, Bertis was confused about Ryker visiting two days before she went missing, or Bertis is talking about a visit that happened later. Why didn't she see that? Maybe it happened outside, where the memories couldn't be captured.

Brynn had no doubts about Lanea's love for Marshall or the possibility that Ryker was a factor in the breakup.

She knew by the way Lanea looked at her father after the phone call that he had just forced her to sever the line to the lifeboat that would carry her to her dreams. Marshall was Lanea's dream. If Lanea had run away, it would have been to Marshall. Ryker had to be involved.

"Where have you *been*?" Jackson said as she entered the kitchen. He was not happy. Jackson set his mug of coffee on the counter and sent Buddy to play with Bingo in the living room.

"Bike riding."

"In blue jeans and boots?" He looked skeptically at her, her clothing, and the dirt she was unable to brush away.

"What? A person can't wear boots while riding bike? I wanted to scope out some new spots to take pictures." The ease with which she could tell the lie bothered her more than the lie itself. "I'd better get cleaned up. What do you want for supper?"

"You can't do that with a car?" Jackson followed her into the bathroom where she proceeded to shed her damp, grimy clothing. "Brynn, we aren't done talking. What's going on? You have been gone a lot, you've been acting strangely, and I feel you're not telling me something."

Brynn turned on the shower.

"What do you want to know, J? I'm an open book. I'm always here, I take care of the kids, cook, clean, do dishes and laundry, and swim in poop the rest of the time." He had no idea how true those last words were. "I'm taking my life back. That's where I've been." She stopped, naked and gripping the glass shower enclosure, and stared at him. "What do you want to know?" Her black, stringy hair hung in her face and she could see remnants of the barn's cobwebs clinging to it. Jackson had to be curious, confused, and probably more than a little worried. She knew that she hadn't been as responsive and forthcoming as she was before she'd discovered her gift, but this is the way it had to be for now. If Jackson found out about her abilities, there would be a lot more issues than cobwebs in their marriage. Telling him might mean an end to her investigation and her newfound freedom.

"I want to know where you've been." Jackson said.

Brynn felt as if the words she should say were choking her like a chunk of dry meat. She shook her head slowly, clambering to find an explanation that would pacify him but not add to the mounting untruths.

"Because even when you're here, you're somewhere else," he said as he walked out of the bathroom.

Brynn stood under the hot water, relishing the scent of the white jasmine and mint bath gel and the solitude. She realized then that although Jackson had suspicions about her whereabouts, his main concern was her distractedness and distance. She just needed a little more time. *Time for what? When would there be a good time to tell your husband that you see ghosts? Maybe not actual ghosts—and that alone seemed enough of a contradiction in terms—but phantom memories that belonged to someone else? "I'm psychic, Jackson." Yeah. That'd go well.*

Supper was an easy fix: Steaks on the grill and sweet corn from last fall's garden that had been stockpiled in the freezer. Small talk over the dinner table was not so easy. Light and chipper conversation was exchanged with the children, but the exchanges between Brynn and Jackson were civil and brief. After chores and getting the children to bed, their own bedtime was equally awkward as well, but soon, Brynn was snuggled up to Jackson. The cold of the rain, the cold of Bertis' empty house full of stuff, and the cold of loneliness that plagued the lives of everyone touched by Lanea, had seeped into her bones. Brynn was gripped with a crushing need to be embraced and absolved.

Jackson pulled her close, but said nothing. His silence was the best argument he possessed, and Brynn felt the sting of guilt, knowing that there was nothing, other than the truth, that could appease him.

She would know when the time was right, when Jackson would be accepting of her abilities. She needed proof, and she needed to know more facts before she could get that proof. Tomorrow, she hoped, Jackson would be planting, Buddy would be with him, and she would have an opportunity to talk to Ryker.

The wet ground kept Jackson from the field until after dinner. As soon as they had gone, Brynn left for Ryker's house.

As her car pulled into the yard, Brynn saw Fern hanging clothes on the line. Brynn parked and got out of the car and began to walk toward her.

"Hello, Brynn! Beautiful day!" Fern shouted, waving a sparkling white sock. Brynn wondered if Fern ever had a bad day. Did she just breathe in the air and convert it to happiness like a daisy?

"Hi, Fern. How are you?" Brynn sauntered closer as Fern finished hanging the socks in hand and dropped the extra clothespins into the basket of damp clothes.

"Just fine! What brings you out?"

"Oh, I'm just out scoping out a few abandoned houses for my artwork. I thought I'd stop since I was in the area."

"It's nice to see you again." Fern's bright expression never dimmed, but Brynn had the feeling she was waiting for more.

"Is Ryker home?"

"Yes, he's inside having a ... oh! Here he is now." Fern smiled broadly as Ryker stomped toward them. She seemed unfazed by his apparent displeasure at finding Brynn there. Brynn looked back and forth at the opposing forces in this bizarre realm: Miss Bliss and the Hulk, and wondered who was stronger. She felt oddly compelled to step closer to Fern.

"Ryker, Brynn would like to talk to you." Fern's voice was pleasant but firm. Ryker didn't argue with her, but his face was twitching like a demon was trapped inside, trying to punch its way out. Fern moved toward the clothesline. "I'll be right over here," she said, with a smile to Brynn and a quick but meaningful glance at Ryker.

Ryker walked toward Brynn's car, and Brynn recognized this as an attempt to keep the conversation private. She could respect that, especially since Fern probably didn't know all of the details of Ryker's involvement in Lanea's disappearance. Brynn didn't know them all either, but she could pretend as well as the next guy.

Brynn opened her mouth to speak and Ryker's hot breath hit her in the face as he leaned in to make himself heard without shouting. "I told you not to come around no more."

With the blissful watchdog hanging laundry nearby, Brynn felt a little more emboldened than she would have otherwise. "Look. I don't want to get anyone in trouble. I just want to know what happened to my friend and I think you know more than you're telling me. I know that you worked for Bertis now and then. And I also know that you were there just before she went missing."

Brynn paused for effect, squinting and keeping eye contact, and trying to remember some of the tactics of interrogations she'd seen on television. Big difference was, she wasn't a cop. And he was twice her size. And she was on his property. This might not work out the way she hoped.

"How do you know that?" Ryker asked, scowling but a little calmer.

"Bertis told me. Why were you there?"

"I was working with Wade. Hegebak. We were loading hay into the hayloft. I didn't do anything wrong." Ryker's expression had softened. It was understandable that he would be frightened.

"Did you see Lanea or talk to her?"

"Why?" he asked after a brief silence. Brynn recognized the question as a way of avoiding a fib. She herself was becoming all too familiar with this maneuver.

"Because her father seems to think you had something to do with her disappearance. Did you?" Brynn was feeling rather proud of her multipurpose "did you"—*did you* see Lanea or talk to her, *did you* have something to do with her disappearance—until she realized that it offered him the opportunity to skirt the truth.

"I didn't do anything wrong," he said again. It sounded rehearsed and safe.

Brynn stared back at him defiantly, but the truth was, she was stumped. There was nothing left to ask that he couldn't answer with that response. At this point in television interrogations, when the authorities were out of questions, they stated their case, stated facts.

"Lanea told me she was thinking of running away," she blurted. It was called bluffing, a little trick, a method of opening the floodgate. But she could almost feel the happy flames of Hell licking her sorry soul.

Brynn shifted from one foot to the other, glanced away for a second, and looked back at him, hoping Ryker wasn't reading her body language as much as she was feeling it. She found he was too busy trying to hide his reaction to notice Brynn's gaffe.

She'd struck a nerve as sure as tin foil on a filling. It was subtle, but it was there. If Lanea had run away, he was off the hook. Unless he had found her walking and abducted her, which would explain his restrained reaction. If he had read her journal and found in there her plans to run away, it would have been easy to intercept her and have her for himself. He was hiding something.

Lanea's journal had answers to those questions, and Ryker had probably destroyed it. But if the journal detailed her plans to run away, why not let it be found? It would only benefit him to have people thinking Lanea ran away. Unless Ryker was named in it somewhere.

All of the "ifs" and "unlesses" were making her dizzy. The whirling theories raced through Brynn's mind like a tornado, while the idyllic Land of Oz carried on at a leisurely pace. Abduction, secrets, anger, and mystery amidst the dazzling white socks, sunshine, smiles, and daisies ... . Opposing forces indeed.

"So," he said bluntly. A well-placed cattle prod wouldn't have made him say more.

Damn it!

"Ryker, please. Just help me out a little here. When was the last time you saw her?"

"When I was helping fill the hay loft. That's all I know." It would have been the perfect time for Ryker to turn and walk away, but matching Brynn's posture, he stood his ground, clearly asserting that it *was his ground.*

In a move she had never seen on any detective show, and that which she knew she would never see sanctioned as a legal strategy, Brynn pulled out the only card she had left.

"I saw you take Lanea's journal."

Ryker's eyes narrowed, and his face mutated in expressions of confusion, anger, and *"How could she know that!?"* fear. Brynn could almost taste his shock and horror. The fear seized him, and swift as a mongoose on a snake, he seized Brynn. He gripped her shoulders in his titan-sized hands and slammed her against her car.

He held her there, his massive fingers pinching her arms and crumpling her upper body like a flimsy paper bag. His body pressed against hers, pushing her bony shoulder blades into the door of her car. She could feel him trembling. His lips quivered and he looked close to tears. Spit sprayed her face as his words exploded from his mouth, "You don't know *shit!*"

CHAPTER NINETEEN

"RYKER!" FERN'S VOICE WAS AS swift and sharp as the crack of a whip. She marched across the lawn toward Ryker and Brynn as he released his grip.

"Apologize to her, Ryker. She's our guest." There was no smile on her face, and it was obvious from Ryker's reaction that it was not a common sight.

"Ma—"

"Now."

"Sorry," Ryker said, but his countenance contradicted him. He turned and left.

"I'm so sorry, Brynn. I don't know what happened to make him so panicked, but fact is, that's how he gets when something scares him. He's a good boy. Man." She smiled. Fern's sunshine-y disposition was returning, as if she called upon it to bring about harmony throughout all the land.

Brynn almost expected immense, glistening bubbles to start forming in the air to take Fern away to wherever good witches go in their off hours. Her perpetual euphoria was getting downright creepy.

"Are you all right?" Fern touched Brynn's arm in an earnest effort to soothe her.

Brynn could do nothing but nod.

"Can I get you some water? You look pale."

"I'm fine. Really." Brynn felt as though the trembling that had begun in Ryker's hands had traveled into her and settled in her knees, amplified. She opened the car door and sat down.

"Brynn?" Fern was slightly bent, looking at Brynn in the car, and for the first time, Brynn saw a look of something other than rapture. "Is Ryker in some kind of trouble?" Fern's smile twitched, and had dimmed to something more melancholy, imploring.

More than the ache that was sinking into her muscles and the dread that was filling her belly, Brynn felt relief to see that Fern was, after all, normal. For the most part. Just as Brynn was beginning to wonder if Fern was one of those flawless mothers who had been born in heaven and raised by angels, a mother who never spoke above a sweet murmur and chuckled at misbehavior, a mother who was blind to imperfection, out came normal. *Thank God.*

"I don't think so," Brynn said flatly. Dazed, she shook her head, and then said, "I don't know."

"We raised him right. His anger was never met with anger. He's big and he ... was never very good at dealing with stress ... but he wouldn't hurt a soul. I know it," Fern said quietly. Beneath the mother's diminutive, fragile form was a steely skeleton of resolute belief and undying optimism. Although Brynn had her doubts about Ryker's innocence, she had no misgivings about the magnitude of Fern's influence on him.

Fern rested her hand on Brynn's shoulder for a moment. "I'm sorry. I will talk to him. We'll get this misunderstanding worked out. All right??" Fern nodded as if Brynn had agreed or responded in some way, then turned and walked back to the clothesline to brighten the disastrous day with her luminous laundry.

Brynn left the farm, and once out of sight of Otten's, pulled the car over to the side of the road, turned off the motor, and got out of the car to walk off her wobbly knees. A wonderful cup of coffee and chocolate of any kind would soothe her, but with only a couple hours before Ellie was to get off the bus, she also knew that she would regret squandering that valuable time.

Frightening as it was, Brynn's ploy worked. Ryker reacted like that of a guilty person. Brynn had more than enough reason now to suspect Ryker in Lanea's disappearance. But still, there was no journal, and nothing other than Brynn's own vaporous illusions to account for those suspicions.

Brynn suddenly recalled a name that popped up in every conversation related to the Covey's: Wade Hagebak. He had to be a valuable source of information, whether he was familiar with details of the case or not.

After racing home to check the phone book for the address, Brynn left for Hagebak's farm, which, although only 10 miles southeast of her home, was as far south as she could go in the county without ending up in the next state. The hills in this part of the county rolled like unfurled sheets over an unmade bed, and valleys and ravines made lush creases in the silky, quilted plains. Patterned sections of row crops, pastures dotted with cows and new calves, and hay fields rose and fell around her as she drove the highway to Wade's farm.

Jackson had land on the hem of the rolling hills, rich with black soil that produced excellent crops. Farming land that was deeply terraced was time-consuming and costly, but crops produced in the hills, on an average, yielded better throughout both wet and dry years. There was also an occasional surge of competition for land from city-escapees who sought the pristine vistas for rural acreages, not for farmland, but for privacy and space. Admiring the views as she drove, Brynn could easily understand the allure of this area of the state. A vacation home 10 miles from their farm, though, would be completely silly.

Wade's farm was tucked into the side of a hill, a windbreak wrapped protectively around it like a green, woolen scarf. Brynn drove up the long, winding driveway. The building site, closed in on three sides by the hills and trees, was crammed with buildings, equipment, and livestock, all which threatened to swallow up the small house. The farm was depressing. Numerous buildings lacked paint, and most were obsolete and ramshackle. Wooden and metal gating and barbed wire fence was attached to every upright structure on the building site, including the old wooden corn cribs that stood near the edge of the farm yard. The cattle yards sat directly behind those fences. The

Hagebaks seemed to make use of everything they had, which, in Brynn's opinion, wasn't much, but admirable just the same.

The recent rains made for a sloppy welcome to the property, as it did for most farms, but more so with this one, creating a moat around the home. The house itself was wrapped in dingy white, wavy vinyl siding and a blue metal roof, and was surrounded by a shallow yard. Two large dogs of undistinguishable breed also guarded it. The dogs barked, their bushy tails dipping with every yelp, but the raised hackles that ordinarily went with ferocious behavior were absent. The numerous cats lounging in the sun on the nearby lawn offered some reassurance. They weren't acting—they were supremely unimpressed.

Brynn got out of her car slowly, letting the dogs come to her and sniff her, her scent the secret password. They followed closely as Brynn walked up the sidewalk to the cement steps at the front of the house. Brynn knocked on the door as the dogs pressed their noses against her, annoyingly intimate at times. The pungent aroma of fresh manure hinted that what she'd been walking in was not only mud.

By the second knock, Brynn realized that perhaps the front door was not the door that was most often used by the Hagebak's. She took the stepping stone path to the door on the side of the house, nearer the detached garage, where a dirty minivan and a dirtier pickup were parked on the approach. As she rounded the side of the house with the dogs on her heels, Brynn noticed a man working near the doorway of a machine shed twenty yards from the back door. As she turned away from the house to walk to the shed, a woman came out of the house wearing green rubber boots, baggy sweatshirt, and sagging jeans. She was carrying a large, shallow box of cheeping chicks.

She saw Brynn and instead of speaking to her, turned to the dogs. "Puck! Zeus! Go lay down!" The dogs tucked their tails and sulked off to lounge with the cats.

She gave Brynn the once-over. "Can I help you?" She looked to be in her late forties or early fifties, plump, but as hardy looking as a Clydesdale. Her face was cherub-like, cheeks high and full, and her shoulder-length hair was a faded brown with streaks of gray running through it. She wore no makeup, and her eyes, the color of faded blue jeans, drooped in a lazy, half-closed position.

"I'm looking for Wade Hagebak?"

With her head, the box, and one finger, the woman pointed to the machine shed where Wade was working.

"Thanks," Brynn replied, " ... Mrs. Hagebak?"

"Yup. What's this about?"

"Oh, not much. Just wanted to ask him about a friend of mine." She was getting really tired of rehashing all of this, and she doubted Wade's wife would know anything.

"Who is—" she asked.

"Lanea Covey."

"Ah," she said as if she didn't care in the first place. "He's right over there. Gotta get these chicks to the brooder house."

Brynn walked down the muddy driveway to the machine shed where Wade worked on a windrower.

"Wade?"

"Yup," he said as he wiped his hands on his jeans and waited for Brynn to reach him. Wade was not a big guy. In fact, he looked small, short, and wimpy, although his arms were lean and veiny. His hair was cut short and thinning on top, but Brynn suspected he was younger than his wife. He put his hands on his narrow hips. His jeans hung low, revealing the dingy band of his underwear.

"Hi. I'm Brynn Young. Jackson's wife?"

"Yeah. Hi."

"Looks like you got more rain than we did. Jackson's out planting today." Brynn tried to avoid launching into a line of questioning that, in the past, hadn't worked out the greatest.

"Yeah, we got a couple inches ... " Wade responded, now looking more wary than friendly.

Way to warm him up, Brynn ...

"What's this about?" Wade asked.

"Oh. Yeah. I wanted to ask you about something. I don't know if you know what happened to me, but I was hoping I could find out more about my own case, you know ... try to piece together what happened ... "

"I heard about that. I'm sorry," he interjected.

"Thanks. Uh ... I'm thinking, and the police are, too, that it might be related to Lanea Covey's case. So I wanted to ask you if there was anything you could tell me about that time." Brynn squinted into the sun, wishing she'd brought her sunglasses so she could bravely hide behind them.

"I told the police back then that I didn't know anything that could help them. What did they tell you?"

"They told me very little because I'm not immediate family. I talked to Bertis, Marshall, and Ryker. I know you worked—work—for Bertis. I was just wondering if you remembered anything that might have happened shortly before she went missing. Did anything happen that sticks out in your memory?"

"Like what?"

"Anything. Like were there any strangers around, any unfamiliar vehicles going by, anything happen that was unusual or weird … " Brynn hoped the last part of her question didn't sound too loaded.

"No, I don't recall any strangers around, but I don't normally look for stuff like that, and it has been sixteen years."

Brynn knew that she would have to be more specific if she wanted to jog his memory.

"I heard that Ryker Otten worked with you on occasion. Is that right?"

"Yeah, I hired him now and then for Bert. Why?"

"Did he work with you at Bertis' right before Lanea went missing?" Brynn asked.

"Yeah, we filled the hay loft the week before she disappeared, if I remember right," Wade said.

There it was again. The inconsistencies in the time line. Unless Bertis is confused about when they filled the loft, Ryker came back after that and Bertis saw him. Ryker lied to her.

"The week before? I heard it was a couple days." Brynn was getting excited, and it had nothing to do with Wade's puny physique.

"Who said that?" Wade, apparently becoming bored with the conversation, picked up a socket wrench and started working on the windrower again.

"Bertis. Do you know if he saw Ryker there after you guys filled the hay loft?"

"Must've. We were there the week before, but if Bert said Ryker was there a couple days before, then he probably was."

Brynn felt like someone had hooked a tractor chain to her chassis and pulled her from the mud. Progress, forward momentum, even an inch felt like enough headway to gain traction and drive onward in this search for her friend. The outlook was bleak for Lanea's safe return, and after sixteen years, Brynn held little hope for that, but she felt closer than ever to a revelation. She searched her mental notebook for another productive question.

Fumbling for words, avenues to take this lead, Brynn stuffed her hands into her back pockets as if she might find some there. If only she'd thought to bring a notebook and pen.

Just then, an older model pickup pulled up near the door of the metal shed and a young man climbed out as the dogs ran to greet him in a merry reunion. Dressed in jeans, t-shirt, and tennis shoes, the teenager looked to be of high school age. He playfully roughed up the dogs then walked over to where Wade and Brynn were standing.

"Brynn, this is Collin, our son," Wade said, then to Collin, "This is Brynn Young. She lives north of here."

"Hey," said Collin.

"Hey." Brynn spoke high school as well.

Collin and Wade had a brief dialogue about what chores needed to be done as Brynn waited. Unless Collin had the manners and hygiene of an ogre, which he didn't appear to, he had to be one of the most sought after young men in his school. He had the smooth complexion of youth, and the chiseled features of maturity. He stood at least six inches taller than his father, with dark hair and striking eyes. Brynn felt slightly embarrassed at her fascination with him. She'd seen it before and it never ceased to amaze her: Nature found a way, somehow, to draw from deep within the DNA of two unappealing people the most hidden, infinitesimal, beautiful qualities they possess and create from that a creature so stunning, even God would be astounded.

Brynn was snapped back to the present when Wade's wife walked into the shed and interrupted the men in their discussion.

"Collin, as soon as you get changed, the cows will need bedding in the yard, after all this rain. Check to see if there are any new calves, and tag any that aren't tagged. And your dad's busy, so you can give the cattle silage tonight."

"'Kay," said Collin, seeming to understand the hierarchy in the family. Brynn felt a little jealous of the authority this woman wielded, albeit a tad emasculating.

"Do you have homework?" she asked him, and he nodded. "Okay. You can do that after supper."

They stood around for a moment, staring at one another as if Brynn's presence was an insulator that disrupted the flow of current needed to spark some movement.

"Let's go!" Mrs. Hagebak clapped her hands.

Collin went into the house, Wade went back to repairing the windrower, and his wife smiled at Brynn self-consciously, her apple cheeks glowing. She probably wore the proverbial farm pants in the family, but Brynn saw this often as well. Strong farm women were not a rarity. More often than not, it was a necessity, and Brynn realized then, with a small measure of pride, that she herself was one.

The arrival of Collin was a reminder that school was letting out and Ellie would be home within the hour.

Brynn glanced at Wade who was thoroughly absorbed in his work, if not hiding in it, then back at his wife. She wasn't leaving.

"So, Wade, is there anything else that you can think of that might help me?" Brynn was tired of waiting.

"Naw, that's all I know. Ryker might've come back after we filled the loft. But I don't know anything about Lanea or what happened to her."

"All right. Maybe I'll talk to Bertis again, see if he remembers anything more. I was by his old place taking pictures and he stopped by. He and I both would benefit from some ... closure." *Closure. I hate that word.*

"Yeah, he mentioned that. Be careful, there. He's pretty leery of anyone going on the place." Wade was politely reminding her of his duty as Bertis' watchdog.

"Right, right. I was taking them from the road. No worries." Brynn didn't think there were any more memories to be seen there anyway. "Well, thanks."

"Good luck with your case," Wade said as Brynn walked back to her car.

"Thanks," she repeated.

As she turned to wave goodbye, she saw Wade and his wife deep in animated discussion, both of their mouths moving at once. She, probably telling him what needed to be done, and he, probably repeating the requisite words, "Yes, Dear. Yes, Dear."

At four a.m., Brynn was completely out of sleep. The warm, heavy, lazy pull of slumber was gone and her mind told her body to get up and do something. Her eyes, unable to remain closed, stared at the ceiling as clues, theories, and possibilities hovered in the darkness, hiding and taunting her.

So many details to remember and connect. Why wouldn't Lanea take her own Bible when she was packing to run away? Exactly what day did Lanea break up with Marshall and when did she disappear? She had nothing more than conflicting stories of Ryker's last visit, and none of that was proof of anything. It's possible the police followed up on all that anyway. The journal was the only evidence she knew of that the police didn't, but that was likely long gone. This whole saga was like a dog chasing its tail.

Brynn shifted in bed, but the bothersome pressure wasn't on her behind or her back or her hips. It was on her mind, and no amount of tossing and turning was going to cure that. The pea under the mattress was her own case.

If she believed half of what she was telling everyone else, that the cases may be related, then she had to pursue the truths in her own abduction and attack. Having no memory of any of it had been convenient until now. It's easy to live with something that takes up no space in your vault. No need to push it aside to get at something you wish to retrieve, no need to look at it, examine it, dissect it, or use it. Help was unwarranted in trying to ignore it, hide it, or lock it away. Other than the dust left behind by the viewing of her files, it wasn't there. It probably never would be.

There was a key, however. A key to the empty vault that, upon turning of it, would flood it with answers, fill it with undeniable realities, and threaten to bury her in an ugliness that she was unsure she could endure. The idea prickled at Brynn's subconscious since seeing her file—the photos, the notations and speculations. For the first time since entering Bertis' house, she understood, if only dimly, his need to hoard. Those things filled the empty space where everything he held dear once lived. It was like he was trying to push out pain by replacing it with treasures of another kind, any kind.

Brynn knew she had to go to the house where she was held. It was Wednesday, and school would be out early on Friday afternoon. That left two and a half days to work unencumbered with children and babysitters. Two and a half days to get up the nerve to witness her own attack.

She got up, dressed, and made coffee. Seemed the right thing to do. It was her grandmother's response to everything distressing. Neighbor died of a heart attack, make coffee. Cow got hit by lightning, make coffee. Mail came late, make coffee. How a stimulant miraculously calmed the nerves was another mystery for another time, but for the moment, she would imbibe, and think.

Brynn thought, and along with that, she folded laundry, polished the granite in the kitchen, dusted, and unloaded the dishwasher. She was sorting socks when Jackson shuffled into the kitchen around 6 a.m.

"You're up early. You okay?" he asked, wiping the last cobwebs of sleep from his face.

"Just a bit of a headache." Brynn wasn't in the mood for deep conversation, but neither did she feel like being alone. Jackson's presence offered a wonderful distraction from her plaguing thoughts.

Having just dressed, Jackson had not yet combed his hair and it stood up like spikes and horns. Brynn smiled in spite of herself. He was the most handsome thing, even with stubble on his face, wrinkled hair, and puffy morning eyes.

"Where are you planting today?" The light talk felt as soothing as a warm bath.

"Hebner's. What are you doing today?"

"I don't know. Buddy driving you nuts yet?" Brynn knew Jack Jr's tendency to talk a lot, and the inside of that tractor cab had to feel pretty confined at times, even if it had only been two days so far that week.

"Oh, he's pretty good. Want to ride with for a bit today? We'll be done planting by Saturday or Monday. Now's your chance." He smiled, flirting.

"Smooth talker. Planting, rides in the tractor ... what's next? You gonna show me your silo?" They chuckled. "Sounds like fun. I better get Ellie up."

"I'll start breakfast. Say, should we tear into that bathroom next week? It's been on your list for a year now. You could run to town this week sometime and look for fixtures, if you want."

"Sure," she said, and went upstairs to wake Ellie for school.

After breakfast was finished and Ellie had gotten on the bus, Brynn cleaned up the kitchen while Jackson finished his coffee at the table.

Brynn draped the rag on the edge of the sink and turned to her husband. "Jackson, where is the house where I was held ... after ... when I was attacked?"

Jackson swallowed hard, startled by Brynn's abrupt question. He set down his cup.

"Where's this coming from?"

"I want to know."

"Why? Is this what all the secrecy and distance has been about?"

"Part of it. I know you know where it is."

"I do. But there's no reason for you to go there." Brynn could see the look of concern in his eyes. She hoped he could see the look of determination in hers.

"Tell me. Please." She blinked slowly, already feeling the short night and the long day ahead.

"You don't need—"

"J." She leaned against the counter, prepared to wait out the day, if necessary. "I need to know."

Jackson stared at her for a moment. "I can't."

"Sure you can."

"Okay, then. I won't."

"Why?"

"Brynn, there's nothing to be gained from that."

Brynn turned away from him, grabbed the rag, and wiped out the sink. "There is and that's what you're afraid of."

"Maybe. You should be, too." Jackson picked up his cup and took a last sip of his coffee before turning to leave.

"It's like it didn't happen ... " she murmured.

The cup slammed on the table. "What? Did you say it didn't happen?" Jackson moved close to Brynn, but she continued to wipe the sink. His voice was low, but intense. "You tell that to your kids who were without a mother for several weeks. Tell that to your own mother who practically lived here from the moment you disappeared until you were able to take care of yourself. Or your brother who wanted to find someone and kill them with his own hands! But don't you *ever*—"

She turned to him. "I meant it feels like it didn't happen. I want to feel *something*, Jackson. Fear, rage, something that feels real, even if I shouldn't. Even if you don't want me to."

They glared at each other. Jackson's breathing was heavy, quivering.

"No." Jackson shook his head, his jaw set and twitching.

This was a standoff that she wasn't going to win.

Brynn went to him and wrapped her arms around his waist. After a moment, his arms pulled her close.

"I'm sorry," she said.

"We can go there sometime together. When we're ready. Please try to under—"

"I'll bring lunch out later. You gonna get Buddy up and take him with you?"

"Sure." Jackson kissed the top of her head as she pulled away and went to the bedroom to change.

After Jackson left with Buddy, Brynn drove to town. Chores could wait for an hour.

Brynn settled into a chair across from Sheriff Raske as he opened her folder.

He paused. "Coff—"

"No." She heard the curtness in her answer, but was past the point of caring.

"So ... change your mind? Remember something?" He slid the picture of the house across the desk.

"Just curious," she mumbled as she studied the picture. She felt his gaze upon her; it wasn't altogether good. "So where is this place?"

"Why?"

Brynn tipped her head to the side and looked up at Raske. This was getting old.

"I can take you there, if you like. It's abandoned, maybe not safe. Who knows what's in there."

Brynn steadied her breathing, but could feel her pulse throbbing in her head. She waited.

"On Archer Road. Across the interstate from you, then 4 miles south of the corner of Archer Road and 320th ... "

"Fondue Corner ... "

"What?"

Brynn smiled faintly. "Jackson and I call it Fondue Corner. After that cheese truck flipped and burned ... stained the road ... " A tiny twinge of guilt struck her at the thought of Jackson. She rose from her chair, threw the photo down onto the desk and headed for the door.

"If you remember anything, Brynn, you let me know. Best not go in. That'd be trespassing."

Brynn pretended not to hear.

After chores, Brynn showered and changed, taking her time and drying her hair, even curling it. She dressed in a pale blue striped, brushed cotton blouse and her favorite faded, ripped jeans, and her scuffed boots—also her favorite. She applied a touch of mascara and lip color, dabbed some Clinique Happy cologne on her wrists and neck—maybe it would soak into her soul—and made a dinner to take to the field.

She arrived at the field just before noon. Jackson, smiling, stopped the tractor near the car, and opened the door for his second passenger and the heaving lunch tote. Buddy excitedly explained to his mother every function of every gadget inside the tractor. They rode to the other end of the field where the pickup sat loaded with seed, and they all sat on the tailgate of the ten-year-old Ford and ate dinner in the spring sun.

The house would be there. Brynn wanted to enjoy the emptiness of ignorance and denial just one more day. She felt as if it was her last day to be normal.

Another short, restless night plagued her, and Brynn did her best to hide her anxiety, lying still and not getting up until Jackson awoke. After chores and everyone was gone for the day, Brynn prepared for her trip to the house. She made toast, but left it on the plate. The cup of coffee sat untouched. Getting dressed and making mental notes stretched the limits of her abilities that morning.

Should I take the dog? Should I take a notebook and pen to take notes? A camera would be handy, if only it could see the things I see. That would be a nifty invention: a camera that records the past, not just the present.

What does one wear to witness an attack?

All of her thoughts and questions whittled down to one sharp, pointy spear—a fear that jabbed at her heart.

What if it's someone I know?

Chills ran down Brynn's leg, the right one, and only the right one, as chills always did for her.

Lanea deserves to be found. The cases might be related. God help me if it's someone I know.

Or love.

Brynn took the dog, and left the pen and notebook at home. Equipped with her camera and phone, she drove to the house and parked on the sparsely graveled driveway. Sitting in her car, Brynn said a prayer. She couldn't—wouldn't—name her concerns. God knew them. She prayed for strength, which she knew meant trials, and she prayed for wisdom, which she knew meant lessons. A small part of her prayed that she wouldn't need either. Perhaps the house would reveal nothing, and she could leave here serenely ignorant and blessedly happy, and go order parts for her bathroom.

She left the camera and her phone on the front seat. She leashed the dog, then got out of the car with her and locked it, stuffing the keys deep into her front jeans pocket.

The house.

She stared at it. This is where it had happened. Apparently. The one from the photo in the sheriff's file. She waited, hoping for something.

Nothing. Not a whisper of past sounds, not the faintest prickle of past pains, not even the slightest inkling of her own recognition of the place came to her. Other than what Brynn thought to be the expected eerie feeling of standing at a crime scene, there was nothing.

Brynn clutched Bingo's leash as she slowly walked to the porch of the house. She watched the front door. The place reminded her of the children's movie, *Monster House*. The house seemed to wait for her to enter, itching to swallow her up and spit back the car keys.

She ascended the wide wooden steps carefully. Bingo pulled her ahead, her large, hard claws scraping hollowly on the wood. They moved toward the open front door, and Brynn peered in. At one time, this was a gorgeous home. Solid wood doors and trim, nine foot ceilings, mullioned windows, and open staircase. Now it was a house of ghosts and garbage, a house that Bingo alone was anxious to inspect.

"Knock it off!" Brynn barked at the dog. Not the right command, didn't sound anything like "heel" but just came out that way and whether the proper command or not, it released some of the tension in Brynn. And the leash as well—Bingo knew the inflection, therefore the meaning, and did as she was told.

Brynn took a deep breath and stepped over the threshold with the dog.

Brynn took in the atmosphere as she walked around the perimeter of the living room. Rain-stained floors and walls and broken windows replaced the once beautiful room. Leaves blown in through years of wayward winds, and grass and feathers from interloping birds and their nests littered the dirty hardwood floors. A dirty, sagging mattress lay in the center of the room, pieces of its covering cut neatly away. She glared at the mattress, vaguely noticing discarded alcohol cans and bottles and fast food wrappers, and animal droppings in her peripheral vision.

Before her eyes could finish scanning the room, visions, like a dark cloud, a swirling, shifting murmuration, fluttered and flowed throughout the room. They descended upon Brynn with a darkness so bleak that it threatened to consume her.

Slow down ... slow down ...

Brynn fought to control the rush of images and memories that enveloped her like a tornado. She grasped at individual scenes, focusing all of her attention and effort on one attempting to slow the pace of the memories. As they decelerated, the visions of separate events began to take form in front of her. The potential to control this gift of hers, if even in a limited scope, lifted her spirits. Slightly. But that capability also scared her to death.

Individual scenes began as a shadow on the wall, a flicker of movement in the corner of her eye, but then began to assault her mind like a horror movie inside her head. What happened first was not yet clear. In one scene, her other self was here alone, and in another, she was being dragged through the room by her hair, but in every scene, she herself seemed to be the token victim of that horror film, destined for gratuitous slaughter, with no hope of survival.

Brynn stood motionless, afraid any movement she made would alter the outcome, although she knew that she was watching history, memories that were untouched, unchanged by exaggerations, embellishments, or emotions. This house seemed like a terrified child who told his nightmare in one breathless sentence—it came fast and furious like an explosion, and deciphering the chain of events was secondary to listening patiently and trying to understand. The story, violent, frightening, and heinous.

A tsunami of memories now flooded her mind, her vision, and this room, and kept coming and coming, drowning her in vivid details. She had turned the key.

It played as if she were the camera, catching every detail, every movement in fast, real, and slow motion all at the same time. Her eyes flitted around the room as the waves hit her, though all of the scenes she witnessed were only in her mind's eye. Her breath hung in her throat, in her chest, in the air, and all life and time outside this room was suspended while her own drama was performed in front of her, as if for her approval.

She saw herself. Not like a mirror image, not like a shadow or nebulous figure. It was her. Her other self. This Brynn saw herself as if through an out-of-body experience. That Brynn was feet away from her. The memory was as clear as if she herself were standing here seeing the events in real life, real time.

The other Brynn entered the room, half walking, half dragged. Blood oozed from her nose and mouth, dripping slow and thick from her chin. Her eyes, watery and red, wide with the fear she'd seen in animals that were startled and panicked. *What causes that? Is it nature's response to fear that makes us all open our eyes wider to see all of our options, maybe a way out?* She wondered if the other Brynn was searching for options. Brynn saw her arms tied behind her, her tank top and shorts dirty and speckled with her blood. Her dark hair, a matted tangle of mud, dirt and leaves, stuck in strands to the crusted blood on her face and neck. The struggle had obviously not started here.

Only one of her running shoes remained, and her feet were caked with mud. Even rabbits scream in moments of sheer terror and pain, but the other Brynn didn't so much as open her mouth. Without remembering any of it, the real Brynn understood why.

Don't scream ... Don't fight back ... .

She knew the importance of not flicking the taut string that kept her assailant tethered to just-this-side-of-sanity. She felt an odd kinship with her other self, like she was quietly rooting for her, here for her support and guidance.

But in reality, she was just an audience, an ineffectual observer—a mere bystander witnessing a crime, unmoved and detached, waiting for the sick entertainment to be over so she could go back to whatever she was doing. Nothing she could say or do would change what was about to happen.

The man in control of the other Brynn had one hand hanging loosely, casually at his side, the other hand embedded in a tight grasp of Brynn's hair, shoving and twisting and turning as he steered her toward the mattress. He could have been taking out the trash—as if dragging a woman by her hair was commonplace for him. With a final, violent thrust, he pushed her to the mattress and she landed face-first in the stained and filthy ticking.

Nothing about him said abductor, rapist, or psychopath. The man was so *average* in build, height, and appearance. He looked somewhat familiar, but his mediocre appearance likely made him familiar: young—early to mid-twenties—5'10, perhaps 180 pounds, with thick, groomed, light brown hair.

His eyes, though, were mesmerizing. To think anything positive about a monster seemed wrong, but she found his eyes beautiful—a light, ethereal blue-gray, outlined by the long, thick eyelashes. What he did with those eyes, however, made them evil. He lusted with them, searched Brynn's body with them. She could see it, feel it. His plan shown in them. The other Brynn lay on the mattress, too much in shock to muster the level of fear that he craved. Anger grew, his eyes narrowing to slits, as he fed off his rage, working it into his demented plan to break her.

That Brynn endured physical assault as This Brynn suffered the visions of her own attack. The house was unrelenting, seemingly hurling the visions at her in no particular sequence as if to be free of them.

The visions came in flashes and clips so intense Brynn felt as though she were being burned.

The man undressed, not seeming self-conscious, hurried, or nervous in any way. This was part of his excitement, no doubt. That Brynn, though still wide-eyed, didn't move. This Brynn threw her hands up to her face, unable to look. Shifting from one foot to the other, though panic electrified her heart, her nerves pinned her to the floor. The visions playing in her mind, she could do nothing but watch. This Brynn silently wept as the man ripped the clothes from That Brynn and savaged her, the words from the police report flashing in her mind as she witnessed each and every repulsive act.

This Brynn spoke quietly to the unseeing, unhearing memory of Brynn, "Get up! Get up!" as if she herself might be heard through the impenetrable barrier of time.

A sudden, loud hacking startled Brynn. First thinking she was hearing That Brynn choking, she realized that she'd tightened the grip on the dog's leash, reflexively holding her back from the traumatic deeds happening in front of them. Brynn loosened her grip and rubbed the dog's head, thankful for the moral support and bodily warmth.

The assault before her continued, unaffected by the interruption. Brynn was rapt, sickeningly compelled to see it through. She'd seen the man— too young to be a suspect in Lanea's case. But This Brynn felt that to leave now would be an abandonment of herself, an act of cowardice. She owed it to herself to unburden the house and take what was rightfully hers, however horrific.

Through tears, she watched as he defiled her. Boiling anger and revulsion built in her gut, and she suddenly felt something tear loose from her throat.

"Get off her! Leave her alone!" she screamed at him, screamed for herself, as if her other self were indeed someone else, where no greater case of deniability existed. Neither of them heard her. Not a flinch, not a sideways glance, not a glimmer of recognition of her outburst shown in his action. She knew it was a memory she was reacting to, another time she was witnessing. She couldn't make herself real to that time any more than it could be changed by this one. The screaming felt useful—an act of fighting back, and louder than the deafening silence that pretended the ghastly act was noiseless. She screamed and screamed until her throat was seized in a fit of coughs so deep they racked her entire body.

Brynn squeezed her eyes shut against the onslaught of gruesome visions, but it continued to play out in her mind. Leaving the room would be the only way to make it stop.

She opened her eyes. Blow after blow, he continued his attack, biting, pinching, punching, and slapping her, tossing her body about like a rag doll. This Brynn jolted with adrenaline and small but sharp twinges of real pain shooting through her for every strike That Brynn must have felt. The brutality continued until the man reached his sordid satisfaction.

The man got up, brushed the dirt from the mattress off of his sweaty body. He watched That Brynn as he dressed, not as if he expected any fight to rise up in her, but with a sense of accomplishment. That Brynn was broken. Just like he wanted her. She was bruised, bloodied, grotesquely swollen, and almost unrecognizable. It was over. This Brynn wanted to throttle him or dig out his eyeballs with her fingernails. She wanted to pick up a pipe or a two-by-four and club his face until he resembled fresh ground chuck. She wanted to stab him with a long, jagged shard of glass until his rotten guts slopped from his body. Instead she threw up on the floor.

Brynn stepped back to the wall as her body began to shake uncontrollably. She felt chilled to the bone. She sank to her knees and gave into the spasms, as fighting them made them worse. The dog nudged her boxy head under Brynn's arm. The vision remained. Why was she still seeing something so ordinary as a man dressing, smirking to himself—a memory so clearly forgettable?

Then she saw another man enter the room.

"No." The plea—a sob, a sigh, a low, mournful gasp— came from the split, swollen lips of the That Brynn.

Brynn struggled to her feet, trembling and leaning against the wall for support. It had happened again. A noise from the past. Brynn looked at the dog, hoping she had heard it too. The dog simply stared at Brynn, neither alert nor alarmed. Bingo had heard nothing.

How in the world?

Along with the tremors and the shock of hearing herself speak, Brynn was now horrified at the sight of another man. Two men. She couldn't bear to look at him. It didn't matter who he was. It was too much. She couldn't imagine living through this, though she knew she had. Her injured brain wouldn't allow her to remember it, no more than her soul could bear to imagine it.

Two men. There was a reason Brynn didn't watch horror movies. The images it scorched into the brain could never be scrubbed away. This was the revving chain saw poised over someone's head. This was the meat hook dangling from a rafter. Impending evil looked like this, and she could see it all coming. She saw it in their eyes, in their anxious twitching, their excited pacing. She herself wanted to run, but there was no escaping the horror that was about to occur—again, but worse— in her mind, a horror she had lived and refused to remember.

Weeping softly, This Brynn closed her eyes and slid to the floor, allowing the images to be seared into her mind as the men raped and tortured the other Brynn. This Brynn felt as if she were being raped for the first time. Revulsion, rage, humiliation, sadness, helplessness—they heaped upon her until she couldn't move, and she joined That Brynn in the bleak and blessed detachedness that had saved them. The innocence of ignorance was gone.

CHAPTER TWENTY

L ED BY BINGO, BRYNN STUMBLED out the front door onto the porch. She had seen more than she expected inside the house. Even with her eyes closed, the visions had been more frightening than any nightmare skillfully crafted by the most depraved imagination on the bestseller list or film circuit.

Still in the throes of violent shudders, she reached the steps. From the edges of her vision, the glaring world around her began to turn dark. Her legs became flaccid beneath her.

If I can just get to the car ...

The sun was behind her, but her face suddenly felt hot. The sounds of the chirping birds and soughing winds became a muffled hiss, and the air, sauna thick.

The steps in front of her danced and swayed, and Brynn's aching head fought to get a steady fix on them. Then they rushed at her face as if in attack.

Brynn awoke to the sky. And Bingo's worried mug blinking back at her. Brynn was sprawled on her back, legs still on the steps as if the house sought to keep her. Her head throbbed. Placing her hand on the pain, she felt the sticky warmth of blood oozing from her forehead.

"Bingo," she groaned. It could have been a call for help, or sarcastic exclamation of her lack of coordination. It certainly wasn't a pronouncement of a winning card at the old folk's home. She wasn't sure why she said it or what she expected the dog to do, but it felt reassuring. The dog hovered over her, tongue lolling from the side of its mouth.

Getting up, Brynn noticed that the tremors had subsided slightly, but her head was pounding now and her stomach was clenching. She reached the car with the dog prancing nervously as if to hurry her in their escape. The car doors were locked. Had she locked the car doors?

Keys ... keys ...

With trembling hands, she searched her pockets, found the keys, and fought to unlock the door, pushing the alarm button instead. The horn blared and a panicked Brynn dropped the keys and pressed her hands over her ears as the dog howled. She bent over, close to fainting again, and finally pulled her hands from her ears, snatched the keys from the ground, and turned off the alarm. She pressed the remote opener at last. She opened the door, ushered Bingo in, and sat behind the wheel. Her breath came in shudders and gasps. She felt the tickle of blood dripping down her face.

Brynn fumbled in the console and glove box, found a wad of fast food napkins, and pressed them against the gash in her head. She had to get home. Shower. Throw up. Shower.

After a few tries, Brynn got the keys in the ignition, started the car, made a wide circle, and began to drive out of the driveway. At the edge of the road, she jerked the car to a stop, flung the door open and vomited on the gravel—a final parting gift to the house.

"Daddy?" It was Ellie. Jackson pressed the phone hard to his ear, straining to hear his daughter's timid, quivering voice over the noise of the instruments, the tractor motor, and Buddy's constant chatter.

"Yeah, hun. What's up?"

"Can you come home?" She sounded small and distant.

"Well, honey, I'm right in the middle of planting a field. I'll be home for supper, though. What do you need?"

"Something's wrong with Mommy," she said and started to cry.

Jackson pulled the tractor to a stop. "What?" His heart kicked like a rabbit.

"I'm scared."

"What's wrong, Ellie? Where's Mommy?" The mature calmness belied what he felt, but he didn't to shout and scare her any further. Buddy stopped the conversation between his friends, Buzz Lightyear and Woody, and looked at his father.

"She's in the shower. But she sounds funny. I think she's crying or sick or something. Can you come home?"

"I'll be right there. Are you okay?" Jackson felt the panic rising in his chest.

"Yeah, but I don't know what to do. She won't talk to me," she said, sniffing loudly.

"Is the door locked?"

"I don't know. You told us ... " she said.

"I know what we told you about knocking, but see if it's locked. You don't have to go in."

The pause lasted no more than a few seconds, but translated to hours on Jackson's end of the line.

"It's locked."

A chilling thought suddenly occurred to Jackson.

"Did you see anyone there? When you got home, did it look like anyone had been there?"

"No. Are you coming home?"

"I'm coming right now. Keep the phone with you, okay? And stay by the bathroom door in case Mommy needs you." Jackson prayed that Brynn would not need Ellie. And that she would.

"I'm scared." Ellie was crying again.

Jackson's heart felt as if it had been ripped open with a scythe. "Don't worry, Baby, I'm calling your grandma right now." He hung up. He had every intention of calling

Adelle, but it would have to wait until after he called Wes. If someone had been—or God help them, was still—in the house, Adelle would be walking into a trap. Jackson hung up and called Wes, though planting in a field that was near his own home, was still too far away, but closer than Jackson was. He gave the details to Wes, asking him to get there as soon as he could, and hung up. Then he called Adelle.

Jackson lifted the planter and sped, as fast as a three-ton tractor could go, back to his pickup.

With Buddy strapped into his seat in the back of the pickup, Jackson cut across the neatly spaced furrows, driving straight toward the entrance to the field, bouncing and jostling, the seed bags in the bed of the truck sliding off their tidy stacks.

Reasons, explanations, possibilities raced through Jackson's mind. It might have something to do with her abduction and attack. The doctors had warned him that there was a risk of seizures after head trauma. Had she had a seizure in the shower?

It might have something to do with her abduction and attack …

What if the man or men responsible had heard of her interest in finding out more about her case, and had come back?

Ice-cold terror and the heat of rage blended and hardened into stony determination. He would find them, eviscerate them, and feed the entrails to the pigs. He'd seen it in a movie, and thought it particularly grizzly at the time, but now …

Jackson hunched over the steering wheel, leaning forward in his seat as if that would get him there faster, driving as fast as he could without endangering his son's life. Buddy sat in his car seat, clutching his companions, his wide, bright eyes looking at Jackson in the rearview mirror.

"It's okay, Bud. Mommy's not feeling very well. We need to get home."

Gravel sprayed as Jackson skidded to a halt in front of the house. Wes' pickup was already parked in front, with Adelle in the front seat clutching the dashboard, looking as scared as Buddy.

Jackson jumped out of the pickup and, running toward the house, glanced at Adelle and pointed at Buddy in his pickup. She got out, went to Jackson's pickup, took Buddy from his seat and held him.

Wes stood outside the bathroom door holding Ellie in his arms when Jackson came in. Ellie's face was wet and red, and her weeping had subsided to the head-jerking spasms that come after a really good cry.

"Did you check the house?" Jackson asked Wes, taking Ellie from him and smoothing her damp curls away from her face.

"Yeah, briefly. I didn't see anyone or anything out of place." Wes didn't look much better than Ellie.

"Mommy's going to be fine, El. Promise." It was a stupid thing to say. He didn't know anything, and his promise was as hollow as a drum. Jackson gave Ellie a hug, kissed her, then pulled her loose and handed her back to Wes. He knocked on the bathroom door and checked the knob. Still locked.

"Brynn? Honey, open the door," Jackson pleaded. He could hear the water running in the shower, and the faint echo of a sob.

He didn't know what was wrong, but standing outside the door wasn't improving the situation. Jackson felt around the top of the door molding and found the emergency key. The children were not allowed to lock the door, which meant it happened a lot. The small, metal T-shaped pin had not felt like an actual lifesaver until today.

Jackson popped the lock, and slowly opened the door.

The lights were off, and the closed blinds blocked out most of the daylight. Through the faint light, Jackson saw Brynn's clothes scattered around the room. Both the seat and cover of the toilet were open, and ribbons of toilet tissue dangled from the holder and the edge of the toilet.

He found Brynn huddled in the darkest corner of the shower with her knees pulled up to her small body. He felt the water, still spraying down on her, and it had long lost its warmth, now as cold as a November rain. Reaching into the shower, he groped until he found the handle and turned it off. He could hear Brynn's shuddering breaths between the intermittent sobs.

"Brynn? Brynn. I'm going to turn on the light." Jackson turned for the light switch, and heard her voice.

"No! No ... "

"Honey, we have to get you out of there," he said softly.

He flipped the light switch to on and saw Brynn clearly.

Her body looked shrunken in its pose, arms and legs pulled in and crossed over each other in a fetal, protective wrap. Her head rested on her knees, her face buried, and her dark, wet hair, a tattered, veiling shroud. Jackson looked to the back of the bathroom door for her robe. Not there. He went to the closet and grabbed an armful of towels, then poked his head out the door.

"Wes, have Mom come in and watch the kids, and throw a blanket in the dryer." Wes quickly moved to carry out the order as Jackson returned to his wife. And

He knelt down in the shower in front of Brynn, "Brynny, here. Let's get you wrapped up. Honey?" He lifted her face to his.

Feeling hot tears spring to his eyes, he blinked, blinked, trying to take in what he was seeing. Brynn's eyes were puffy and red, her cheekbone scraped raw, and from her forehead a jagged cut trickled rivulets of watery blood down her face.

Jackson cleared his throat, hoping his emotion, his anger and fear and helplessness, wouldn't be detected in his words. "Who did this to you? *Who?*" His quavering voice cracked on the last word.

"I fell. I'm not feeling very well ... I fell."

"*Fell?*" The word didn't compute. They could talk later. Right now, he needed to get her warm. Jackson draped the towels over her and lifted her from the floor of the shower.

Had she lost weight? What's going on!

He held her close to him, wishing he could warm her, heal her, cleave her to himself where she would be safe forever.

As he neared the door, he heard Brynn's urgent raspy whisper, "The kids ... "

"They're okay. Mom's got them. Let's get you to bed."

Wes awaited the signal to fetch the blanket from the hot dryer, and Jackson gave it to him when he left the bathroom. Adelle and the children were out of sight when Jackson carried Brynn to their room and laid her gently on their bed. Wes, ready with the warm blanket, saw Brynn, and his big-brother-heart broke, sending a rush of tears to his eyes. Wes stood by the bedside, uncertainty gluing him to the floor.

"Can I do anything? What can I do?" Wes rubbed his head in frustration.

"Just help Mom with the kids and I'll be out in a second," Jackson said softly.

Jackson wrapped the warm, fuzzy blanket around Brynn, pulling the covers from the bed over her as well. Erratic waves of tremors gripped her. Her eyes fought to remain open.

"We should get you to the hospital, Brynn."

"No!" she yelled. Her forcefulness surprised him.

"You could have a concussion. How did you fall? Did you faint? What happened?" He peppered her with questions, but he couldn't stop his mouth from saying what his mind was screaming.

"I felt sick, then I fell. That's all. Just a ... stomach thing ... " She closed her eyes.

Jackson left the room and quietly pulled the door shut behind him. He ran both hands through his hair as Wes greeted him with the same questions he'd had for Brynn.

"I don't know what happened. She said she fell. She felt sick and fell. I should have been here!"

"You can't be here twenty-four-seven, Jack. Do you think something happened? Do we need to call the police or a doctor?"

"She seems to be okay, just some cuts and scrapes, and she looks pretty chilled, but I don't understand what's going on with her. She's been kind of quiet and distant lately … .and she's been crying." He shook his head. "It's too soon! She shouldn't have been out on her own!" He rubbed a hand over his face, stopping on his mouth and squelching his tirade. "I shouldn't have let her quit therapy," he said, more to himself.

Adelle came into the hall where the men huddled outside Brynn's door. "The kids are watching a movie in Ellie's room. They're fine. What happened?" she whispered.

Wes repeated Jackson's details.

Adelle didn't wait for permission. She entered her daughter's room and went to her bedside. Jackson sent Wes to get the first aid kit and followed Adelle into the bedroom.

"Binny?" said Adelle, putting her hand on Brynn's forehead.

"Mom?" Brynn said quietly, her eyes still closed.

"Yes, honey. What do you need?" Adelle answered hopefully.

"Don't call me that … " she whispered, and rolled over to face the wall.

Adelle's brief laugh was a quick breath that came out her nose. A feeble smile touched her lips, but faded when Brynn turned away.

Wes came in with first aid supplies and handed them to Jackson, who sat next to Brynn on the bed. "I'm going to make some soup. You need to sit up and eat something, get warmed up … "

"I'm not hungry," she said to the wall.

"Well, you can sit up and eat something or I can have your mother feed you."

Adelle's face lit up, and she looked as though Jackson had just handed her the keys to a brand new grandbaby.

Brynn rolled onto her back and stared at the ceiling, new, huge tears welling up in her eyes.

"Please," she said, "Can I just be alone?"

Jackson tried to keep the frustration from his voice. "Brynn, you just gave us all a scare. What's going on?"

"I just … " Brynn shook her head.

"What?"

"I just don't feel well. Nothing more than that."

He dabbed the cut with an alcohol prep and applied a square bandage to her head. "Fine. I'll be back with some soup and you can eat it if you feel like it."

He went to the door and watched as Adelle tried to get through to Brynn. Adelle sat on the edge of the bed in his place. "Honey, he just wants to help. We all do."

"I'm really tired, Mom. Okay?" Brynn pulled the blankets up to her chin and rolled over again.

Jackson knew Brynn was done talking. Adelle must have known, too. She met Jackson and Wes in the hall and they went to the kitchen.

"She's been acting weird lately. Then yesterday she asked where the house was. The house where she was held. Maybe she ... went there, maybe she remembered something." Jackson said, unable to look Wes or Adelle in the face. "I wouldn't tell her where it was. She must've gotten the information from the sheriff. If I had just told her, I could have gone with her. Do you think she went there?"

"Maybe, but what would that do? With 'head trauma,' they said ... " Wes tried to relieve some of Jackson's guilt.

"I know what they said, Wes. It's unlikely that she would ever remember, but not impossible. We'll just have to wait and see what she tells us," said Jackson.

"Should I stay with her?" Adelle asked.

"No, Mom, I'll stay home. You and Wes can go. We'll be fine. Thanks, though, for coming."

"Why don't I make some coffee? You boys go sit. I'll get some supper started, and bring the coffee in when it's done." Coffee and mothers trumped rhetorical questions and nonsensical answers.

Jackson didn't sit. He went to his office to call Sheriff Raske.

Brynn gazed at the wall, at a spot where there once hung a picture, and the hole where the nail had been had been patched. The smooth spot had never matched the texturing on the wall after that. She would have to try to do a better job at stuff like that. She blinked, wishing she could sleep, but only if it meant a dreamless—or rather, nightmare-less—sleep. She wished the water heater would hurry up and make some more hot water so she could shower again. 18 months of waking, sleeping, working, laughing, eating, living, and not near enough of it had been spent showering. She had 18 months' worth of cleansing to do. All this time, she was fine, not knowing all the details. She hadn't known exactly what had been done to her, what had happened in that house, and the photos she had seen did not give her, or *anyone*, the slightest *hint* of all that had happened to her. The house knew. The *damn house*. Those boys knew. Oh, they knew. And they relished it. All of it.

She didn't know them. Youngsters. College age. *How do boys that age dream up the evil things they did? Who were their parents? What had they seen in their lives to think this was fun or fulfilling?*

Ropes. Lit cigarettes. Knives. Lighters. Tape. Tools. They seemed to have it all. And they knew how to use it all. Things that were innocent, practical, and commonplace held sinister potential for them.

" ... *no* ... " *How was I able to hear that? Of all the haunting sounds that room had heard, of all the sounds I could have heard, I heard that one.*

Brynn recalled her feelings at seeing another man. She remembered the attack and the look on That Brynn's face, imagining the terror she must have felt, and it became glaringly clear why she heard that one word at the appearance of a second assailant. It was the vocalization of utter hopelessness and unimaginable aloneness. It had been the breaking point for That Brynn and the tipping point of her own capability. It was that pivotal moment that caused her to hear the memory.

She was thankful for the mute button in her ability. It was her protection from the unmitigated brutality of the combined effects of the memory, not unlike her tendency to mute the scary parts in her movies. This aspect of her skills, the silencer or muffler of sounds, was too coincidental to ignore. Brynn felt as if, whether God-given or self-administered, it was intentional, perhaps even controllable.

Another thought occurred to Brynn: maybe the gift was indeed that—a way for her to find her assailants. The abandoned house, the way the gift only works in abandoned houses—it was all so terribly convenient. *Nicely played, God. Nicely played. I would have been fine without it.*

Feeling "real" was overrated. She had been completely happy not knowing. They'd been completely happy. But Brynn didn't know how much Jackson knew.

Jackson. What must he be thinking? How could he stand to be with me after that? What does he know? And what would he think if he knew what I know now. I wanted to tell him. I want to. But how can I? I can't. I don't remember it. And if I try to explain how I know only what happened within those walls, he would never believe me. He would nod, ask polite questions, and then go make quiet arrangements for a neurological exam. He wouldn't want to know. Not what "gifts" I have, not what those boys did to me in that house … .

It didn't seem to end, the savagery. They fed off each other's pleasure and sickness.

I don't remember seeing when I'd stopped fighting. I just remembered seeing that any movement at all only spurred them on. Play dead … play dead … I must have heard myself … my other self.

There are things worse than death. Death is merciful in so many ways. Death would have been preferable to the brutality in that house. I know now how easy it would have been to play dead when I would have wished I were. When I would have prayed for it. When I would have welcomed it. When I thought it was an escape, a peace, a way of winning. My conscious mind might refuse to remember, but my memory, the one borrowed from the house, knew. I know that those boys planned on me dying in that house. They tortured me, beat me, kicked me, and when they thought there was no fight, no life remaining in me, they spat on me and left.

My other self was … is … stronger than me. I'm stronger than I want to be.

She was proud of her other self. Pangs of empathy at the loss of the innocence of her other self stung deep, but she felt a burgeoning pride in her ability to find a way to live with the horrors that two sick young men imposed upon her, even if it was her mind's reflexive response—outside of her control. Only an unfortunate few will ever see their other self and witness the resilience of the human spirit within them. Even though This Brynn now bore the images of the cruelties done to her, she was no doubt insulated from the sharp, icy fear and desolation that That Brynn must have felt. And she was grateful for that as well.

How did she … I … have any fight left? How could I live through that? Where is the fight that I had that day that I crawled from the house out onto the road? Where is the fight that kept my heart beating in the hospital when I wasn't awake or even aware I was alive?

Brynn closed her eyes because the nightmares didn't belong to sleep anymore. The nightmares were loosed into the light. They were part of her waking moments, her sleep, her laughter, her work, her eating, her living, and her showering. Real or borrowed, they were now a part of her.

I'll fight tomorrow.

School was out for the summer. Saturday. Until mid-August, every day was Saturday unless it was Sunday. Brynn sat on the porch in her robe, sipping a cup of coffee with extra cream. She'd slept the past two days away, helping to dull the memories, and the morning sun warming her bare toes afforded her a bit of tranquility, normalcy. The cut on her forehead was healing nicely, the scrape on her cheekbone was an angry brown scab that she hoped wouldn't scar, and her eyes were now black and blue with the settling blood from her head wound. Jackson hadn't pressed the subject of what happened, but she could see his lips fighting to hold back the words behind them.

She had to tell him. She knew that. But when? And how? And most importantly, how much?

Brynn finished her coffee and went inside to shower and change. She had to go talk to a friend.

With the children in tow, Brynn entered Perris Manor after dinner and went directly to Cole and Spencer's room. The men were engaged in a meaningful discussion about the practicality of peas in a place where the majority of people struggled with simple sandwiches. Brynn and the children stood in the doorway, hesitant to interrupt. When the men turned, their expressions changed immediately from the misery of menu choices to the pure joy at new faces.

"Brynn!" Cole shouted.

"Kids!" Spencer joined the chorus.

Noticing Brynn's sunglasses, Cole urged her in, and Spencer, employing his 80-some years of experience at reading body language, invited the children to help him with a rather difficult jigsaw puzzle in the lounge.

Brynn took a chair next to Cole's and removed her glasses.

Cole winced at her face. "Oh, dear Lord ... "

"I fell," she said.

"I should say."

She looked up at the wall and noticed her painting hanging above his bed. "That looks nice up there."

Cole looked away from Brynn and glanced up briefly at the painting. "Yes, I get a lot of compliments on it." He turned back to Brynn.

She felt him watching her as she attempted to avoid his gaze.

She knew he wasn't naïve enough to believe that she preferred to go visiting in this condition. He waited until her gaze met his then asked, "How are you?"

Brynn looked down at her hands and toyed with the rings on her fingers. "I'm fine." Her lower lip pulled up hard against her upper lip in an effort to control her emotions. His words and the loving, fatherly look of worry began to melt the stiff resolve she had been carrying in front of others since witnessing her attack.

"Cole, I saw … " She looked at him. "I went to the house where I was held. I saw who … I saw my attack." Brynn's eyes glimmered.

"Who was he? Do you know him?" He spoke softly, as if the words could summon the devil there in person.

Her head jiggled in a negative response and tilted toward her shoulder as if it were too heavy.

"What is it?"

"Them. There were … two." Brynn searched his eyes for any sign of repulsion or horror. She found only pain— pain which mirrored her own. Cole put his trembling hand to his mouth. In a release of grief, she exhaled the fetid air she felt as if she had held for two days, as though she were expelling swarms of wicked creatures hatched from seeds planted by the assailants. She exhaled the truth. She exhaled the burden of knowing, that which could never be unknown again. The breath for which her lungs hungered was waiting, but she couldn't allow it. She forced every molecule of tainted air from her lungs. She tried to purge herself of every ounce of anger and sorrow she contained. And with the last trace of air in her, she cried, *"Why?"*

"Oh, my dear, my dear … " Cole reached out to her with both hands as Brynn collapsed, bending over in her chair, in long, breathless sobs. Her shoulders jerked as she wept, her face buried in her hands. Cole leaned over in his wheel chair and rested his hand on her back.

When her weeping had subsided, Brynn sat up slightly and began to talk to her only confidant.

Without any gory or intimate details, Brynn recounted some of the horrific things that she had endured. She told him she didn't recognize the men and explained how she got hurt. She freed herself from the shackling secrets that she couldn't share with anyone else. She focused on a pattern on the tile floor that resembled a small, abstract heart, and when she finally looked at Cole's face, she saw sadness, but more than that, she saw utter helplessness. His droopy eyes were wet with tears and his head was lolling back and forth in disbelief.

Cole's voice was hoarse. "My God," he said with such conviction that Brynn accepted it as a prayer on her behalf. "Who knows this? Have you told Jackson?"

Brynn leaned back in her chair, stared at the ceiling, and wiped her face on her shirt sleeves. "No. I don't know how."

"Does he love you?"

"Yes." She plucked a tissue from a nearby box and wiped her nose. "Of course."

"Then it doesn't matter how. He'll listen. He'll believe you. You need to tell him."

She nodded. "You're probably right. I just don't want him to … " She couldn't go any further.

"Pack you off to the bughouse?" Cole smiled, though his eyes were still moist.

"Well … yeah." A small grin touched her lips.

"He won't, but if you're worried, you can bring him here and we can tell him together."

The reassurance of a man who was as sound and trustworthy as a national monument calmed her nerves.

Brynn found herself feeling hopeful that Jackson would be as receptive as Cole had been.

"I'll tell him tomorrow, after church. I hope."

"Sounds like an excellent plan. I'm here if you need me," He looked around and smiled broadly. "Always."

"Thank you, Cole." Brynn got up from her chair, went to him, and kissed him on the cheek. He grasped her hands in his and held them for a long moment.

"You take care," he said.

Homemade pizza sounded halfway good. Brynn's appetite was improving, and the kids were always game in helping mess up the kitchen. Jackson had finished planting, with a little help from Wes, and was moving equipment home. A quiet evening at home would be pleasant—movies and popcorn maybe, and later, snuggling in bed until church in the morning. Then the conversation. The details were still a bit fuzzy, however, in that part of the plan.

Brynn started the conversation several times in her head throughout supper. She imagined all of the possible scenarios: disbelief, horror, outright skepticism, laughter, a queer look that turned into passive indifference or sympathy at her apparent lunacy ... None of them included the passionate empathy and acceptance she needed. Brynn decided to go for a run to work out her anxiety.

"The kids are on the porch playing Barbies. Let's hope some of those shoes fall through the cracks," Brynn said to Jackson, who was in the machine shed cleaning up his planting equipment before putting it away.

"My son is playing Barbies?" he asked.

"Don't worry. He's the horse. I'm going for a run, okay?"

"You sure you're feeling up to it? Brynn, we really need—"

"To talk," she interrupted, "and we will. Soon. I'm fine. Popcorn and movie tonight?"

"Sure." Jackson went back to work emptying the seed boxes on the planter. Brynn saw the disappointment and frustration in his expression. Tomorrow would be the day, though, no matter how fuzzy her plan was.

She pushed the headphones into her ears, set her phone's music settings to the "Run!" playlist, and turned up the volume. The evening sun was low in the sky, but she hadn't planned to go far, perhaps only a couple miles. Except for the bugs, it was a perfect night for a run—warm day, cool night, and just a slight breeze, although she would need to remember to breathe through her nose.

Walking briskly out the driveway, Brynn warmed up slowly, then once on the road, began a steady jog in sync with her tunes. The activity felt good. Her songs challenged her to a brisker pace, and she enjoyed the dare. She reached the corner at three quarters of a mile then turned to go north. She had a whole mile to decide if she wanted to go further or not. The weather, the tunes, the tingle in her legs, they all joined together in an energizing triad of autonomy. She felt a strength that had eluded her for the past few days, and felt more determined to foster that feeling by telling Jackson everything. He would understand. He would believe her. And if he didn't, he wasn't the man she thought he was. She would still have the knowledge that she gave him her honesty, and she would still have her gift ... for better or worse.

Probably best not to overdo it the first time out after such a long break. At the half-mile mark, the corner, she would turn around, and by the time she reached home again, that would make three and half miles. Not bad. A pickup drove toward her and she moved over to the edge of the road to allow it to pass.

As the pickup neared her, however, Brynn noticed that it had slowed significantly. She glanced behind her to see if there was traffic keeping him from passing her safely, and moved onto the gravel shoulder. No traffic. She could feel her body tensing up.

The newer model, metallic brown pickup was not one she recognized. She knew the vehicles of her neighbors, and this one was completely out of place. The license plate showed it belonged to the same county, but it was a big county. It could be anyone. Probably someone who was lost, looking for someone to give him directions. She avoided looking him in the eye, glancing quickly. She didn't see the driver well, with the darkly tinted windows, but what she could see through the darkened windshield was a man with a farm cap pulled down low on his brow.

The truck went past her, still moving at a reasonable speed for a paved highway, but too slow for comfort. Brynn braved another glance after it passed. She saw the taillights come on, and the pickup slowed to a crawl. She neared the corner. Another quarter of a mile and she would be there. Brynn wondered if she should turn around and run back toward home, possibly running straight toward the pickup, which had now stopped at the corner behind her, or if she should round the corner onto the gravel going east again, and go past the Kludt farm, and go around the section. Neither of the options appealed to her. It was probably nothing. He'd be gone by the time she got to the corner. He was probably answering a phone call or a text or something.

She removed her headphones and concentrated on staying calm. She kept her pace and faked nonchalance. As she neared the corner, she turned to see if he had gone, but he was still sitting at the corner. She'd have to turn the corner and go around the section. And go past the spooky farm site.

As she reached the corner and turned, she heard a vehicle behind her, and hoped it was someone she knew. No such luck. The brown pickup turned the corner onto the gravel road and, slowing when it reached her, passed her as it had before. Its taillights brightened again a quarter of a mile ahead of her.

Brynn stopped running and took her phone from the armband holder and dialed Jackson. "Jackson? Honey, do you know anyone in a metallic brown Dodge Ram pickup? ... I don't know ... it's just passed me a couple times and I'm a little nervous, that's all. I *am* coming home ... okay ... I will." She hung up and began to run again.

Jogging on gravel now, and seeing the pickup inching along ahead of her, Brynn looked around frantically, trying to weigh her newest options. Empty buildings or trees she could hide in at the farm site stood on her right, or she could turn around and race for home. Nothing but open road remained on the stretch behind her, and nothing to save her if he wanted to stop and snatch her up. *Oh, my God! Could this be happening again?*

The pickup pulled into the driveway to a field ahead of her and stopped. The taillights went off. The pickup waited for her. If she turned around and ran the other way, it would follow her again. This was not her imagination. This was someone stalking her. Perhaps the same man or men who had taken her before. Is this how it had happened the first time? She'd been wearing jogging clothes.

Brynn slowed to a walk, not caring if it looked suspicious or insecure, and kept her eyes on the Dodge.

People know I've been asking around about my case. What if they heard about it? What if they realize I might have remembered something?

Brynn saw the taillights flicker from red to white. He was backing up. *Please let him go the other way ... Please let him go the other way ...*

She stopped in her tracks.

The pickup backed up onto the road, facing her yet again, and started coming toward her. Brynn turned around and began to run, her legs suddenly feeling heavy.

Brynn, desperately scrambling with her phone, called Jackson again, her panic, her cry, and her footsteps jarring her voice. "J, it's coming back. Someone's following me! He's coming back!"

CHAPTER TWENTY-ONE

ACKSON'S PHONE RANG AGAIN ONLY minutes after Brynn's last call. He looked at it, puzzlement and alarm registering simultaneously as he noticed Brynn's number on its face.

"Hey, what's up?" he said, hoping it was a fluke or she'd forgotten something.

"J, it's coming back. Someone's following me! He's coming back!"

Jackson heard her breathless words being knocked out of her by her footsteps, and worse, he heard the panic and fear in her voice. He looked around, frantically searching for his next move.

"What? Who's coming back? Brynn?" He hurried toward the house where his pickup was parked in the driveway.

She didn't answer in words. She answered in her cries, in the sound of footsteps in gravel and the rustle of grass or leaves. Then nothing.

"Brynn!" Jackson stopped, pressed the phone to his ear, waiting for some sound to tell him what to do.

Hurrying while juggling the phone, Jackson hung up and tried to dial her back. It went to voicemail. Time after time, her polite recorded greeting was his only response. *It's entirely possible that she realized she was imagining things and was too embarrassed to answer … . Maybe she dropped her phone and didn't realize it or it broke.*

Maybe she can't answer it.

How would he look for her without alarming the kids? If he took them with to look for her and didn't find her, what would that do to *them? This can't be happening again!*

Jackson reached his pickup and called Adelle and explained that he needed to have her come over and watch the kids for a minute. Right now! He didn't give her any details. He didn't have any to give. He only knew that he was going to go pick up Brynn from her run, bring her home, and they were going to watch a movie and have popcorn, just like they'd planned.

Hopping into his pickup, he shouted to Ellie and Buddy on the porch, "Kids, I'll be right back. You *stay* on the porch. Your grandma is coming over. *Got it?*" They agreed and he jumped into his pickup and started it. He shifted into drive as soon as it caught and fishtailed on the gravel as he roared out the driveway.

He couldn't wait for Adelle. He could be sitting here waiting while some stranger was abducting his wife. Again!

Turning right, the route Brynn most often took, Jackson scanned the road for Brynn, but knew she had to be farther than he could possibly see. He reached the corner where she usually turned around and saw nothing, no one. *Which way ... which way ...* She often went north, but didn't like jogging toward the old Kludt farm. It gave her the willies, especially toward dark. But that was on the other side of the section, around the corner. She might have just gone a different way.

Jackson turned left, going south on the highway, and called Adelle, who'd just pulled in the driveway at home.

He drove slower than he wanted to and faster than he should have, looking left and right into fields and driveways and trees, hoping to see Brynn in her white tank, black leggings, and bright pink runners.

Please, God ...

Jackson took his cap off and ran his hands through his hair in desperation. *"Where are you?"*

Oh my God, he's coming after me! I have to hide!

Her feet carried out the orders her mind shouted, but like a new recruit at boot camp, they floundered in frenzied panic, uncertain what to do first. Brynn weaved back and forth on the road, wanting to get away from the pickup, but wanting just as badly to stay away from the abandoned farm. She finally gave in to the lesser of the two evils and ran through the water in the ditch to reach the dark cover of the thickets and trees surrounding the farm.

Her shoes, now soaked and oozing stagnant water, slipped on the grass coming up out of the ditch. She fell hard on her stomach, then clawed her way up the slope, scrambling to get into the trees. Branches and new saplings whipped her arms and legs, snagging and pulling on her clothing, as if colluding with the abductor. Her white tank top, though now muddy, would show up like a glow stick in the dark cover. She hunkered down close to the ground behind the stump of a broken tree, and pulled her knees up in front of her, using the black color of her leggings as camouflage.

The pickup cruised up slowly, the driver obviously aware she was hiding in the trees. In no time, he'd be searching for her on foot. Brynn held her breath. Even with the rumbling motor, the closed windows, and the heavy brush, he would somehow hear her breathing. She covered her mouth with both hands and pressed them into her knees to guarantee no sound would escape.

It stopped. The Dodge stopped at the side of the road. He was looking for her. Brynn felt the tears squeezing from her closed eyes, and the quivering breaths leaving her nose. *Surely* he would hear her terrified heart slamming against her ribs, or hear the rustle of her shaking. He would find her. And. She couldn't bear to imagine the rest.

A prayer floated through Brynn's thoughts. She reached out, grasped it, clung to it and whispered it, but only in her mind. The pickup finally left. It was near dark, but Brynn couldn't risk that he, whoever he was, was still nearby, waiting for her to emerge.

She stayed there, motionless, until dark. What seemed like hours could have been no more than ten or fifteen minutes. Stiffness had settled in her legs and feet. She slowly stood, taking a few steps toward the edge of the woods yet keeping cover, looking for the Dodge. Her extremities tingled as blood flow returned.

She had to call to Jackson. In the panic, Brynn had lost track of her phone, realizing now she didn't know where it was. She must have dropped it. Didn't matter. She needed to get home.

As she emerged from the trees, she saw headlights. *Hide!*

Brynn ducked down in the brush and waited as a pickup drove by slowly. This one sounded different from the Dodge. Familiar. *It was Jackson!!*

Brynn ran from the woods, waving her arms and shouting as the pickup went by. As she clamored through the flooded ditch and scrambled to get to the edge of the road, she watched the retreating taillights and felt a sick desperation rising up in her.

Then she saw the bright red glow of brake lights. The white backup lights came on and she heard gravel spraying as Jackson slammed it into reverse. He'd seen her.

Crying, she ran toward the pickup as Jackson stopped, got out and ran to her. They collided in an embrace that neither wanted to relinquish.

Brynn saw tears in Jackson's eyes, reflecting the pickup's interior light.

"I'm so sorry, J! I'm sorry, I'm sorry ... " Brynn rambled.

"Sorry for what? It's okay. It's all right ... let's go home." She could feel him trembling when he helped her into the pickup.

They both climbed into the driver's door of the truck and Brynn held Jackson's hand as if she wished they would grow together. As he drove home, Brynn recounted what had happened.

"This pickup followed me, Jackson. It passed me twice and waited for me up the road. Then I turned and ran into the trees, and it ... he ... stopped on the road by where I was hiding and waited. He was looking for me! I lost my phone ... "

"We'll find it or get a new one. You didn't know the pickup?"

"No. I thought they were coming back for me ... " She heard the quiver in her voice as she spoke, and the feelings of helplessness made her angry.

"They, who?"

"The men who abducted me."

"*Men?* What makes you think it was more than one?"

Brynn looked at Jackson, wondering if he knew more than he was letting on, or if this was news to him.

"There were two."

"How do you know?" he asked cautiously as he turned into their driveway.

She swallowed, pausing and recognizing the opportunity before her. "I saw it ... them."

"You *remember?* My God, Brynn. Why didn't you tell someone! Is that what was bothering you the other day?"

Jackson stopped the pickup in front of the house, put it in park, but left it running.

"Yes. No ... yes. I saw what they did to me. There were two of them—young guys. I didn't recognize them. But I didn't remember it. I went to the house and ... saw it." She paused to see his reaction. She could feel the emotion churning in her chest. She didn't want to cry; she wanted to be sane and in control and rational-sounding.

Brynn was glad for the concealing, dim lighting of the dash, and the subdued atmosphere it offered. She saw Jackson's face, and it was the same one she loved and trusted and needed. She saw his love for her in the slight furrow in his brow, in the damp eyes, and in the mouth that was set in the thin line of a grimace.

Jackson waited. When no explanation came to him, he quietly said, "Saw it?"

She nodded. It wasn't Sunday. She still didn't have a plan. But she knew that what she had to share with her husband wasn't fuzzy. It was as clear as her love for him. It was as solemn and honest as the prayer she whispered in the woods. He loved her. She trusted it.

The words tumbled from Brynn's mouth, from the discovery of her ability, and Cole, Lanea, Marshall, Ryker, Bertis, and Wade, to seeing the events in the house where she was held.

His reaction was the same as Cole's: horror, shock, and profound sadness. But something else.

Jackson stroked his eyebrow briefly and looked out the window, avoiding her gaze. They both saw Adelle peeking outside from the living room window.

"J?" Brynn was still holding his hand.

He turned back to her, saying nothing for a moment. Tears streaked his whiskered cheeks. She knew the something else. He didn't have to say it.

"I'm sorry I didn't trust you enough to tell you. I'm sorry I hurt you and lied to you." And with that, Brynn felt the lump growing in her throat and the guilt burning in her eyes.

Jackson leaned over and pulled her close, hugging her tightly. He finally said, "You know ... you can tell me anything. *Anything.* I might not always agree, I might not always like it, but I'll always listen and try to understand. Okay?" He held her for a while, then leaned back and swiped at the wetness on his face.

"Okay."

"You can trust me." He tried to smile. "And I believe you. Not just because I love and trust you. I know about ... the two men. Raske told me, after evidence confirmed it, but I didn't want to tell you. I'm sorry."

Brynn attempted a thin smile through her tears and shook her head quickly. "It's all right."

"We should call the sheriff," Jackson said. Brynn nodded, but hated the idea.

Adelle peeked out the window yet again.

"We better get in there before she dies of curiosity," Jackson said, squeezing Brynn's hand. She took the hint and let it go and they wiped their sweaty palms on their pants.

Sunday was an even better day. No plan to adhere to, no nervous chatter leading up to an awkward conversation, no guilt, no secrets, and no cooking. After church, the Young family went to town for dinner and later to Perris Manor to see Cole and Spencer. Cole and Jackson took an immediate liking to each other. Brynn saw that coming. Maybe she *was* psychic.

On the way home, they stopped to look for Brynn's phone, finding it in the ditch where she'd fallen. Broken beyond repair. Arriving at home, Ellie and Buddy went out to play in the yard with Bingo. Jackson and Brynn grabbed some glasses and a pitcher of lemonade from the refrigerator, and went out onto the porch to enjoy the late May weather. The daylight held a haze, the humidity and heat promising a beautiful thunderstorm. The dwarf Korean lilacs next to the railing, heavy with blooms, carried the intensely sweet fragrance through the veranda.

"An inch of rain would be perfect right now," Jackson said, "with all the crops finally planted. A nice, slow rain would be sweet."

"I know what would be sweet ... " Brynn teased.

"An inch and a half?" Jackson smiled.

"You know that's not what ... " Brynn stopped mid-sentence, staring out toward the road. She set down her glass and slowly got up from her wicker chair as Jackson turned around to see what had stunned her into silence.

A metallic brown Dodge Ram pickup was coming in the driveway.

Brynn and Jackson looked at each other. "Is that the pickup that followed you last night?"

"Yes."

Startled as Brynn was, she knew it was unlikely that someone who was stalking her would dare drive onto their farmyard and try to abduct her in front of her family. It was just as unlikely that he would reveal himself to her family now if he had indeed tried to abduct her the night before.

Jackson shot out of his chair and out of the porch, hollering at the unseen occupant as he stomped down the sidewalk toward the truck that was now stopped in front of the house.

"Hey! Come out of there, you son of a bitch! Who do you think you are, following my wife and chasing her down! Come out of there! Now!"

Brynn looked around the yard; the children were not within earshot. She had never seen Jackson so angry. She was impressed. Flattered, even.

The truck door opened and Ryker stepped out of the cab.

Jackson looked like he might punch Ryker in the throat—or the belt buckle, whatever he could reach. Brynn hurried down the stairs after him.

"What the hell were you doing, stalking my wife? You scared her half to death! Don't you know what she's been through?"

Brynn caught up to him. "Jackson, this is Ryker. Honey, it's okay. Calm down!" she said, finally shouting.

Ryker stood in the open door of his truck, stunned motionless.

Although shaken, Brynn was dying to know what Ryker was doing at her home. For someone who had every conceivable reason to avoid her, avoid the whole subject of Lanea, his showing up at her home was unexpected. Not to mention, contrary to the assumptions she'd made about him.

"I'm sorry … about the other day. I didn't mean to scare you … then. *Or* last night. I came lookin' for your house to come and tell you in person, then I seen you on the road, figured that was you, and wanted to stop and talk. Then I seen you run into the trees, and wondered if you was okay … sorry I scared you." His cheeks flushed. He looked everywhere but in their eyes.

"Okay. I appreciate that. You could have rolled down your window and hollered, you know." Even if she'd known it was him, she would have been frightened.

"I'm sorry," he repeated. "What happened to your face?"

"I fell."

"That happened last night?" Ryker looked alarmed.

"No, a couple days ago. But it's okay now."

"Anyway, I'm sorry," he said again.

"Thank you," she said. Now what? He seemed hesitant to leave. She invited him to stay. "Would you like some lemonade?"

Jackson looked at her in disbelief. Brynn smiled at him.

"Sure," Ryker shut the door to his pickup.

On the porch, Ryker relaxed a bit and began to talk. He talked about his mother, and how she'd encouraged him to come and talk to Brynn, how she was good to him and always believed the best in him—in everyone, really. Ryker's apparent love for his mother was a direct reflection of the love she had for him.

Eventually, Brynn got up the nerve to mention Lanea, and it was her turn to apologize to Ryker.

"I'm sorry I startled you with the detail about the journal."

"How did you know that?"

"It's just something I can ... do. I can't explain it. It's kind of like a psychic thing."

"Wow! I've heard of stuff like that! For real?"

Brynn nodded.

"Guess that's the only way you could know. I was the only one there. I know that," he said.

"When did you take it? And why?" she asked.

"I came to see if it was still there after she disappeared, after I heard it on the news, to see if she took it with her. It was still there, so I took it."

"But why did you take it?"

"I wanted to know why she wanted to run away, what was goin' on that would make her want to leave. I thought I could help, but also, I wanted to know if she said anything in there about me helping her run away. 'Cuz if she did, I didn't want no one thinkin' that I had somethin' to do with it. 'Cuz I didn't."

Brynn felt a bit guilty for thinking it, but it was really quite logical and intelligent reasoning on his part. Socially awkward, yes; dumb, no.

She picked up on a part of his explanation. "You were going to help her run away?" She remembered the exchange in the tack room. "That's what you were talking about? Right after she hid her journal?"

He was quiet for a moment. "You saw that, too?" He blinked in amazement.

"Yeah. She looked panicked, scared, like she was pleading with you."

Jackson watched the conversation like a person watches a tennis match. "The back and forth likely made him dizzy, but Brynn knew he knew too little to ask any questions.

"She was. She begged me to help her run away. She was actin' real scared, too, but I don't know what she was scared of." He sat, staring into his lemonade. A bug floated in his drink. Brynn hesitated to take the glass from him, feeling any move would change the course of the conversation.

"She wasn't scared of … you?" Brynn hoped she wasn't touching on something that would make him angry.

"No. We was friends. She liked me. I *really* liked her, but she said she didn't like me like that, so we was just friends. She liked Marshall. She loved him."

Buddy and Ellie suddenly appeared on the porch with the dog, all of them breathless and sweaty. Ryker's face brightened at the sight of them.

Jackson said, "Ryker, this is Buddy, and this is Ellie, our children. And this is Bingo, our … watchdog."

Bingo jumped on Ryker's lap, knocking the glass of lemonade out of his hand and spilling it down his pants. Brynn and Jackson lunged for the dog, but not fast enough. They hollered in unison, "Bingo! Down!"

"Whoa, Nelly," said Ryker, laughing, patiently pushing the dog to the floor.

"Her name is Bingo," said Buddy, indignant.

"Isn't Bingo a boy name?" Ryker asked him.

Buddy turned to Brynn. "Mom, is Bingo a boy's name?"

"Well, I guess it could be both … "

Ryker, obviously sensing a dispute, came up with a proposal. "Bingo is also the name of a game, and since both boys and girls can play it, then I think it can be both."

Buddy and Ellie nodded in agreement, pleased with his sensibleness. The three ran off again, leaving the visitor sitting on the porch in wet britches.

"I'm sorry about that." Brynn said. Jackson went into the house for a towel.

"No, that's okay. It'll dry. And my mom loves washing stuff. Makes her happy," Ryker smiled. It was the first time Brynn had seen him smile and she began to understand what Fern loved about him. Not completely, but it was a start.

"So, Ryker, getting back to what we were talking about … " Brynn asked as Jackson appeared with a towel, "You were going to help Lanea run away?"

Ryker started wiping at the lemonade with the towel, although it was thoroughly soaked in. "Yeah. She asked me to help her on Friday night. She asked me on Wednesday, and I was supposed to meet her at the corner that Friday near their house."

"And?" Brynn prompted.

"She didn't show up. I waited for a long time, too. Took my daddy's pickup, without askin' even, and they didn't know. I was just supposed to give her a ride to town. That's all. But she didn't show up."

"But … " Brynn had to think a moment. Marshall said that she'd disappeared about two weeks after they broke up. "She was reported missing over a week later. Are you sure about the dates? The days?"

"Yes, ma'am. In two days, I was supposed to come pick her up. She never came. Then a week or so later, I heard she was gone. I figured she changed her mind and ran away the week after, but I don't know how."

"Why did she ask you to help her? What about Marshall?" Brynn remembered then that she had broken up with Marshall that day. "She still loved him, didn't she?"

"Yup. She did. But her daddy wouldn't let her go out with him no more, and wouldn't let him come around, wouldn't let her even talk to him. She needed someone to help her and that was me. I said I would. We was friends."

"So let me get this straight. You worked there loading hay into the hay loft with Wade on Wednesday, the same day she broke up with Marshall, and she asked you to help her run away on Friday, right?"

"Right."

"Bertis said you were there a couple days before she disappeared. Did you go back? After you worked with Wade loading hay?"

"No. What for? I didn't work there much and she knew that. Just went that Wednesday, and was supposed to come back that Friday night, but nobody saw me, pretty sure. And I waited at the corner. When she didn't come, after a long time, I went back home. Never saw her after that."

"Ok, let me ask you this," Brynn was getting excited now, and so was Jackson, judging by the way he was leaning forward in his chair, "do you remember what *date* you loaded hay into the loft with Wade? Is it possible we have the weeks mixed up?"

"No," Ryker said, rolling his eyes a little, as if he believed Brynn was a little thick and he needed to go slow to help her understand. "Could'na. We loaded hay the Wednesday after school got out for the summer. It was late gettin' out that year 'cuzza snow days. We got out on Monday and loaded hay on Wednesday. Friday she was gonna run away," Ryker was ticking off the timeline on his fingers, "and she disappeared or ran away or whatever the next weekend. Don't know how, though, 'cuz I didn't *help* her."

Jackson decided to get in on the action and asked a question. "Have you told all of this to the police?"

Ryker raised his hands in a defensive position—the most expressive that they'd seen him since he arrived. "Noooo, sir! I wasn't tellin' no police that I was gonna help her run away. They woulda' for sure thought I took her. My mom had a *good* long talk with me about that." So Fern wasn't dumb either. She'd eventually learned of Ryker's plan to help Lanea run away, and knowing that the plan had failed and Ryker had nothing to do with it, didn't feel a need to make him more of a suspect by admitting it to the authorities. Lanea's plans to run away made it easy to justify not divulging the failed plan to them once she'd disappeared. She had probably succeeded in running away without Ryker's help; therefore, he had nothing to hide. Nothing to *divulge*, but nothing to hide.

"I didn't do anything wrong," Ryker said. There was his rehearsed statement, his reaction to accusation and pressure. The fact that it was a *grammatically correct* rehearsed statement led Brynn to believe it was Fern's tutelage at work.

"Does Bertis know any of this?" Brynn asked.

"Nope. That would be like telling the police. He already didn't like me. Or Marshall. Never did. Why would I do that?"

"Maybe so he could find his daughter?" Jackson said incredulously.

"She was runnin' away from *him*, though."

"Why would you say that? Maybe she was just angry at him," Brynn said.

Ryker was shaking his head, sure of his ideas. "Nope." He stood up.

Brynn suspected that Ryker was reaching the edge of his patience and she either needed to talk him down or grab his suspenders. "Ryker, we just want to find Lanea. I know you didn't have anything to do with her disappearance. I'm not going to tell anyone anything. Okay?"

He breathed heavily, shifting his weight back and forth from one leg to the other like a lame horse. "Okay."

"So, I have one more thing I want to ask you." She waited until he looked her in the eye. "Did you read Lanea's journal?" She knew he probably had, but she hoped he would be able to admit it and maybe share some of what he'd gleaned from it.

He tipped his head back like he was going to sneeze, mouth open, looking up at the porch ceiling. When honesty finally overruled guilt, he lowered his head as he slowly said, "Yes."

"You did?" Brynn was elated. She hoped he would remember enough of it to give her some clues.

Ryker nodded, embarrassed.

"Do you want to read it?" he asked.

Brynn and Jackson looked at each other in astonishment.

"I brought it with me 'cuz I figured you'd want to read it, since you're her friend, and you're wantin' to find her and all. Not sure it will help, but it's in the pickup."

They all walked to Ryker's pickup, he retrieved the thick book and handed it to Brynn. She looked at the dirty floral print of the journal and the wrinkled, worn pages, and felt the heft of possibility in her grasp. She held Lanea's words in her hands. It wasn't just a book of thoughts and fervent dreams; it was a book of potential answers.

"Does anyone else know about this journal?" Brynn thought of Fern. "Has anyone else read it?"

Ryker shook his head and stared at the book, seemingly lost in thought. It seemed there were some things Ryker held sacred, and his feelings for Lanea were as private and cherished as the words in the journal. Not even his mother knew of it.

"Why did you keep it all this time?" she asked. "I thought you might have gotten rid of it."

"She was my friend. This is like ... a story ... of her life. That she wrote. I couldn't throw that away."

As the day promised, the storm came: Booming thunder, cracking lightning and beautiful rain. It came hard at first, but had tapered off to a slow drizzle, while the flashes of fading lightning gave an encore performance. Brynn sat in the window seat of her living room watching the storm and reading Lanea's journal by the light of a flashlight. The electricity had gone out before dark, and the family had constructed a blanket fort in the family room, where Buddy and Ellie now slept: the perfect beginning to summer vacation. Bingo, her usual brave self, slept in Brynn's room on top of Jackson to protect him from the storm.

As anxious as Brynn was to read the journal, she also wanted to take her time with it, to give Lanea the respect she deserved with Brynn's complete attentiveness. She'd waited until everyone was asleep and the house was quiet, save for the lingering storm, which only worked to soothe her. The journal was also a welcome distraction to her plaguing flashbacks of her own attack.

Reading the diary, she couldn't help but feel like a voyeur, though, peeking into the intimate parts of Lanea's and Marshall's lives. She didn't belong here. These were Lanea's private thoughts and feelings, and moreover, the thought of Ryker reading it gave her a sick feeling.

Brynn skimmed over the parts where it described in uncomfortable detail Lanea's passion for Marshall and vice versa, which accounted for most of the first half of the book. She was able to spot random entries that stood out on the pages, however, like names, dates, and excessive punctuation, the hallmark of successful journaling. Brynn was relieved to see that Lanea hadn't reduced herself to hearts and flowers.

While not initially fond of Ryker, Lanea found he'd grown on her, and became—if not a close—at least a trusted friend. Brynn also discovered in the journal that Lanea did not particularly care for Wade Hagebak. She resented the fact that although her father didn't have enough money to buy her a car, they had enough to pay for a hired hand. Bertis apparently treated him like a son, taking him to town for lunch, giving him free reign with livestock, crops, and equipment. She'd even heard Bertis refer to Wade as the son he never had. Lanea had even admitted however, that it was hardly Wade's fault. She did say that he was a hard worker and he never acted disrespectful or inappropriate around her. It was obvious that the bitterness was mainly directed at her father. The subject of Bertis was prominent in the second half of the journal.

The years dripped away with the rain as Brynn read the graceful, florid handwriting, feeling as though she were sitting behind Lanea in math class, reading a note that Lanea had secretly passed back to her by scratching her head and dropping it on her desk.

" ... *Daddy never lets me out of this DAMN house!! He recites his Bible verses, pounds the scripture down my throat, and insists on praying before everything we do! I don't think he was ever a teenager. He was born old and grouchy. I bet he was a joy as a child. (haha!!) His mother had to be in misery* ... "

"... *Devotions twice a day. Daddy is getting to be a fanatic. Mom goes along with it. She's so patient. I would have beaned him with a frying pan by now ...* "

"... *I think I'm going to have Marshall teach me how to drive. Daddy won't. He says women don't 'need' to drive. We only have one vehicle and HE'S the only one who gets to use it. Wonder how Mom puts up with him and his old fashioned ways ...* "

"... *School is the only time I get to see Marshall. HE won't let Marshall come around, won't let me talk on the phone to him for very long, for SURE won't let me date!!! It's like he doesn't trust me or thinks I'm a tramp or something. GOD!!! ...* "

Brynn looked up from the book occasionally, and in spite of the melancholy of seeing these words from someone probably long gone, she felt herself smiling. Don't all teenage girls hate their dad's protectiveness? Brynn imagined Jackson reacting quite the same way when Ellie finally reached dating age ... like nineteen or twenty.

The tone of the journal changed dramatically at the mention of her mother's illness. From the normal lament of an angry teenager, it turned to the darkness of anger, hopelessness, and fear.

"... *Mom's sick. She collapsed in the kitchen a few days ago, and we took her to the hospital. We found out she has leukemia. It's pretty serious. Daddy says that prayer can do more for her than medicine, and even with the treatments they have for this kind of leukemia, she wouldn't survive. So they're not doing anything. GOD DAMN IT!!! WHERE'S YOUR GOD, NOW,*

DAD! WHY WOULD HE GIVE THIS TO <u>HER</u> AND NOT YOU!!! ... "

" ... *Mom's not getting better, and I didn't really expect her to, but Daddy's being a JERK and I need to talk to someone. HE insists that we pray all damn day and do devotions two or three times a day, and he preaches to me and hints about how Mom is being punished ... he sometimes acts like it's my fault she's sick ... "*

" ... *Mom's always tired. I make her food, bring it to her, but she won't eat. Sometimes she will, but she mostly sleeps. I need Marshall so much right now. He snuck over yesterday and we went into the hay loft and 'talked' for a long time. I love him so much ... "*

The quotation marks could just as well have been stick figures drawn in lurid poses. Brynn understood their meaning, pleased she hadn't had time to explore the hay loft. That's one place she would be avoiding in the future. Both at Lanea's *and* everywhere else.

" ... *Daddy's getting really really weird! He sits at the table all day and reads the Bible, he hands me my Bible whenever I sit down to do homework or eat or anything, and he keeps harping on me about MY sins. Doesn't HE have any?? Why won't he shut up and help Mom?? I spend all my extra time with her, and I don't mind that at all. I help her bathe, I feed her, brush her hair, read to her, pray with her, I love it all. It feels good to know I'm making her happy, and honestly, it's so good to have her all to myself. And I know Daddy helps her during the day when I'm at school, but when I'm home, he prays. That's it! He acts like prayer is the only thing she needs ... "*

" ... *Mom and I had a good day today. It was almost like normal. She sat up and ate, I helped, but then we talked and laughed and I read to her when she got tired. God, I'm going to miss her soooo much! What will I do without her??? I need my mommy!!! ...* "

" ... *I don't know what to do. I just ... forgive me, God, but I wish she would just ... die. For her sake. I feel so guilty for feeling this way, but I can't take it anymore ... watching her wasting away like that. I LOVE HER, I NEED HER but I don't want her to suffer anymore! She's so sad all the time, worrying about Dad and me. I'll be a wreck. I'll be lost. HE has God and all his STUPID Bible verses and his prayers and devotions. HE'LL be fine! I HATE him ...* "

Brynn looked up from her reading. The lights had come on. Her vision blurred with the sadness of the words she'd read, she turned off the flashlight and got up and stretched. She neared the end of the writing in the journal, but knew it was probably the most important part and wanted to be alert.

The storm had passed and the rain continued in a soft mist, the sound, like a mournful whisper. Brynn felt comforted by the night's company. She got up and wrapped herself in her grandmother's knit afghan and settled into the deep, comfy reading chair and turned on the table lamp.

" ... *Mom's dying. I can tell. She is so weak, she's hardly awake anymore, and she's so thin I could pick her up and carry her like a 4 year old. Oh, my God. Tell me what to do. I'm so scared. I don't know how to live without her, and worse, I don't know how I can live with my father. He's nuts. He mumbles and prays and rants and raves and PREACHES all the time.*

I get that he's upset, I think, I know, he probably loves her, but doesn't he see how WEIRD he's acting?? ... "

Brynn read several more entries that ripped at her heart, imagining Lanea's fear and sorrow, but also her own at the prospect of losing Adelle. The anguish she read in Lanea's words was especially poignant, remembering her own father's death. Moreover, she was grateful to have had a father that was nothing like Bertis. She turned back to the book, knowing Lanea still hadn't lost her mother to the finality of death, but she losing her every day to that lingering non-life that kept them all hostage.

" ... I'm so scared. I need my mom now more than ever. I want to tell her things and have her hold me and rock me and tell me everything will be ok, and I want her to stroke my hair and kiss my cheeks and wipe my tears and hug me so tight that I can't breathe. But she can't. She's so frail, so small, so weak, and I'm so afraid that if I go to her and tell her anything, it will kill her. It will kill her! I will kill her. How can I do that?? Oh mommy mommy mommy take me with you!!! ... "

Brynn cried for her friend, cried for her friend's mother, and cried for herself at the loss of two beautiful women, and in between the tears and tissues, she continued to read. Then she stopped. She looked up as if even more lights had come on. She re-read the entry.

" ... I told Mom today. I went to her, and she was so weak, I wasn't sure she could hear me. But I had to tell her before ... Even if she couldn't hear me, I had to let her know. I just whispered it in her ear. She opened her eyes and I know that she heard me. She understood me. She knew why I couldn't say it out loud. Her eyes got real big and I thought for a minute

that she was so disappointed in me. I saw tears in her eyes, those dry, sunken eyes that I thought were almost gone from me. She looked at me with such love and pride and joy that I knew she could never hate me, or hate anything about me! She loves me and that's all that matters. I started to cry and so did she and I saw a little bit of a smile on her lips, and she reached up with her weak, little bird arms and put her cold, tiny hands on my face and wiped my tears away. She held my face like she was memorizing it to take with her to heaven so she would know me right away when I come. She forgives me. She loves me no matter what. She pulled me into her arms and cuddled with me and we slept in her bed. Mom needed to know that she was going to be a grandma before I could even tell you. Marshall and I are going to have a baby ... "

CHAPTER TWENTY-TWO

B RYNN SAT UP AND WIPED her eyes. It was about as important as a clue could get without saying "Duh": Lanea was pregnant! It hit her like a palm slap to the forehead. So much for being psychic.

Without even finishing the journal, Brynn could deduce that Lanea had almost certainly run away, but since she couldn't trust her psychic abilities any more than she could trust her dog to protect her from storms, Brynn continued reading.

"... I can't wait to tell Marshall! He's going to be so happy! Of course, he won't be thrilled with the timing, but we have always talked about getting married once we graduated, so this shouldn't be a big deal ... to us. To DADDY, however, it will be HUGE. I'm sure he'll flip out and I'll be grounded till I'm 30. Wow! If I thought his preaching was bad NOW, I'm sure *that once he finds out about this, he'll REALLY be unbearable ... "*

" ... I haven't had a chance to talk to Marshall yet about the baby. I do NOT want to tell him over the phone (impossible anyway, since Daddy is always around) and I do not want to tell him in school. I'll wait till he comes over and we'll go talk somewhere in the barn or the trees. I want to tell him in person ... "

" ... Daddy. He's going to drive me inSANE. He hovers over everything I do! He's gotten so protective and paranoid about everything I say and do and won't let me out of his sight. It's like he thinks he has to be Mom AND Dad, and like he thinks if he doesn't control every part of me, he will lose complete control and I will be gone like Mom. He acts like I don't know how to cook or clean or be an adult. He lectures me about school work, about behaving like a 'young lady,' he checks my homework, he takes me to school and picks me up, he talks to my teachers all the time! What is wrong with him??? He treats me like I'm a baby!!! Or an idiot. If I'm doing something that HE doesn't think I'm doing right, he steps right in and takes over and makes me watch while HE does it right. Then he explains everything in detail till I want to scream! HE'S the reason I would go away. I can't help but feel that Mom got off easy ... "

" ... It's getting close to the end of the school year. I'm not very far along, only about three months, but I will start to show pretty soon and I need to tell Marshall before the end of May, which is just two and a half weeks away. If I can just get to the end of the school year without anyone knowing, I can move out of here and move in with Marshall once we're

married. He will graduate in May and we can be together! If I have a baby girl, I'm going to name her Genny after Mom … "

Brynn read several more entries that gushed with excitement, curiosity, and dreams of her future. Lanea wanted a baby girl for herself, and a boy for Marshall, but she didn't care if she had a litter of each. She was beside herself with joy at the new life that was growing inside her, joining her and Marshall together forever. *Where was she?*

" … Daddy's acting weird. Weird-ER. He's quieter, angry almost. He's still preaching, making me read the Bible allllll the time and do devotions twice a day, all the crap he's done before, but he won't look at me. He misses Mom I'm sure, but why punish me? Doesn't matter. I won't have to live with him much longer. I'll move out this summer … "

" … Oh, my GOD! I hate him! He's on my back every minute of every day. Clean this, clean that, do this, cook that, work, work, work, get up, go to bed, I can't take this anymore. If he's like this NOW, what's he going to be like when he finds out about the baby? I can't hide my pregnancy much longer. Ha! He's such a religious freak, he'll probably perform an exorcism on me to drive the demon out! Like it's not mine and Marshall's baby, but an evil seed planted into a "virgin" by Satan himself! Haha. Whatever! I'm not giving this baby up and I'm not having an abortion. I doubt he would make me have an abortion anyway, knowing how 'GODLY' he is. But then again, he's always so worried about how I behave, act, dress, and talk in public. This would be a <u>huge</u> humiliation to him. He'll probably try to make me give it up. Or send me away to have it, even though I can't see him letting me out of

his sight for one second. He won't even let me talk on the phone or go outside alone. I don't know what he's so afraid of ... "

Brynn puzzled over the last entries. Nothing was ever reported about Lanea being pregnant, which wasn't surprising, but Marshall never said anything either. If he had known, why would he be so angry toward Lanea? She obviously never got the opportunity to tell him. Or she lost it. Or she left intending to go to him and explain everything and never arrived. Somewhere between her house and Marshall's something happened.

" ... I'm thinking that Daddy might have read my diary. I can't believe he would do that! (Actually ... I can.) It's the only thing that would explain how weird he's been acting. So from now on, I've been hiding this so that he can't read anything else I write in here. It's possible he hasn't read it, but I'm hiding it anyway ... "

" ... I'M RUNNING AWAY! I HATE THAT MAN! Today, when I got home from school, he sat right there at the kitchen table and made me call Marshall and then he took the phone off the wall and left. He takes the phone ALL THE TIME so I can't call anyone, but today, I just wanted to HIT HIM WITH SOMETHING! I NEED TO CALL MARSHALL AND TELL HIM THAT IT'S ALL A LIE! HE made me lie and tell Marshall that I didn't love him and couldn't see him anymore! I do love him and now there's no way to tell him that Daddy made me do this, so I'm going to run away. Ryker is working here with Wade today, so I'm going to ask him to help me. He will, I know it. I'm going to get to Marshall and tell him everything. I just need to get ... "

It was Lanea's last entry. She didn't need to finish the sentence for Brynn to know what happened next. Bertis came into her room and took the journal from Lanea's hands and handed her the Bible. From her room, Lanea watched him put it in the burning barrel. She had retrieved it and hidden it in the barn, hoping that he hadn't read it, that his actions were merely those of a fanatical, oppressive father. Brynn knew something that Lanea probably hadn't known for certain. Bertis had read the journal. He knew she was pregnant. It still didn't explain what had happened to Lanea.

It was late. It was past one a.m. and Brynn and Jackson were planning to begin construction on the bathroom in the morning. Brynn went to bed, pushed Bingo onto the floor and snuggled up to her husband. The warmth of the covers, the murmur of the rain, the snoring dog, all elements conducive to sleep. Brynn's body welcomed the environment, but her mind shunned the notion of dozing off.

She mulled over the things she'd seen in Lanea's house and the things she'd read in the journal and they should have matched up. She'd seen Lanea had enlisted Ryker's help to run away, she'd seen her pack, and she'd seen her walk out of her room. She hadn't seen Lanea come back, but that might not have been a memory that she would have picked out of the memories as abnormal or emotional. Perhaps Lanea never left.

If Lanea's father had stopped her from running away, that would have been a powerful memory—one that the house would have shared with me. Lanea may have changed her mind. Or

Lanea had not been able to leave the night that Ryker was going to help her, but decided to stash her bag and leave the following week. If she left on her own, it might be possible that an unsavory character intercepted her or she hitched a ride from someone whose idea of an ending destination was different from her own.

Go to sleep! ... but try and fail to run away one week and be abducted the following week? Maybe Lanea *had her dates mixed up! Maybe she showed up the following week and not two days after she'd spoken to Ryker ... no, that doesn't make sense. She would have spelled it out to Ryker. She had to have known. Then again, I don't know which week I was seeing when I saw her packing to leave ... maybe she* couldn't *run away the first week and tried to do it on her own the next ...*

Brynn finally succumbed to the lure of all the unconsciousness around her and fell asleep.

Like a song upon the lips at bedtime that is upon the lips at rising, Lanea was still on Brynn's mind the next morning. Chores, children, and household duties were slated for every day, and this one was no different. With the rain the previous night, there would be no fieldwork today for Jackson. The bathroom was a go and Brynn could not put off picking out fixtures any longer.

Brynn welcomed the distraction of the trip to town. In short order, the plumbing fixtures, lights, and tile had been either ordered or purchased, and Brynn and the children arrived home by early afternoon. Jackson was amazed at her focus, her ability to decide on everything in one trip.

"It's a bathroom. A small three piece bathroom in the back of the house that will be used mostly by us after chores. Not a big fashion statement to be made there ... " she said with a grin as they grabbed bags and boxes from the car. *I'm forgetting something.*

"Mommy, take me with you ... " Did Lanea commit suicide? No ... she wouldn't. She loved the baby, loved Marshall ... she wouldn't. What am I missing?

"Did you get shut-offs for the sink faucet?" asked Jackson. "Brynn?"

"What? No. No, sorry. Forgot that. Do you need it today? I can run and get it ... " she said distractedly.

"No, I don't need it today. Not till we start putting it all back together again. So did you read the whole journal?" Jackson asked now that they were alone.

"Yes. It was interesting." Brynn felt somewhat covetous of the contents of the journal, like it was a secret pact between her and Lanea that somehow never ended when Lanea disappeared. Like Lanea's messages dropped on her desk, folded neatly into secret note squares that allowed access to no one, Brynn wanted to keep all of Lanea's confidences and innermost feelings to herself. But she was done keeping things from Jackson.

"She was pregnant." She couldn't bear to elaborate, but it was enough, since there wasn't much more to tell. She felt guilty, though, for divulging that, as if she had betrayed her friend.

"Pregnant?" Jackson stopped and looked at Brynn. "Whose was it?"

"Jackson! It was Marshall's, of course."

"How would I know that!" he said, slamming the trunk lid.

"Because she wasn't a tramp, that's how. You know that. You were interested in her, too. Is that the kind of girl you were interested in?"

"So did you find out anything from the journal about what could have happened to her?"

Brynn knew he was avoiding her last question because it looked an awful lot like a landmine. *Wise decision.* They stepped around it and went inside.

"No, not really. She complained about her dad being so controlling; he got really weird after her mom died, and she wanted to run away. But you know how that ended. I don't know any more about that than I knew before I read it."

Along with the missing shut offs, the nagging feeling that she was failing to remember something or see something that was important tugged at Brynn's conscience. Short of returning to Lanea's house, which was way, way at the bottom of her list, she was stymied as to her next course of action.

"Do you think Marshall knows about the baby?" Jackson asked, breaking Brynn's trance.

"No. And I'm not going to tell him. Not until and unless I know what happened to her. What purpose would that serve?"

"What about Bertis?"

"What about him? He doesn't deserve to know any more than Marshall, and in fact, he doesn't deserve to know *anything*," Brynn barked.

"What did Bertis do?"

"More like what didn't he do ... " she said almost to herself.

"What?"

"Nothing. He did nothing except preach, and lecture, and punish, and *control*, and drive her out of her own home, and she probably ended up being taken by some creep like the guys who took me, and God only *knows* what happened to her after that!"

The short night and the frustration of the forgotten valves had finally caught up to Brynn. She needed a moment alone. She went to her room and shut the door. Jackson began dismantling the bathroom as the children played in the mess.

Brynn threw herself into an easy chair in their room. She was in over her head. Who was she kidding? How could she hope to solve someone else's case when she couldn't deal with her own?

She picked up a magazine, flipping unseen pages, and finally throwing it across the room.

Shit. I don't want to go back to Stokes. Can't get those visions out of my head. I can't tell J about the things I saw. Not sure I want to tell anyone, Stokes included. It was humiliating and horrifying to watch. And it would be even worse to talk about it. But what they did *... What if they did it to someone else? Where are they now?*

What if they found out I remembered?

What would her world be like if it got out that she had this weird ability? To what lengths would her perpetrators go to keep her quiet? What about *any* criminals, especially those in the area? There were a number of unsolved crimes in the county and surrounding counties. A whole family, except for the husband, was slaughtered in their sleep near Mandert, in Tanka County, the one next to theirs. Everyone suspected he did it, but there wasn't enough evidence to indict. What if ... ?

Goosebumps covered her bare arms. Enough sitting around. She got up and paced, rubbing her arms.

Anger surged in her.

Do something, damn it!

Brynn forced her thoughts back to Lanea. She simmered in those juices, getting angrier by the moment.

Mad that Lanea needed a father but got a warden. Mad that it looked like she'd have to go back to that crap-packed, mouse-infested hole to see what she'd forgotten. More than that, she was mad at everyone, herself included, who could have helped Lanea and hadn't. Bertis deserved most of that. He'd deflected everything he'd felt onto Lanea and made her carry the burden of his guilt, despair, and fear. He was responsible for Lanea's disappearance, maybe in a small way, but responsible, nonetheless.

What was Bertis thinking, treating her like that? What did he hope to accomplish with all the punishment and pulpit pounding? Did he think he would convert her to his way of thinking? That she would see the error of her ways by making her memorize every word in the Bible as penance?

That's it!

Brynn came out of her bedroom and found Jackson in the bathroom, pulling grungy, twenty-year-old shower walls off the sheetrock.

"J, I need to go back to Lanea's house."

"Seriously? After all that, you want to go back?" He dropped the pry bar on the floor.

"Want to? I wouldn't exactly put it that way. I think I used the word 'need.'"

"I don't think that's such a good idea. You don't *need* to get arrested for trespassing."

"I won't. I'm going to take my camera, just run in and check something, and run out. I'll take the car so it doesn't look suspicious, you know, like I'm trying to sneak."

"Wow, Brynn, I don't know if I like this side of you."

"Come on, J, just a quick *zip-zip*, what do you say? Okay?"

He brushed off his pants and checked himself. "I'll come with you. Get the kids."

"No. I got this. Be right back." She kissed him and ran.

"Take the dog!" he hollered. "And the phone!"

With the dog and the camera in tow, Brynn got out and started taking pictures from the fence line. She looked both ways and dropped the leash.

"Bingo! Rabbit!"

The dog sprang like a greyhound out of the gate toward unknown, unseen prey in the direction of Brynn's pointed finger. As if fetching a faked throw, Bingo bounded into the last season's dead scrub that grew between the rusted remnants of Bertis' life. She dashed back and forth, trying to catch the scent of the precious fuzz she planned to gleefully shred and scatter to the winds. Brynn took the opportunity to race toward the house.

She reached the back door as Bingo eagerly explored the area nearby. Pushing on the door, Brynn winced at the smell that she had so conveniently tucked away in her mind.

Brynn stepped over the mounds of junk, and into the kitchen. She wished she could pick and choose what she wanted to see and get the hell out. Knowing she only needed a couple minutes made the mission more nerve-wracking. The car, the dog, her unpreparedness; she was tempting fate.

Like a gift, wrapped in filthy vestiges, it came to her. She unwrapped it, gratefully accepted it, smiled, and turned to leave.

Brynn's instincts saw him before she did. She jumped, and a scream she didn't recognize flew from her mouth. Standing nearby was the figure of a man not from the past.

Wade stood in the doorway.

"What are you doing here?" His relaxed, affable manner was gone.

Excuses, justifications, and possible colorful embellishments—numerous and loosely gathered on her way here—were nowhere within reach of her stammering mouth. "I ... I ... the dog ... she took off with the leash when I, well, ... got out to ... I was taking pictures. There was a rabbit." Nope. Not near as smooth as she had envisioned.

"Get off this property. You have no business coming in here and snooping around." He went to Brynn, grabbed her arm, and roughly, clumsily shoved her over the refuse toward the door. Outside, Brynn saw Wade's wife holding Bingo on her leash.

"You want me to call the sheriff, Wade?" she asked, eyeing Brynn and looking all too happy to oblige.

"I don't know. Brynn, do you think Ardis should call the sheriff?"

"The sheriff? Really? Because I came to catch my dog? Look, I didn't take anything or even *touch* anything, *trust me on that.* I'll just be leaving, I won't be back, I got some pictures, got my dog, thank you very much ... I'll just go." Brynn pulled her arm from Wade's hand, took the leash from his wife and turned to leave. She walked casually to her car without looking back. Her racing heart felt anything but casual, but fortunately, it wasn't visible from where they were standing.

The dog tracked mud into the car, and brought with her the sweet, mildewy scent of the root cellar, but a bath for the both of them and a thorough cleaning of the car was worth what she'd seen in the house. She finally looked back at Wade and his wife when she was pulling away. Ardis, he said. *I've heard that name before ...* They were carrying items from the house to their pickup. Odd.

"I'm back!" Brynn shouted as she arrived in the house.

"So you didn't get arrested for trespassing?" Jackson's voice echoed from the gutted bathroom.

"Just about."

His head poked out the bathroom door. "Are you serious?"

"I smooth-talked my way out of it," she said with a smirk, which he would deduce that she probably ran for it.

Jackson, who was shirtless and covered in dust, came out of the bathroom and met her in the kitchen.

"Nice." Brynn smiled as her eyes traveled his body. Now was not the time. "Her dad stopped her—at least the first time she was leaving anyway, that Friday that Ryker was going to help her. I think her dad overheard their plans and stopped her." She looked at his smooth, muscular chest. "Why do you have your shirt off? It's 73 degrees outside."

"Wardrobe malfunction." Jackson winked and opened a can of soda, taking a break from the bathroom. "So how do you know that?"

"When I saw her packing to leave, in her bedroom, she was packing her mother's black Bible. I saw her put it in her bag. And when I saw her dad talking to the police in the kitchen, the Bible is sitting on the kitchen table."

"Could it be a different Bible?"

"No, it's the same one. Same cover, book mark, it's her mom's. It's the same one he handed her when he took her journal. I'd seen her reading it and writing in it, and when she left, she took it. I'm thinking since it was her mom's, she wanted it with her." Brynn paced, looking at the floor, trying to figure out how this was important and what it all meant.

"What does *that* mean, though? He caught her trying to sneak out. He stopped her from running away."

"But then why didn't I see that? That would have been a pretty big deal. They wouldn't have just walked arm-in-arm upstairs together and said goodnight. There would have been a big argument. I would have seen it."

"True."

It was odd seeing Jackson so accepting of her abilities and trusting in what she said she had seen. To know that someone could accept even the craziest parts of her and love and believe her anyway was more phenomenal than her ability.

Brynn asked, "If he had caught her trying to run away, would he have mentioned that to the sheriff after she went missing?"

"Why wouldn't he? It wouldn't prove that she'd run away. What difference would it make if she ran away or was taken?"

"Because running away would make him look bad?" Her eyebrows arched. "If she was taken, it gets more attention, she is found faster, and so on, but if he says or even implies that she ran away, that brings up more questions about *why* she would run away." She smiled and pointed at Jackson.

"True again. You're good at this. But either way, she's still gone. And he'd still want her back ….Unless he didn't … but then why report her missing?"

"Because people would notice her gone and ask questions. Right?" she asked.

"Who would notice her missing? It was summer. She never went anywhere. No one ever went over there either."

"Good point." Brynn said, pacing again. She stopped and her eyes snapped back to Jackson. "What if he sent her away to have the baby?"

"Why report her missing then? That would be pretty easy to trace. And if she came back a few months later, that would look fairly suspicious, and they would *both* have questions to answer."

"*Dang* it. What does this mean? I know he knows more than he's saying. If Lanea packed the Bible ... but it was sitting on his table when he was reporting her missing ... Why would she take it the first time and not the second time?"

"You're assuming she tried to run away more than once."

They stared at each other, searching each other's eyes for an inkling of understanding.

"You're right. I only saw her packing to leave one time." She paused in thought. "Unless she stashed her bag for the next time. But how? Her dad would have taken it or I would have seen that, maybe. But, then again, what are the odds that she would try to run away one week, and get abducted the next? Right from her yard, no less. I would have seen it if she was taken from the house."

"Okay. Let's back up. We're confusing ourselves here. So you saw the Bible on the table. And that means—"

Brynn smiled at him. He reminded her of Mr. Huff, her high school science teacher, who would recite half-sentences and wait for the class to fill in the blanks.

"What?" he asked.

"Nothing. Okay: it means," she said, holding her hand out to count, "one, Bertis caught her and/or she changed her mind and never left that night; so the Bible was still there, which would mean that she forgot it the next time, or there wasn't a next time. Which brings us to two: If there wasn't a next time that she tried to run away, she was abducted. From her yard, because I would have seen it if it was from the house or … wait. I never checked any other buildings. She could have been taken from one of the other buildings. But with Bertis knowing her plans, because he read her diary, the *big jerk,* he would have been watching her like a hawk. He wouldn't let her out of his sight. She even said so herself. So that leaves abduction, somehow. I don't know how. Or who."

"What about Ryker or Marshall? Ryker could have come back and taken her. Marshall could have been mad enough at her breaking up with him to come and hurt her or something … "

Brynn sat down at the kitchen table. The endless possibilities numbed her brain.

She shook her head. "Why would Ryker admit to having her journal and knowing her plans to run away, even if it was just to us, if he had anything to do with her disappearance? He wanted to help her. And Marshall was hurt and angry that she broke up with him, but I didn't sense that he was *that* mad at her. I sensed that he was hurt and still loved her. She had no doubt that he'd be thrilled about the baby. They were going to be married as soon as they could. That doesn't sound like the same Marshall that would hurt her. Besides, both Marshall and Ryker had to have had an alibi for the night Bertis said she went missing or they would have been arrested."

"You're probably right. But I don't have any other answers. It had to be a stranger then." Jackson dropped his can in the recycling bin under the sink and turned to go back to work on the bathroom.

Skepticism twisted Brynn's face as she watched him retreat. "Right. A stranger that shows up within a week of her wanting to run away. It could happen."

Brynn propped her chin on her hand and stared out the window. After a moment, she shouted, "J, do you know Wade's wife, Ardis?"

"Yeah," his voice echoed from the back bathroom, "Why?"

Brynn got up from the table and went to the door of the bathroom and watched her husband dismantle the toilet.

"Just wondering. I heard her name somewhere and can't remember where I heard it."

"Was she there today? Why are you asking about her?"

"Yeah, she was there. After I left, they started carrying things from the house to their pickup. Weird, huh?"

"After what you told me about the filthy house and all the useless junk in it, I would say so, yeah."

"So was it you that mentioned her to me?"

"I don't think so. Don't know why I would."

"How well do you know her?"

"You insecure, honey?" he smiled, "I don't know her that well. She's kind of a homebody, she works with Wade, or I should say, he works with her ... she wears the pants, from what little I've seen." He chuckled.

"Kind of like me, huh?" Brynn laughed. Jackson rolled his eyes.

Brynn turned and went outside to wash the musty sweetness and mud from Bingo and vacuum out the car. Anything to burn off the fog of confusion.

Progress in the bathroom slowed with the drying of the fields and Jackson's farming responsibilities, which drew him away for hours or days at a time. Brynn assumed bathroom duties.

Brynn mulled over the details of Lanea's case as she labored, working and thinking, the happy twins, whistling and skipping hand in hand. She wanted to scream.

I'm not going back there. NOT going back. Imagine what they'll do if they find me there again! There's something I missed, though, if I didn't see what happened to her. Or how that Bible got on the table. I might not have stayed long enough to see her pack a second time. I might have confused two different times for one. How could I have missed anything though? I. Am. Not. Going. Back.

With Jackson in the field spraying, Brynn had constant company with the two children. Only a little more than a week into summer vacation, and Buddy and Ellie were already bored with each other.

She'd had enough.

"Kids, get in the car and get buckled up. We're going for a ride. Let's go take some pictures." Brynn packed a lunch, her camera equipment and the dog, and drove out the driveway.

She stopped at Cole's house and showed the children where her muse for his painting had been born. She then drove to the old school house, took photographs, and explained how, at one time, classes for several grades were held within one room by one teacher, which Ellie vehemently refused to believe. After juice and cookies on the steps of the schoolhouse and checking their clothes for ticks, they piled back into the car to drive to one last house: the house that had been Brynn's bane in every possible way.

Pulling up to the driveway, Brynn noticed that the stretched-fence gate barring access to the property was draped off to the side, and equipment was now parked in the grassy farmyard.

"Stay in the car, kids. I'll be right back." The children pressed their faces to the windows, gawking at the massive yellow machinery that outsized anything their daddy owned, as Brynn got out and surveyed the grounds.

No one appeared to be around. The tractor-trailers that had delivered the bulldozer and backhoe were parked at the edge of the property, but there were no operators for the equipment that sat waiting.

Bertis was planning on bulldozing the property and burying it. The equipment must have arrived within the previous day or so, waiting for dryer ground or operators with an open schedule.

I'm so close! I just need a little more time! If they tear it down now, I may never find her!

Suddenly, it occurred to Brynn that the timing of the apparent demolition seemed not only inconvenient for her, but also eerily convenient for Bertis.

Brynn turned to walk back to her car, but stopped. She walked to the semi and read the name of the wrecking company on the door, got in her car and drove straight home.

"Aggie Dozer Service? ... Hi, I live south of Perris. I saw you have some equipment sitting at a nearby farm site, and I was wondering what kind of services you offer. I have an old barn that I've been thinking about pushing over ... M-hm ... yes ... Wonderful ... can you tell me when they will be done with my neighbor's property?"

Jackson walked in while Brynn was on the phone, his frown asked a question she didn't have time to answer. She put Jackson on hold with her raised pointer finger.

"My neighbor's property? I believe the name on the account would be Bertis Covey ... Yes, that's right ... Oh. That soon ... . So how much notice do you need, like when did Bertis call and order thi ... M-hm ... Oh ... I see ... Well, thank you so much ... I'll be in touch ..." Brynn hung up before she was minus a barn and a few thousand dollars.

Brynn put the phone on the counter and faced Jackson. "He's pushing the place in. And burying it. On Friday."

"Hm. Wonder why."

"Something's fishy, here, J. How many years has that place been sitting there accumulating crap, *literally*, and now all of a sudden he wants to tear it down? Right after he finds out I was asking around about Lanea?"

"The timing is a little ... fishy, but it is his place. Maybe he's been planning this for a while." Jackson said.

"She said it was ordered just a few days ago. Right after Wade caught me on the property."

"Yeah, okay, that's kind of odd." Jackson got a cold drink from the refrigerator and grabbed the box of Wheat Thins from the cabinet to take back out to the field.

"Kind of? Why tear it down now? They don't know about my ability. This just makes me wonder what he has to hide." Brynn gaped at Jackson, standing near the door with his soda and box of crackers looking like a little boy who wanted to go build a tree fort with his buddies and his mom was holding him up.

"I gotta go ... " he said apologetically, "fuel pump is running, tank's about full. Ok, Hun? We can talk more tonight?"

"Yeah, that's fine," she said but didn't mean, waving him on.

A supper of roast with potatoes, carrots, and onions remained a wonderful stand-by when Brynn didn't feel up to anything fussy. After supper and chores, Brynn busied herself in the kitchen and bathroom with cleaning, another wonderful stand-by when she was frustrated or restless.

In two days, the house would be rubble in a hole. Probably nothing more to be done or seen at the house, anyway. She would have to use whatever info she had or forget about finding Lanea.

Bertis knew more than he was admitting; they had determined that. Brynn realized there were as many clues in what she *didn't* see in the house. She hadn't seen Bertis catch Lanea trying to run away, she hadn't seen Lanea packing to leave a second time, and she hadn't seen anyone else taking Lanea from the house. She also hadn't seen a devastated Bertis finding the note that Lanea had left on her nightstand. Either Lanea had taken the note after a failed attempt, or Bertis had casually strolled into her room and taken it. He didn't want the authorities to assume she'd run away. If they suspected it, then so be it. But if there were proof that she'd wanted to, even if she hadn't, that would raise red flags.

What if Bertis was getting confused about the time that Ryker was seen at the house? He was *confused or forgetful about a few things when I'd talked to him. If something happened to Lanea the night she planned to run away, and Bertis was thinking of Ryker's visit a couple days before that—when he was working with Wade ... What if Wade had something to do with it! No, why would Bertis lie for Wade when it came to his own daughter. They both know something, or at least Bertis knows something and has Wade to do his bidding, which is probably the case. He doesn't want anyone snooping around his place, and has Wade guarding the place. Bertis is hiding something. Or some ... no.*

The thought of Lanea possibly hidden within the house sent icy fingers down Brynn's spine. It seemed inconceivable, though, that she wouldn't have seen a memory of her body. Tearing down the house was a fairly drastic measure if there wasn't something to be seen or found there. Brynn could think of hundreds—heck, *thousands*—of reasons to bury that house. After dousing it with gasoline and sticking a match to it. Maybe even throwing a few gallons of bleach and a sprinkling of holy water on the ashes for extra measure. But to push it in because someone was asking too many questions seemed absurdly extreme.

In the end, though, Brynn found it hard to believe that Lanea could be anywhere on the grounds. Bertis was a raving fanatic and control freak, but she doubted that he could hurt his daughter or be a witness to some violent act against her, or still, know anything about her disappearance and not say anything about it. She would have to let it go. Lanea was gone, probably forever.

Satisfied with the cleaning that she had accomplished, Brynn made a cup of coffee with an extra shot of cream for a job well done, and joined Jackson and the children in the family room. The next day would be full enough without the added chore of solving missing persons cases. But she was absolutely sure that's exactly what she would be doing, if only in her head.

Chip.

Hammer and chisel in hand, Brynn picked away at the tile floor in the bathroom.

What am I missing? What do I know? Maybe Lanea sneaked out of the house and fell and got hurt. I suppose it's possible she did *fall down a well, like Cleo speculated. Maybe she managed to sneak away, but not in time to meet Ryker. She may have shown up late and tried to make away on her own, and someone found her.*

Scrape.

Something had to have happened to her outside the night she left.

Chip.

In that case, I'll never find out what happened to her.

Scrape. *Dang it! Why was the hideous always so well made?* She would never get done scraping this disgusting hunter-green tile off the bathroom floor.

It had been a long day and it wasn't over. Hog chores had taken longer than usual with the sorting out of some culls, dinner was fast and furious, and Jackson had gone right to work on the bathroom. Throughout the afternoon, Brynn sanded and painted an old dresser she'd planned to use as a vanity in the remodeled room as the children played nearby. Supper consisted of leftover roast beef sandwiches with barbeque sauce and chips. While she did evening chores, late, Jackson had read to the worn-out kids, put them to bed, and had gone to bed himself. Brynn worked alone, the ugly tile poor company, but an easy target. And she, a willing aggressor.

Brynn's back and knees throbbed, but she needed to finish tonight. Jackson was starting work on the new tile in the morning. *Thank God for thick walls and sound sleepers.* The pounding didn't seem to stir anyone from their sleep, and Brynn needed the hammer more than she realized.

Brynn chiseled and scraped at the old floor tiles that fought her every inch of the way. The adhesive holding the tiles was as tenacious and stubborn as Brynn's haunting thoughts. Today was Thursday. Tomorrow the house would be gone. Undoubtedly, the crew would be there before eight a.m. and within mere minutes the house would be nothing more than a pile of kindling. Tears stung Brynn's eyes, knowing that within a couple of hours of pushing the house over, a hole could be dug and most of the farm would be committed to earth, like a soon-to-be-forgotten loved one, conveying the aged, lifeless home to an unmarked, eternal grave. In the time it takes to sing a couple hymns and say a prayer, generations of memories turned into the loam like compost, memories of Lanea that would never be seen again.

Brynn got up from the floor and dusted off her pants. She stretched, pulling her arms up over her head, bending over at the waist and pulling the hamstrings that seemed to be connected to every nerve in her body. Jackson would not be upset if she didn't finish chipping off the old tiles, she knew.

This floor was not going to win, however. It had tested her patience and plagued and taunted her long enough. Brynn looked at the hammer, lying there on the cracked tiles so innocently, so patiently. She picked it up, raised it over her head, and smashed it down onto the mocking tiles. Shards flew out like crows after a gunshot, striking Brynn's face and arms. She pounded and pounded, slamming the head into the cracking and splintering pieces of porcelain as she cursed and sputtered against all that is unfair and wretched in the world. She finally dropped to the floor, exhausted and somewhat victorious. She took up the chisel and scraper and began to pick away again at what remained of the horrid past.

There would be no sleep tonight. The demolition of the bathroom became the execution watch for the demolition of Lanea's memory. Brynn wedged the chisel under the stuck tiles, prying and grunting in angry determination. The chisel slipped and sent her arm glancing over the razor sharp shards of porcelain, giving her almost paper-cut-thin slices in her forearm. Dark blood dripped on the tiles and the underflooring. Blood. Images of her attack and the crime scene photos flashed white hot in her mind. Her heart raced and tiny beads of nervous sweat broke out on her face. Brynn shook her head, and blew a slow breath out of her mouth. *Not happening. No.* She wiped her forearm on her jeans and forced her thoughts back to Lanea.

" ... she fell in a well," Cleo's words rang in her head.

Yes, that's possible. It's also possible that someone came to her farm and took her. Options ... options ... Ryker or Marshall ... possible. Wade ... even that's possible. Bertis ... Bertis. That possibility was becoming more and more likely. The biggest tipoff yet to that suspicion is the planned demolition of the farm. If he's hiding evidence, I would challenge the world's finest forensic experts to find it in that mess, and what if it's not evidence, but Lanea herself?

Brynn allowed herself one last reverie of investigation into Lanea's disappearance, as if she hadn't already obsessed for the last few hours.

Think! What did you do, Bertis? When: the night she planned to run away, probably. There is no evidence that she disappeared a week later simply because he reported her missing a week later. Why: because ... she was pregnant and soon to disgrace his family name? She was about to prove that he wasn't perfect? Would he kill her for that, though? Maybe he didn't intend to hurt her at all, but something happened. He is hiding something, that's clear. Okay, what about the how: he probably intercepted her outside the house. It's the only place that makes sense. I can't imagine a where ... I just can't imagine a father burying his little girl's body on his farm or keeping her body in his house. Where would he put her?

The question of where was chilling, but the why and how were unimaginable. How a father could submit his own child to a life of isolation and condemnation was reprehensible, but to know her fate and lie about it, unforgivable. Brynn didn't know for certain that any of her suspicions were founded on truth, but Bertis' actions gave her no other choice but to believe them.

The bathroom floor was almost finished. Only a section of flooring the size of a Monopoly game board was remaining in the corner, and Brynn was spent. The sun would be up in a few hours and she knew she would be worthless for the rest of the day. But at least the floor would be ready for Jackson. Brynn leaned over the tiles around the hole in the floor where the sink drain had once been. She pried and picked as the pieces scattered about the floor and fell into the hole. Brynn looked into the hole, curious to know where those hideous pieces of tile would end up. She went to the mudroom, grabbed a flashlight, and peered down into the basement from the two-inch-sized hole. Nothing looked familiar from this angle, from this small viewpoint. A fine haze of dust drifted in the flashlight beam within the dark and dirty space. It was the old part of the basement, the four-foot deep crawlspace under the original section of the house. She knew every inch of it; she knew there was plumbing that fed this bathroom underneath this floor, but nothing looked the same from up here. It was like looking through a keyhole into secret chamber. It looked mysterious and undiscovered. *Funny ...*

Stunned, Brynn suddenly fell back on her butt, sending sharp splinters of tiles into her backside and her hands. She popped up off the floor, banging her head on the towel bar, sufficiently dismantling the last disgusting item in the room. The clattering of the polished brass bar resounded off of the walls of the empty room.

Holy crap! I know the where!

CHAPTER TWENTY-THREE

3:18 A. M. WAKE JACKSON?
No.
Wait until daylight.

No!

The workmen would never let her inside the place if they were already there when the sun came up.

Brynn snatched her pullover hoodie off the hook near the back door and yanked it on. She pulled on her boots, grabbed some gloves, a flashlight, and the wrecking bar and headed for the door.

She stopped at the door. What else? She briefly questioned her sanity at going to an abandoned house in the pitch black of the night. It wasn't ideal. It wasn't wise, or fun, or even adventurous. But it was her only option.

The dog. Brynn trotted into the living room and whistled softly for Bingo. "Car ride?" she whispered loud enough to get the dog excited but not enough to wake anyone. The dog danced in place while Brynn puzzled over what else she needed to do or bring. Bingo would help her feel brave. The wonder dog that was scared of thunder. Better than nothing.

She would be home before anyone woke up. She needed only a quick look to prove her theory and stop the demolition of the property.

A phone? Hers was broken, still not replaced since she dropped it while running from Ryker. Jackson's was charging on his nightstand, but if she went to retrieve it, and he woke, he would never let her leave to check out her suspicions. *I'll be home before anyone even knows I'm gone.*

A note. Her excuse was as versatile as the pry bar, and it worked for this too. *Before anyone knows I'm gone.*

If Jackson found the note before the sun came up—for some reason—her "be right back", which would be all she would dare to write, would be as woefully insufficient and feeble as her flimsy theories. Why bother?

Brynn went to the garage and pushed the button to lift the door. It squealed and clanked as it went up, and Brynn held her breath and hoped that she wouldn't soon see a bleary-eyed, ratty-haired Jackson poking his head out the door to see what was going on. Being on the far side of the house from the bedrooms, no one appeared to have heard the garage door opening.

She opened the car door and motioned for the dog to get in. Bingo hopped in the car, tail wagging and tongue flapping in Brynn's face, the dog's something-died-in-there breath mingling with the precious air Brynn needed to survive. "Sit," Brynn told her, pointing at the other side of the car. Bingo took her place on the passenger seat and couldn't have looked more ready for a road trip if she'd been wearing a seat belt and sunglasses.

She arrived at Covey's at precisely 3:42. Two hours until sunrise. Plenty of time to find what she thought was hidden. Brynn weaved the car through the rusty graveyard and parked it between the semi-truck and the thick row of trees at the edge of the lot. If anyone were driving by, they wouldn't see it, and *if* someone showed up before she was done, they would probably—hopefully—assume that it belonged to one of the crew. Besides ... *long gone.*

She hooked the dog to her leash and pulled the flashlight and wrecking bar from the floor of the passenger side of the car.

"Let's go, Girl," Brynn whispered, feeling a little ridiculous for being so covert.

The beam from her flashlight didn't go far. Not *near* far enough. The night greedily gobbled up the light and opened its maw to show her that there was nothing left of it. She shined the light back and forth on the ground as she walked toward the house. The items of junk on the site crouched like beasts in the dark, the house, the scariest beast of all. It was filled with blackness. It seemed to watch her. She paused in her step. The toads and frogs paused in their calls. Except for the dog's panting, all was quiet. In the distance, she heard an animal cry out, a sound she'd never heard. *This is a stupid idea! Anything*—anyone!—*could be in that house. Or anywhere on the place!*

Bingo wasn't scared at all. She panted and pulled at the leash. *You're too stupid to know when to be scared, you dumb dog.*

Last chance, Brynn! Stop being such a sissy! Brynn took a deep breath and continued, her steps crackling and crunching in the grass.

She lit her way to the back door with the flashlight and pushed the door open as far as the junk would allow. The rooms inside the house, black as a grave and deathly quiet. The moon had long since moved on, abandoning Brynn to explore the dark house without its help or comfort.

Once inside, she kicked the clothing and rubbish away from the door, pushing some of it outside and some of it into the kitchen. Although she hesitated to touch it with her hands, even gloved, she picked up damp, stinking trash and threw it out the door and on top of the already huge mound on the shelled-out washer and dryer and into the tiny bathroom. As soon as the sun came up and the crew was here, no one would give a second thought to why there was a clean spot on the floor.

She hoped that she could peel up a section of the floor and look, then lay the section back down as neat as a trap door. It didn't appear to be that simple. Nothing ever was, was it? *Laws of gravity, laws of nature, laws of Murphy.*

Memories of the comings and goings of the Coveys and their help swirled in the room, adding to the chaos of flying clutter. As if she were standing in the doorway to a mall, the traffic flowed around her, constant and unmoved by her presence.

"Go away!" Brynn shouted. *It's me. It's me. I need to control it. Control.*

Brynn shut her eyes, thought of home, and took a few calming but shallow, tentative breaths. The visions lessened, the smell did not. She got on her hands and knees next to the clearing on the floor.

Vinyl flooring covered the surface. She'd have to peel it back to expose the wood flooring underneath. Brynn dug the beveled edge of her pry bar into the old vinyl flooring and skinned back a small chunk of linoleum, scraping and scraping until she had a section that was big enough to excise some of the floor boards and look underneath.

Who in the world put vinyl over floorboards and not sheeting or subflooring? Bertis. Visions of Bertis in the room popped into her mind. Brynn shook her head. *Keep working, Brynn. Don't think about him or the dark rooms around you!*

The floor planks were soft and not well seated to the joists, so prying them loose took little effort.

Lifting the boards was not the issue. Keeping them lifted to allow her to see underneath proved to be the challenge. Time ticked on and Brynn stopped caring about exactly how she needed to do it, she just needed to do it. She used the wrecking bar to hammer at the soft boards, and crack them enough to break them off. The hammering seemed louder than the booming thunder days ago in this house. She had no way of knowing if anyone from the crew was staying in one of the semi's sleepers. Probably not. *Now you're just scaring yourself. Hurry up!*

No one came to stop her; most normal people were still sleeping. She might be waking other occupants in the house, though. She couldn't avoid it any longer. Brynn stopped what she was doing and shined her flashlight into the house, hoping that she wouldn't see the familiar glow of two luminescent eyes, or *more*, staring back at her. Nothing. She could only hope that the hammering would keep them at bay.

Just look and go home!

If the entire space underneath the addition were part of the original basement, it would be approximately six foot deep by ten foot wide. It might only be a crawl space, but since there was plumbing in the addition, it had to be accessible from the main part of the basement.

Thinking back on her visit to the basement-dumpster before, Brynn remembered seeing the memory of Bertis working on the foundation in this corner of the basement. And she could not remember the basement being as deep as the addition would have allowed. He may have built the wall to enclose this part of the basement, and then painted all of the walls the same color so that it would not look new. Was there a door into this section? It could have been buried underneath all of the trash that literally filled the basement. Then again, why would he need a door to a grave? Bury her and wall it back up. Wouldn't be the first time someone had done it. She'd seen enough crime shows on television to know that. Brynn continued to hammer and chip away at the rotten boards.

That was a lot of work to go through to hide a body, especially when he farmed hundreds of acres that would supply endless grave opportunities. However, if he were as controlling as Lanea had accused him of being, he might have wanted her near him. The planned demolition of the house was significant—more telling than Bertis intended if there weren't something here to be found.

Finally, Brynn had a section of the floor removed, a small section large enough to get her head and shoulders into, if necessary. All of Brynn's hopes were riding on this theory. Lanea could be entombed underneath this floor.

Shining her light into the blackness, Brynn peered into the hole, preparing herself for a vision of Lanea's decomposed body that might be forever burned into her mind. The powdery dust from her frenzied work shifted and floated up through the beam of bright white light, like spectral souls released from a crypt. The fine particles lifted, settled, moved, and Brynn squinted against the contrast of bright and dark into the chasm. She could hardly believe the story her eyes wanted to tell her.

The space was not so much a tomb as a room. And Lanea, nowhere to be seen.

She could see a cot with a dingy mattress, a nightstand, a small dresser, and in the corner, a crude bathroom, likely one that was in the basement before Bertis walled up the room. Everything in the room was draped with cobwebs and covered in a thick coating of dust.

Brynn sat back on the floor next to Bingo, who was curious of the goings on, but clearly unsettled.

"What are you panting for? You haven't done a thing to help, you lazy butt," she said to the anxious dog. She looked around once again at the impermeable blackness in the house. There could be an animal in this house besides the one that sat panting next to her. A fox, a coyote, a raccoon, maybe a *mountain lion, which weren't unheard of around here lately …*

Brynn reeled in her self-imposed terror. She couldn't concern herself with that right now. She needed to figure out what to do next. She smoothed back the fringes of hair that had escaped her ponytail, and looked into the hole again.

A room. He had held Lanea here. He obviously knew of her pregnancy and kept her hidden until she had the baby. But what happened to her? She must have died …

A barrage of thoughts bombarded Brynn. So many theories, so many questions, *so little time!*

Without a body, there was nothing to stop them! A simple, secret room was not enough evidence to stop the demolition.

Brynn wanted to cry with the realization of what this meant. *Crap, crap, CRAP!*

She looked around for something that could be used as a ladder. *Crap!*

Nothing. Clothing, broken furniture, trash, and nothing remotely resembling a ladder. If she had a *day or two*, she could tie together all this disgusting clothing to make a rope, but it would crumble before she even got it tied because everything was *rotten with age!*

She could run home and get a rope or the ladder and the pickup, but she might get delayed and the crew would be here by the time she got back.

Crap!

Brynn knew what she had to do. She cursed and muttered as she swung her legs into the hole, hoping her ability had evolved since she tried doing this before in the closet. Even dangling her legs into the dark hole sent shivers up her right leg. But the tingling of the creeps was not the same as absorbing the memories of the room—it wasn't working.

She stuck one arm down into the hole, then two, reaching down as far as she could, as if to grasp whatever apparitions of the past were wandering around within the room. Nothing.

Finally, lacking any other options, Brynn held the flashlight, reaching with it, shining it into the room below, and hung her head and shoulders into the chamber while holding onto the rim of the hole with her other hand. She stretched, hoping that by suspending her upper half into the room she might fool the room into relinquishing its memories.

Come on, room! Come on! I'm right here! Tell me what you know!

Brynn hung there until her head throbbed with blood and her sinuses filled. It wasn't going to happen this way. It might never happen. Other than going home for a ladder, she had no other options. She pulled herself with the one grasping arm to extricate herself from the hole. The board she gripped suddenly cracked and she felt herself sliding into the void.

Nothing stopped the momentum. The laws of gravity and the laws of Murphy were working together in a dastardly plan to see her end up in the room below, and Brynn was powerless to stop it. Grasping and flailing, Brynn tried bringing her other arm up to grab something, anything, but air was the only thing at hand. She was falling, sliding, tumbling into the hole.

"Oh, my God!" Brynn yelled. It didn't help.

Her meager scream barely had time to escape her lungs before the *whump* of her landing knocked the air from her body. The last thing she heard before she blacked out was the clunk of her head striking cement.

Brynn awoke on the floor of the basement room. Her legs were draped over the edge of the cot, but seemingly unharmed. Her right wrist, however, burned. It was broken or badly sprained, she was sure.

Holding her wrist, Brynn struggled to stand, her head pounding with the effort. Her whole body protested, but Brynn didn't want to listen. Her heart was hammering as if in delayed echo of her hammering upstairs. She had no idea how long she'd been out, more than likely, only seconds. It was still dark above her. That meant that she had time to observe whatever visions the room had to share, and more importantly, find a way out.

There has to be a way out. It's dark, but through the memories, I'll be able to see a door or something. Concentrate, Brynn! Oh, my God, what if I'm trapped down here ...

She looked around, though the room was as black as a cave. No visions came to her immediately. She started to panic. *What if the proverbial bump on the head is real? What if I went through all ... this ... and knocked my ability right out of me?*

Brynn backed up until she found the inside wall of the room and waited. Above her, Bingo whined.

"It's all right, girl. Stay." Brynn hoped the dog wouldn't leave her. She was Brynn's only chance of being found before she was buried if she didn't find an exit. The irony of the room becoming a tomb became a sobering possibility.

The darkness of the room was disorienting. The dank odor yanked her mind back to her assault, a trapped, helpless sensation flooding her bloodstream, jumpstarting her heart. Borrowed or not, the memories were branded into her brain, and still searing hot.

I'm not there ... They're not here ... Breathe ... breathe ... Brynn blew trembling breaths from her mouth. Her heart rate slowed as she looked up at Bingo, calmed by the dog's presence. "I'm fine. Don't worry about me," she quipped to the dog.

If I had a flashlight, I could find my flashlight, she thought stupidly. Her legs shaky, Brynn slid to the floor, hoping to see her options in a memory or through a clear head, both of which would be easier if she were seated.

She had no choice but to wait. She sat with her back to the wall, thinking how perfectly appropriate that was.

Within minutes, a flurry of memories began to swirl around her, like cherry blossoms caught in a squall. She saw Lanea for the first time, in the room, on the cot, her belly swollen with child.

She was beautiful in her pregnancy. Brynn could see on Lanea's face that the hopelessness of her situation could not overshadow her obvious hopefulness for her child, her life. Brynn saw her friend soothing the tightening, contracting muscles that worked to force the baby from her womb.

Lanea blew and panted, clenching her teeth when she couldn't bear it any longer. Brynn watched in amazement as Lanea gave birth—sixteen years ago. The memory, being one of the strongest and most powerful of any event on earth, held reverent by this room, as it should have been, first and foremost above all others. For one wonderful, blessed moment, Brynn heard the unmistakable, sweet squawk of a baby's cry. It brought happy but bitter tears as she watched this new mother lift the tiny life onto her chest and kiss him and stroke his thick, dark hair. Brynn watched as Lanea cooed those precious bonding, formative lyrics of motherhood.

Lanea had delivered the baby by herself, and although Brynn felt a pang of loneliness for her, she understood that under the circumstances, Lanea probably preferred it that way. It was the closest thing to privacy and sanctuary that she could hope for. Brynn saw that Lanea had a few hours—sacred and cherished hours—alone with her baby.

She watched her friend tie the cord with a strip of fabric for lack of any other choice, remove her sweater and swaddle the squirming, silently howling infant in it, and snuggle it to her breast to feed as she lay down on the cot to rest.

In the midst of the visions that continued to flow, Brynn was saddened by the state of the room that the new mother had to endure. The cot was the same as the one she'd seen in the closet upstairs: small, metal, with a lumpy, worn mattress. The furnishings in the room were monasterial—a lamp on a nightstand, a bed, a dresser, a sink, and a toilet. No homey touches existed, no warmth of artwork or photos, no personal belongings, nothing. It was a prison cell. Bertis' judgment for Lanea—her sentence handed down by her maker, her magistrate.

Brynn finally looked closer at her friend and her bleak life in this hole. Lanea had become much thinner. Lanea's hair had thinned, her skin was sallow and dull, and her body looked frail—all no doubt attributable to the unhealthiness of the damp, sunless compartment, and exacerbated by her pregnancy. More surprising was the grace and optimism that Lanea displayed here.

Brynn watched the memories play around her. Bertis had come in hours after the birth and taken the child from Lanea's arms, another chilling memory that the house seemed eager to relinquish. Brynn wept with Lanea as Bertis dropped the sweater on the foot of the bed, wrapped the baby in a towel, and walked out the door carrying the screaming baby.

"You lousy pig," she muttered under her breath.

Lanea was not well. Brynn could see that the delivery had taken every ounce of energy she possessed, and the blood loss from the birth was frighteningly profuse. Lanea had tried to staunch the flow with rags and clothing, but it continued. Brynn felt helpless. She couldn't imagine what Lanea must have felt. Lanea was doomed by more than her circumstance. Brynn watched Lanea's lifeblood trickle from her, soaking the mattress that no doubt still held the stains of Lanea's desolate existence here.

The wooden panel door on the other side of the room opened, and a feeble buoyant look crossed Lanea's face. A younger, chubbier or pregnant Ardis entered carrying a lunch and some toiletries, and upon seeing the blood, rushed to Lanea's bedside and sat, helping to stop the flow.

Of course. They both knew. That's why they were talking so heatedly when I was leaving their place that day.

Why would they help Bertis? As the light went on in Brynn's head, something changed in the room's memories as well.

All motion seemed to slow as Ardis faltered in her efforts. Long moments passed, then Ardis slowly got to her feet. She stood at the foot of Lanea's bed, dispassionately staring at the young mother in front of her, her hand over her mouth. Silently, Lanea implored her to help. But Lanea's pleadings halted when she saw the toiletries: a package of heavy-duty sanitary napkins. Grim understanding replaced expectation. There was only one reason Ardis would not want to save her. And only one way she would know the need for the pads. Lanea looked at Ardis' lumpy belly.

Lanea's eyes met Ardis', and a resolve that belied her physical frailty shown in her face. "He's mine." Lanea's words were loud and clear, resonating through time.

Ardis' mien was as cold and unyielding as the walls surrounding them. She spoke, but Brynn heard nothing. Ardis stood for what seemed forever but could have only been a couple minutes, watching the crimson puddle grow beneath Lanea. Then she left.

Lanea, lethargic and slow, strained to reach the sweater at her feet, pulled it to her chest and clutched it tightly.

She breathed in the lingering scent of her beloved son. Her lips moved in silent pleas or prayers. She clung to all she had left of her dreams in her final moments.

In that, Lanea's last, Brynn watched in anguish as the last flicker of hope and joy faded from Lanea's eyes. She saw the tiniest squint of despair that had replaced the wide-eyed fix on the future's dreams in the fleeting moment between life and death. She watched, as the eyes, wet with tears of fading fantasies, became a dry, unfocused gaze.

Lanea's spasmodic breaths ceased. The weak twitch of the pulse in her neck paused for seconds at a time and started again, but after a few moments, stopped completely.

Lanea had escaped, but not to the life she had planned.

Inches from her stretched out fingers, Lanea died in front of Brynn. Whether sixteen years earlier or the present, it was as real and heartrending as if Lanea were actually here, and Brynn could do nothing to stop it. Brynn sobbed, seeing the life slowly wrenched from her helpless friend. Lanea had lost everything. She hadn't been able to tell Marshall of her pregnancy, or that she had been forced to lie to him. Then she had been viciously robbed of her future with him and her child.

Brynn closed her eyes and said a prayer for her friend, pausing after the Amen to gather herself. She stood and stretched her tingling legs, and hugged herself to ward off the chills.

A creak overhead stopped Brynn in mid-motion. Footsteps. Clumping, creaking, back and forth across the room above her. Brynn froze. Someone had found her. She couldn't call for help. Whoever it was would likely find her anyway, and call the police. She had to know either way. She peered up, expecting to see an angry face looking down.

She saw the dark shadow of Bingo, who hadn't moved. The footsteps continued, yet the dog didn't hear it.

That's it. That's what I heard the other day when I was in the basement on the other side of the wall. I was hearing the memory of Bertis walking on the floor above.

Brynn let out the breath she was holding, happy to not be found. For the moment.

Perhaps half an hour had passed since she had opened up the floor and fallen in, providing she wasn't unconscious for more than a few seconds; but that would give her hardly an hour to get out before sunrise, and who knows how long before the crew would show up.

I just hope I can get out!

Brynn had to know more, however, before she could leave. She knew how Lanea died. Now she needed to concentrate on specifics. There would be time to find the flashlight after she saw what else the room knew. She didn't need light to see the past.

Even as her eyes adjusted to the darkness, scarcely more than faint outlines of the items in the room emerged. Through the dark memories and the faint light, Brynn saw the wooden panel door on the other side of the room. The vault smelled of a root cellar, the sweet musk of fermented fruits and root vegetables. Surely, the exit was through the root cellar mound right outside the back door, a viable choice, an escape route when the time came to leave. Hopefully.

Brynn appreciated that she couldn't see everything in the room, sure that the room held its share of spiders and maybe even snakes and mice. If there were no mice, then the snakes would be sufficiently, disgustingly fattened. She held no fear of those things, but nevertheless, she didn't wish to be trapped with them. She tried to convince herself not to be afraid of what she could not see, but plenty of ticks had found their way into her hair unbeknownst to her in the past. She knew better.

As if on cue, Bingo growled a low, rumbling warning at the edge of the hole above. Bingo rarely growled. That frightened Brynn more than her own imagination. Either an intruder prowled above, or a worker had come early to get a head start on the excavation. Perhaps Bingo sensed an animal, hoping to alert her or trying to threaten it. In any case, Brynn hoped that Bingo wouldn't lose her nerve and try to make it home on her own. She heard the dog sit up, its thick claws scratching the floor, the dog's tags clinking as she moved her head.

Brynn realized she'd been holding her breath. She strained to hear over her pounding heart and ringing ears. She heard nothing other than the dog's breathing and low, intermittent growls.

"Shh! Bingo! Stay!" Brynn hoped the dog would be reassured by her master's voice, but hearing it from a dark hole in the floor might be a bit baffling for her. It seemed to work for the moment. The dog settled down with a soft, whistling whine. "Good girl. Stay. Stay."

"What's up there?" Brynn said to herself, more than the dog. She didn't want to know. It wouldn't help to know. *Get what you came for and get out!*

Brynn eased down to the seat again, waiting to capture more of the room's secrets, pulling her knees into her chest to avoid as much exposure as possible to whatever creatures that dwelled there. She began to watch the movie-like events in the room, a time-lapsed film footage of utter sameness throughout the last months of Lanea's life. She watched the comings and goings of Bertis as he brought her food and clean clothing and toiletries, and took laundry and dishes from her room. Never in the entire content of the room's memory did Bertis even once embrace his daughter, or offer any consoling gestures of affection or friendship. He played the heartless autocrat. Czar of The Coveys. She was his prisoner, and furthermore, a seemingly willing one. It appeared, through her passivity, that Lanea felt she deserved to be imprisoned. Except for the first time she was brought into the room, Lanea hadn't fought to escape.

The closest that Bertis ever came to warmth or affection with Lanea was when he sat at the foot of her cot reading from her Bible. He would then hand it back to her and leave. The Bible became Lanea's only source of affection. The only loving words she heard were from a faraway god that couldn't soothe her with a gentle touch, or hug her or hold her close. They were only words Bertis uttered from a book that ruled his life and that he used to rule hers. The God Brynn knew would have rather seen his Word used to press flowers, stabilize a table leg, or even smash a bug than to be used to kill someone's spirit. Bertis' retribution would hopefully be a hell worse than the dungeon in which he stuck his daughter.

As Brynn had already suspected, Wade and Ardis also brought food, clothing, and supplies, evidently arranged by Bertis for times when he was not available.

They both looked younger, and Ardis, in most visions, looked pregnant. She was probably faking the pregnancy for Lanea's benefit. When Lanea finally got to leave the prison, she wouldn't suspect—or couldn't prove—that Wade and Ardis had her son. But once Ardis knew that Lanea was dying ...

Concentrate ...

The business of the Bible plagued Brynn. When Bertis was not reading it to Lanea, it sat on her nightstand, untouched. Brynn puzzled over this. She had seen Lanea in this room, reading and writing in a Bible, but not in the white one that Bertis read to her. She wrote in the black Bible, and she kept it hidden from Bertis. *Why would you hide a Bible from your father, Lanea?*

Like the planned demolition of the house, the motives for hiding the Bible were reason enough to look deeper into the meaning behind them. It didn't take long to figure out what Lanea was doing.

Lanea was a journaler. She had been using the black Bible as a journal. That explained why she would have taken it with her when she left. One of the reasons, at least. And somehow, she had gotten it back after Bertis reported her missing. Would he have given it to her? She had her white one. He surely would have thought it odd for her to request the black one, so it had to have come from Wade or Ardis. Brynn waited, and waded and sorted through countless memories, looking for this one. Patience and practice won, and the vision eventually came to Brynn. Ardis had delivered the black Bible and a pen to Lanea, probably because Lanea innocently asked her to bring them. And being a Bible, especially Lanea's mother's, Ardis would have no reason to deny that request. Or even feel compelled to announce it to Bertis. No harm in it. It was a Bible.

Brynn could see that Lanea had depended on her mother's Bible as if it were her mother herself. She wrote and sang and read and talked with the Bible.

Brynn looked up. She could faintly see the outline of Bingo's nose sticking over the edge of the opening now, which meant that it was near dawn. It had to be about five, and the sun would be shining bright by five forty five. She didn't have much time. She would have to look for a way out within the next few minutes. The room continued its performance of Lanea's last months. Brynn saw Lanea massaging her growing tummy and singing, rocking, swaying. She was infusing her love into her child every day, determined to have him feel it, know it forever, even if he didn't ever know her.

Brynn strained against the shackles of time to control this gift of hers, to hear the soft tune Lanea sang to her baby. How does one listen hard? Brynn listened hard. She heard Bingo's breathing, she heard crickets, a faint howl of a coyote, but no lullaby.

Listen ... listen ... soft and sweet ...

Bits and pieces, first a word, then a short melody, and finally, suddenly she heard it: The murmur of Lanea's voice singing to her unborn baby.

She hummed and sang a tune about walking in the middle of the night and searching for something.

The tune was familiar, but it wasn't a lullaby. Lanea sang to her baby and Brynn listened quietly, solemnly. Eventually, Brynn laughed sadly, knowing the tune, finding it silly, yet fitting at the same time. It was Billy Joel's "River of Dreams."

This was perhaps Lanea and Marshall's song, passed down to her—their—child now. The meaning was not lost on Brynn, and it was more prophetic than even Lanea knew it would be, given the situation she'd been in and all that had happened after she gave birth.

Brynn cried as Lanea sang to her swollen belly and later to her newborn infant, the song that she wanted him to somehow hear and to know and carry in his heart. It was a prayer, a promise that she would find him.

" ... *something, taken out of my soul, something I would never lose, something somebody stole ... "*

Once she'd heard Lanea's song, she heard the chorus repeated over and over in Lanea's voice, when the baby was in her arms and after Bertis had taken the child from her. She sang it until she was too weak to move her lips. The song belonged to the baby, and Brynn was determined to deliver it to him.

" ... *I don't want to walk anymore. I hope it doesn't take the rest of my life to find what it is that I've been looking for ... "*

Brynn knew the song well. The ending was as chillingly foretelling for Brynn as it was for Lanea, and Lanea sang it to Brynn.

"... *it can only be seen, by the eyes of the blind* ... ."

Brynn became the eyes of the blind. And Lanea's last hope. Lanea's son was out there and Brynn would deliver the song to him and tell him it was from his mother.

Wiping her eyes with her sweatshirt sleeves, Brynn glanced up at the hole and saw the dim blue light of dawn creeping into the room above.

Hurry! Hurry!

But she had to see more! So much of the same, so much to sort through!

What happened to the black Bible? What happened to Lanea's body?

Brynn grasped at whatever memories looked different and watched Lanea's movements away from her bed.

If only there were a fast-forward button ...

At last, she saw Lanea hiding the black Bible. She had wrapped it in a wrinkled, worn piece of tin foil that had come from one of Ardis' sandwiches and stuffed it above the cement blocks where the plumbing came into the room from above. Unless Bertis was standing on a chair, *or the toilet,* he would never see it.

Can I be that lucky twice? Could the Bible still be here? Oh, please, God, if you ...

Brynn knew better than to ask God to prove Himself to her. There was no reason why it would not be here and she could not imagine any god of hers rejoicing in the lack of justice. Lanea knew what she was doing when she hid it.

Wrap it in foil to keep the mice out, and keep it high off the floor, away from moisture.

Spurred into action, Brynn began to fumble in the dark for the flashlight. Over the mattress, under the bed, she could feel the bumps and lumps through the gloved fingers of her one good hand. Dead mice, gargantuan spiders or maybe even ticks, snake carcasses, who knew? Thank God for the gloves. Dust wafted up into her nostrils and Brynn coughed until her head throbbed again. She finally located the flashlight on the other side of the cot. She flipped the switch, on, off, on, off, and tightened the lens and the bulb compartment cover. As a last resort she banged it against her hip and it finally came on, instantly blinding her. "Of course," she said.

The light flooded the tiny room and Brynn looked around at the present condition of the room. She was surprised that it didn't look much worse than it had 16 years ago. From up above, it hadn't felt real. Now that she was standing in the last place Lanea had been alive, the reality struck her like a brick dropping on her head from the floor above. She looked around. It suddenly occurred to her that this was the one place that Bertis hadn't polluted. He had filled the house, the entire farm with his garbage— his guilt, she hoped—the filth spilling into every area of his life but here. The one place he couldn't or wouldn't dare corrupt: Lanea's room and his grandson's birthplace. *Did his conscience stop him from coming here? Or was he simply afraid of her accusing ghost and the chance that he would be found out?*

She shook off the anger and questions. Brynn's wrist still stung and she could feel the swelling stiffening her fingers inside the glove. It was useless in helping her get out, whether it was broken or not. She needed to keep moving.

Brynn looked up at the spot where she'd seen Lanea hide the Bible, over the toilet and slightly to the left. Too high to reach. Lanea needed only to stand on the toilet, being at least six inches taller than Brynn. And the sink was too far away from the toilet to stand on it and reach the hiding spot.

Brynn shined the light onto the small table that was used as a nightstand. Barely two feet high, if it didn't fall apart, she could use it to set on top of the toilet and reach the Bible. *Be there! Be there!* She lifted the table with her good hand. Lightweight and rickety, it only needed to last another ten minutes. She set two legs on the toilet and leaned the table against the wall. Precarious and lopsided at best, but it was the only way to reach the top of the wall.

She climbed to the top of the toilet lid, stepped on the tank with one foot, then onto the wiggly table edge with the other. Hanging onto the block wall with her good hand, she fumbled above her with the crippled hand, her fingers tingly and half-numb.

She swept back and forth on the ledge and in the blocks, standing on her tiptoes on the edge of the slippery toilet tank and dusty table. She felt the crackly foil, nearly falling in her excitement, as she pulled the book from its hiding place.

Clutching the Bible like a baby to her chest with her injured hand, she carefully stepped down the wooden and porcelain stairway. "Thank you, God," she whispered.

Again, the sound of Bingo's low grumbling echoed down the hole. It came out as a rumble, and the phlegmy inhalation sounded just as fierce. Whatever Bingo growled at would be seeing her back teeth. It should be scared. Brynn was.

She heard a scuffling, tags jingling and Bingo's nails sliding on the floor and a snapping, snarling nastiness from above. The sound left the room and went into another part of the house. Then nothing.

She needed to get out of here. Where was Bingo? What's happening?

Brynn heard the tick, tick, tick, and occasional *foof* of the dog's footsteps on hard flooring and soft garbage as Bingo came back to the room above. Bingo lay down next to the hole again.

"That's it? You're not going to tell me what was going on up there?" The dog just barked. "What was it? A opossum?" Who wouldn't be afraid of an animal that looked like an enormous rat? Bingo barked again as if to tell her to hurry up. "I'm trying! Shut up!" The dog stared down at Brynn.

"Just stay right there. I'll be right up ... " Brynn shined her flashlight at her surroundings and took a harder look at her situation. "Maybe."

The door, which she hadn't tried yet, led to the root cellar. Hopefully, it wasn't locked, and the passageway wasn't blocked. And if it was locked or blocked, then what? The bed was too short, and stacking the furniture would not get her close enough to the ceiling to lift herself out with one arm. Maybe she could use the bed like a ladder … if the hole weren't in the middle of the room. There was nothing to lean it against and it wouldn't be sturdy enough to stand on end.

It was soon light and Brynn needed desperately to find a way out and read the Bible. Read the Bible. She had a few minutes … *No! You need to get out!*

What if I read the Bible and find out I missed an important memory? By the time I get home and read this, the house will be gone and so will every clue this room has to offer! If I read it and discover something that can stop the destruction, it's worth staying a few minutes more! And if I read the Bible and all it has is Lanea's handwriting, that's probably not proof enough. Without the room, there is no proof that Bertis held her here while he was insisting *that she was missing.*

The argument continued in Brynn's head as the dog waited patiently.

Find a way out, then read the Bible. Find a way out!

Brynn knew she was right. On both counts. She would find a way out, and read as much of the Bible before the crew showed up. Then she would stop them. Somehow.

Wait! Maybe you should see if there's anything written in the Bible first?

She unwrapped the book from the brittle foil, tenderly, eagerly, as if opening a much-anticipated gift from her friend. Brynn marveled at the book's pristine condition. She opened the book and shined her flashlight on the pages, immediately finding Lanea's familiar script tucked deep in the inside margins of the Bible. It was a Bible intended for margin notes, of which Lanea made good use. Seemed only fitting.

Briefly, Brynn scanned the onionskin paper, engrossed to the point of distraction from her most pressing matters. Lanea had written early in the book about her suspicions that her father had found the journal, and how she had hidden it and would go back to get it when she left to run away. But, as Brynn suspected, Bertis intercepted her outside the house and took her to the basement room straight away. He had moved the furniture in after Lanea arrived in the room so he wouldn't tip her off. She never made it to the barn. And she had no way of knowing that she would never make it out of the room.

Brynn hastily scanned the short entries detailing how, at first, Lanea wanted to find a way to escape, but reasoned that it would be easier to go along with Bertis' plan. And when she finally gave birth and was allowed to leave the basement, she would find a way to get the baby back ... after she and Marshall got married.

She had accepted her sentence, her penance, but she had no intention of honoring Bertis' plan to the end. She would find her baby after she got out of this hole. No matter what. It made her song, their song, much more poignant, especially seeing the words to the tune written in these margins. She believed every aspect of the opus—from the meaning it held for her and Marshall to the message she intended for her son.

Lanea would find her baby. She had even named him.

The writings produced in Brynn a surge of rage and profound grief. She felt hot tears welling up. Lanea had no idea of her fate, no plan of dying in this vault. Brynn suspected that even Bertis hadn't planned on that happening, but it didn't make him any less guilty. Lanea wasn't guilty of anything. She had acted out of love for Marshall, which created a child, and she had planned to live her life with them both. Bertis had acted out of self-serving, zealous beliefs and shame. And Ardis ... *There's a special place in Hell for you.*

She'd read enough to know that the room needed to be saved. It was all evidence, and there would be justice. Brynn shined her light on the door. She set the Bible on the cot and went to the door and turned the knob. It wouldn't budge.

"Damn it!" she shouted.

She looked around. There had to be something she could hammer at the doorknob. A wonderful wrecking lay just above her that would work perfectly. Naturally. Lassie could run home and tell Timmy's mom that he'd fallen in a well, but Brynn was pretty sure that Bingo wouldn't have a clue what "wrecking bar" meant.

She saw the toilet tank lid. Did she dare whack the doorknob with that? What if it broke off? *Then* what?

Brynn decided to use the toilet tank lid anyway. It was all she had. She picked it up with both hands and hit the door near the latch. She repeated hammering and checking the knob, with no new results. Her wrist screamed.

The doors hinged from inside. Brynn attacked the hinges with the tank lid, hoping at least a pin would work loose, and her last option, other than shouting for help when the bulldozers bore down on her overhead. *Not ideal, but ...*

She hit and hit, most of the time missing the upper hinge altogether. Occasionally, a well placed hit offered some movement in the pin. She finally lifted one pin out and began on the lower hinge, which was by far a harder target, having to strike from below.

Relief overwhelmed her when the lower hinge broke with much less effort than the top, and the door hung hinge-free. Maybe she could pull the door open or even off. She yanked on the knob. Nothing. Wedged tight with the spring moisture. "Shit!" As if she didn't have enough to worry about—the expletives were coming far too easily of late.

Upstairs the sun shone brightly into the entryway, probably well past six by now and the crew would be here soon. Not only that, but Jackson would also be waking up soon, and he would have a *fit* when he found she was gone! She needed to get out. Now!

Jackson awoke at six ten, alone in bed. He saw that Brynn's side of the bed didn't look slept in. She'd probably worked late on the bathroom and fell asleep on the sofa. He rose, used the master bath, and dressed quietly. He checked on the children, who were sleeping soundly, and went downstairs.

Bingo was noticeably absent from the scene, usually whining to be let out by the time they woke up in the morning. As Bingo's loyalties dictated, she was probably sleeping with Brynn on the couch, or rather, *on* Brynn, on the couch.

On his way to the kitchen, Jackson found Brynn wasn't on the couch and neither was Bingo. Bingo wasn't his concern.

Checking the bathroom, he found the floor almost done. But no Brynn.

He went back to the kitchen and stood in the center of the room in a quandary.

She was doing chores ... probably wanted to get them done early since they would be working on the bathroom all day. Bingo was probably with her. Not unusual.

He started the coffee and turned on the television to watch the early morning news.

Every blow prompted a scream of pain from Brynn, the wrist now excruciating. She banged and banged on the door until the tank lid cracked and her throbbing hand, barely movable. Completely exhausted of energy and options, Brynn sat on the cot, close to tears.

She attempted to rub her aching wrist, but her wrist would have none of it. *Maybe someone will come along and find my car hidden behind the semi and realize it isn't one of the crew's. Maybe someone will give the house a final inspection before tearing it down and find me. Crap. I'm going to be found out. Then again, being found out is better than being buried alive.*

Above her, Bingo waited. She was no more helpful than a lump of warm clay, but Brynn felt comforted to have her there, regardless.

I've got to get out of here! Brynn jumped up from the cot and paced. This must be how a caged animal felt. Pacing was pointless, but felt useful. *What was it Grandma always said about worrying? Something about a rocking chair ... how it gets us nowhere.* "Well, Grandma, I think I *should* be worrying!" she said to the ceiling.

Worrying and waiting were the only things she could do, however.

By seven, Jackson was near panic. Brynn was usually home within an hour of leaving for chores. He went back to the bathroom and puzzled over the scene. As he looked, he noticed droplets of blood on the floor. Little splashes of dark red on the tiles and on the underlayment. He put his hands on his head in desperation and rubbed his hair.

Could something have happened to her? *And* the dog? He called the hog house office. She wouldn't hear the phone from the pens, but he had to try. While the phone rang on the other end, Jackson realized that he hadn't checked to see if the car was there. He went to the garage. No car and no answer at the hog house. She had to have gone somewhere. Maybe out to shoot photos of houses at sunrise? That was logical. He hung up the phone.

He went to Brynn's art room and found her camera, still in the bag.

Where else ... where else ...

He looked in their room for her purse and found it hanging on the doorknob to her closet. She wouldn't leave without at least ...

Jackson went back to the kitchen to look for a note. Not on the table, the counter, not even blown onto the floor. He rummaged through every scrap of paper there was, searching through the artwork and snapshots on the front of the refrigerator for a scribbled note from Brynn. Nothing.

"Where are you, Brynn ... " He paused to think, hands on his hips. He ran a hand through his hair.

No car, no dog, but that didn't necessarily mean Brynn was in danger. Blood was not a good sign, however. However conceivable it was just a cut that bled, a minor injury during the demolition of the floor, the entire picture was far too unsettling to ignore. Given her history.

Jackson dialed Brynn's mother. Adelle's sleepy hello told him immediately that Brynn was not there. He asked her to come as soon as she could.

Jackson opened the door for Adelle six minutes later. She looked as though she had been twisted into her clothes, her hair remained uncombed, and her eyes were still puffy. "Is everything all right? Why did you need me to come?"

"It's Brynn." He couldn't bring himself to say more. They walked into the kitchen.

"What's going on, Jackson? This is the third time now, and I need answers. I'm trying not to be nosy, but I'm her mother." Adelle sat down at the table. "Is she okay?" She didn't look quite awake yet.

"I'm sure she's fine. I just don't know where she is."

"What! What do you mean, you don't know where she is?" Adelle was very much awake now.

"She was working on the bathroom floor last night and never came to bed. This morning, I can't find her or the dog. The car is gone, but not her purse. Or the camera. And she's not answering at the hog house. I'm going over there to see if she's there. Can you stay with the kids?" He left out the part about the blood.

"Of course! Go! Go!" Adelle got up and shooed him out the door.

The car wasn't at the hog house, and he knew that she was probably with the car. And the dog. Just to be sure, though, he ran into the building and looked and shouted for her. Not there either.

Could someone have heard that she was looking into her own case? And would that someone be ballsy enough to come into our home and take her? And the dog? And the car? Really? That's absurd!

Jackson returned home within five minutes, and Adelle opened the door for him, coffee in hand.

"Anything?" she asked.

"No. Did she ca ... " He shook his head. He realized she couldn't call. Her phone was broken. He went into the kitchen to pace.

Adelle followed him, peppering him with questions. "Call? No. Does she have a phone yet? Does she have yours?"

He showed her his cell phone and rubbed his forehead as if to stimulate his brain. "Damn it, Brynn!"

Adelle was quiet. Jackson knew she probably didn't want to add to the stress of the moment by demanding explanations. Especially when it was obvious that he didn't have any.

After a couple minutes of silence, Jackson finally spoke. "She's probably not in any danger. She has the car and the dog. I mean, who would come into our house and take her, the car, and the dog?"

"Then where is she? And whose blood is on the bathroom floor?" She'd seen it.

"That's probably just ... It's not very much. She'll probably be back any minute," Jackson said.

They decided together they were overreacting ... and that they should call the sheriff.

Raske assured Jackson that he would be there within the half hour. It was 7:25.

Brynn finally sat down on the cot and waited, much like Lanea had. But Brynn wasn't weak and dying. Trapped and in danger of being really, really embarrassed, but not weak and dying.

Brynn heard a rumbling, and Bingo heard it too. It sounded like thunder.

Was it supposed to rain today? Then Brynn realized what it was.

The dog whimpered. Oh, lord, the dog. She would probably crawl into the hole just to get away from the noise.

"Bingo, calm down. Stay, you big baby."

The thundering didn't stop. It continued, constant and ominous.

Brynn knew it wasn't thunder, but Bingo didn't. Brynn knew the sound of a bulldozer running. Bingo whined a little louder, in competition with the "thunder" she couldn't escape.

The crew had arrived. With the machinery warmed up, the crew would soon be in the house to inspect … hopefully.

"Hello! I need help!" Brynn hollered up to whoever might be nearby.

The rumbling continued for a few minutes, but still, no one appeared over the hole to laugh at her and then rescue her.

The dog inched closer to the hole as she sought comfort from her greatest fear.

The rumbling vibrated the ground, getting louder and closer. Brynn realized that they were not going to inspect. It was probably a flagrant violation of demolition laws, and she would have to report it to the proper authorities. If she made it out of this hole alive.

She got up from the bed and began to jump up and down on the cot to help her voice reach the edge of the hole, her wrist and head throbbing together. "I'm here! … I'm here! … Hello!" Bingo's whistling whine neared a howl. Any second, Brynn expected the dog's quivering body to land on her.

Brynn could hear the crunching of wood and feel the trembling of the earth around her as she stood on the basement floor looking up at the ceiling of the mudroom above. She had to try one more time to break down the door.

Brynn lifted the cracked tank lid once again, ignoring the shooting pains from her injured wrist, and began hammering at the center panel of the door. The door cracked, cracked, and the lid appeared close to breaking as the building shook and dust drifted down from the floor overhead.

Brynn grabbed the Bible from the bed, stuffed it into her waistband and tucked her shirt in around it. She went back to pounding on the door.

Dying here became a very real and frightening thought. Sweat mixed with tears of frustration and sadness ran into her mouth as she desperately pounded on the wedged door. She thought, of all things, the poor dog. Jackson would take care of the kids and they, him. The dog would sit up there, paralyzed by fear, and let the bulldozer run her over.

Brynn, sobbing, turned around and looked up at the hole. Bingo peered down at her, her paws hanging over the edge of the hole.

"Bingo, go home! Go!" she cried.

The dog trembled and panted, her sad eyes imploring.

Brynn had only one other trick, if it would even work. She climbed on the cot and jumped up, faking a throw out the hole.

"Rabbit, Bingo!"

The dog sat up, turned and looked, but lay down again, whining and shaking, when the thundering grew louder.

"Oh, my *God*, dog! How stupid are you? You're going to get run over!" Brynn looked around her for something to throw at her. She snapped the leg off of the nightstand and got back on top of the cot.

The house above her creaked and squealed and snapped as if it, too, were angry.

"Get out of here, you idiot! Git! *Go on!*" she screamed and threw the table leg, hitting the dog in the snout. Bingo sat up and shook her head. She gave Brynn a look that broke her heart—a look that would haunt her until the end. Which seemed to be soon.

"Go on!"

Bingo looked away momentarily, back at Brynn, and then ran away from the hole.

Maybe she would run into the trees, maybe she would hide under the car, but at least she wouldn't end up buried alive. At that moment, she almost wished the dog had jumped into the hole. *At least I wouldn't have to die alone.*

Maybe someone will see her and know I'm here! I couldn't be that lucky. I can't depend on that.

Brynn wiped her face and went back to pounding on the door and with one substantial *whack*, the tank lid busted in her hands.

Jackson waited for the sheriff to arrive as he and Adelle went through routine motions with the children—breakfast, getting dressed, watching television, and Adelle making more coffee. When Sheriff Raske arrived at the farm, Adelle took the children upstairs to read to them. Jackson met him at the door and explained as much as he knew.

Raske seemed calm. Annoyingly so.

"10-8," the sheriff muttered into his lapel microphone. He pulled a pen from his shirt pocket and start making notes in his black notepad. "When did you say you noticed her missing?"

The information Jackson had already given him seemed to have gone unheard.

"Don't we need to put out an APB or something?" Jackson asked.

"That's a little premature. You say the car is gone? What would that license plate number be?"

Jackson answered Raske's questions much quicker than the sheriff asked them. His patience was wearing thin.

The sheriff inquired about the make and model of the vehicle, whether Brynn had been in contact with any friends lately and who they might be, if she often took the dog when she went out, if there was anyone she could have confided in. Jackson gave him clipped answers, and took the sheriff on a tour as he did, showing him the blood spots on the bathroom floor.

"How's your marriage?" the sheriff asked.

Jackson stopped and stared at him. "What?"

"It's a standard question, Jackson. Just doing my job."

"Then do your job and get some people out there looking for her!" Jackson could feel his blood surging through his veins. Like months before when Brynn had gone missing, no one was taking it seriously other than to suspect he had something to do with it.

The sheriff continued to scribble on his notepad. He pressed the button on his lapel radio and spoke calmly, "10-29 on one Brynn Young ... "

Growing more aggravated by the moment, Jackson waited and listened as Raske murmured his monotone jargon into the handset. He fleetingly wondered what the penalty was for hitting a cop.

When Raske finished, he turned to Jackson. "What's she been involved with lately? Has she been talking about or worried about anything in particular?"

Jackson's eyes flew open. *Of course! I'm so stupi* ... Then the phone rang.

When he hung up, he turned to Raske and said, "I know where she is! We need to go. *Now!*"

"Heavenly Father, forgive me for all my sins. Forgive me for not leaving a *note!*" Brynn grunted as she jabbed the sharp point of the broken lid into the splintering wood of the door. "Forgive me for not bringing a phone! Forgive me for calling the poor, stupid dog an idiot! At least *she's* not down *here! Help me out of here!*"

The rumbling intensified to a reverberating roar as the machines worked above ground, seemingly all around her. She saw splinters of the house and pieces of trash falling into the dark room behind her. There was no way anyone was going to hear her shouts or her pounding now. If she didn't get the door open, she would be crushed under the debris like an earthquake victim.

Brynn continued to pray and pound and pick as the house crumbled around her.

Jackson and Sheriff Raske pulled up to the Covey home as the bulldozer pushed the last of the house in. Jackson jumped out of the patrol car before it had even stopped moving and ran to the dozer operator, pointing and shouting. The operator finally stopped and turned off the machine, gaping at Jackson as if he'd lost his mind.

Wade and Bertis stood nearby as Jackson and the sheriff scrambled to find Brynn. Little more than the back portion of the house stood as the operator climbed down from his massive machine and looked around at everyone, scratching his head.

Jackson was near tears when he heard the dog whine and finally saw someone coming from the root cellar at the back of the house. Brynn emerged with the dog, dirty, shaken, but singly focused on only one thing and it wasn't Jackson.

Brynn charged at Bertis, her emotions plastered all over her face along with the dirt and tears.

"You *son of a bitch! You cowardly, Godless, piece of crap!* You shoved her in that hole, all because of how it might *look* to have a pregnant daughter!" Brynn shouted at Bertis as she stomped toward him, ignoring Jackson and the sheriff on her way. She reached Bertis and shoved his chest with both hands, but this pain was worth it. She nearly knocked him over, and Wade grabbed Bertis' arm, steadying him before he could fall.

"Whoa, now. Take it easy. You don't know what you're talking about." Wade said, annoyingly calm. Bertis stood with his mouth hanging open, apparently shocked at the sight of Brynn, but probably more shocked at the truth now being broadcast to all the confused onlookers.

"*You* shut up! You are part of this!" she said, turning to Wade, poking him in the chest, "You knew all along that she was there, so I would think that makes *you* an accessory to a crime, you *asshole!*" Brynn was shaking and crying, her hand burned, her head throbbed, but she felt triumphant.

She walked over to Jackson, finally, and hugged him, clung to him, whispering fervent apologies, love-yous, and thank-yous in his ear. Then she turned to Sheriff Raske.

"Sheriff, right over there is proof of what happened to Lanea. He held her prisoner in that room because she was pregnant and *he* was too ashamed of her to let her be seen by anyone. He filed a missing persons report while she was locked up down there in that room! She died down there, and he carried her out and buried her body."

Sheriff Raske looked at Bertis, who was shaking his head and mumbling.

"She knew it was best … it was the right thing to do." Bertis was looking at the ground.

Raske went to the back door and peered down into the hole at the room.

The following morning, Jackson poured the coffee as Brynn rewrapped her wrist.

"Remind me to thank your mother for taking the kids for a couple days." Jackson said.

"Oh, I will. Trust me. So ... " Brynn said, pulling her bathrobe around her, "do you think I was wrong to not tell Sheriff Raske about the Bible?"

"Yes. No. I don't know. Bertis admitted to everything. They found her body, they know what happened. What difference would it make now? There won't be a trial." Jackson carried the coffee to Brynn and she took it from him, added extra cream, and settled back in her chair.

"How did you know I was there? Sorry I didn't leave a note. That would have been so much easier, huh?" She smiled, having already been properly reprimanded *ad nauseam*.

"Ya *think?* Actually, Wade called, screaming at me that our dog was running loose over there and someone needed to come and get her or he would call the pound, which is kind of funny, since we have no pound. Anyway, he hung up before I even had a chance to ask him about you, but I had no idea that you were trapped. Apparently, it never occurred to him that you might be there. Nice job hiding the car, by the way. No one saw it, including us. Good thing we came when we did."

"Yes. It is." She smiled again, knowing full well she'd saved herself.

Brynn spent the day in her fuzzy robe and slouchy socks, cuddled up to her dog and reading the Bible-made-journal. It may not have been meant for her, but she needed to know how much of the story she hadn't learned from the room.

No matter how much she saw or read, she couldn't get over how suddenly things could change—how one minute, there was life, and the next, it was gone. Plans, dreams, ideas, memories, feelings, all wiped away like chalk from a chalkboard, turned to dust like cremated ashes. Instantly gone. Lanea's plans, her wishes and love and thoughts—swiped from existence. Not even those plans chiseled in stone are permanent enough to withstand the erosive force of death. And other than a journal, no lasting testament of those ideas and dreams remained. Brynn felt grateful to at least have that to give to Lanea's son.

Brynn thought as well of her own almost-demise, both in the cellar and at the hands of her attackers, how quickly her children could have been motherless like Lanea's child. She had, if nothing else, found justice for her friend … with the help of an old house that sought only to share the one thing it had left: Memories.

Even in her fuzzy robe and thick socks, a chill traveled down Brynn's neck. The memories of her own attack, the house, the nightmare—they waited for her. Just down the road. Now that Jackson knew what she'd seen, now that she couldn't try to deny it had happened, she would have to face it. An appointment with Dr. Stokes didn't sound half bad. What would she do with the facts she'd learned? Would anyone believe her? How could they *not?* They *were her* memories. Now and forever. They just didn't come from her own head. They were borrowed. And no one needed to know that.

The faces of her attackers flashed in her mind, and Brynn drew a sharp, painful breath. Her body ached in places she didn't know she had. She scratched the dog's neck, snuggled deeper into the chair and refocused on the journal.

Later that day, Brynn got off the phone and turned to Jackson and said, "You ready to go?"

"Yup. Let's do it." Jackson stuck his phone in his shirt pocket, grabbed a jacket, and went to the pickup with Brynn.

Dena answered the door, with Marshall behind her.

"Jackson. Brynn. What's up?" Marshall spoke, stepping in front of Dena.

"Can we talk?" Brynn gripped the door handle, hoping it would stop her hand from shaking. Her wrapped arm cradled the black Bible and Lanea's journal.

Marshall pushed the door open. "Yeah. Come on in."

They all followed Dena, who led the way to the living room. Brayden and Ella ran into the room, chasing a gold kitten. "Kids, can you go to your room and play for a bit? We need to talk to our company for a little while." The kids grabbed the cat and left, and Dena turned to Jackson and Brynn. "Have a seat. Coffee?"

Brynn accepted, the men did not. Dena left the room and Brynn took a deep breath, wishing she'd asked for creamer, sugar, anything to stall.

" Well," she began, "as you know, I've been looking for Lanea. Sheriff Raske said he wasn't going to release the information until later today, but I didn't want you to hear it on the news." She swallowed. "She's been found."

Marshall blinked, his eyes jumping back and forth between Jackson and Brynn. "Are you kidding? Where is she?"

Brynn cleared her throat, and her eyes flooded.

"She's dead." Marshall's words were more confirmation than question. They stabbed at Brynn's heart. She suspected his, too. Death was bitter consolation to the pain of rejection.

Brynn nodded.

"What happened?"

"She died at her home. Bertis had locked her in a secret room, in the basement." Brynn wasn't sure how much she should dump on him at once. "Because ... she was pregnant."

"What?" Marshall frowned. "What?"

He exhaled and leaned back in his chair.

Dena came back with the coffee. All faces turned to her. She looked at Marshall, his bewildered expression. "What?"

Marshall didn't hear his wife. He tipped his head. "Pregnant?"

"What?" Dena repeated, setting the coffee on the coffee table and slowly lowering herself to a chair.

"Was it ... mine? Do you know? What happened?" Marshall leaned forward again, eager for answers.

Brynn couldn't tell him the end of the story without the beginning. She owed him that.

"She broke up with you because her father forced her to. After he found out she was pregnant, he decided to hole her up in the basement until she had the baby. She died right after child birth."

"Pregnant?" Dena said. She looked near tears.

"He didn't know, Dena. Lanea never had a chance to tell him. I'm sorry to drop all this on you both," Brynn said. "Yes, Marshall. It was yours."

Marshall looked at Dena, who finally asked, "What about the baby? What happened to the baby?"

They both turned to Brynn.

"He's alive. Lanea named him Leath. Leath Marshall Nord. It means "broad river." After your song, Marshall. But the people who took him called him Collin. Collin Hagebak."

Marshall and Dena exchanged glances.

"We know him! He's done some work for us," Marshall said. "Collin? Are you sure?"

"Sure as we can be without a DNA test. Lanea wrote about everything in her journal. Journals. It's all right here." Brynn handed the journal and the black Bible to Marshall.

Marshall and Dena were looking at the books as if afraid to open them.

Jackson finally spoke. "Bertis confessed to everything. He was just going to keep her down there until after she had the baby, then claim she had run away and come back home. Says he gave the baby to Wade, his hired hand, and his wife, Ardis because they couldn't have kids. He claims he was just trying to do the right thing, but we think he just couldn't handle the shame of it."

"Now what?" Marshall asked.

"Well, I suppose that's up to you," Jackson said. "Wade is at the police station in Perris right now. There's no proof, yet, that they knew anything about Lanea being held captive or dying in the basement, so they may never be charged with anything,"

Dena put her hand to her mouth, tears filling her eyes. "That poor girl."

"Since Bertis confessed, the courts will order a DNA test if you want to pursue this," Jackson said.

"Leath." Marshall, his eyes watery, took Dena's hand, and she clutched his back.

Brynn took a shaky sip of her coffee.

They arrived at Wade's farm a few minutes after leaving Marshall's, and went to the back door and knocked. The dogs were still as obnoxious as ever, and the lazy cats were even more plentiful than a few days earlier.

Ardis came to the door. She wore baggy jeans and a sweatshirt, her stringy hair pulled up in a clip. Her sour expression spoke before she did.

"What do you want? Wade's not here." She tried shutting the door, and Brynn held it firm with her good hand.

"I imagine he's in town, answering questions at the sheriff's office, huh? That's okay. I wanted to talk to you. Can we come in?" Brynn glared at Ardis, and Ardis was unmoved.

"I don't have to talk to you. I think you should leave."

"That's fine. We can talk to your son." Brynn heard the tractor nearby and looked around, coercing Ardis' cooperation.

Ardis opened the door and Brynn and Jackson walked into the kitchen. It was modest and cluttered, but clean. The Hagebaks held a liking for old, rusty farm implements and gadgets. Tools hung everywhere in the rooms that Brynn could see. They covered the walls: chicken catchers, hay hooks, sickles, corn knives, two-man saws, hay knives, yokes, pulleys ...

No wonder they got along so famously with Bertis. He was their inexhaustible supplier of junk.

Ardis walked into the room and leaned against the counter, crossing her arms. Brynn and Jackson pulled out chairs and sat down uninvited.

Jackson motioned to one of the chairs and Ardis slowly sat.

Brynn stuffed her hands in her pockets, stared at Ardis, and finally spoke. "I know everything, Ardis."

"Oh, really? What do you *think* you know?" Ardis said smugly, but Brynn could see sweat beading on her upper lip.

"Everything. I know that son of yours isn't really yours, is he? Bertis arranged for you to get him after he was born, and you faked your pregnancy so that no one would know he wasn't yours. Lanea suspected it. Also, I remembered Fern was the one who told me that you had infertility issues. Funny how those issues suddenly went away, *years* later, when Lanea was pregnant." Brynn's eyes never left Ardis'. She didn't want to blink and miss one glint of Ardis' reaction.

"You can't prove anything. How do you know it wasn't an open adoption?"

Jackson spoke this time. "Oh, come on, Ardis. With all the DNA evidence in that basement and Bertis' confession, you really think the courts are going to believe all that?"

"So what," Ardis quipped. "Collin is almost full grown. We're the only parents he's ever known. No one's going to take him away."

They were at a standoff. Brynn braved a blink. "They might not need to. He's almost an adult. He can decide to leave all by himself."

"He wouldn't." Ardis fidgeted in her chair. "What do you want, anyway?"

"I want Lanea's son to know everything we know. I want you to admit to everything you did."

"What I *did?*" Ardis got up from her chair. "I think you need to leave. Now."

Brynn ignored Ardis' last statement. "Did you know Lanea kept a journal? She wrote everything down. It was her only friend in those last months of her life."

"So? I didn't do anything to her." Her voice was shaky, not as confident any more.

"I know what you did, Ardis. I read everything she wrote in those journals. Bertis was the one who stuck her down there, but you're not blameless, either, are you?" Brynn squinted at Ardis, hoping her intense gaze would be enough to make her admit to something.

Ardis stared at the table, eventually not focusing on it at all. Her gaze drifted inward and Brynn knew Ardis was someplace else. Her voice was flat and cold when she finally spoke.

"She was almost dead when I went in there."

"And you let her die all alone. You knew she was dying and did nothing!" Brynn leaned forward in her chair. "I know what happened and soon the sheriff will, too. I just want Collin to hear it from you, not the police. I know about Bertis bringing the baby to you. Lanea wrote in her journal, her mother's Bible, that he was going to town to get antibiotics and medicine for her. She was hoping to get better and find her son when she got out of that hole.

"But you went over to that basement after Bertis left the baby with you and Wade. You went there to help, but you saw that she was dying and knew if she died, she couldn't take her son from you. She saw the pads you brought. She knew there was only one way you could know she needed them. When Bertis left with the baby, he was screaming. She would have heard if he went upstairs and called you. So he went to your house, and minutes later, you showed up. You saw she was bleeding out, and when you stopped helping, you confirmed her suspicion. You left without helping. You could have saved her or at least tried!"

Brynn paused to catch her breath and let the truth soak in to Ardis' head—her soul seemed impermeable.

Tears trailed down Brynn's cheeks. "You only needed to help her to your car and take her to town, but you left her alone to die. What Bertis did was bad enough, but you let him think all this time that he was too late bringing medicine, that she just died. Wonder what he'd think if he knew."

"She was going to take him from me. I couldn't ... ."

The only sign of emotion in Ardis' face was that of disbelief that Brynn could know so much of what had happened. The same look of horror and amazement that Brynn had seen on Ryker's face was evident in Ardis'. None of what she saw here, though, looked like remorse.

Suddenly, the back door opened and beautiful Collin, Lanea's son, walked in. "Cows are fed, Ma. What now?"

"You can go out and ... " Ardis began, but Brynn cut her off.

"No, I think he should stay." Brynn said.

Ardis shook her head slowly, desperately. Her lips trembled. Collin looked back and forth between the three people in the kitchen, confused by his mother's emotions. Finally. Some emotion.

"What's going on?" he said softly.

Brynn couldn't do it. She wanted so badly for Ardis to pay for her crime in the highest court ever: the court of adoration, respect, honor, and love of family. She couldn't tell Collin everything she knew. Collin—Leith—would maybe, eventually, know the truth, but it didn't have to happen today, and it didn't need to come from her.

Ardis looked at Brynn and Jackson in silent appeal.

"Ma?"

Brynn and Jackson got up from their chairs and moved toward the door. "Ardis can tell you," Brynn said quietly.

Ardis followed them to the door. "What are you going to do? Are you going to tell the Sheriff?"

"We're not going to tell him anything," Jackson said, patting his pocket. "You are." He pulled his phone out and showed her that they'd been recording the conversation. "Incidentally, Marshall, *his* father, has the journals. He'll probably be over to talk to him soon."

Brynn and Jackson walked back to their vehicle, shooing the dogs off their legs and stepping around the cats.

Jackson helped Brynn into the vehicle. "Did Lanea write in the Bible about Ardis not helping her?" he asked.

"No, she didn't have a chance. She was too weak after the baby was born. But Ardis doesn't know that."

They looked back at Hagebak's house as they drove out. Ardis was still standing, motionless, on the step.

CHAPTER TWENTY-FOUR

COLE'S BED WAS EMPTY. THE bedclothes were gone, and the room was dark. Brynn swallowed. She could feel the fluttering of panic rising in her chest. She stood in the doorway, flowers in hand, dread holding her to the floor. Spencer was absent as well, but his bed was neatly made, the knit afghan folded at the foot as usual.

"Hi, Brynn!" Brynn jumped as an aide carrying sheets and blankets came in behind her and flipped on the lights.

"Hi, Emily. Um, Cole Emmick? He's usually in this room ... " She couldn't bring herself to say the words that might suggest the ultimate end to their friendship.

"Patio." Emily pointed to her right.

"Thanks. I'll ... Thank you." Brynn took a deep breath and felt the fear settle like a well-trained pet.

Hunched over in his wheelchair on the patio, Cole sat with a slice of dry toast in his hand, breaking off pieces and throwing them to the birds.

"Hello, Cole! Beautiful day!"

Cole looked up and paused. "Hello," he said, his usual exuberance absent.

Brynn waited until she got closer to address him again. He probably couldn't see her well enough.

"Cole? How are you?"

Cole squinted. A long, uneasy silence followed.

"Well, hello, Brynn!" Cole sat up and smiled.

"They told me I'd find you here. I was wondering where you were." Brynn handed him the spring bouquet of alstroemeria, gerbera daisies and tulips.

"Thank you! They're lovely." He closed his eyes as he sniffed the flowers. "Where else would I be?" He looked up at her.

"I don't know. Bowling ... grocery shopping ... " Brynn chuckled at her own joke and smiled, hoping he wouldn't catch the implication.

"Morgue."

He'd caught it. She felt her face flush.

He gave her a wry smile. "Someday, but not today. Good to see you. How are you? I haven't seen you since you told me of your attack."

Brynn hadn't the heart to remind him that she'd stopped in with Jackson after confessing to him.

Cole glanced at her bandaged wrist. "And what have you done to your hand?"

"I'm doing well." She held up her hand. "I hurt it when I fell into Lanea's room."

Cole's eyebrows shot up. "You fell *into* her room?"

"Yeah. It's a long story. Sorry I haven't been here for a while. I wanted to tell you all the news in person." She pulled up a patio chair and sat.

"News? Have you made more progress in Lanea's case?" He threw the crust of bread to the birds, brushed off his hands, and gave Brynn his complete attention.

"Definite progress." She leaned forward in her chair. "I found Lanea. Well, I found out what happened to her, and the police found her. Her body."

"That's terrible. What happened to her? Was it Marshall or Ryker? Or someone else?"

"You won't believe it. Bertis is the one who took her. He built a secret room in his basement. He hid her because she was pregnant and he didn't want anyone to know."

"Pregnant? Oh, my goodness. Does Jackson know now? About everything?"

"Yes. He knows everything. We're ... good—*great,* actually." Brynn then recounted everything from her confession to Jackson, to the journals, her discovery of the secret room, and her visions of Lanea's life in the room and Bertis' part in the disappearance.

"So what happens to him now?" Cole asked.

"Well, he pretty much confessed to everything. I'm not sure, but I don't think he'll be charged with murder. Maybe neglect, I don't know. He's so old, I doubt he'll go to prison.

He didn't kill her, but he might as well have. She died right after childbirth. But he wasn't the only one responsible."

Confusion crossed Cole's face.

"Wade's wife, Ardis, went there after Bertis brought the baby over, saw she was bleeding heavily, and didn't do a thing to help. She was afraid Lanea would take her son back."

"*What?* They had the baby?"

"Bertis was giving the baby to them because they weren't able to conceive. Wade was like a son to him, and this cemented it. And he'd get to keep the child in the family. But just to be sure that Lanea couldn't take him back, Ardis let her die. I got a recorded confession ... kind of ... from her on our phone, but I don't know if that will do any good. At least the sheriff has that information now. Maybe he'll know what to do with it, since there's no physical proof."

Cole clucked and shook his head. "Oh, that's just a shame. That poor girl. So what of the boy? Is Marshall the father?"

"Yes, Marshall's the father. I told him about Collin—or Leith, which is what Lanea named him—before I went to Wade and Ardis' house." Brynn clenched her hands. "Oh, man, I really wanted to tell Collin about his mother, but I couldn't. Ardis is the only mother he's ever known and I couldn't hurt *him* like that. I honestly don't care what happens to her. But it's going to be so hard for him to learn all of the details. At least he'll know who his real father is, and find out he has a little brother and sister."

"Have they met?" Eagerness brightened Cole's face.

"They already know each other. Distantly. But this will be so ... I don't know ... gratifying. Marshall had always thought that Lanea had broken up with him. Even if he did suspect her father was behind it, he never got over the feelings that she should have tried harder or that she ... abandoned him. Now he knows why. And he knows that Lanea had his son, and that all she ever wanted was a life with them. Marshall and Dena have Lanea's journals. They know everything now." Brynn's voice trailed off, her mind and focus drifting to another time and place.

"Brynn? Are you all right?" Cole asked, dipping his head to look into her eyes.

"Yeah. I just feel so bad for Lanea. I watched her die right in front of me ... well, it seemed. She was so weak, so tired, but she *fought*. She tried so hard to hang on to her life. Her dream. And Ardis, she didn't think a thing of leaving Lanea to die alone. She only cared about getting and keeping that baby. I hope she goes to jail." She shook her head and swiped at her eyes. "But if she doesn't, at least she knows that Collin will know the truth, and that will be punishment enough."

A frown pulled on Cole's features. "I'm confused. If there is no proof, how did you get a confession from her? And how did *you* get it and not the police?"

"Well, that's where it gets a little dicey." Brynn grimaced. "I told Ardis that Lanea had written everything down in her journals and that I read it. So when we went over there to confront her, we got a recording of it on Jackson's phone."

"And the sheriff? How did you convince him to go along with it?"

"I didn't exactly tell him I was going to do it."

"Oh. Gotcha." Cole nodded and smiled. "But he has all the information now."

"Yup. I just left there. I had a long, long talk with him." Brynn paused, watching Cole's face for a reaction.

"He knows?" His eyes widened.

"He does. I'm not sure he believes me *completely* about my ability, but how else would I know so much? He's willing to give me the benefit of the doubt. I questioned whether to tell him or not, but we've known Arthur most of our lives and it would only help our situation to be honest with him. He won't tell anyone, mostly because it would affect *his* credibility. At least we can help each other now."

"'Now'? So you told him what you saw in the house where you were held?"

Brynn nodded.

They looked into each other's eyes, exchanging silent words, felt and not spoken.

Brynn spoke first. "Sometime ... soon, I'm going into his office and looking through some mug shot books to see if I recognize anyone."

"I'm sure that won't be easy." Cole's eyes welled.

"I'll be okay." One side of her mouth pulled up in an attempt at a valiant smile. "I'm going to find them."

Cole cleared his throat and leaned forward and took Brynn's good hand in both of his. "Well, my dear, I wish you all the best." His voice caught.

Brynn sniffed and patted his hands with her free one. "I wish you all the best, too, Cole cuz I think they're serving liver for dinner today." She laughed. "Need me to bring you more black licorice and Cheetos next time I come?"

Brynn's legs burned right to the bone. She'd never gone this far. She should have brought the car. She felt exposed. Defenseless. Watched.

She stood for a long while, watching the house, waiting to see if there was any movement inside. When her legs stopped shaking, she stepped quietly up onto the porch and peered through the glassless picture window. It was safe out here. No unbidden memories to bombard her mind. She peered into the room where she'd been held captive. It looked the same: dirty, disgusting, cold. The only memories she saw now were the ones that had been forced upon her weeks ago by a malicious and perverse fate. Another rape of sorts.

She felt the bile rising in her throat, and the tug of a gag. Saliva filled her mouth and her gut and jaw clenched simultaneously. She backed away and stepped off the porch. She wasn't going in.

I remember the men well enough; there's no need to see them again. She fondled again the flap of the heavy paper folder in her pocket, caressing the coarse striking surface of the matchbook. *Not yet, anyway.*

THE END

ABOUT THE AUTHOR

Christine Mager Wevik lives on a farm in southeast South Dakota with her husband, Doug (the other Clint Eastwood) and her dog, Livie. She's mother to 4 and grandmother to 3.

She is the author of *It's Only Hair*, a humorous, self-help book about living and coping with hair loss, and is also published in C. Hope Clark's *Funds for Writers*, a nationally recognized newsletter for writers, and *The Link*, a quarterly magazine for the American Hair Loss Council.

You can also find Christine on Facebook and Twitter, as well as at her author website (*www.ChristineMagerWevik.com*).

Made in the USA
San Bernardino, CA
23 September 2018